tex and molly in the afterlife

Other Avon Books by
Richard Grant

IN THE LAND OF WINTER
KASPIAN LOST

tex and molly in the afterlife

Richard Grant

SPIKE

AN AVON BOOK

AVON BOOKS, INC.
1350 Avenue of the Americas
New York, New York 10019

Copyright © 1996 by Richard Grant
Cover illustration by Haydn Cornner
Interior design by Kellan Peck
Published by arrangement with the author
ISBN: 0-380-80706-8
www.spikebooks.com

Library of Congress Cataloging in Publication Data:

Grant, Richard, 1952–
    Tex and Molly in the afterlife / Richard Grant.
        p.   cm.
I. Title.
PS3557.R268T48   1996   96-13682
813'.54—dc20   CIP

First Spike Printing: September 1999
First Avon Books Mass Market Paperback Printing: October 1997
First Avon Books Hardcover Printing: October 1996

SPIKE TRADEMARK REG. U.S. PAT. OFF. AND IN OTHER COUNTRIES, MARCA REGISTRADA, HECHO EN U S.A.

Printed in the U.S.A.

OPM 10 9 8 7 6 5 4 3 2 1

I

The spectacle of Nature is always new,
for she is always renewing the spectators.

—GOETHE, quoted by T. H. HUXLEY
in the first issue of *Nature*, 1869

&
time ran out.

Wizard or no Wizard, the ritual had to begin. The great sun god Belenos was not going to wait for Guillermo to find a parking place where the cops wouldn't notice his inspection sticker or whatever else the little mortal hangup might be. Gods and seasons and celestial bodies have their own gigs to get on with, their own (totally alternative) lifestyles to lead. When noon arrives on the 1st of May, and Beltane is due to come down, it *comes down,* and that's the end of the story. Molly had gone over this with the Street Players way beforehand. But you know how it is. There's always somebody who doesn't get the word.

"He's done this before," Tex reminded her.

Right, Molly thought: life is cyclical. She gave Tex a smile and smoothed her black feathers down. No sense getting ruffled over things that can't be fixed.

"I *told* you that guy was wrong for the part."

Tex obviously was not letting go of it. Molly stroked his fur.

"Okay, everybody," she said. "The shoe must go on."

—forcing herself to sound jaunty, adjusting the jut of her raven beak. Sacred bird of the Dagda, right? Bosom bud of the Sandman? Two major demos taken care of right there. A committed player to both pit and gallery, Molly did not neglect the obeisances.

Tex, though, was hung on the testosterone thing. "We ought to get rid of him," he growled.

"You can't just *get rid* of a Wizard," said Molly. Her beak clacked at him. Quite an edge on that papier-mâché. "Remember: they're whatever it is, and quick to anger."

Tex looked at her for a moment blankly. Then (getting the Tolkien reference: *ha*) he smiled. When he smiled, a glint like starlight shot from the dark centers of his eyes. Mysterious, twinkling energy. Fetishes danced at his ears.

"Come on, Bear," Molly said, patting his furry shoulder. "Put your head on."

"Rrrr," he rumbled, companionably. He slipped the big toothy headpiece onto his shoulders, inhaling the comforting trace of taxidermic chemicals, and stared through the gap in the jaw. Raven claws scratched his neck, soothingly. Tex felt like himself again.

"Let's go, gang," Molly called to the rest of the troupe.

And so the four Seasons and the five Elements (including Akasha, a sort of Vedic phase-space, just added for this performance), along with the cardinal Directions, Mother Earth, Father Sky, the Moon, the Sun, and an assortment of totemic Beasts— the entire roster of the Cold Bay Street Players except for the Wizard, who was late—shuffled out of the C-Vu Cafe into the principal intersection of Dublin, Maine: until last year, when Wal-Mart opened, the only place in the county with a traffic light. It was just before noon on Beltane, the pagan planting festival. The sun (actual sun) poured down on them like a full-spectrum fluorescent bulb, bright but not warm enough. An offshore breeze carried fresh memories of mountains and of winter. The street was almost empty; the air was quiet; tourist season was six weeks off and the local economy was still in hibernation. Everything was cool.

Without the Wizard, the performance was going to be a little strange.

Well, it was strange anyway. But it did proceed according to a certain internal logic.

SCENARIO

Like:

MOTHER EARTH, lying cold and lifeless under the dark spell of WINTER, is summoned to wakefulness by the SUN, who passes across FATHER SKY with a retinue of ELEMENTS. The SUN's way is impeded, however, by various BEASTS who represent the vested interests that resent the coming of springtime. A fat tusked PIG, for instance, stands for the vendors of heating oil, who ritually jack up their prices each Novem-

ber; while Molly's RAVEN embodies those spirits enamored of
darkness—Death, struggling bards, talk-show hosts. Against
these, the BEASTS of Light and Warmth rise up: a ROBIN, symbol
of migrating second-home owners, and a MOUSE, which has got
cabin fever from spending the winter behind your refrigerator,
and naturally a BLACK FLY, champion of those heroic tiny creatures that keep Maine green and beautiful by driving normal people away.

The contesting BEASTS dance in ritual combat, reaching a frenzied stalemate that is broken when the WIZARD (who up to now's
been standing like a calm center of the whirling cosmos, directly
beneath the traffic light) leaves the safety of his magic circle to
awaken the BEAR—i.e. Tex, in his genuine *Ursus americanus* pelt.
Then BEAR, who not only enjoys ancient associations with the
pan-Eurasian Goddess but also important Native American connections, bestirs himself lazily, sniffs at the AIR, paws the EARTH,
investigates the angle of the SUN. Time to wake up, he figures.
And so with a roar he drives away the BEASTS of Darkness and
Cold. Then he rumbles off on his inscrutable way, ready (though
in no big hurry) to get on with the business of eating and procreating and casting spoor about.

Exultant, the ELEMENTS join SPRING and SOUTH in a dance of
birth and renewal into which, if all goes well, the PLAYERS together with members of the AUDIENCE, including perhaps the
local MEDIA, will be drawn. Until at last

[*Exeunt frolicking*]

everyone skittles out of the street and into vehicles parked
nearby and away down Route 1 before the SHERIFF gets really
pissed at the drums and chants and blocked traffic.

Finis. Cast party at Eben's barn.

HOWEVER

Without the Wizard things were different.
Leaving aside questions of dramatic logic—such as,
who wakes the Bear up now?—the loss of that central
figure, planted like a Maypole in the middle of the intersection,
left the Players without a visual reference point. These costumes
were quite elaborate and it was hard to see from inside them.
Plus, you could always count on Guillermo Gobán (the Wiz's
street name, also a made-up one), being the control freak he was,

to use that long staff of his to zap any herbed-out or otherwise errant Players back into line.

So now what?

"Break a leg," said Molly.

And the Cold Bay Street Players went [*Jangling. Rattling. Intoning mantras. Waving wire-and-muslin wings. Shaking staves and wands cut from oak and ash and rowan. Waving smoldering bundles of sage and cedar. Thumping stretched-skin drums and acrylic-headed doumbeks. Humming snatches of this and that. Feigning animal stances.*] out into the middle of Water Street.

And everything in Dublin stopped.

Which is not to say that much had been happening in Dublin to begin with. Only:

(7) shift-workers in rusty cars heading home from the paper mill
(2) lobstermen and (3) rangy kids hanging out
at the public landing
(1) brick mason w/ponytail perched on 2 x 6 scaffolding
above the sidewalk
(1) same-gender couple (female) browsing the Polaroids
tacked in the window of a real estate office

Surprised, then alarmed or amused or totally flummoxed by the neo-Pagan processional, these folks stared and others began to emerge from the Fleet Bank and the Real Food Co-op and other places in Dublin's micro-downtown. Mostly they smiled as the Players with their neon nylon banners and musical contraptions and sheaves of desiccated straw paraded by; and the Players got into it big-time now as they twirled and dragged their trains of flowing muslin, leapt onto the hoods of parked cars, tapped at plate-glass windows and beckoned shop clerks and other bored wage-slaves to join the festivities. Reaching now the intersection at the center of town, they arranged themselves in a circle around the spot where the Wizard should have been. Those carrying straw made a pile of it, and Molly swooped down on this with a butane lighter. *Whoosh.*

The air, damp and breezy and quite cool (because the first of May is only marginally springlike in these parts), filled with sweet white smoke.

The audience fleshed out.

The Players waxed shamanic.

A deputy sheriff named Doug poked his head out of the station on High Street and exchanged looks with a Fleet Bank loan officer.

Two or three car-lengths back from the blocked intersection, a biker laid on his horn. Someone in the crowd shouted at him, and after a second or two he stopped. Old hippies in the audience whooped and clapped. On his scaffold, the brick mason shimmied and carved the air with his trowel.

The loan officer sighed, and Deputy Doug shook his head. He said, "I guess it's that time again."

6 O'CLOCK REPORT

The recap on the nightly news out of Bangor takes up right about here. The reporter who looked like Gidget in a Nautica parka arrived in Dublin a little early (expecting traffic, meeting none), but there was some problem with the camera and by the time it all got straightened out Molly had already decided that—Guillermo still being a no-show—she would have to attend to the seasonal deed herself. So on the screen you see her, out-of-focus at first and then disconcertingly zoomed in on, flapping around the snoozing Bear, who you have to figure is ready to get up and bite somebody on the ass by this time anyhow. Molly plays to the camera nicely, though the prancing Beasts keep screwing up her sight lines. That's show biz.

Suddenly now—you don't catch this at first; the focus is too tight—who but the Wizard should stroll magisterially onto the scene. He spreads his robe and waves his long rowan-branch staff in a wide circle, clearing the space around himself with the dangerous efficiency of an NBA forward in the free-throw lane. He now delivers himself of a loud and portentous announcement in, presumably, wizard-speak—

"HOOMDAYA. FIGDIS WAPPAPPAH! BLONG DEE MOSKOYAI!"

—and by now even the slow-uptake camera operator cannot help noticing this flashy new presence. The camera swings around *just* as old Bear is starting to rouse himself. So what *should* have been the center of attention—Tex going into his twitching and shuddering and stretching routine, the powerful forces of life beginning to stir in a new year, waking into a world remade by winter, et alia—instead is fairly tossed offscreen; then we

CUT TO:

Dancing and carousing at the end of the performance. Deputy

sheriff visible in the corner of the frame, glancing at his watch. In the foreground, our Channel 5 correspondent in a tight two-shot with who else, the Wizard himself.

"Gidget" (not her real name) smiles into the camera, looking like someone who's having a little more fun than she's being paid to have. Guillermo's costume allows plenty of room for his impressive jaw (a bit like Gaston's in *Beauty and the Beast*) to thrust itself this way and that.

"So would you say," Gidget wants to know, "that the goal of your performance goes beyond just, mere entertainment? I mean would you say that you have any message, maybe a political message, for the people of Maine?"

"We are *here*," says the Wizard, so loudly you can picture the meters red-lining, "to call attention to the devastation being wrought upon the North Woods by corporate interests out to make a profit by plundering our common natural heritage."

"Are you referring to the Gulf Atlantic Corporation and its plans for the former Goddin Air Force base?"

The Wizard takes a breath, fueling up for a lengthy reply.

"Fucking Guillermo," muttered Tex. This was later, catching the telecast in Eben Creek's rented barn, which served as the Cold Bay Street Players' storage and rehearsal space. Animal masks stared down luridly from the walls. A non-UL-approved extension cord from the distant farmhouse powered a television and a lone electric light, reclaimed from the dump, that Molly called the Equity Lamp. Also there were candles and the glowing embers of hemp and tobacco. Ragged lifestyles galore around here.

"*Shh*," hissed Molly.

On-screen, the Wizard was talking about the destruction of native habitat, a great opportunity that will be lost forever, selling out the heritage of our children and grandchildren for a favorable quarterly earnings report—it was as though he were reading from a TelePrompTer balanced, like a pirate's parrot, on Gidget's shoulder.

"You were really great, Guillermo," one of the women in the barn said. Pippa Rede.

"Sublimely, bro," Indigo Jones concurred.

Guillermo acknowledged the compliments with a weary nod and a smile, becomingly strained, assuming what Tex thought of as his Sandinista War Hero mode.

"What an ass," Tex muttered.

"Be *quiet*," commanded Molly.

"You be quiet," said Tex. He stood up and swayed a bit, reorienting himself to an upright position after having spent the last hour cross-legged on the floor. Middle age (if that's what 49 was called these days) had visited upon Tex this slight but seemingly permanent sense of dislocation. It was like his body was off-kilter by just the tiniest amount—fractions of a degree or something—in relation to the world it had grown into. The way Tex looked at it was, life had been supposed to evolve in a certain way, a particular direction, and instead History at large had made some incorrect turn—this might have happened one afternoon while nobody was paying attention, possibly during one of those dark evenings of the national soul when John Ritter was in prime time—so that now, as the years slithered by, life became increasingly, though subtly and insidiously, different from the way it was divinely intended to be. Another way you could look at it was as though you were dealing with two great tectonic plates—

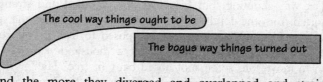

The cool way things ought to be

The bogus way things turned out

—and the more they diverged and overlapped and strained against one another, the greater the pressure and the danger and the need for a release, a realignment.

Molly tugged at a fold of his cloak. "Are you okay, Bear?"

Tex did not ignore her exactly, but he did not answer her either. Recovering his equilibrium, he made for the way out—a hatch that opened to a ladder going down from the loft, covered for safety purposes by a sagging remnant of plywood.

"Hey, Tex," young Ludi called out to him. "Look, it's you! You're on TV!"

Had it been anyone but Ludi, Tex would have continued on his way. But there was in Ludi's voice—indeed, in Ludi in general—this appealing quality of Midwestern openness that he found it difficult, or inadvisable, to resist. Besides which, Ludi was long-legged and sparkly-eyed and cute, not unlike Molly a couple of decades ago.

So he turned to look, and yo: there was himself, as Bear, on the mutant tube.

Gidget was still trying to interview Guillermo, who was now, in Wizard mode, explaining something about *the delicate interlocking of species that characterize a mature woodland, that fragile web of connectedness that will be ripped asunder if Gulf Atlantic is allowed . . .*

Suddenly the Bear, his great toothy head bobbing in the middle-ground just over the Wizard's shoulder, began yelling:

"Tell them about the Little People!"

A few moments of confusion ensued during which Guillermo continued to talk *(. . . advances in biology have taught us that it is the super-organized system, the meta-organism if you will, rather than its species-level constituents, that is the crucial . . .)* and Gidget politely to listen while glancing back in a discreet but anxious effort to zero in on this fresh commotion. It was the camera operator who resolved the issue, finding the Bear too viewer-friendly to ignore. He zoomed in on Tex and evidently cued Gidget as well, because she aimed her microphone into the wired-open bear jaw and called out, "Little people?"—flashing a distinctly nervous smile back to the imaginary audience out there in TV News Land.

"Sure, you know—the elves and dryads and wood-sprites!"

Tex was shouting, but his voice rose muffled and strangely distorted from the depths of the bear-head. "You know, the spirits of the forest. Where are *they* supposed to live, if you go in and wreck their homes? You expect a thousand-year-old Oak Man to move into some snot-nosed baby fir tree? Ha!"

"Ha," said Gidget, uncertainly. "Spirits of the forest. So you object to the North Woods Project on, would you say, religious grounds?"

"What *lunacy,*" Guillermo moaned: real-time Guillermo, there in the Players' barn. "Here we had this wonderful opportunity, this *media exposure,* and he completely blew it."

"Who blew it?" said Tex, moving a step closer to where Guillermo sat in the blue glow of the television screen. (On which, in extreme close-up now, the Bear was outlining the tenets of Druidic Animism.) "You think you can turn people on by reciting things you've memorized from the Sierra Club calendar?"

Guillermo rose with a grand show of weariness—as in, weighted down by his battle fatigues and his trusty Khalashnikov—and said, "Turning people on. Is that what you think we're trying to do here?"

"What I thought," said Tex, thrusting himself forward, a full head shorter than Guillermo but not willing to let this guy shout him down in body language, "what *I* thought was that we were having a Beltane festival to welcome back the spirits of growth and make some noise and have a good time. And if people come away from that with a feeling for what spring and green leaves and regeneration are all about, then that's cool. That's great. And if they don't, then the spirits can dig it, anyhow."

Guillermo shook his handsome head. Sickened with regret, like. "The world is dying," he said, "and you want to celebrate."

"The world can't die." Tex mustered a smile. Not a happy smile. Stalwart, at best. "Nothing can die. Everything in nature is alive. Rocks, atoms, light-waves—*everything*. Only the forms change. This world, *our* world, may be a little sick—"

"*This* world is the only world there is," Guillermo said, louder and more forceful now. "And we are the only ones who can save it. If you can't get serious, even about that, then God help you."

"The Goddess helps," Molly said, inserting herself hopefully between the two of them, "and the Goddess nurtures. And sometimes the Goddess bites you on the ass. We all have our parts to play in the great drama."

This shut the boys up long enough for her to whisper to Tex, "Come on, Bear. Let's go get some fresh air. The show's over."

Channel 5 News, she may have meant. The fat weather dude was on screen now, doing his folksy live broadcast from the back deck, where pots of Fischer geraniums, pumped up on high-phosphorus time-release fertilizer, bloomed so lustily you could practically hear them panting. Then Molly gave him a nudge and he stepped onto the rickety ladder.

Someday this thing is going to break, he thought, and somebody is going to fall and get hurt.

"So what do you think?" said Molly, easing up close to him, moving into the little niche between his side and his left arm. "You want to go back to the boat?"

Tex shook his head. Together they stepped out into the chilly evening.

The moon was up, though there was still a good bit of daylight left; a couple days short of full, it sailed high in the sky with a few scrappy pieces of cloud drifting far beneath it. The air smelled like spruce needles, like damp earth, and like stones. In back of Eben's barn a field sloped down to the ocean, which shimmered eerily in the gathering dusk. It was as though some of the day's sunshine had been absorbed by the water and now was seeping back out.

He stopped where he was—boot heels sunk in mud scented with wintergreen, as dark and sweet as chocolate—and turned to Molly. The two of them looked at one another. Moonlight, ebbing dusk and ancient sparkling suns made a fitting light for them. Molly with her Guatemalan peasant vest, a raven feather braided into her straight brown hair, was attractive in an unfussy, earth-mama sort of way. She looked to be early-40ish, softening with age, serene. Tex was a few years older and a piece of work. His hair was still dark, dangling like a rope to his bottommost couple of vertebrae. His mostly gray facial hair was sculpted into side-burns and moustaches that dangled like walrus tusks. He wore a fetish in each ear—little silver likenesses of Bear, the guardian of strength and medicine—and from a leather cord around his neck a Tibetan skull pendant, carved from human bone. He was of medium height and stringy, so that his clothes tended to flap. But what you really noticed were his eyes: so full of energy they appeared to beam messages out at you, independent of the rest of his face.

"Bear?" Molly asked him again. "Ready to go home now?"

He smiled at her. Something mischievous there. The eyes flashed their unbreakable code. "No," he said. "Not yet. Let's go up to the Well."

THE MOON & MARIJUANA

The rusty Saab scraped its butt as it creaked off the town road onto a rain-gullied dirt-and-gravel fire lane marked only by an aged, 3-trunked white birch onto which people had nailed placards announcing, usually, the names of their summer cottages. There was a certain art to this.

CHUTE INN (No Vacancy)
LOCH MESS MONSTERS
CAMP KERFLOP II
OKIES IN EXILE
THE *OTHER* PENDLETONS
ULTIMA TOOLEY

The moon was close to straight overhead now. Peering down through the almost absolutely black webwork of needles and branches. Beautiful. And scary, sort of. So far away; so ancient and powerful. Inhumanely serene. This would be the moon known as Little Frogs Croak by some Native Americans and as Too Cold to Plant by others, as Willow by the pre-Christian Norse, and as Faerie by the Witches, or at least the Witches that Tex knew personally. (The idea, he guessed, being that now that the weather was relatively decent the Fair Folk would come out again to dance at night in their enchanted glades. And so would the Witches behind the hedge at Pippa's place in Pickup City.) To most people now, of course, this moon tonight had no name at all—no color, no tree, no totem animal, no seasonal handle or magical aspect or anything at all tagged on to it. And there you have the whole sickness of the world, the starvation of its spirit, metaphorically speaking, anyhow. So Tex believed.

Now over the next-to-biggest hill and down into a dale as black and deep as the night itself the old Saab bumped and lurched and scraped its underbelly. Molly began to look alarmed though she had been here before, had made the drive herself under worse road conditions than these. But the physical state of the road isn't everything; there was something about this night distinct from other days and nights; there is always a certain immanence in the instant, the *now,* and Molly felt the presence and the strangeness of this in a different way than Tex, perhaps (at any rate she was less inclined to blame it on anything), but she felt it all the same. The blackness *within* the dark. The empty spaces gaping unmarked and hazardous between one quantum of passing time and the next.

Along the bottom of the gulch between the biggest and the next-to-biggest hills the spring runoff had carved a channel for itself. Water gushed through, more clearly heard than seen. Before them the headlights picked out fallen logs, rocks laid naked by erosion, and a set of muddy fissures made by the tires of somebody's ATV. The snowmelt revealed itself as a chain of ripples, slithery, like the skin of some faintly glowing snake, as colorlessly effulgent as moonlight. The Saab crept closer, halted inches short.

"Think you can make it, Bear?"—sounding much more anxious than she had expected or wanted to, Molly asked him.

Tex said nothing. In truth, he *thought* nothing, one way or the other. Nothing he could have said. He yanked up the hand-brake and left the engine chuttering in neutral, stepped onto the wet road, and leaned down to plumb the water with his hand.

It was *so cold* his fingers felt severed from his body. When they brushed the pebbly bottom of the ditch his nerve endings barely signaled it. He kept his hand down needlessly long, just for the sensation of doing so. Digging it: the altered state. Finally he stood back up because his back began to hurt. Middle age & such shit. Up in the air again, the fingers felt changed into something different, shards of thrilling pain, the sort of feeling that energizes you.

"It's cool," he said, climbing aboard and slamming the door too hard. "It's not too deep. Just freezing."

Molly rubbed his fingers on the gearshift knob. (Wrong hand, though.)

"I love you, Bear," she said.

"I love you too, Raven," he told her. And they splashed through and over the water and up again, ascending the biggest hill.

At the top was a good place to park—the disused driveway of the oldest cottage in these woods, a Craftsman-style, mail-order bungalow, probably put together back when the ghost village of Applemont, down the other side of the hill, was still breathing. Tex swung the Saab into the drive and only belatedly noticed twin sets of tire tracks leading through the grass and goldenrod stalks and baby fir seedlings ahead of him. "Somebody's been sleeping in *my* bed," he growled.

"They sure have," said Molly. "In fact, they're sleeping in it right now."

Barely, near the limit of their range, the headlights caught something way up the drive, something that glinted back, red and silver.

"Too much," said Tex. "Who could it be?"

Molly shrugged. "I wonder if it's still cool to park here."

Tex made a scowly face and he said, "I'll just leave it in the road, I guess."

The second weird discovery of the evening was that, right where the path branched off into the woods that led, eventually, to the Well, a sign had been posted. And not just your ordinary tacked-up plastic NO HUNTING sign, but an elaborate custom job.

NOTICE
Private Property
Trespassing for any reason
is <u>strictly prohibited.</u>

"*Property rights,*" Tex said darkly, as though uttering an epithet.

Molly took his hand and they started up the trail together.

Even with the moon as high and bright as it was, you could barely see where you were walking. It was easier to let your eyes lose their focus and your feet find their way by pure bodily intuition. This was an excellent path, that way.

After they had got into the rhythm of it—left foot, right foot, mashing down and springing off the loam, bodies swaying, breaths and heartbeats in sync—Tex produced from somewhere in the mysterious depths of his vest an awesomely fat finger's worth of last year's homegrown. He fired it up with his Navy Zippo, a relic older than the Saab, and Molly was glad to take it. Somehow the skunky smell and the mold-and-must taste (it had been an *indica* x *sativa* clone, selected for its pretty purple-tinged leaf color as well as its truly Plutonian head) seemed to normalize the situation, to reattach her to the things that were most pertinent. The buzz coming on felt like when you raise your head suddenly, realize you've half nodded off—still groggy a little, confused for a second or two, so you make a sort of cursory psychic inventory, a rapid mapping-out of the gestalt.

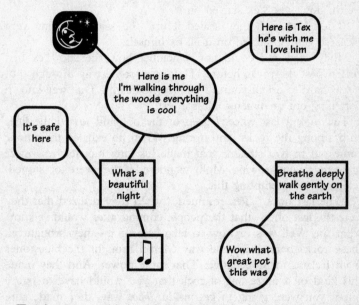

Tex began to whistle. Molly strained to identify the melody. Something wistful: it eluded her, though the memory of what it was seemed close at hand.

The path curled leftward, widdershins, and became a sort of fissure etched in the downward slope. Big rocks stood around them, luminous with condensation and draped with opulent velvet coverlets of moss. Ferns raised their fiddleheads toward the moon, and the whole schmeer of ice-white spring wildflowers—trillium, blood root, foam flower, Canada mayflower, goldthread, creeping anemone—sparkled against the dark forest underfloor like a reflection of the stars overhead. All of these plants had older names and older uses than anyone now remembered. Tex's business partner Jesse knew some of them from his grandmother but there was so much even she had forgotten; nobody explained to her as a little girl that an Age of Information was dawning in which Wisdom and Understanding would count for zip, and that she and girls like her were the only hope that something would be saved. Anyway she was gone now. Gone to the Summerland, as the Witches would tell you. Or perhaps simply dead.

Down, down. At the bottom of the hill the path did a peculiar thing, sort of tucked itself into this giant heap of boulders that just seemed to have *plopped* here. Really, it was hard to think of a plausible geological explanation for this place. It was pretty weird: don't get Tex started on it.

"Look how well they sealed it up," he said, sounding very pleased, getting started on it all by himself.

Molly tried and could not remember how she and Tex had gotten past the rocks before. There was some way through, but it was hard to orient yourself by just moonlight. That well-known flattening-out or dimensionless effect.

Tex took a last wheezy gasp of the pot and tossed the little stub among the rocks: an offering. When he exhaled the smoke came out in two streams that made his long moustache appear to be magically growing. Molly wondered if they were too stoned, really, to be attempting this.

"The last ones," Tex resumed, "when they realized that they *were* the last ones—that the people coming after wouldn't know what the Well was or how to take care of it—they brought all these rocks here, the same way Merlin brought the bluestones from Ireland to Stonehenge. That same power. And they made this kind of a maze out of rock that you would have to figure out if you were going to get inside. *That* way, they made sure the spirits would be safe and they could sleep in peace for as long as it took till they were needed again."

Molly said nothing and began to hope that Tex would not remember the way through.

"They were ultra-cool, the Old Ones," he said gravely.

He flashed his dilated pupils in her direction, as though inviting a challenge or an Amen to this. Then he laughed: that chesty, always surprising Bear laugh that was so rich and spontaneous that you couldn't help, usually, laughing along, even if you had *no idea whatsoever* what was so funny. As was generally the case. Molly smiled and she thumped him on the arm, hard enough to test his balance. He did not move or flinch at all; it was like knocking against a wall.

Tex halfway turned to confront the wall of rocks, then he stopped himself. He patted the part of his chest where his Tibetan bone pendant should have hung.

"Damn," he said.

The story with these pendants was, as long as they stayed on you, you were fine. But when the bone wore away, or the pendant came loose, or you otherwise got separated from it—then *boom.* It wasn't carved out of bone for nothing.

Carefully Tex moved backward, reversing his last couple of steps, to where he had stood when he flicked the roach away. A thumb-sized object caught the moonlight near his feet. *Thank you,* he thought, scooping it up, slipping it deep into one of his pockets.

"That was close," he said. "The cord must've broken or something."

Then so easily—barely seeming to glance where he was going—he turned and stuck his foot into a notch in one of the boulders, grabbed some invisible handhold, and pulled himself onto the narrowest of ledges. And he took it from there. The way through the rocks was not actually hard—each step of it was quite doable, given a certain mood of abandon and the absence of gross physical impairment. It only, at every step, *seemed* impossible. Being high helped you to overlook that.

Soon they were inside: past the stones, peering into the darkness of the Well. They stood shoulder to shoulder on a gently sloping face of rock, wide enough but a little slippery. The mouth of the Well was a pace in front of them, so big you could drop the Saab into it. (And how long, Molly wondered, would you have to wait to hear the splash?)

"Hey," said Tex—loudly, to hear the way his voice sounded, swallowed up by blackness. He always did this; a matter of personal ritual. "Dig *that.*"

"I dig it, Bear."

Tex dug around in his pockets and flaps and other hiding places and came up eventually with a small object that glinted in the moonlight. Molly could not guess what it was.

"It's a copper fitting," he told her. "From a gas line, I think."

"Nothing important, I hope."

She could feel his shoulder twitch in a shrug—so characteristic. Molly was surprised to realize, all of a sudden, that she was *tired* of this shit. Some of it, anyway. Tired of the endless hippie trip, the traipsing from one thing to the next with no map, no mile-posts, no destination.

"Now when the Druids came here," Tex was saying—picking up his Well rap—"they would usually offer like pins or clasps or something to the Spirit Behind the Face of the Water. So see, I figure this connector doobie is sort of the same thing, sort of a thing that clasps one thing to another, right? And that's the important idea, you know what I mean?"

Molly would almost always, invariably, have said "Right" or smiled and rubbed his arm fondly. Tonight, though . . . tonight for some reason she felt like: I may be stoned, but I'm not *that* stoned.

"How could there have been Druids here?" she asked him. "This is *Maine,* remember?"

Tex drew back a tiny bit, insofar as the width of the rock allowed it. "Of course there were Druids here. Can't you feel it?"

Molly shook her head. All she felt was damp. And tired. She wanted to be in her bunk on the houseboat. "Besides, even if there were," she said, "how does anyone *know* what the Druids did? I mean, are there eyewitness accounts or something?"

She thought this was a rhetorical question, but Tex had a quick answer. "Sure there were: the rocks were the witnesses. And the trees, and the Well. Some of those old Druids, you know, they were practically immortal. They could go to the Summerland and then come back whenever they wanted to. Or they could transfer their souls into a rock or an oak tree and wait basically forever for the right time to come. That's how we know. The rocks and the trees tell us."

"Oh, come on, Bear."

"You come on." He looked down into the void of the Well—bottomless, for all they knew, for all you could tell by staring at it—and his eyes blinked quickly as though a brief light or vision had danced across them. "Mmm," he said, very softly.

"What?" said Molly.

He looked up at her as though surprised. "What? Oh, hey. I just had this—I sort of flashed onto this—"

His arm stretched out, holding the copper connector. "Make a wish," he told her.

Molly wished to be home in bed.

Tex closed his eyes, wishing his own thing. He wobbled a little. His eyes popped open. "Whoa," he said. "I almost—"

He seemed to gesture way out over the lip of the Well, as

though calling Molly's attention to something. She looked where he was gesturing

—a mistake: took her eyes off Tex for *one second*

—and when she looked back again he was leaning in an odd way against the damp slope of the rock, the way you lean against a swell on a rocking boat. It came to her slowly, in a stoned-out way, *he is trying to grab on to something*

—then Tex gave her a funny sort of expression, a quizzical or bemused flickering smile

—*he has lost his balance and he is falling*

"Bear!" she yelled. Grabbing for him.

"What the fuck," he said, still apparently not getting it. The arm that was above the Well, pointing or reaching, waved helplessly, grasping for something that was not there

(of course this all happened

very

quickly)

and then he was falling, really falling.

Molly thought she shrieked, though she did not hear herself. Tex's body was way over, half-toppled into the blackness. She held him by pieces of clothing, but it was like grabbing an empty husk, a Player's costume. Inside there's a body writhing away, a skeleton doing its bone-dance, but that's in a parallel universe.

Stop, Molly willed.

She willed it hard enough that for a moment Time did come to a halt. Tex was not sliding into the Well and she was not losing her grip on him.

Then Time gave a lurch, and they were *both* sliding into the Well. The slope of the rock got steeper as they inched closer to the big drop-off.

"Let go!" Tex yelled to her. "Let go or you'll fall! Listen to me—Raven!"

She did not listen to him. She called out "Bear!"

and she held on, and
they both fell in
together.

&
there was no Time.

Time was not theirs.
There was no Time there, and there was no There there.
What was *was*.
But it was not Then.
& actually, while there was no There and no Then, there were many somewheres, neatly superposed like a deck of cards; and there was a single drawn-out, loop-the-looping *when*. This *when* soared and plunged like a roller coaster. Or like the flight pattern of a paper airplane. That's what Time was, here: all motion, convolution, a kinesthetic labyrinth.

So where, or when, exactly, were Tex & Molly?

TEX (0')

An enfoldment of black: a caress.
Motion. Carrying, rocking, mothering motion.
Throaty *krr krr krr* like an incantation, song without melody or words, stripped down to sheer timbre.
Going away. Going . . .
And something else. A familiar . . . what?
Ah:
Wing-beats.

MOLLY (0')

Perfect light. Pure liquid golden sunlight glinting off all the jewels that ever grew in the belly of the Earth.

Dream blanket soft and warm spangled with stars, cutout moons, beautiful patterns, swirling and swelling, growing, *knowing*—

How exciting it felt to her! A thrill, a tingling that might be in her heart, or entering her heart from outside, filling her, fulfilling her—

Oh. Like a pang of joy. Agonizing, orgasmic. Too much, almost too much. Too full, too complete. And yet she could never get enough of this.

This.

Blinking something like her eyes.

Light streaming through where her eyes might have been.

Warmth. Growth. Plenitude.

Hugeness.

Gentle, overwhelming power.

Like a thing she knew. A texture she remembered.

Like some . . . not a *what*. Some *who*.

TEX (1')

"Raven?"

Heard his own voice and that was something. Reassuring or whatever.

"Raven, are you there?"

Hollow and dark. Bottom of the Well? Things coming back, bits and bytes.

"*Ow!*"—as all of a sudden remembering. Trying to reach down, figure out where *down* was. Straining for a sense of body.

Had there really been wing-beats?

"Raven," he said—words more clearly audible now, the larynx forming itself around them, then the throat, the chest, the diaphragm. "Raven—my head hurts."

A rustling. The darkness moving, unfolding and refolding itself. His face brushed as if by feathers.

My face? he wondered. Touching it. Feeling fingers probe the skin. Still apart from him, though, some way. And still so dark, so vacant and still.

Whispering, "Raven?"—in a voice at once too loud, ringing, metal-edged with reverb.

And the *Darkness* answered:

I AM HERE.

MOLLY (1')

Lying on the breast of that unbounded plain. Breeze moving soft through her hair: warm against her forehead: sweet as it entered and escaped her lungs.

Knowing the taste of it. Primordial recipe of minerals, earth-salts, amino acids, dissolved in water, drawn up in the air and scattered in rain, simmered under a younger, yellower sun.

Beginning over. (She understood now.)

Sinking new roots in the Underworld and unfurling upward, stretching open-armed for the heavens where light and music beckoned her. Retracing that old path, the ancient living pattern.

And gradually, by a process of steady and piecemeal accretion, retrieving the knowledge, the lessons and morals and memories that lay strewn about her like pebbles. Like popcorn. Like nuggets of gleaming white light.

Bear, she remembered—neither first nor last among the thoughts that came to her. She held on to it, though. Bear.

Bear. A mantra, of sorts.

Bear.

And sometime, anytime, the plain rose up and its grasses and flowers became a coat of fur. Its soil became flesh, its sunlight crystallized in two huge eyes, terrible and irresistible to look back at. The warm sweet breeze became breath. And then the monstrous *Being* lifted Molly up, unhurriedly examined her, and set her easily on her feet.

Molly felt herself whole again, though tiny and naked.

The *Being* was huge and clothed in an earth-colored hide. The two great eyes peered down at her; the nostrils tested her scent.

"Are you real?" Molly asked. She was surprised that she could talk, and somewhat more surprised that she had the nerve to.

The *Being* dropped suddenly onto its four paws, dug at the ground with its claws. This seemed to make the ground more real, more tangible. Solidity rippled outward in waves. Soil and rocks took shape, then trees and ferns and mosses. Like a bubble, the sky expanded over their heads. Birds cried down. Bugs buzzed. A snake emerged from a hole and coiled itself tightly up, holding its pose with infinite reptilian patience, as though waiting to see what would happen.

Molly felt as though she were starting to get the picture. She looked at the Being and said, "Are you the Goddess?"

The *Being* snorted. Like thunder. Like war-hammers.

Then that Voice—too loud and full of power to have been merely sound—came out of the *Being*, and It said:

WHERE AM I?

TEX (2')

 "Who's there?" said Tex.

All was still darkness, with a deeper *Darkness* at its core.

WHOM DID YOU CALL?

—sounding distinctly impatient, the *Darkness* replied.

"I . . . I don't think I called anyone."

THEN TELL ME WHO I AM. AND TELL ME HOW I CAME TO BE HERE. I SUGGEST YOU CONSIDER YOUR ANSWERS CARE-FULLY. I AM ACCUSTOMED TO BEING RECEIVED WITH RATHER A GOOD DEAL MORE CEREMONY.

Tex groped. He groped first at himself, counting and sorting his body parts. (They were all present.) Then he groped for some clue as to what was going on here. Like, was this a world-class hallucination? And if so, then why could he not *see* anything so as to better enjoy it? He remembered a bumper sticker he had once proudly displayed, on some rustbucket or another. The memory made him chuckle.

YOU LAUGH?

roared the *Darkness,* incredulous.

"Sorry, man. I was just thinking—you know, 'I brake for hallu-cinations,' remember that?"

The *Darkness* caused the entire world (or so it seemed) to shudder.

THIS IS NO OCCASION FOR JOKING. WHERE I GO, SUCH AN

OCCASION SELDOM ARISES. NOW I ASK: DO YOU HAVE AN
OFFERING FOR ME?

Tex figured by this time there was no way things could get
any weirder. This was more outrageous than that time in Katmandu—getting off on something reputed to be no-bullshit *soma*
while dying of malaria at the same time. The old *rishi* fucker that
sold him the *soma* brought him back to life in the nick of time—
or perhaps just after the nick; there were some pretty cool death
rushes there for a little bit—and so he lived, or lived again, to
tell about it, though of course words could never do a thing like
that justice. But that was *nothing* compared to this.

Could it be (it came to him to wonder) that this time, it's the
Real Scene?

ANSWER ME

demanded the *Darkness*.

"Right, right," said Tex. "But if you don't mind my asking:
who are you?"

Then there was light.

And Tex was hanging upside down from a gnarled, naked-
limbed thorn tree. The branches of the tree were full of ravens.
The ravens screamed in mockery. Tex recognized the scene from
a tarot painting.

It changed.

Now he was being held down under a river. A huge fish—a
salmon—was staring him in the face. The water was icy and Tex
struggled not to breathe, but in vain. Slivers of pain laced his
lungs. The salmon had a know-it-all expression on its scaly face.
Tex writhed as his lungs imploded. Something like this happened
to somebody once before, he recalled.

It changed again.

Bound securely with what appeared to be his own stretched-
out intestines, Tex could not look away from the aged and terrible
Crone that stood before him with a long, rusty knife. The end
of the knife was bent, forming an unpleasant-appearing hook, like
some kind of bird claw. Cackling, the Crone plunged the knife
into Tex, twisted it around a bit, dragged it out with some of
his liver attached. Do not imagine that Tex did not acutely feel
all this.

Well, he thought, that ought to do it. The Triple Death. Quite
an honor, sort of.

He yowled in unbearable excruciation.

It changed once more.

Now he was on his feet again. Liver back in place. Lungs empty. Blood pumping. Mind awfully, and for once completely, clear.

He stood in a small round chamber. The walls were of stone, glistening with moisture, crawling with vile forms of life, or half-life. On the floor, amid sordid effluents, lay hundreds of coins, old and new, a few beads and lesser-grade gemstones, decomposing scraps of paper on which little messages had been scrawled, a terra-cotta goddess figurine, a Ken doll, and a small copper pipe connector. Everything was coming into focus.

"I dig it," Tex said, to the *Darkness* that was now assuming a visible form close, very close, in front of him. "I yelled 'Raven,' right? I meant Molly. But I got *you*."

Huge: hideous: stinking of carrion: so utterly black that ordinary blackness would have seemed to glow in comparison: the *Darkness* stood before him. It lifted a leg and clawed at the feathers underneath one vast wing. Unsavory little things fell out, hit the ground and scurried off into crevices.

YOU GOT ME

the *Darkness* concurred.

YOU INVOKED ME, TO BE PRECISE. YOU AWOKE ME. NOW PLEASE DO NOT DETAIN ME HERE UNNECESSARILY. WHAT DO YOU DESIRE OF ME? AND WHAT ARE YOU PREPARED TO OFFER IN RETURN?

On the whole, Tex was mind-blown. In some measure he was also scared shitless, and certainly he was way confused. But you couldn't help getting into this, a little bit. This was, after all, the Ultimate Trip. This was the mystery of the ages. This was the Underworld. Tex was pretty sure about that, at least, if nothing else.

NEVER MIND

said the *Darkness*.

OF COURSE I KNOW WHAT YOU DESIRE. IT WAS IN YOUR MIND WHEN YOU UTTERED YOUR INVOCATION. YES, OF COURSE, I CAN IF I CHOOSE FULFILL YOUR WISH. EXPLAIN FIRST, HOWEVER, IN WHAT WAY YOU PROPOSE TO SERVE ME. YOU ARE NOT, AFTER ALL, ARE YOU, STANDING BEFORE ME IN A POSITION OF STRENGTH.

No doubt about it, thought Tex. The *Darkness* raises a very significant point here.

"Woo," he said. "So you mean, you want me to like, promise you my immortal soul for all eternity, or something like that?"

The *Darkness* appeared to quake. (With rage? or laughter?)

I'M AFRAID THAT SORT OF THING IS NOT MY STYLE. INDEED, IT REFLECTS A RATHER SAVAGE AND VENGEFUL MIND-SET, IF I MAY SPEAK IN SUCH A WAY OF A FELLOW DIVINITY.

"No, hey, I can relate," said Tex. "I should have known you'd be cooler than that. No offense, okay?"

Better shift focus, he thought. Get in the appropriate god's-eye p.o.v. What were the old Pagan guys into? Music, feasting, ecstasy, sacrifice . . .

"I could throw a really big party for you," he suggested, hopefully.

A PARTY.

"Or I mean, a festival, you know? A whole big holiday. Do it again every year."

The *Darkness* appeared to contemplate this. It smacked its beak thoughtfully. Its orbicular, slightly bulging black eyes skittered this way and that, as though looking for a small living entity to snack upon.

IT COMES TO ME THAT YOU ARE IN AN EXCEEDINGLY UNFA-VORABLE SITUATION TO INSTITUTE ANY NEW HOLIDAYS. YOU WERE SCARCELY AN INFLUENTIAL PERSON, THERE IN THE WORLD OF FLESH AND TIME. IS THAT NOT SO?

Tex felt totally cast-down. Even your ancient, long somnolent deities had not failed to notice this. " 'Fraid so," he admitted. "Raven was the only one who took me seriously, and that was only about a third of the time."

YOU REFER TO YOUR SEXUAL MATE.

"Right. I mean, but it was more than that, though. But sorry. I guess that's what got me into this, isn't it?"

I BELIEVE YOU RATHER FELL INTO THIS YOURSELF, DIDN'T YOU.

"Ha!" You've got to love this *Darkness* dude, Tex thought. Or is it dudette? Would it be impertinent to ask?

I AM OF FEMININE POLARITY

the *Darkness* said,

> THOUGH I SHARE MANY TRAITS WITH MY SIBLINGS AND COUSINS WHO ARE ALLIED WITH BOTH SEXES—OCCASION-ALLY AT THE SAME TIME. WE CORVIDS ARE UNIQUE AMONG DIVINITIES, THAT WAY.

"Far fucking out," said Tex. "I wish you could like, manifest yourself to the Dianic separatists and lay this out for them."

> I FIND SUCH SECTARIAN BICKERING OF NO INTEREST WHAT-EVER. ANOTHER LATTER-DAY PERVERSITY, I SURMISE.

Scratching at the stone floor; flexing Her huge and rather grue-some body as though loosening up for some amazing feat of devilment; lastly cocking Her head sideways to regard Tex with a single onyx eye.

> NEXT TIME YOU INVOKE ME, PERHAPS YOU MIGHT SUMMON ONE OF YOUR MORE UP-TO-DATE GOD-FORMS AS WELL. FOR EXAMPLE, THE ONE WHO ENGENDERED THAT CULT OF RIT-UAL CANNIBALISM—I SHOULD *LOVE* TO MEET HIM.

Tex thought, Well, at least I've come to the right afterlife. He said, "*Next* time I invoke you?"

> I HAVE HAD ENOUGH OF BANTERING. I AM GOING TO GRANT YOUR DESIRE BECAUSE IT WILL ENTERTAIN ME TO OBSERVE THE CONSEQUENCES. I SHALL EXPECT TO BE THANKED IN SOME APPROPRIATE WAY. THE WELL HERE COULD DO WITH A LITTLE REFURBISHING. I HAVE NO WISH TO SPEAK TO YOU AGAIN. HOWEVER, IF YOU CANNOT HELP YOURSELF, AS I EX-PECT YOU CANNOT, YOU MAY ADDRESS ME AS *NEMAN*. IT IS NOT MY REAL NAME, OF COURSE. BUT IT WILL AVOID SUCH PROBLEMS AS YOUR ACCIDENTALLY INVOKING ONE OF MY SISTERS—OR OUR DREADFUL COUSIN FROM UP NORTH.

Even as the *Darkness* spoke, the small circular room was grow-ing brighter. Light spilled down from above, growing nearer and clearer as the objects close at hand grew faint and dim.

> NOW I SHALL MARK YOU

said the *Darkness*

> IN THE CUSTOMARY MANNER.

And with a rapid swipe of the great swart beak, the *Darkness* snapped at Tex's thigh. The bone broke with an audible pop.

"AAAAGGGHH," Tex roared. But he did not fall to the floor. He found to his surprise and bafflement that he was able to stay on his feet, even to balance his weight on both legs, the broken and the unbroken. His pain was, of course, indescribable. "What did you do *that* for?" he wailed.

BE HONORED. YOU HAVE BEEN KISSED BY A GODDESS.

"Wow. What a turn-on," uttered Tex through gritted teeth.

NOW GO

the *Darkness* said.
And you better believe
Tex obeyed
Her.

MOLLY (2')

"Where *are* you?" repeated Molly. As in, why are you asking *me*?

The *Being* stretched and yawned. Ripples of long-dormant power traveled down massive flanks as the muscles beneath stirred and tightened. Overhead, the sun flashed many colors, an unfamiliar spectrum, as if the sky were made of polished jewels. Winds gathered force, shaking the treetops, though the air close at hand remained calm.

THE WORLD I FELL ASLEEP IN WAS VERY DIFFERENT THAN THIS. CAN YOU TELL ME WHAT PLACE THIS IS, AND HOW I HAVE COME TO BE HERE?

Molly's eyes opened wide. She did a thing she often did when nervous or uncertain: curled her lower lip upward and gently bit it, rabbitwise, with her two front teeth. In doing this she tasted traces of the makeup she had worn for the performance. She ran quickly in her mind through the various Elements and Seasons and Potencies the Street Players had impersonated, trying to find one that approached the awesomeness of *This*. All she could think was, Maybe we didn't know what we were fucking around with.

"So, ah, where are you from?" she heard herself saying, stupidly.

The great *Being* might have laughed, or the world around may simply have shaken in some unrelated seismic event.

COME

the mighty, divinely gentle Voice said.

WALK WITH ME.

Before Molly could take a step, the Earth began to move. Trees and rocks and stands of tall grass passed by them. Watercourses spilled, clans of furry creatures scampered out of their way, wide skeins of geese and pairs of milk-white swans flew nobly across the sky. The *Being* moved at a magisterial pace, giant paws touching the ground, barely resting there, moving on; and wherever the paws had lain, the ground instantly sprouted yellow-green grasses and sunflowers.

Then they stood at the edge of a shining sea. The waves rose and dove in spuming furrows. Sunlight danced in a billion ever-born and ever-dying prisms of salt spray. Molly recognized what ocean this was. Somewhere, in some distant Time, her own houseboat rose and fell on these same waters.

I AM FROM THERE

the *Being* said, holding out one giant forepaw.

ACROSS THERE. I KEPT COMING WEST AND WEST, MOVING WITH MY PEOPLE. FINALLY I CAME HERE. I THOUGHT NONE OF MY PEOPLE HAD FOLLOWED ME. I MUST HAVE SLEPT FOR A VERY LONG TIME. I COULD FEEL MYSELF BECOMING BURIED IN IT, THAT SLUMBER. SINKING DEEPER AND DEEPER. AT LAST I BELIEVED I WOULD NEVERMORE AWAKEN. BUT NOW ...

(Peering at Molly. And *smiling* now. No shit. The smile of a god, can you dig it?)

NOW I AM HERE BEFORE YOU. AND I SEE THAT THINGS HAVE CHANGED VERY GREATLY. PERHAPS YOU CAN HELP ME UNDERSTAND.

Help a deity understand? Molly couldn't imagine it. Then she thought, Wait a minute. The Goddess is in everyone. I am strong, I am invincible, I am quoted in the last edition of Bartlett's.

"I'll give it a try," she said. "By the way—my name is Molly."

The *Being* appeared to laugh again. Like, of course *It* or *He* or *She* would already grok all that. Still, sounding not terribly unkind:

YOU MAY CALL ME *ARTH VAWR*. IT SIGNIFIES 'HEAVENLY

BEAR.' AND YOU MAY THINK OF ME AS MALE, THOUGH THAT
IS NOT HOW I BEGAN. YOU MAY ADDRESS ME AS YOU WOULD
A VERY OLD KING, THOUGH WHAT KINGDOM I ONCE HAD I
FEAR HAS LONG VANISHED. HERE, SIT BESIDE ME AMONG
THESE ROCKS. THIS WILL DO FOR A KING'S TABLE.

Around them, Molly now noticed, stood a ring of weathered
stones. When she looked at them they seemed to become larger,
as though they were growing like trees out of the substance of
the Earth. She turned around and around, watching the stones
form a sort of protective wall about them. Finally, safe and surrounded, the two of them, mortal and immortal, gathered themselves up before a massive central rock that was broad and nearly
flat, like a table. Or an altar.

"Will you eat?" said *Arth Vawr,* indicating a steaming and sa-
vory banquet that materialized on the flat stone.

Molly's understanding was that you had to be extremely cautious in dealings of this type. "Um, no thanks, I don't guess I'm
really hungry."

NO? THEN AT LEAST TRY A BIT OF THIS. I CAUGHT IT JUST
NOW MYSELF.

On a platter of gold lay a giant salmon. It was obviously fresh;
in fact it looked only half-dead. One eye stared up at Molly as
though daring her to dig in.

Something about the expression of that fish . . .

"Sure," said Molly. "I guess I'll try a little."

Seeing no flatware, she reached out and gouged out a piece of
the salmon's flesh with her fingers. It was the most delicious food
she had ever tasted.

"How do you *do* that?" she marveled. "Some kind of butter
sauce? Is that rosemary? And something tart . . ."

Lying on the platter, the salmon looked dismayed. Molly had
a sudden quirky feeling—a little niggle of intuition, as though she
had just become aware of, you know, *everything.* Which would
have been cool, except that it made her feel more confused
than ever.

"So it must be hard," she said to the *Being,* conversationally,
"this whole omnipotence trip. Do you just start right in on it, or
do you have to sort of work your way up?"

WHAT AN EXCEEDINGLY ODD QUESTION.

Arth Vawr leaned back, scratched himself a bit, appeared to deliberate.

> I CAN SPEAK ONLY FOR MYSELF, OF COURSE. MY OWN EARLI-EST MEMORIES ARE OF BEING A WIDELY HELD NOTION AMONG SCATTERED BANDS OF NOMADIC HUNTERS RANG-ING ACROSS A VAST CONTINENTAL PLAIN. FROM THERE I GREW TO BE A PRIMAL TOTEMIC FIGURE, A REPOSITORY OF AWE AND TERROR. I WAS STILL ESSENTIALLY FEMALE, IN THOSE DAYS. THEY FED ME MEAT AND GRAIN, A BIT OF FRUIT. THEY DANCED AND SANG TO ME. I GREW FAT ON THEIR DREAMS AND THEIR VISIONS. BY NIGHT, THEIR SHAPE-SHIFTERS CAME TO VISIT ME, AND I SENT THEM BACK WITH A BIT OF THE POWER I HAD COLLECTED OVER THE CENTURIES. THEN, OF COURSE, THINGS GREW COMPLI-CATED, THE WORLD LOST ITS INNOCENCE. I FELT MYSELF SPLITTING INTO SEPARATE ENTITIES, GOING SEPARATE WAYS. I UNDERWENT A SEX CHANGE. I TOOK ON NEW ATTRI-BUTES, WHILE SOME OF THE OLD ONES WERE LEFT TO AT-ROPHY. HOW I CAME TO RESIDE IN *ARTH VAWR*, AND TO FALL ASLEEP IN THAT GUISE, IS SURELY TOO LONG A STORY TO TELL. NOR IS IT PARTICULARLY A HAPPY ONE. IT HAS ITS VILLAINS. I SENSE THAT SOME OF THEM ARE AROUND US.

Molly looked up worriedly. A great deal of Time, or whatever passed for Time here, seemed to have moved by very rapidly. The sky had fallen into purple dusk, and the air had the pregnant hush of evening. Molly thought she could just make out the sil-houettes of black birds, coasting silently against the shadowy backdrop. There was no sound, no way to be sure.

> NOTHING TO FEAR

said *Arth Vawr*.

> I AM AWAKE NOW. I AM BACK IN THE WORLD. THOUGH I WISH I KNEW MORE ABOUT THIS WORLD I HAVE RETURNED TO. CAN YOU NOT HELP ME AT ALL?

"Sure," said Molly. "I'll give it a shot. For starters, though, I'm probably not the best person to be talking to. 'Cause you know, everything that's been happening for like, the past 30 years, I guess, I've been on the side that's come out on the bottom. I kind of feel like I'm waging a losing campaign against History, or something."

> I KNOW THE FEELING.

(Letting go a long divine sigh.)

"Right, I guess you do. So anyway, from my perspective things seem to be going to hell in a clutch purse. Only of course a lot of people probably see it differently. Or they see it happening for different reasons. It's like, everyone agrees that the world is sick, but nobody can get together on the diagnosis or treatment or anything."

PERHAPS THAT IS THE NATURE OF THE DISEASE.

"Yeah, maybe. I figure—or rather I used to figure, back when—anyway, I'm just an actress, you know? An entertainer: a Player. I figure that's my part, that's what I can do and it's what I've *got* to do, to make people feel a little better and make the world a better place. I mean sure I recycle and buy unbleached coffee filters and all like that. But in the big scheme of things, I feel like my real contribution is more to try to affect people's *feelings,* if that makes any sense. So when they would look at a tree, for example, they'd just naturally feel like: Wow, a *tree*—you know? They'd feel a different way about the world, so they'd act differently, without having to actually change their rational thoughts and ideas first. Because it seems like that's what people overlook—they argue with each other in *words,* when words are really pretty much secondary. I used to disagree with Bear about that, though, because Bear always says—"

BEAR?

"Ah, sorry. Tex. My sort of husband, only we weren't actually legally married, in a real church. Anyway, he always said, you only see what you believe in. If you don't believe in magic, then magic won't happen for you. If you don't believe in the holiness of the natural world, then you're not going to see anything there but maybe a pretty backdrop for your vacation photos. And he said the problem wasn't that people don't *care* about the Earth, it's that most of them don't *believe* in it, as this great holy sentient-mother-goddess-living-being. They think it's all just this *system,* this big complicated glob of interacting parts that you can control or tinker with or reprogram, like a computer. So he was coming at this out of a totally different head. *Belief,* you know, instead of *feeling.*"

YES, I SEE. NOW YOUR HUSBAND—HIS NAME IS TEX, BUT YOU CALL HIM BEAR?

"Sure. That's his clan name, you know? His power-animal. And he called me Raven."

BEAR AND RAVEN.

Molly did the thing with her lip and her teeth again, waiting this one out. Finally she ventured, "Is there something weird about that?"

That quaking again: the god's laughter, or whatever.

> I SHOULD SAY THAT IT'S AN UNLIKELY UNION, TO SAY THE LEAST. AND IT MAY EXPLAIN CERTAIN THINGS. AND IT MAY MAKE CERTAIN THINGS A BIT MORE DIFFICULT. OH, DON'T WORRY—IT'S JUST, AS ONE MIGHT SAY, A BIT OF A FAMILY QUARREL. OF VERY LONG STANDING.

"Sorry," said Molly, wondering where that all-knowing feeling had gotten off to. "I didn't mean to make things hard for you."

> DON'T BE FOOLISH. IT IS PLEASANT TO HAVE SOMETHING TO DO, AFTER ALL THIS TIME. AND I AM AFRAID, YOUNG MORTAL, THAT YOU HAVE SOMETHING TO DO AS WELL.

I do? Molly started to say. But the world was changing again, and somehow her vocal chords were caught up in it. Around her, the circle of stones seemed to move, to spin, and the stars just popping out whirled above her eyes like fireflies swept up in a cosmic whirlwind. Then things began moving in a new direction as well—neither side to side nor up nor down; a different, spiraling way that maybe they had moved once a long while ago, before the sleeping and the reawakening of *Arth Vawr*. The spiraling movement grew faster and faster, drawing the whole world and Molly herself into it.

As she felt herself falling, or being dragged away, she saw for a single instant a horrifying flash of light. The flash came in only one eye (the right one, the one with better and longer vision); it was as though she had collided with one of those tiny swarming stars. Before she could cry out the flash was over, and she blinked her eye (which did not hurt at all), but all she could see was blackness.

Then, at a certain moment—an inevitable instant, long foretold but no longer much expected or even believed-in—

The *Heavenly Bear* reared up on two legs,
and its shattering roar broke the world into pieces,

and all things under the Sun
were changed forever.
But not at
once.

&
they were back in Time.

The clock radio aboard the good ship *Linear Bee* flipped on promptly at 10:00 A.M. It was tuned as always to WURS, the nonprofit community radio station out of Awonadjo, up the coast from Dublin Harbor. Reception was terrific, also as always after a storm cleared out the atmosphere. Goblin the Cat-Person lay curled on the chart table in the pilot house, where the morning sun made a puddle of warmth, and Molly's stellar geranium "Strawberry Fayre" bloomed its miniature head off.

If there was anything to tip you off that this was not a totally ordinary wake-up call, it was just this: the total ordinariness of it all. The mundanity. The lying there, staring at the seams in the planking overhead, listening to tunes straining out of the tiny speakers, feeling the boat gently rise on top of the swells then settle back into the troughs: the whole scene felt so perfectly homey and comfortable and all's-right-with-the-world that you had to chew the apple a little harder, looking for the worm in it. Because it *shouldn't* have felt so 99.9% sweat-free, right? Whatever had really happened last night (and still only half awake, Tex and Molly had not had time to mind-lock on *that*) it had been decidedly weird and you would think it ought to have mattered in some fashion, to have jiggled their world one way or another. To have changed *something*. And yet, to all appearances, it had not.

Molly felt Tex stir beside her and she peeked over at him. Out of custom she glanced with her left eye, the one with the better close-up vision. Tex's own bright small eyes were slitted, appraising and sly, peeking back at her.

"Morning, Bear," she said.

"Morning, Raven."

There: that had done that.

"So," said Tex.

"*So,*" said Molly. "Some night, huh?"

"I guess."

She could read him like a book. She could tell that he was waiting for *her* to be the one to bring it up. Whatever it was, that needed to be brought. She rejected a couple of options—starting with, I *told* you it wasn't a good idea to go out to the Well (because she had not in fact told him this, though she had thought it)—and finally settled upon:

"Um, Bear. Do you remember anything about the drive home?"

He wrinkled the skin of his forehead, which came down in a V-shaped crease to the place where his two eyebrows had mostly grown together. He allowed: "Not much."

"Much?"

Tex closed his eyes again, perchance to think; he lay there in pregnant silence.

"Bear," Molly said. Her mind set now. She nudged Tex with an elbow, squeezed the open left eye into a forceful squint. "Bear. Try and do something."

"What?" He frowned, still not looking. "What do you mean?"

"*Do* something. Like I don't know. Try to levitate or something."

"*What?*"

At this at last he jerked his head up and intercepted her eye and grokked that she was serious. He sighed.

"Okay, Raven. I'm trying to levitate. Right, *now.*"

His body strained. His grizzly face got a little more wrinkled. The dangling skulls and fetishes in his ears (why had he worn them to bed?) shook and jingled with the effort. But he did not levitate. He just lay on the bunk. After a while, he let his breath out.

"There," he said. "See?"

"Okay," said Molly. "Now try something else. Try—let's see. How about putting your hand through that bulkhead there?"

"Anybody can put their hand through that bulkhead. It's as thin as paper."

That's not what I meant, she started to tell him. Instead she laughed. "Bear," she said. "You are terrible."

"Bear the Terrible," he murmured happily. He rolled onto his side, away from her, signifying an intention to go back to sleep. Bogus, probably.

On WURS, the way-cool voice of the announcer said, "This is Bad Cathy at the mike, and your radio is in need of an attitude adjustment. Let's dig some extinct reptiles, shall we?"

"I think I'll try making some tea," Molly said. "That ought to prove something."

Tex grunted. "It'll prove there's still propane left in the tank."

"Be quiet."

"On the outside," groaned J Mascis, "that's where they always hide."

"I hate this guy," said Tex. He wiggled a foot under the covers, keeping time. "But I dig the Mellotron."

Molly rolled out of bed. One foot down, then the other. So far, no surprises. She rose to her feet and just stood that way for a moment, feeling vertical. Did one usually feel so vertical upon rising? she wondered. Maybe I'm thinking too hard.

Padding into the galley, where the sun was doing wonderful things with the Vaselineware, whose luminous yellow glow comes from traces of uranium in the glass, she set about the daily decoction of caffeine from *Camellia sinensis*. They had switched from black tea to green after they read a couple of years back that this would be better for Tex's prostate. Molly popped open the white Gevalia jar and stuck her nose in. A damp, gardeny smell. Nothing much, really. She missed her Earl Grey.

Afterlife Factoid #1
Making tea is *much* more complicated than you imagine.

Just lifting the teapot required an unbelievable amount of concentration. Molly found herself staring at a spoonful of leaves—tiny gray-green, balled-up nuggets of Gunpowder, the cheapest variety at the Co-op—and thinking about *splendor in the grass, glory in the flower;* she had to nudge herself to get going again, turn on the burner, adjust the flame, position the kettle—it was all so *complicated,* and every twist and turn in the plot came as such a surprise to her. Such a . . . revelation!

Whatever this is, she declared to herself, it is *definitely* the strangest trip I've ever been on.

After eternity, or half an hour, the tea was made and she

dragged Tex up and they ventured out onto the little deck aft of the galley to drink it.

The day was beautiful. Molly could not remember a more beautiful day. Snatches of conversation, music, windows being opened, daily life being lived, came from widely separated points about the harbor. There was a sputter of lobster boats working their trap lines just outside the sea buoy, and an almost transparent veil of haze softened the ice-sharp edge of sunlight, as though the pure spring air had by some miraculous happenstance been rendered visible. Even the seagulls, a.k.a. Cold Bay chickens, looked sleek and graceful, and Tex (a further miracle!) was not annoyed when one of them chose the deck of the *Bee* to bomb with a mussel. (That's how they open the shells.) He sat and Molly sat beside him as the tea steamed up from the his & her, Sun & Moon mugs, wearing the peaceful look of an aged acid freak glad to be hanging out, mildly buzzed, with nowhere in particular to hustle off to.

"I guess I'm not really in the mood for tea," Tex said, staring down into his mug (the Sun: a bear connection) as though its contents were completely unfamiliar to him.

"Me neither," said Molly. "But still. Tea's kind of comforting, isn't it? Like a ritual or something."

Tex did a mouth thing, a Mick Jaggerish pucker. Agreement, but with something held back. Molly smiled to see this familiar, well-worn look; then she dropped the smile before Tex could catch her wearing it.

It seemed to Molly that the Thing [unspoken, unnameable] that she was worried about—secretly deep in her belly terrified of—could not possibly be true on a day like this. Or rather, a day like this could not be possible if the Thing were true. If It had really happened. Because here, stretched out before her like a brightly painted canvas on its vast hardwood frame, you had the very web of life, the curious network of interdependence and rivalry, ceaseless bickering and provisional, moment-to-moment compromise, by which the whole biosphere was knitted together. And just as plainly you had You—You the person thinking this— who must be a part of that web, who indeed could feel the strands of the web quiver in response to the least movement, the most infinitesimal change, even something as tiny and ghostlike as a thought. And if You were part of everything, connected with everything, flowing and changing with the All, then mustn't you be—

"Yoo hoo!"

—came a voice from the *Bee*'s brow. Young woman's voice. Tex and Molly turned, and although they could not see her through the pilot house, they recognized the voice as belonging to Ludi, the fresh-faced 20-nothing Street Player.

"Molly!" Ludi called out. "Tex! Is anybody home?"

"Out here," Tex called back to her. "On the aft deck." Rather *eagerly*, it seemed to Molly.

Ludi pulled open the hatch that led down to the living quarters. "Hello?" she said, more cautiously. "Hey, are you guys ready? Are you still asleep?"

"We're back here," Tex yelled, a bit louder.

"Ready for what?" Molly wanted to know. (Setting her teeth, invisibly.)

He pretended not to recall. The imposture was obvious. Molly had not spent a lifetime in the theater to be taken in by such facile deceptions.

"Where could they be?" Ludi said, speaking to herself now. She moved through the living quarters into the galley. Molly could see her beautiful long brown hair, with possibly genuine sun-gilded highlights, through a window filled with angel-wing begonias.

"Oh, right," said Tex, glancing sideways, the picture of innocent forgetfulness. Butter wouldn't melt in his mouth. "The protest at the Goddin base. You know, the place Gulf Atlantic is turning into a gene-splicing operation?"

The aft hatch popped open and Ludi emerged into the sunshine. She blinked, raised a slender, long-fingered hand to shield her face. Every motion (Molly was obliged, professionally, to admit) a study in natural, unaffected elegance. All she needed was a bit of training. A stint in a city somewhere. And a good dose (Molly appended, tossing professionalism overboard) of artistic suffering.

"*Good* morning, Ludi," Tex said, shifting his feet a bit, hitching his middle-aged back up straight.

Good morning, Dad, thought Molly.

But Ludi appeared to ignore him. She took the two paces over to the tea table and she looked down at it, as though no one at all were sitting there. Molly could smell the agreeable pungence of patchouli oil, the warmth of an athletic body beneath rumpled denim and wool. Ludi reached down with one of those graceful hands and picked up a teacup—the Moon, a raven thing—wrapping her fingers around it, measuring the heat, sniffing the steam that wafted up to her nostrils.

"That's funny," she said. "I must have just missed them."
Tex and Molly stared at each other across the table.

Afterlife Factoid #2
Dead hippies are invisible.

Ludi plopped the mug down—carelessly, sloshing tea, now that
she found herself alone—then briskly retraced her steps through
the houseboat. Tex and Molly followed her with their eyes, even
while she moved unseen through the living quarters, and did not
look again at one another until they heard Ludi's orange VW bug
sputter to life and take off with an energetic ratcheting of its
ancient gearbox.

"I wish she would learn how to drive that thing," Tex said.

But this did not annoy Molly now. Because all of that—all of
Everything—was beside the point. *Way* beside it. She fixed her
left eye upon Tex and she hammered him with her attention until
he was forced to return her stare, to snap into phase with her.

There was no more shucking and jiving. And Tex knew it—
had known it all along—Molly now understood. He had just been,
Bear-style, taking his time about coming around to this. But he
was around to it now.

Tex looked at Molly and he gave her—out of nowhere—a
funny little side-of-the-mouth smile. Just a jerky little thing.

"Woo boy," he said.

Somehow—you figure it out—this relieved her. She managed
to smile back. She said, "So, what do we do now, King Farouk?"

Bad Cathy at the mike said, "Is it just me, folks, or do you
think that song is really about *frogs*?"

"Of course it's about frogs," Tex said. "What an airhead."

And Molly figured there was no point, at this stage of the
game, giving him a hard time about talking back to a radio.

ANGER, DENIAL, & SEQ

They sat on the built-in sofa in their living quarters,
taking stock. (For starters, did the term *living quarters*
still apply?) They lifted objects and put them down.
They noticed, for possibly the first time ever, what a peculiar

place the houseboat was—i.e., for adult human beings at the end
of this millennium actually to call their home. Its décor fell somewhere between Hiawatha and Jimi Hendrix. There were

(3) framed Day-Glo posters, including (1) autographed
Peter Max
Stacks of LP's, still acquiring scratches from regular use
Shelves stuffed with New Directions paperbacks
(Patchen! Rexroth! *The Lime Twig*!)
A Sarah Nickerson hooked rug in a yellow-on-black
peace sign pattern
Painted parchment wall hangings and other souvenirs
of Katmandu
The Invisible Landscape, original 1975 edition
The Complete Marijuana Grower's Home Handbook
A steer skull from Jerome, Arizona
A bong
The Sri Yantra
The *I Ching*
A quilt made of old T-shirts too precious to throw away

None of which, if you want to know, provided any notable
consolation.

Where Tex and Molly sat, the sofa's foam cushion was worn
into channels by the familiar shapes of their bottoms. Goblin the
Cat-Person lay curled in the space between them, where a tiny
declivity marked his own settled-in spot. He seemed totally oblivious to their presence; but then, what else was new?

They tried to adjust, to accommodate themselves. They imagined there must be some protocol. Tex found his copy of the
Tibetan Book of the Dead, and Molly picked up a hand-me-down
paperback by Elisabeth Kübler-Ross she had not bothered with
before now.

"None of this stuff seems to apply," said Tex. "I mean according to this, we're supposed to be, you know—on our way
out of here."

He tossed the book onto the coffee table, a gnarled spruce burl
sawed through the roots, upended, and rubbed shiny with bay-
berry wax one long-ago Samhain. The *Book of the Dead* touched
down with a satisfyingly physical THOOMP.

"That's just Anger," Molly assured him. "Perfectly natural."

"I just can't *believe* it," Tex said.

"Ah. You're already on to Denial."

This phase persisted for several minutes. Molly considered Bargaining.

"Do you suppose if we . . ." she began, absently plucking Goblin's fur. "Nah, forget it."

What came next? Ah:

"What a bummer," said Tex.

"I hear you."

The Cat-Person mewed. Automatically Molly stroked him in the skinny part of the neck. Goblin purred. He raised his head a little.

"Nice kitty," said Molly.

"Hold on a minute," said Tex.

Afterlife Factoid #3
Death is no big deal to a cat-person.

"Well, what did you expect?" said Molly. She smiled, playing a game with Goblin's ears. She felt Acceptance coming along.

"You know what?" she said. "I think I might try going for a walk. Maybe just up to the Co-op or something. See what's new in the bargain bin."

Tex sighed. He propped his feet up on the coffee table. He said:

"Ah, yes. The afterlife goes on."

THAT FAIR DISTANT SHORE

Poised at the *Bee*'s gunwale, where a wooden gangway led up to the worn timber pier behind the chicken-processing plant, now closed-down and derelict, Molly paused. She turned like an actress preparing to deliver her exit line.

But what she said was, "Come to think of it, maybe not."

And she backed down from the gangway onto the deck.

"What?" said Tex. "Aren't you going?"

She shrugged. "I don't know, I just don't feel like it. I'm kind of afraid that . . ."

"That what?" Tex was irritated, mostly at not understanding. Molly looked at him solemnly, silently calling for attention.

Over the years she had developed a way of doing this, a certain intimacy-inducing manner of tilting her body forward, getting into Tex's space, while meanwhile making her eyes round and raising them to look up at him, ingénueishly. He continued to find this endearing.

"Suppose," she said, "I were to crumble into dust as soon as my feet touched the ground."

"*What?*"

She raised her chin, all dignity now. "It happens."

"It happens? How do you know? To who?"

"To people who have crossed the water and come to the Blessed Isles. You know, afterwards they can go back to the land of mortals, but only as long as they remain on their magical steeds. If they ever set foot on the ground—*pffft.*" She rubbed her finger and thumb together, watching the imaginary dust drift down.

Tex could not believe this. He determined to be reasonable. "Those are fairy tales," he said. "They're just *stories.*"

"Just stories? Where do you think everything we know comes from? If people had honored the old stories more, we wouldn't— I mean, *they* wouldn't—be in such a mess today."

"But Raven. Listen. We did not cross the water and come to the Blessed Isles. We drove up a dirt road and fell in a well. In *Maine.*"

"Ha!" Molly gestured with full dramatic vigor, though Tex suspected it was a smoke screen. "We crossed that little creek, didn't we? Where the snow had melted and made a gully in the road? And everyone knows that wells are entrances to the Otherworld. That's why people throw pennies in them—it's a folk memory, seeking the favor of the gods and so forth. Didn't you know?"

Tex felt dizzy for a moment. Something blurry came about halfway back to him. Pennies in a well. He had seen that, some-where. And something else. A figurine. A plastic doll.

He shuddered. Too weird.

"I don't believe it," he said. "I mean, if we're dead, we're dead. That's cool. That's the end of the story. There's no way we could get any *deader*. Crumble into dust—what does that mean?" He hoisted himself onto the gangway.

"But it can't be the end," Molly said (so weakly, though, that he didn't quite register it). "Otherwise . . ."

Tex said, "Look, if you're not going ashore, then I am. I'll just stroll up to the Fleet Bank and—hey, dig this—I'll see if I can sneak some money out of a drawer. Just to check," he added quickly, seeing Molly's disapproving gaze about to fall on him. "Anyway, I'll be right back. Then you'll see."

He took a step up the gangway. Another step. So far so good. More confidently now, he pulled on the safety ropes and forged ahead with a swagger, reaching the end of the plank in half a dozen steps. With a little flourishy wave back at Molly, he set his right leg on the thick old timber of the pier

and fell down screaming

in unbelievable

agony.

"Bear!" Molly cried. She came scrambling up the gangway after him. "What happened?"

"I broke a leg," he groaned, twisting from side to side. "You told everybody to, remember?"

His right leg flopped uselessly, making a zig and then a zag in very unnatural directions. Molly felt slightly nauseous but also fascinated.

"How did you do that?" she said. "How could it possibly have happened? In the Well, do you think?"

"A goddess kissed me," he said—harshly, not sure altogether what he meant by it.

"She *did*?" whispered Molly. As though she had *known* there must be more to the story. "When? What goddess?"

"I don't know." Tex paused in his writhing about to look up plaintively at her. "Could you help me back on board? Please?"

"Oh. I'm sorry." She reached down—being very careful not to touch the pier—and grabbed Tex by his upstretched hands. He was a scrawny thing, not much to lug around. With a couple of heaves she got him back on the gangway. She paused for a breath.

Tex felt his pain evaporate. He looked down and saw that his leg was miraculously mended: straight and solid like always. Cautiously he flexed it, pressed downward against the plank. *Ninguna problema.*

"I'll be damned," he said.

"I hope not," Molly said sweetly. And she turned and sashayed back to the living quarters without so much as a told-you-so.

"Women," Tex said to a visiting seagull. "Women and goddesses."

The seagull cocked its (his? her?) head sideways and looked down superciliously. But then, a seagull would.

KNOWING IT ALL

 "Maybe we're not *supposed* to leave the boat," Tex said. Thinking aloud, mostly. "Maybe this is where we have to stay. Forever, I mean. Maybe we're ghosts, and we've got to hang out and haunt the *Bee*."

"I don't think so," said Molly.

Tex looked up at her, moderately annoyed. She was watering her royal purple streptocarpus.

"I think it's more like a riddle we have to figure out," she said, without looking around at him. "Like a puzzle, a labyrinth, whatever. That's how the gods communicate with humans, generally. Plus, it's a characteristic feature of visits to the Otherworld."

"What do you mean, *visits?*" Tex said. It came out sounding less sarcastic and more like a real question than he had intended. "And how did you get to be such a know-it-all, anyway?"

Molly spritzed a rosemary topiary with the pretty copper mister she had found at the dump. She guessed somebody had thrown it away when the green patina started to spread on it, like lichen. Turning, she gave Tex a playful spritz as well. She didn't figure a little water would do him any harm.

"I guess it must have been something I ate," she said.

"*What?*" Tex raised a pillow to defend himself.

"Something I ate." Molly paused, thinking over what she had said. "That's odd."

Tex lowered the pillow, cautiously.

Molly spritzed him again.

"Stop it, Raven."

"Ask me something," she said.

"I am asking you something. I'm asking you to stop squirting me."

"No, I mean . . . ask me something real. A question. Something you really want to know."

Tex got it that she was serious now. "Okay." He reached into his patchwork Spindleworks vest and pulled out an acorn. He rolled it between his fingers: brown, egg-shaped, thickly capped. "What I really want to know is, how did this acorn get in my pocket?"

Molly took it from him. As soon as she touched it she said, "That's easy. You picked it up in the dark last night, thinking it was your bone pendant."

Tex opened his eyes, feeling something like panic. "My bone pendant! Holy shit! I've lost it!" He patted his vest pockets, but there was no doubt about it. He looked up at Molly in dismay. "So where's the *pendant*, then?"

"Ah," she said. "Good question."

She narrowed her eyes in an effort to . . . what? To remember? To intuit, to dowse, to scry? Whatever it was, the effort made her feel woozy. She sat down on the sofa next to Tex and she closed her eyes.

To see, she realized. She was trying *to see*.

Okay, she thought. Addressing herself as though to a person, a Being, hanging around somewhere, just waiting for this. She thought: Listen up, now.

"Ask me again," she told Tex.

And from somewhere, outside, in the distance, she heard his voice say

(Where's my pendant?)

and she felt Time begin to change direction, to spiral around her. Presently a great blackness began to grow, to swell from within, like a photo-negative universe, filling the space in Molly's brain where she was accustomed to forming images with her right eye, the one that was good at distances. And in the middle of the blackness was a single mote of light, way far off but painfully bright even so. She did not want to look any longer at this but she understood that she must. So when the light spiraled inward closer and closer Molly struggled against the urge to turn away, and the pain ripped down her optic nerve like a claw tearing its way into her eyeball. And then very suddenly

she was through it

and out again

on the Other Side.

She saw it clearly—and heard and smelled and felt it again, too: a land where furry creatures roam and blankets of moss lie on ancient boulders and mighty trees thrust their limbs a hundred feet and higher into the sky. Where music throbs down the high-ways and whispers in the ears of nursing mothers and floats from the drop-tile ceilings of supermarkets. Where water gurgles se-cretly in woodland streams, in sewer pipes, in the ABS tubing of irrigation lines. Where energy hums in wires. Conversations fly and bounce within light-waves. Colors rain like tiny droplets onto phosphorescent glass. Where children play and firearms pop and there is danger at every breath;

where the sky is melting and the seas are bursting their bounds;

where eagles soar with quicksilver tarnishing their blood;

and where the Worm that gnaws at the heart of the Rose has evolved resistance to the incantations long used to banish him.

And Molly dared not blink, because the vision was marvelous though it was also terrifying. And she knew that she had returned

if only in spirit

with only her one good eye

to the enchanted land
that was called
Life.

&

there was time.

Plenty of time: It was just past 8 o'clock and there was no need to hurry to the office, so Eugene Deere, Ph.D. (Bot.), decided to get his 20 minutes of cardiovascular ya-yas by hiking up the logging trail into the forest near his rented bungalow. This was a good time of year for identifying native plants—deciduous forbs, now starting to leaf out, as well as the smaller evergreens that had been until very recently concealed by a lingering snow cover. He slammed the heavy ash-wood door of the house and had to remind himself (for it was not yet a matter of habit) to leave the door unlocked. After all, this was rural Maine. The Great North Woods. And there was no sense taking a job way out in the toolies like this if you were going to keep glancing over your shoulder all the time like folks back home in the heart of Civilization.

Keys clinking in his pocket, Gene set off down the driveway—could you call it a driveway? parallel groves mashed into the mud by his oversized radials—whistling a little snatch of the Handel piece they had been playing on "Classical Morning."

The morning was fine: sunny and cool, sky deep blue, with a few cumulus puffs crossing the mountains at high velocity. But was it *typical*? Gene had only lived up here since last July, when the position at Goddin opened up. This, then, was his first spring. Locals had told him winter was not what it used to be. They remarked upon this with an odd lack of emotional inflection—neither grateful for relief from the god-awful cold, nor worried by the possible connection to global climate change—as in fact, now that Gene came to think of it, they remarked upon most everything.

Passing his dun-brown Range Rover, Gene gave the hood an affectionate pat. He glanced down at the vanity tags, a late-winter whim. **GRN GENE,** they said.

«Oh, come on»
thought Molly.
«Who *is* this guy?»

She felt as though she were floating—just a presence, bodiless: a mere *point of view*—just behind Gene's right shoulder. And yet she seemed also to be inside his head, effortlessly surfing his thought-waves. Too weird. But definitely worth hanging on to, just for the ride.

At the end of the driveway Gene noticed a second, noncompatible set of tread marks. For an instant, a whimsical thought flitted through his mind. Somebody's been sleeping in *my* bed, it said, in the mock-ferocious voice of a cartoon bear.

Gene allowed himself a smile. Frivolous thoughts were not entirely unfamiliar to him. He was a normal person, after all. Still, the mental sidestep made him uncomfortable, as did many day-to-day workings of the human brain. Gene was beginning to entertain serious doubts about the mind-as-self-organizing-neural-network model, currently in vogue among cognitive science types. But this was no time to get into that. He glanced at his khaki-strapped L. L. Bean field watch and strode briskly onto the roadway. Half a mile in, half a mile out, then on with the day's itinerary.

Less than a dozen strides in front of him, tilting measurably as its passenger-side wheels sank into the oozy shoulder, an old Saab hunkered down on its ruined suspension. Mid-70's Model 99, Gene judged. The car's advanced state of oxidation was partly masked by the baked sienna color that its paint had, presumably, once been. Its decrepit rear end looked as though it might owe much of its structural integrity to a generous bandaging of bumper stickers:

SUBVERT THE DOMINANT PARADIGM
AS FAST AS A SPEEDING OAK
DOING MY BIT TO PISS OFF THE RELIGIOUS RIGHT
DON'T BLAME ME—I VOTED FOR ELVIS

POG MO THOÍN
QUESTION MICROSOFT

Gene chuckled: he liked the one about the religious right. He approached the Saab cautiously, half expecting some unmedicated Nam-vet psychopath to come lunging out at him; but it appeared that the old car was empty. (Empty, that is, except for an amazing backseat's worth of old clothes and cardboard boxes and . . . could that be an actual *bear pelt?*) Gene passed the Saab in a museum-style sideways shuffle, marveling at this anthropological showpiece. Somewhat reluctantly he crossed the road, walked past the tree where a sign had until recently declared STRICTLY PROHIBITED, and stepped into the damp and shadowy forest.

PATH WORK

The local woodlands were a secondary-growth forest of mixed hardwoods and conifers. The tallest trees were spruce that Gene guessed to be in the 60- to 75-year-old range. Seen from below, their thick skirts of needles were such a deep green as to be almost black. Scattered among them were stands of balsam fir, as improbably fragrant as one of the tourist traps down in Glassport, and white pine, which had given Maine its old nickname of The Pine Tree State. Nowadays it was Vacationland. Simple economics, Gene supposed. The hardwoods were a mixed lot: red oak, sugar maple, red maple, white birch, quaking aspen, beech, ash, and a couple others he could not identify by their bark alone; he would have to come back in a few weeks after the leaves unfurled.

So much for the aerial survey. Closer to the ground was where the action was—a greater profusion of species, and a better chance of spotting something exceptional. With a practiced eye, Gene ticked off

Cinnamon fern
Royal fern
Ostrich fern
Reindeer moss
Club moss (actually a lycopodium, relic of dinosaur days)
Lichens—pale green on tree trunks, brown and gray on stones
Creeping dogwood

Partridge berry
Wintergreen
Sheep laurel
Bearberry
Wild *vitis*
Bloodroot
Violets (white)

Mundane stuff: Gene was disappointed. Then he noticed, where the trail made a sharp turn leftward, a broad patch of daylilies, the common orange *Hemerocallis fulva* so ubiquitous along New England roadsides that most people take it to be a native. It is not (having straggled along with the Europeans), and a daylily patch so deep in the woods could only mean that there once had been a homestead nearby—and also, by extension, that these very woods, old and permanent though they might appear, were relatively young. This land had once been cleared for farming, maybe not all that long ago. A lot of farms around here had survived well into the present century, until the kids grew up and joined the Army or moved to cities in what was not then called the Rust Belt. Again, simple economics. But try explaining *that* to eco-weenies who like to believe that a forest is some kind of hallowed ground. Gene pressed his lips together. Best to keep Nature and politics separate, he thought.

He high-stepped through the emergent daylily blades, careful not to snap their tender stalks—and nearly tumbled into a gaping cellar hole. He laughed out loud, just at the surprise of it, the pleasure of turning something up.

An old granite foundation lay before him, remarkably intact, though engulfed by suckering alders. Unmelted snow lay ankle-deep at the bottom. The spaces between rocks were stuffed with emerald moss, so thickly that it seemed to be pouring out of the black recesses, like some luxuriant green crop overflowing the Underworld.

Gene kept still for a minute or longer, as though some echo of vanished lives might still be trapped in that old stone pit. He heard no such thing (of course), but his own silence made him aware of a remarkable abundance of bird calls. Chirps and squawks and twitters came from everywhere, at least eight or ten species, though Gene could see none of the birds themselves. He was better at patterns than particulars. Taken as a whole—plants, stones, bird sounds, moist air, splattering sunlight—the whole scene was, it seemed to Gene, supremely beautiful.

After that, belatedly self-conscious (the way you feel when you begin to suspect someone may have been watching you while you were doing something private), Gene turned and moved quickly back to the path.

«Well what do you know?»
thought Molly.
«We must have walked right by here a hundred times and never noticed that place.»
And she wondered again:
«Who *is* this guy?»

Gene moved onto the downward slope, where the trail dog-legged counterclockwise around the western face of the hill. He was a couple of minutes off his normal pace (dallying at the old homestead had cost him) but he liked to see things through to their logical conclusion, and the logical conclusion of this particular hike was the big pile of boulder-sized rubble, some sort of glacial moraine he supposed, that lay at the end of the path. It was a place that could fairly be described as "moody," if any place could. (Gene was aware, as a scientist, that what was actually being described here was not so much the place itself as his own reactions to it—which in their turn were built up of layers of personal and evolutionary history. For example, he had read as a young boy the *Narnia* books. The Green Witch retained, in his memory, a pleasurably chilling frisson, like mnemonic soda pop.) Anyway, there you had it. Gene found the pile of rocks at the end of the trail to be mysterious and moody. If that was some sort of antirationalist category error, then CSI-COP could issue him a citation.

At the end of the trail, as was his habit, he pressed both hands against an upright slab of marvelously eroded greenstone, to go through his routine of stretching exercises. He had barely gotten to work on the first set of ligaments, though, when his eye happened to fall, almost straight down, on a small white object that at first he took for a bird's egg. When he bent to examine it, he discovered that it was actually a minuscule sculpture—a piece of ivory or bone that had been carved into the semblance of a grinning skull. The skull looked cheerful rather than ominous. Gene turned it slowly in his hand.

«Hey, I found your pendant»
Molly said triumphantly to Tex, though she could not tell

whether her voice came through audibly or not, back on the Other Side.

For a moment, in the morning sunlight, the tiny skull appeared to wink. Gene closed his eyes and opened them again. The illusion did not repeat itself. Nonetheless Gene winked back. He felt jolly. He felt as though he had made a serendipitous discovery; though he was not at all sure what he had discovered. Into both sides of the skull's white cranium, tiny holes had been drilled, and Gene found that he could look right in one ear and out the other. Probably the thing was meant to be worn as a pendant. Probably its cord had broken. Gene wondered if the skull and the old Saab might belong together; or rather, if they might both belong to the same person—an unmedicated psychopath, as he had first supposed, or more probably a harmless back-to-the-land type who had taken refuge here during the twilight of the Counterculture, when the Woodstock Nation made its slapdash retreat. If so, should Gene take the skull back up the trail and leave it on the dashboard, where the old (and perhaps imaginary) peace & love & marijuana type could find it?

He did not bother answering this question. Leaving off his stretching routine, he set off up the trail with the small piece of bone—it could only be bone—cradled loosely in one hand. It felt at home there, like something that was meant to be touched or worried-at. Gene had a faint sense, just short of consciousness

«You can't fool me, though»
said Molly.

that he was *not* going to leave it in the Saab—that for reasons that would never be clear to him (so maybe they were not "reasons," in the sense of rational causes, at all) he was going to hang on to this skull and eventually thread a shoelace through the hole and wear it around his own neck. A strange and secret personal token: a memento mori.

Which he carried quite happily.

Whistling Handel while he walked.

TIME OUT

"Where have you been?" said Tex. Molly propped herself up on the sofa. "Hmm?" she said, rubbing her eyes. At first her vision was watery, as though the world around her had not yet taken solid form; then it swam into focus, and Molly found herself staring at a primitive (c. 1969) black-light poster. On the poster, two vultures leered at one another from the shoulders of a saguaro cactus. Tumbleweed, a pile of bones, and luridly colored rocks lay scattered around them.

"I'm tired of just sitting around," one of the vultures said, as it had been saying for decades now. "Let's *kill* something."

Molly noticed for the first time how anatomically screwed-up the birds were.

"Where have you *been*?" Tex asked her again.

"I've been . . ." Her mouth felt as parched as the psychedelic desert. "I'm dying of thirst," she said, realizing right away what a twisty expression this was. She actually might have died of drowning.

"Have some tea. You didn't touch it this morning."

Molly tipped her Moon mug and trickled some of the lukewarm liquid down her throat, where it seemed to transubstantiate. Green tea sort of did that anyway, though. "It doesn't do any good," she said. "I need something . . . *wet,* you know?"

Tex looked at her in a funny way. "You mean, like blood?"

"No, *not like blood.*" She felt cross at him. She felt addled and out-of-sorts. "What do you mean, where did I go?"

"I mean, you just lay down on the couch with your eyes wide open—sort of jerking and twisting, like you were having a seizure. I thought you were maybe going to, you know—" (snapping his fingers) "—disappear on me."

"Well, I didn't, it seems." Molly sat up straighter and drained off the rest of her tea. "The famous unquenchable thirst of the dead," she said.

"Never heard of it," said Tex.

"Well, you've got lots of time to read now."

Tex tightened his mouth, then appeared to think twice about it. Sliding closer to Molly, he began stroking her arm, her shoulder, working his way up to her neck. She bent herself, catlike, curling into him.

"Raven," Tex murmured. "Raven, what's the matter? What's been going on with you?"

She made a purring noise. His fingers moved up to her temples, creeping through the fine hairs there.

"I found your pendant," she told him, after she had gotten her fill of this.

"You did?" Tex turned enthusiastic as instantly and easily as a boy might. "Did you bring it back?"

"I, no—I don't think I could have. But I was with this guy, see, this some kind of scientist, and it was him who found it, only I think maybe I might have led him to it, in a way. I'm not sure."

"Some kind of *scientist*?" Tex was looking at her the way he did: like, are you high on patchouli oil or what?

"What I'm saying is, he was a real person. A real *living* person. And he picked up the pendant, and now *he's* got it. Back *there*. I think he's sort of adopted it. Although he doesn't understand that yet."

"And you could see all this? You could see this guy when he took it?"

Molly patted his hand. She put on her Pearl Bailey voice. "Honey, I could see *everything*."

"Far out." Tex's eyes darted here and there, as though he were scoping out a whole new territory. "So did you see where he went? With the pendant, I mean."

"Sure. He drove off in his car. It was the car we saw last night. Or almost saw. When we were looking for a place to—"

"Wait a minute. You let him just climb in a car, with my genuine Tibetan Death Head carved out of the thigh bone of a lama, and *drive away*?"

Molly shrugged. "What did you want me to do? All I could do was watch. It's like I wasn't even there, really. Like I was seeing it on TV, only this guy's head was the only station I could pick up. His name is Gene, by the way."

"His name is Gene."

"Green Gene is his nickname."

"I see." Tex obviously did not see. He did not see *at all*. "So can you—I mean are you able to—tune back into this person now? Can you pick up on him whenever you want to, and tell me what he's doing with my pendant?"

Molly lowered her lashes at him. She still had great lashes, no matter what else might have fallen by the wayside. Dark brown, like her hair. With only the lightest touch of mascara, you could see those lashes from the back row. Slowly, meaningfully, she batted them.

"Maybe I could," she said. "Maybe I couldn't. Why do you ask?"

Tex eased off, expertly. He scuffed his feet like an amateur improvving Nonchalant. "I'm only interested," he said, "because it concerns you. And anything that concerns you, concerns me. Plus, you know, I'm just naturally curious."

"You're naturally sneaky," said Molly.

And when he looked quickly around at her she noticed something different
something new
—a Darkness—
in the deepest hollow
of his eyes.

COMMUTE

Range Rover. The ultimate toy.

Okay, okay—so there were glitches in the electrical system. You had to expect that. And so the radio had problems with multipath interference: it was these damned mountains. And so people tended to look at the car somewhat askance, as though Gene were flaunting an unwritten local ordinance against owning any vehicle more ostentatious than a Jeep Cherokee—though if you were old enough and drove poorly enough, you were entitled to one (1) white Cadillac. Nonetheless, Gene loved his car and he loved taking it down the back roads, fairly shitty to begin with, that by the end of winter had been rendered almost impassable by crumbling and frost-heave. And he loved his immaculately preserved (albeit through neglect) Arts & Crafts bungalow; and he loved his incredible new sound system; and he loved (though more guardedly) the generous salary that made all of this possible; and he hoped he might someday grow to love the job that generated the paycheck.

True, it was hard to love an entity as abstract as the Gulf Atlantic Corporation. It was hard to feel reverence before the official portrait of Burdock Herne, C.E.O., that hung in his boss's office. And true, there was not much professional or scientific challenge in his current (midlevel and overspecialized) niche in a multinational timber-products conglomerate. But the hours were decent, and the working environment—well, just *look* at it. These woods, these hills, these soggy meadows: Gulf Atlantic owned all this, as it owned other, almost inconceivably vast tracts of land throughout Maine and New Brunswick, and also as it owned, since last year, the former Goddin Air Force Base, where Gene's coffee mug was hangared—a place with the distinctive atmosphere (cheap and oppressive and creepy, all at once) of a post-Cold War ghost town.

Gene sighed as the chain-link and barbed-wire perimeter of the

Goddin base came into view. He shifted down and brushed his hair away from his temples. For an instant he felt something strange, a tingling, there—as though someone else were in the car with him, so close as to be brushing against him—but the sensation quickly passed. A cheery, acrylic-on-plywood sign hung over the security shack:

WELCOME
GODDIN FOREST RESEARCH STATION
A Gulf Atlantic Company
"Growing the Future"

Gene hit the brake.

The Rover jerked to a halt.

Today there was something new. *Another* something new, besides the old Saab and the tiny skull. It was quite a morning for new things, and if you were so inclined, you could see them all as being somehow of a piece, like little threads snagged out of a common fabric.

What the *new* new thing was, was a demonstration. A *direct action,* in the parlance of the day.

It was a group of maybe a dozen individuals wearing absurd costumes that were intended (Gene gathered) to represent endangered animals or some such thing—though also there was a person wearing a sort of Gandalf-meets-Chief-Seattle outfit, and a long-legged creature of nonspecific gender who appeared to be a species of flower fairy. Daffodil, perhaps? Dandelion? *Doronicum,* or was that too educated for this crowd? Something yellow and open-faced, anyway. Gene gave the flower a professional nod.

　　　«And she loved it»

Molly thought. Surprised to find that some of the old resentment still throbbed in her, like a hangover, even now. Molly recognized Ludi wearing her neon yellow warm-up suit and Leopard Bane headpiece with its daisy-petaled golden mane; and she was fascinated by how rapidly Gene's male p.o.v. scanned and categorized those long, jogging-tapered legs.

The little mob came rushing forward to surround the Rover. They shouted at Gene, their masked faces angry, and the whole thing seemed ready to turn unpleasant. But then a couple of 3rd-party contract security people came out of the shack, vectoring in on a spot between Gene and the direct-actors, looking competent and courteous. Gene snapped the shift lever up into first, eye to eye with a short blue Elephant, a couple of strides away.

«That's just Deep Herb»
Molly thought helpfully.
«He's harmless.»

But Gene did not hear.

The Elephant's trunk curled sideways (stage right). Two opaque Dumbo eyes mooned at Gene imploringly. Also accusingly, he thought. As though ready to let loose with baleful—and litigatory—tears. The little actor (whose own eyes you could just see as shiny dots behind a screen of black gauze) yelled something at Gene, but the driver's-side window efficiently filtered that out.

On an impulse of irritation, Gene rolled the window halfway down. "There are no elephants in Maine," he said.

The actor continued his diatribe-in-progress exactly as though Gene had not spoken. ". . . and a further symptom of the decline of theme-park capitalism. People need *reality* and not some bogus synthetic target-demographic thing. Because you can't genetically engineer *Nature,* man. Nature's got a mind of her *own,* man, and boy, is she pissed. You can't keep her knocked up and in the kitchen forever."

Gene said, "What in the world are you talking about?"

Another Player—a Crane, or other peg-legged bird—stuck her head in and said, "We're talking about *you,* friend."

And Big Chief Gandalf said, "But we're not just talking—we're doing something about it."

"About what?" said Gene.

"If you work here," said a Squirrel, quietly, "you're a rapist."

"You're a technophobe," said Gene.

"Murderer."

"Luddite."

"You have no heart," said the Crane.

"You have no brain"—and with that, finally, popping the clutch and *leaping,* with a very discreet crunch of tires lifting off from the asphalt, past the demonstrators toward the gate and finally beyond it.

Back to work.

DAY JOB

"You're late," said Sefyn Hunter, Gene's admin assistant, perkily. He had rearranged the office again: now Gene's desk was scenically located behind a huge whiskey-barreled specimen of the Chusan palm, *Trachycarpus fortunei*. Gene suspected that Sefyn must have applied for this job at least in part because the old WWII-vintage Quonset hut was roomy enough to accommodate his barely manageable collection of potted exotica.

"How can I be late?" Gene said.

"You tell me." Sefyn rolled his eyes. "I tried to stall them—I said you were out checking your control plots. That *usually* works." With a conspicuous sidelong stare he appraised Gene: apparel, general bearing and comport. He made one of those ambiguous teeth-and-tongue noises, approximately ducklike. "Oh, my. I'm afraid this won't do at *all*."

"Do for what?"

"Do for meeting the *public*, for heaven's sake."

"What public?" said Gene.

"Oh!" Sefyn threw his hands up, literally and with dramatic flare. He addressed himself to his computer, as though here at least he might find an appreciative audience. The monitor was full of fish. At a touch of Sefyn's ring finger, softly striking the **s**, the fish shimmered away and a daily organizer sprang into view.

> 9:00 Community outreach reception
>   Sauvage greets C.O.C. reps
>   Deere briefs on company ops, plans, economic bennies

"Oh, fuck," said Gene.

Sefyn scratched the mouse pad with his fingernails. "You ain't whistling Dixie, Pixie."

Grabbing some papers and disks, more or less at random, from the debris on his desk, Gene sprinted from the room back into the open bay of the old hangar. At the distant end, near bomber-sized garage-style doors, an ad hoc meeting area had been set up, complete with folding metal chairs and wall-size display screen and battalion-sized giant coffee urn.

They had not started without him. They had been standing around drinking coffee for the past three-quarters of an hour, and now Gene's boss, Chas Sauvage, had about him the look of a man who wants to pee. Sighting Gene, he slapped the shoulder of the person standing next to him—a large, slightly overweight and imposing man wearing a really terrible suit—and said loudly:

"Well, here is our wunderkind now. Ladies and gentlemen, let me introduce Dr. Eugene Deere, who will be filling you in on our operation here. He'll also be happy to answer any questions you may have. And if you all will excuse me, I'm afraid I've got a few brushfires to put out. You know, the sun never sets and all that."

He did not bother throwing any sort of look in Gene's direction. Under the circumstances, there was no need to. The gentleman in the bad suit was holding out a big loin-chop of a hand, and a couple of the others were circling behind him, waiting to strike.

"Banebook is the name," the meaty man said. "People call me Hoot. Isn't that a hoot?"

Gene smiled, while his hand was palpated.

A smartly dressed woman whose age was totally irrelevant, if she had an age at all, examined Gene at close range with a level gaze. "Reverend Banebook is very active in local causes," she said, in a tone of voice that implied she was speaking in code. If you understood the code, you would know what "local causes" and "very active" meant. Gene was still coming to terms with "Reverend."

"Please," said the Reverend, to everyone, it seemed. "Call me Hoot."

Gene could not imagine himself or the smartly dressed woman or anyone else consenting to call this man Hoot.

"I am Donna Di Fuora," the woman said. She did not offer her hand. It was clearly not a case of Call me Donna.

Further introductions ensued. Gene cruised through them on autoparty, using these precious few minutes to organize some kind of presentation in his head. Ultimately he supposed he would see what was in the papers and disks he had snatched up, and just wing it. Chamber of Commerce types—what would they care? In any case he knew what Chas Sauvage would say; he could practically hear it:

"Be sure to employ at least twenty-seven times the phrase *job creation*. You can mix it up a little—*creating new jobs, bringing jobs to the community, fostering opportunities for employment*. Just make sure the seed gets planted, and then tamp the sucker down. *Job creation*: want to say it with me now?"

There was still one fellow who had not introduced himself, a man about Gene's age, wolfish looking, somewhat out of context

in this crowd of small-town gentry. He was wearing rubber boots
and a ball cap and a camouflage hunter's vest, typical seasonal
attire of the just-plain-Mainer, and he hung back far enough that
Gene could not quite get a fix on him, but close enough to hear
what people were saying. Finally Gene noticed that the man was
wearing a company name tag—the kind with the blaze orange
border that identified an outside contractor. Squinting, he could
just make out

JAG ECKHART
STATION SECURITY
Access: All Areas

Gene looked up and found the wolfish man staring back at him.
Locking eyes, Eckhart gave him a slow and not at all friendly nod.

Great, Gene thought. Absolutely top-notch. I'm a half hour
late for a meeting and they've got the rent-a-cops tailing me.

"*Well,* Mr. Deere," said Donna Di Fuora, as though she were
now completely in control, "perhaps you'd like to get this meeting
under way."

Gene smiled at her. People had often told him nice things
about his smile. Donna Di Fuora narrowed her eyes, but even
she was not immune to it. She ventured a thin and wary smile
in return.

"Would you like to sit up front here?" Gene suggested. "In
case you have any questions."

"Thank you," she said.

He wondered if it hurt at all, plunking down on a butt that
hard. He decided not to think about it. He switched on the computer connected to the large-screen display and, with high hopes,
popped in a disk labeled "Slide Show" in Sefyn's #2 (Strictly
Business) handwriting. There was a full-color shot of the Gulf
Atlantic logo, together with the company's current theme music,
a clip of "Mars" from *The Planets.* This made Gene think of *Star
Wars,* but it did drum up the attention of the community reps.

"What we're doing here," said Gene, as the thunder of tympani
faded and some rumbling commenced in the lower brass, "is all
about growing trees. *And,*" he added, jauntily lifting an eyebrow,
"creating jobs."

Donna Di Fuora nodded gravely. Hoot Banebook folded his
big arms and rumpled his jowls. You got the idea that he was
listening carefully for something to disapprove of. Which at least
put him a step ahead of the other folks in the audience, who

appeared to have no idea what they were doing here at all. Out in marginal territory, neither part of the briefing space nor apart from it, Jag Eckhart, the contract security man, prowled for meat.

You cannot, thought Gene, take this kind of shit too seriously. After all, it's only a day job.

DEBRIEF (1)

"So what happened?" asked Tex.

Molly's right eye throbbed from the intensity, the psychic weight of her vision. That strange feeling of entering someone else's consciousness left her disoriented, unsure whether she had altogether returned to herself. Or whether she even wanted to. The allure of the living, she thought.

"What did you see?" said Tex.

For an instant, a flash, she heard his voice the way someone else might have—the way Green Gene might—and it made her smirk. Just a little: discreetly: a refined and private amusement.

"*What?*" demanded Tex.

"Shh," she said, "wait. There's something else, I think."

DEBRIEF (2)

"So what happened?" asked Chas Sauvage, Gene's ever-dapper boss. He had appropriated Sefyn's desk, upon the edge of which he perched as though it were a stool, swinging his legs. Behind him—as though placed there for this occasion to lend authority to his every brainless utterance—hung a department-store-grade portrait in oil of Mr. Burdock Herne, the Chairman and C.E.O. of Gulf Atlantic. The Old Master trick of piling up layers of translucent paint, so as to lend depth, had given him a shifty look about the eyes. Gene feared to behold the model in the flesh.

Sefyn, passing on a gilt-edged opportunity to get up close and personal with the executive rump, had undertaken to visit in turn his red-petaled passion flower, which had entirely overcome its trellis, then his miniature banana tree, *Musa velutina*, and finally his pot-bound night-blooming jasmine, whose scented blossoms, mostly spent, were turning brown and floating to the concrete floor.

It struck Gene that there was something undeniably sexual and something also melancholy or wistful about Sefyn's horticultural orientation. He regarded the Chusan palm, whose massive fanlike leaves threatened to engulf him, in an adjusted light.

"I bet Di Fuora lapped it up," Chas was saying. His bronzed and confident top-of-the-food-chain features crinkled becomingly. "And that Fleet Bank fellow, what was his name? The one that was wearing the funny hat."

Gene had no idea who Chas was talking about. Mainers as a class all seemed to wear funny hats. In fact, the very habit of wearing hats, year-round and in all kinds of weather, seemed funny to him. Was it a cold-climate thing? Did people in Scandinavia do likewise? Russians, of course, you always pictured in those flat-topped fur helmets, those Nikita Khrushchev caps.

"Deere? Are you with us?"

Gene's head jerked. He must have missed some pearl of Sauvage wit.

"Where else would he be?" asked Sefyn, glancing aside from the task of pinching out side-branches from a datura cultivar known as "Dr. Seuss."

"Earth to Deere," said Chas.

"Come in, Deere," said Sefyn, with a deftly implicit wink.

Gene smiled self-deprecatingly, as though embarrassed by his own driftiness. People expected scientists to be off in a world of their own, he had noticed. And they generally did not hold it against you, as long as you played it like Einstein (the genial eccentric) as opposed to Frankenstein (the obsessive weirdo). But you had to be careful, because in the popular mind it tended to go one way or the other. You couldn't just be normal.

"The one that worries me," he said, "is that beefy preacher. Banebook."

"Hoot?" said Chas—and he stopped swinging his lags.

Gene nodded.

"Why?" said Chas. "What did he say?"

"Oh, you know. He just kept asking these questions. For example, I was explaining the mechanism for genetic enhancement of harvestable species—I mean not *explaining* it, but I was doing this once-over-lightly about the insertion of growth regulators, the extra vigor that you get from tetraploids, the general considerations involved in determining desirable traits, whether you go for optimal growth or take into account competition from weed species and the danger of infectious agents . . ."

"Right," said Chas, waving such considerations aside. "And Banebook wanted to know what?"

"Well, he kept wanting to know if it was *natural*. And you

know, I could have delivered a whole dissertation on the question of exactly what *natural* means. Or whether it means anything, in this context. But I just said, Of course it is natural. God has given us the ability to affect the genetic makeup of these trees— trees that were put here for the use of humankind, and that our ancestors have been cutting and building into homes and schools and churches for hundreds, even thousands of years. The temple of Solomon, you know, was built out of logs. *Cedrus lebani,* in fact. Of course, that's just about wiped out in the wild, now."

"Did you say that?" asked Chas sharply.

"Of course not. I just said that since we've been *given* this ability—to control the growth characteristics of trees—then it is our duty to *use* it as wisely as we can, for the benefit of everyone. And for the creation of jobs."

Gene smiled, but Chas seemed not to recognize his own tag line. "So how did he take it?" Chas said.

"Who knows? He took it fine, I guess. He didn't smile. But he let me get back to what I was talking about. I figured that was what mattered."

Chas slid down from Sefyn's desk and walked over and slapped Gene a couple of times on the shoulder. "It sounds like you handled it very well. Very well indeed. Of course, only time will tell. And there's still the Attack of the Greens to fend off."

At this, Sefyn reentered the conversation. "You mean the Cold Bay Street Players? Aren't they a riot?"

Chas gave a brief nod and then a dismissive shake of the head. "Not *just* them," he said. "There's a more serious sort of opposition, too. There are questions of long-term strategy, harvest sustainability, that sort of thing. Not that I expected those things to come up today. But it won't be long now, will it? Before you know it, it'll be sweaty-palm time. In the meanwhile, I want to make sure you're fully up to speed on Company philosophy."

Gene weighed these words carefully. They seemed to portend something, though he couldn't divine what. The workings of Chas's corporate mind remained mysterious to him, and on the whole he was content to let them stay that way.

"But what *about* harvest sustainability?" he could not help asking. "That's pretty much up in the air, isn't it? I mean, isn't that what my trial plots are supposed to be helping us to evaluate?"

What he really meant was, Isn't that what you hired *me* for?

"*Nothing* is up in the air," said Chas. There was about him a certain persuasive serenity: an air of being in the know about something Big. "We can always change our minds, of course.

But at any given moment, our minds are fully made up. Our course is set, our strategy is determined. All that remains is an ongoing assessment of tactics, within the purview of our overall philosophy. Remember that. And consider your trial plots from that perspective."

Appearing satisfied with this—the Sauvage Wisdom of the Day Desk Calendar, May 2nd installment—he turned and strolled purposefully from the office. It was a big office and it took a long time. Sefyn and Gene stood together and watched him recess.

"I can't decide," said Gene after the boss was well and safely gone, "whether I like that guy or not."

"Oh yes you can," said Sefyn. "You can always change your mind. But for now, your mind is fully made up."

AND BACK

Molly wished she knew what he looked like.
She could see him only from behind, from over the shoulder. She only knew him from the inside out.

More than that, Molly wished she knew who he was. Not just the résumé stuff. But who he was to *her*. Why she was locked in on him like this.

And more than anything, Molly wished she knew what she was doing here. In this post-everything place where neither "here" nor "doing" nor even "Molly" had any longer a fixed and clear meaning.

She sighed.

She opened her eyes.

The right eye was blinded now, totally. It could see only the Other Side, the living world.

Her left eye was attuned to the world she now inhabited. The Afterlife. She trained it across the cabin of the *Linear Bee,* toward the row of Shaker pegs where masks and costume hats hung. She studied for a period of time a jester's cap, teal and black, with bells at the end of pieces of fabric that dangled like droopy horns. A word floated across her consciousness, like a leaf in a stream.

Psychopomp.

Molly wondered why jesters' costumes were traditionally two-colored and two-sided like this. It seemed to connect with her own new split-down-the-middle quality, her foot in each world. Perhaps it connected also with Raven the Trickster, a mythic being of the Pacific Northwest who was also a spiritual go-between, known for conferring ambiguous gifts upon humans and for outwitting the greater gods by irreverence and cunning. And Kokopelli, the blind (but visionary) flute player. Tiresias, the blind (but all-seeing) prophet. Odin the One-Eyed. Janus, with eyes pointing both forward and back.

So where was this thing going? Was Molly plugged in now, through her deformity, with the Old Gods?

She felt dizzy. She wished she had never eaten that salmon. She had no desire to know everything, nor even to wonder about everything. All she had ever wanted were the three blessings of the Lupine Lady: to visit faraway places, to live by the sea, and to do her little bit to make the world more beautiful.

Plus Tex, of course. She had wanted a long and happy life with Tex. And she had gotten that. A happy one, at least.

Fondly, she turned to pat Tex on the knee. Her hand brushed over Goblin the Cat-Person and then fell into Tex's empty place on the sofa. He was not beside her. He was nowhere in the cabin.

"Bear?" she called, but her voice came out too weakly.

She rose to her feet with a modest struggle and crossed through the galley to the afterdeck. The two chairs there sat empty.

"Bear?" she called again. Anxiety creeping into her voice.

She stepped carefully onto the gunwale, pulling herself forward, hands on the safety lines. Why she should be worried about slipping into the water was, of course, a complete mystery. But like all mysteries, there it was.

Tex was not on the foredeck either. He was not on the flying bridge above the cabin, and he certainly was not clinging to the flagpole. Unless he had crawled down into the engine space (a nearly unprecedented event), he was nowhere on board the houseboat.

"Bear?" called Molly, soft and plaintively. This time expecting nothing.

A deep, resonant growl passed over her—the rumble of approaching thunder. Dark clouds, gray shading to bloodred, lay low on the western horizon. The weird, unsettled energies that run before a storm were swirling around her, and the afternoon had grown dark and chilly. A breeze came down from the neck of the harbor, where the Route 1 bridge ran across; Molly could smell the cold, unsettled, still-thawing spring earth in it. She shivered then

for the breeze
went right
through
her.

&
times being what they were.

And Time being what it was. And Being being what Time was
not. There was only so much of this sitting around dead on the
sofa that Tex could take. So when Molly sank for the third time
into this ecstatic or stoned-out trance of hers—

"Let's *kill* something," snarled the make-believe bear,

—he left her sprawled there and stepped into the little pilot
house near the bow of the vessel. It had not been used for seafar-
ing purposes for quite a little while, not since Tex had taken it
into his head to steam down to Bar Harbor and try to impede
the docking of the QE2: a political pawn-move in some forgotten
game—no doubt a losing one—that might have proven truly di-
sastrous (as per Molly's prediction) had not the *Linear Bee* come
down with dyspepsia of the fuel pump that required assistance
from the Coast Guard, of all people. Since then, the chart table
had been cleansed with dew collected at dawn on a new moon
from the small declivity in the leaves of lady's mantle, *Alchemilla
mollis,* and consecrated as an altar in the names of various gods,
devas, and other higher-vibration types. Tex could not remember
exactly whom. The altar held

A candle (to represent the element of Fire)
An incense burner (Air)
A Wedgwood teacup (Water)
An arrangement of rocks (Earth)
Photos of Frank Zappa, Howard Ashman and Jerry Garcia
A pot of whatever was in bloom

A Zuni bear fetish
(6) Raven feathers, bound with Molly's hair

Tex paused briefly before the altar. It was his and Molly's custom to light a small piece of incense every morning. Today he wondered whether—being dead and all—it would be safe to skip it. Then he decided, No, it would not. He slid open the drawer and brought out the good stuff: handmade frankincense from India, imported by the good sidhas of Fairfield, Iowa.

You had to be serious about this kind of thing. About magic, and ritual, and other dealings with the Old Gods. If you were serious, your results would be serious. If you were casual, your results might be horrific. As with drugs, so with the Ancient Ones: it was dabblers, not regular users, that tended to get themselves in trouble.

So before striking his Zippo, Tex made an effort to steady himself. He closed his eyes and waited for a mantra to swim up through the tangled layers of his consciousness. There was a bit of static at first and then a name whispered itself—not the usual secret name of Tex's chosen deva, but a different one, with a totally different vibration.

(NEMAN)

the voice whispered, way down inside. The silent sound of it struck deep into Tex, ringing against his spine. He saw whiteness: the empty whiteness of icicles, not the fullness of snow. He felt the north wind on his cheeks.

(NEMAN)

it came again. This time softer. Tex knew what that meant: when a power word starts to fade out, it is not disappearing. It is sinking deeper into you. He tried to pull out, close his mind to it, but

(NEMAN)

he heard once more.

And then his eyes were open and he was unfastening the hatch up to the flying bridge. He felt as though he was choking on frankincense. Whether he was still actually breathing or not, he needed some air.

FLYING BRIDGE

As to Dublin Harbor, you progressed through three opinions.

1st, Isn't it scenic and colorful. Look at all the little boats.

2nd, Isn't it sad how all the plants have closed down and the lobstermen are having trouble making a go of it. I wonder if this town will ever come back.

3rd, Isn't it great how this place is never going to turn into another Glassport or Bar Harbor. The rich people will never be able to live with the Trailer Park of the Gods staring down at them from up there on the hill. And that tank farm across the bay is just too funky. I guess we're safe here for a while.

Tex had matriculated to the third school of thought several years ago and today he stood drinking in the seamy sights like a restorative tonic. The boarded-up and broken-into chicken plant. The biker bar on Main Street. The rusting corrugated-metal warehouse out of which, rumor held, armaments had been smuggled to the I.R.A. The weedy lot behind the Real Food Co-op where a couple of drunks were hanging out, settled comfortably in the holes of discarded tires. Such blessed sights were the salvation of Dublin, and the reason Tex and Molly could afford to moor their houseboat here.

As he stared up the hill, along the old truck-access roads and the railway line, allowed to deteriorate now that they no longer bore much traffic, his eye got snared on a little orange object to which his lower chakras responded energetically, even before the recognition had progressed up to his brain.

Ludi's Volkswagen. Twitching and turning its way down to the waterfront—taking as always the wrong turns at the wrong times, getting fouled in one-way streets and trapped in blind alleys. A smile came across Tex's face as this endearing disaster unfolded; until finally, flustered, still wearing her neon yellow flower costume minus the daisy-petaled headpiece, Ludi yanked the car to a halt and stepped out onto the pier.

Within seconds, her composure had returned. Where did it come from? The windblown hair, which only moments ago looked wildly disheveled, once more fell into its customary charming deshabil. The hot red cheeks faded to an outdoorsy rouge. Or was it all a matter of Tex's transliteration?

"Hi, Ludi!" he yelled down—confident that she could not hear him.

"Hello?" called Ludi, striding heedlessly down the gangway. "Are you guys home yet?"

He could hear her footsteps below, searching the living quarters. He could feel the boat bob gently as her long legs carried her from fore to aft and then back. At last he could see the top of her head through the open hatch, as she stepped guardedly into the pilot house. Her shoulders looked skinny from this angle. You could imagine them breaking if you squeezed too hard. You'd have to be gentle. You'd *want* to be gentle.

"*That's* weird," she said, not too quietly. "Incense."

She picked up the stick of it, still fuming away. She glanced perplexedly up through the hatch—right up through *me,* Tex realized, which was a discomfiting thought.

"Are you guys up there?" she said. Then, "Ooo!"—in momentary fright, as Goblin the Cat-Person snaked his way between her calves. She bent to pick him up, giving him a few long strokes down the sinuous backbone. "How you doing, Goblin?" she said. "You think it would be okay if I left your folks a note?"

Goblin purred encouragingly. Ludi fished around, wreaking ungodly havoc in the drawer full of ceremonial paraphernalia. The only thing she could find to write on was Molly's Book of Shadows, a journal of the various spells and enchantments she had attempted over the years, with the results (if any) jotted down, to the extent that Molly got around to it. Most of the pages were blank. Ludi filled one of these with her blithe, schoolgirlish scratching, then flopped the Book of Shadows onto the altar and took off.

Tex sighed.

Afterlife Factoid #4
The dead are still horny.

"I wish I could follow her," he said aloud, to a seagull perched impertinently on the radar antenna. "I wish I could take off out of here, like you guys."

The seagull cocked its head at him. Its little black birdy eyes looked strangely intelligent. Many birds, of course, can learn to talk. Some of them are highly trainable. They can live a pretty long while, too.

This seagull looked at Tex and then away and then—amazing!

how fast it moved—shot up off the antenna and beat its wings hard, swerving low across the *Bee*'s forecastle and then banking toward the eaves of the chicken plant.

It never got there. From somewhere (or nowhere, as it seemed) a giant bird with copper-brown wings and claws that looked like industrial equipment shot down and snatched the seagull right out of the air. There was a second or two of confusion, a lot of twisting and shrieking, and *feathers flew,* truthfully; and by the time the feathers fell to the pier it was all over. The predator— a peregrine falcon, Tex thought—folded the body of the seagull into a messy bundle and flew away, back toward the Route 1 bridge where its nest was. It rose languidly into the air. The way it behaved—making a slow loop around the *Bee* before heading homeward—you would swear that it was taking a victory lap, showing off its trophy, letting everyone know what a badass raptor they were dealing with.

Tex was astonished, slightly sickened, utterly fascinated. He watched the falcon pass close before him.

Just at that instant Tex thought he saw—he would swear he saw—the falcon give him a look. Sort of a rude eye-shot, a wordless challenge. Like, Let's see what you've got, asshole.

"Oh yeah?" shouted Tex. He swaggered across the flying bridge, hamming it up for the bird's amusement. "Well, you're a predatory scumbag. And you're poaching on my territory. I was planning to kill that seagull myself."

THEN YOU SHOULD HAVE KILLED IT,

said the falcon, in what Tex guessed must be raptor-talk, though it sounded oddly familiar.

YOU SHOULDN'T HAVE LEFT IT FOR ME.

Tex figured there was no sense getting worked up at this—a talking falcon giving him shit. It was the Afterlife; you had to expect this sort of thing.

"If I could fly," he yelled after the bird, "you'd learn some manners."

YOU CAN FLY,

said the bird. Its voice was remarkably clear and loud, though the bird was growing steadily more distant.

AND MY MANNERS ARE APPROPRIATE FOR MY PLACE IN THE FOOD CHAIN. YOU SHOULD LEARN SOME MANNERS YOUR-

SELF. YOUR BODY IS BEING CHEWED UP BY WORMS, RIGHT
NOW.

Tex wondered if there was such a thing as insanity among the
formerly living.

"Hey, wait a minute," he called, though the bird was surely
out of earshot by now. "What did you say? I can *what*?"

The receding falcon spun around, a blurry mass in motion a
hundred wing-flaps away, and its voice boomed in as though it
were right beside Tex's ear:

WHY DO YOU THINK THEY CALL IT THE FLYING BRIDGE,
SUCKER?

SLIDE SHOW

 Molly, meantime, was back in the big converted hangar, hovering above Gene Deere at a makeshift po-
dium. Before her, images flashed across a wall-size
screen.

FRAME #1

Company Logo:

GULF ATLANTIC
Growing the Future

Music:	*The Planets* (excerpt—fades to:)
Voice of Narrator:	"Good morning. I'm Burdock Herne, the Chairman of Gulf Atlantic. Here in Maine and throughout the world, our company is at the forefront of modern forestry. Combining a century of experience in timber resource management with a passionate commitment to maintaining this vital resource for future generations, our team of reseachers and forestry professionals is hard at work planting the seeds of a new millennium."

FRAME #2

Painting:

The Paleo-Indians by Philip C. Paratore. Luminist mural depicting life at a hunting camp in the Magalloway River Valley, circa 10,000 B.C.E. The terrain resembles modern Labrador: open, almost treeless, tundralike. In the foreground, a hunting party, clad in furs, gathers about a fire. We see dogs, children, animal hides, the carcasses of two large caribous.

Burdock Herne:

"This is what Maine looked like 10 to 15 thousand years ago, after the last Ice Age, when the earliest humans arrived via a trek across the Bering Straits and the continent we now know as North America. Nomadic hunters, these original Mainers had an arduous existence whose closest parallel in modern times may be with that of the Tungus people of Siberia. There were no Great North Woods then. The trees that would eventually clothe and soften the rugged landscape were growing in the southeastern corner of what was to become the United States of America. Compared to human beings, the forest is a comparatively recent addition to the Maine countryside."

FRAME #3

Woodcut:

Samoset Greeting the Pilgrims (Anonymous) An Abenaki from Maine approaches the settlers on a wooded shore. The landscape, heavily forested, is depicted in realistic style, though for artistic purposes the trees are shown at 1/3 scale. The gentleness of the shore—sedges and estuarine plants, no large rocks—identifies this as southern New England.

Music:

Changes to *Luminitza* by the Balanescu Quartet. Moody, restive postminimalism.

Burdock Herne: "By the time the English colonists arrived in Virginia and Massachusetts, the landscape of the New World had greatly changed, assuming the pattern of forests and clearings we know today. Though for years it was thought that the Pilgrims encountered the northern forest in a pristine, unaltered state, we now understand that woods already bore an unmistakable imprint of the human presence. We know, for example, that Native Americans, through their selective clearing of land, their cultivation of desirable plant species, their patterns of hunting and trapping and their many other interactions with local ecosystems, had shaped the countryside as surely as we ourselves are doing today."

FRAMES #4–#10

Vernacular images: A series of drawings, paintings and photographs, showing the subsequent history of the North Woods: Trees are felled to build homes and stockades. Long timbers are made into schooner masts. In an 18th-century village, roof shakes are split, mortises cut, a barn raised, clapboards hammered into place. A Paul Bunyan-like figure leads the (unmistakably violent) cutting of dark, ominous-looking woods. A farmstead nestles in a cleared valley; children and domestic animals scamper in the yard. A river is filled from shore to shore with logs being floated to a mill. Grizzled lumberjacks pose amidst the wreckage of a forest. The countryside regenerates, tiny trees emerging from the debris of past cutting.

Burdock Herne: "As the colonies expanded westward, becoming in the process the United States of America, the fruits of the North Woods were harvested at a relentless pace to meet the needs of the rapidly growing society. We look back at those early days of American forestry with a sense of wonder, combined with feelings of chagrin. Back then, loggers did not understand the complex dynamics of life in a healthy forest, nor the importance of ensuring that these resources remain a permanent asset bequeathed to our children and grandchildren."

FRAME #11

Photo:

A Gulf Atlantic forester, wearing a hard hat, supervises the timber harvest. Pointing, he gives instructions to a Site Operations Manager.

Burdock Herne:

"That thought lies at the center of Gulf Atlantic's philosophy of long-range land stewardship today. In all our operations, from harvesting to replanting, habitat improvement to soil conservation, our goal is to achieve the highest sustainable level of forest-products creation, while at the same time making sure that the North Woods will remain a dependable, renewable resource for generations to come."

FRAME #12

Photo:

Establishing shot of gate of Goddin.

Burdock Herne:

"Here at the Goddin Forest Research Station, Gulf Atlantic has established an advanced and innovative scientific facility, devoted to the exploration of new opportunities for preserving the incomparable wealth of the Great North Woods."

FRAME #13

Photo:

Wide-angle shot of a tree-breeding lab. Dr. Eugene Deere, in a white lab coat, stands among trays of spruce seedlings. He holds a tiny plant in his hand, observing the healthy mass of roots.

Burdock Herne:	"By tapping cutting-edge technology in the exciting new field of genome enhancement, and through intensive ecology management, our researchers are expanding the frontiers of human knowledge in their quest for a deeper understanding of the ancient science of forestry."

FRAME #14

Graphic:	Computer-generated image of a black spruce, *Picea mariana*. The layers of the tree become successively transparent.
Burdock Herne:	"The first step in improving the health of the North Woods involves the basic unit of the forest: the living tree. We peer deeply into the plant's genetic structure, looking for ways to improve its vigor and productivity. We also aim to improve its structural characteristics—making it stronger, for instance, or better adapted for specific forest-products applications."

FRAME #15

Photo:	A helicopter conducting weed-and-seed operations along a cut-over stretch of forest.
Burdock Herne:	"The second step lies in improving our basic habitat management. One challenge facing the modern lumber industry is the tendency of the forest, left unattended, to exhibit a pattern known as species drift—in this case, the replacement of highly productive black spruce trees with less desirable species. Regular ecological maintenance is needed to ensure that the balance of species remains close to its natural condition."

FRAME #16

Photo:	Small plane spraying herbicide over a landscape of young trees.

Burdock Herne: "The traditional means of sustaining a natural climax species is through carefully selected herbicides, such as the glyphosate
compound being applied here to eliminate
forest weeds. Although modern herbicides
such as this are almost entirely harmless to
human beings, forest animals and the ground-
water supply, Gulf Atlantic is committed to
the exploration of new approaches which will
achieve the same benefits."

FRAME #17

Photo: Dr. Deere, amid acres of chest-high saplings. He is smiling.

Burdock Herne: "To accomplish this, we look to genetics.
Already, our biologists have made progress
in enhancing the ability of spruce seedlings
to hold their own against the forces of species
drift. Through such improvements in the
competitive abilities of young trees, we reduce
the need for chemical reinforcements."

FRAME #18

Photo: Panoramic view of the Magalloway River
Valley as it exists today, thickly covered
with a dark mantle of trees.

Burdock Herne: "Beyond our laboratory research, our computer habitat modeling, our experiments in
species development and our field trials,
we are digging even deeper, asking the
most fundamental question of all: What do
we want the Great North Woods to look
like 100 years from now. 1,000 years?
10,000 years? Because that is what we
must consider with every step we take,
every tree we harvest, every seed we plant.
What demands will our children and our
grandchildren place upon the forest? What
products will their evolving lives require?
What level of output can the forest sustain?

We cannot hope to answer all of these questions right away. Ultimately, only the future knows what unforeseeable changes the next millennium will bring. But we can begin now to peer into that dark glass, and to make out, however dimly, the shape of things to come."

Fade to: Gulf Atlantic logo.

LIGHTNESS OF BEING

 Dig it: Tex could fly. A killer birdie told him so. Extra cool.

But how?

Thus far, Tex had determined the following.

1. Flapping his arms did not work.
2. Thinking a happy thought (—of himself homing in on Ludi's open thighs, the scatter of golden hair there—) did not work.
3. Trying to leap into the air and *take off* did not work.

He decided that he would have to approach the matter scientifically. He climbed belowdecks, tiptoeing past Molly, still in the grip of her vision. For a few moments he stopped, directly in front of her. Just kind of gazing down at the old girl fondly.

She hadn't lost her looks. Her face had changed, over the years, but not in an unpleasant way. It was as though she and her aging body had come to peaceful terms with one another—each had agreed to let the other go her way, interfering as little as possible.

Beneath the closed lid, Molly's right eyeball twitched. Heavy r.e.m. action there. Tex turned away and moseyed into the galley.

He stared into the debatable domain of the small refrigerator. There, from a forest of Tupperware, he slid out a less-than-aseptic-looking container labeled "Organic Tofu." Decades of experience, supported by an impressive body of ethnographic theory, had convinced Tex that the kind of people who might, on occasion, paw through your belongings in search of illicit substances are not the kind of people who will ever, under any circumstances, open any container known or believed to contain organic tofu. Indeed the very thought of tofu, the spondee of its syllables, the train of associations clattering behind it like tin cans tied to a car, any of these alone would be enough to keep official hands well clear of the offending object. Together, they constitute one of the starkest taboos of modern Western society. Therefore Tex had for years kept whatever aids to alternative consciousness he might possess securely tucked away in this little self-sealing plastic ark, and he had never had cause to regret it.

A few doobers' worth of last year's homegrown—the same stuff that had put Tex and Molly down the Well—lay in the bottom, along with a ceramic pipe shaped like a Shelagh-na-Gig. Tex carried these things up to the flying bridge, where he stuffed the welcoming cavity of Shelagh and got down to serious investigation.

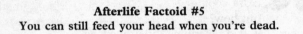

Afterlife Factoid #5
You can still feed your head when you're dead.

Tex entertained the following series of thoughts.

He recalled reading that the well-preserved body of a shaman found in the ice of Siberia had been buried with two bags of *Cannabis* seeds. Two different species, in fact. And that one of those Roman history-writing guys—Heraclitus?—had sojourned up north among the Scythians, one of whose holy men had gotten him toasted by sprinkling hemp on some fire-heated rocks. Same principle as the Native Americans who used two hot knives, inspiring Tex's friend Jesse—during those early days of getting back to his roots—to throw a Hot Knife Party. The joke was, you could post flyers all around Dublin, and only those *truly* in the know would dig what they were getting invited to.

Woo, thought Tex. Super excellent batch. Always sad to come to the end of it. Proof of the impermanence of all things. Ancient planting-and-harvest cycle, rhythms of nature. Blah blah.

But now shamans. What was the thing about shamans? Ah yes: the thing about shamans is that they could fly. Or rather, they could take the form of creatures who could fly. At least, that's the way Tex heard it.

He helped himself to another toke.

Deeper thoughts. The trans-Eurasian connection. Scythians, Tex believed he was remembering, were only intermediaries—they had transmitted the old shamanic know-how from the nomads of Siberia to the westerly migrating Celts (hence all the shape-shifting and other strange goings-on in fairy tales, Arthurian romances and such stuff). But the Scythians had also, in their rampaging across the steppes, passed the secrets along to migrants trekking south to the Indian subcontinent. Where the old Vedic rishis had had the very good sense to encode it for posterity, breaking it into pieces and doling the pieces out to hereditary lines of pundits. Get enough pundits together, and you can read the earliest scripts of human consciousness. You can crack open—allowing for cultural variance, problems of redaction, memory drift—the spellbook of Merlin. Read the Vedas and you can dig why Cernunnos, Horned God of the Celts, is sitting in the lotus position with his eyes closed on a cauldron that turned up in Austria.

One more hit on Shelagh. Then Tex, feeling as though the vitreous humor in his eyes was turning to Jell-O Instant Pudding, opened the most sacred and confusing of all hippie texts, the *Yoga-sutras of Patañjali*.

The dinged-up hardcover was filled with marginal scrawlings, highlighted passages, and assorted doodles reflecting three decades of perusal, chemically enhanced and otherwise. In this respect Tex's study of the book only extended a tradition by which Patañjali's cryptic utterances had been glossed, commented on, reconsidered, and misconstrued over a period of 3,500 years. If you were to believe Patañjali, the answers to the very coolest mysteries in life were to be found among these 195 one-liners. For example, you want to read minds? Turn to Book III, Sutra 19. You want to know about past and future existences? Book II, Sutra 39.

All Tex wanted, however, was to understand what the old shamanic hemp-heads had been up to. He wanted to do what witches did with broomsticks. What any pesky seagull could do without giving it a second thought.

He turned to Book III, Sutra 42:

By Practicing Samyama On The Relationship Between The
Body And Akasha, And By Concentrating On The
Lightness Of Cotton Wool, Passage Through
The Sky Can Be Secured.

Tex frowned. He furrowed his brow. He fingered the place at his chest where his skull pendant should have hung. Cotton Wool? he thought. Weren't there too many fabrics involved here?

It was ever thus with Patañjali.

After a minute or so, feeling a headache coming on, he sighed and gave up and let the whole thing go. He tossed it away, as he had been planning to toss a copper pipe-connector into the Well. As indeed he had tossed his body there instead. He lay down on the flying bridge, feeling spaced-out and bodiless.

He thought how nice it would be to fly. Or not even to fly. To *float*: to simply drift in the air, the æther, the akasha. He saw himself hanging there, empty and clear—sunlight gleaming through him, splitting into rainbow bands of pure color. The earth below was damp and gray, while here in the sky it was warm and bright. Here there were no boundaries, no limitations. No rules to break. No authorities to defy. It was all, indeed, very pleasant.

Pleasant, hell. It was *heaven* up here. Just as he had known it would be, always, somehow.

Still, the earth was important. He could not forget that. It was big and it was solid and there was a lot of complicated stuff going on down there, a lot of important things left to do. Tex looked down, just to check the place out

—he couldn't remember exactly how he had gotten away from it

—and he saw the *Linear Bee* rocking peaceably at its mooring; the network of roads and buildings and patches of green and brown and tiny objects shuttling up and down, back and forth, that was Dublin, Maine, at the end of a millennium

—and he understood at last what had happened.

Tex felt the pressure of air against his wings. He bent sideways, and watched the earth tilt up, the ocean spilling into the sky. He heard the cries of gulls, the chitter of sparrows, and after a while the insolent, interrogatory quork of a solitary raven. He opened his throat and answered it.

I can't believe it, he thought.

Finally, I grok Patañjali.

HOMERING IN

So in some ways, Tex thought, you could say that death was cooler than life. Insofar as, to take one example, you could do *this*.

He followed the coastline southward from Dublin Harbor, admiring its in & out, jaggedy fractal contours. There had been a character in *Hitchhiker's Guide to the Galaxy* who claimed credit for designing the fjords of Norway. A joke: and yet here you could see the hand of the artist unmistakably, in the branching and rebranching channels, unfolding organically as they moved inland. If you looked at it one way, you could believe that the watershed had *grown*—like a tree, or a stag's antlers, or maybe an ultra-retro TV antenna—ramifying inward from the sea.

But blink: and you see that the energy that carved these waterways flows the opposite way entirely. The water collects itself from a state of maximum diffusion, far inland, and gradually organizes itself into runlets and then streams and rivers and finally the great wide trunk of Cold Bay. Just as an oak's branches channel the diffuse rain of photon wave-packets down into a network of chloroplasts, leaf veins, xymatic tissues, and finally the great thick trunk, burying itself in the black earth. And a TV antenna does more or less the same with electromagnetic waves.

What about a stag's antlers, though? What kind of ætheric program is Cernunnos picking up, sitting there cross-legged, antlers lapping up the cosmic run-off?

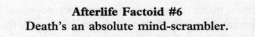

Afterlife Factoid #6
Death's an absolute mind-scrambler.

Tex was glad it had not overtaken him sooner. Now, at least, he had a certain perspective from which to consider things. Death would be totally wasted on the young.

He gave a throaty *krrrk!* He cocked a wing and twirled himself sideways, rolling in the air. Then he shot earthward. He had sighted, in the green-and-dun strip separating Cold Bay from Route 1, the sagging barn that was the headquarters of the Cold Bay Street Players. As he descended he saw the white ghost of smoke coming out of Eben's chimney, the flutter of many-colored streamers on poles.

It was all cool; it was all beautiful.

Easing down on wide, capable wings, Tex alighted upon the ridge of the barn next to a ruined dovecote. Its holes had been stuffed with field-straw by red squirrels. He heard blurred voices from the loft below, and he felt as though he had come home again.

A crack providentially ran between the roof boards next to him. Actually there were cracks everywhere. Without cracks and hidey-holes, perches on cliffs and in trees, doors left ajar, underbrush interposed, and similar aids to hidden observation, much of world

literature would be impossible. Tex beamed a silent prayer of soli-
darity to Angus the Ever-Young, the Irish god who had crouched
behind a tree while the swan-maiden morphed into a beautiful girl
(a beautiful *naked* girl, Tex had always figured). He lowered his eye
to the crack, and prepared to dig what was happening.

DRAMATIS PERSONÆ

GUILLERMO GOBáN, *a sailmaker*
LUDI SKEISTAN, *a part-time bookseller*
DEEP HERB, *a Taoist waiter*
PIPPA REDE, *a welfare witch*
INDIGO JONES, *a community radio station manager*
SARA CLUMP, *a self-realized electrician*
EBEN CREEK, *a freelance geomancer & soil tester*
RAINIE MOSS, *a shade gardener*
TEX DARFFOT, *a magical bird*

The scene is much the same as the night before, when Tex made
his (ostensibly) final exit. Faces of Animals, Spirits, the 4 Directions, the Seasons, the Elements—eyes empty now, souls departed—form a spectral gallery. Dark robes flutter in the breeze,
like curtains. The Players strut, fret, and lounge on cast-off pillows.
Indigo has brought his portable stereo, an antique KLH Model 11,
whose stylus is further eroding the vinyl of *Forever Changes*.

TEX   tries to speak ("Wow") but his bird-self renders the syllable
in a remarkable way, involving a Q-sound and no discernible
vowels.

TEX   *[offstage]* Qwwrw.

EBEN   I mean, we are talking about Midsummer Night. Right?

GUILLERMO   So what? *[With a haughty, dismissive wave of the
hand. He is still wearing his indigo Wizard cloak.]*

EBEN   So . . .

RAINIE   So maybe Ludi's right.

GUILLERMO   *[Scoffs]*
*[LUDI flushes red. A complex current runs between the 2 of them,
as though we are coming late into a long-running quarrel.]*

TEX   Awsswwll. *[Scratches the roof planks with his claws.]*

RAINIE Asshole.

GUILLERMO *[Turns—angry, astonished.]* Excuse me?

RAINIE Sorry, I . . . I don't know what made me say that. *[Thinks a moment.]* On the other hand, it is Midsummer Night.

LUDI Yeah. *[She's trying to stand up for herself: squaring her shoulders, setting her chin, facing* GUILLERMO *straight-on.]* All I'm saying is, there will be all these tourists from everywhere, and people out with their kids, and the weather ought to be nice. So maybe we ought to be thinking in terms of, you know, a joyous celebration of the season. Full of magic and wood sprites and happiness and stuff like that.

GUILLERMO Nobody believes in that kind of crap anymore.

PIPPA *[Almost too faintly to be heard.]* I believe in those things.

GUILLERMO Which is why it's important that we stick to the real issues, the genuine problems of the day.

LUDI *[Angry, but feeling helpless before* GUILLERMO*'s decisiveness.]* Maybe the fact that nobody believes in magic and wood sprites and happiness is the problem of the day!

GUILLERMO *[Sighs. He wears the expression of a martyr, resigned to having his advanced and prophetic utterances misunderstood by the people around him.]*

On the roof, TEX *gets steamed. He pecks at the crack between the planks, trying to widen the opening.*

HERB Hey, man. What's that?

People look at him briefly—cross-legged on the floor, brain obviously weed-infested. They turn back to what they were doing. From above, clawing and hammering continue.

SARA So what's your plan, Guillermo? *[She's very businesslike— a flannel-shirted woman with a no-nonsense haircut.]*

INDIGO *[Buddha-like, rotund and jolly.]* Yeah, dude. Enlighten us.

GUILLERMO All right. All right. *[He puffs himself up, like a tenor about to belt out an aria.]* My plan is, to stage a totally mind-blowing spectacle that will rip the lid off the whole Gulf Atlantic sham.

PIPPA   *[Faintly, as always]* What Gulf Atlantic sham?

HERB   *[Gazing up at the roof, where there are scratching and hammering noises that only he seems to hear.]* I think it wants to get in, man.

GUILLERMO   We'll go public with solid evidence that their plans go way beyond the usual slash-and-burn tree-farm monoculture. What they're planning is a complete ecological takeover of the whole northern forest. They've got a monster tree they're planning to unleash, that'll wipe out everything in its path. The thing is like a plague. Worse than a plague, because there's no defense against it.

EBEN   *[Aside to* DEEP HERB.*]* Probably just a squirrel. They've been apeshit this year.

SARA   You say you've got proof of this?

INDIGO   You know, we did a call-in last week, and most of our listeners were pretty much wait-and-see on the Gulf Atlantic thing. A lot of people seem to feel like there's nothing wrong with turning an Air Force base into a tree-breeding laboratory. At least it's nonpolluting, right? Plus there's the job angle. Half the county got laid off when Goddin closed down.

GUILLERMO   Fools. They're all fools. And we're going to prove that to them on Midsummer Night.

SARA   What you mean we, white man?

HERB   I'm not kidding—I think it's busting a hole through the roof.

GUILLERMO   *[Mysteriously—reaching into his Wizard cloak.]* The proof is right in here. This was made available to me by a— shall we say—very reliable source.

[He holds up a little floppy disk, on which the words "Strategy Briefing—Restricted Availability" are written in a businesslike hand.]

RAINIE   Still, though, Guillermo. Is this really what the Street Players are all about? I thought we were, you know, into ritual and celebration.

GUILLERMO   Don't any of you people understand anything? If we don't stop them now—and I mean immediately, midsummer may already be too late—it doesn't matter what we do.

Rituals, monkey-wrenching, it'll all be pointless. The game will be over.

LUDI   *[Helplessness in her voice.]* Oh, I wish Tex and Molly were here. What could have happened to them?

GUILLERMO   *[Turning on her.]* I'll tell you what could have happened to them. They could have gotten so stoned they just floated off into space. Because that's all they ever do. And that's why this theater has turned out to be such a fucking joke. As far as I'm concerned, it's better if they've gone into orbit, or back to Nepal, or to Uranus, or wherever they came from.

SARA   Oh, please. *[Standing up to depart.]*

HERB   Here it comes, man.

With a rending sound, roof boards fly apart and pieces of rotten wood rain down. Then comes a storm of black wings as TEX *swoops from the rafters. He dives for Guillermo's head, talons extended.* GUILLERMO, *however, shows his mettle. In a dramatic gesture he sweeps his cloak up, entangling* TEX *in the cloth. They struggle, beat wings, strike out at one another. The* PLAYERS *shout in alarm, draw back in fright, gawk in amazement, or (in the case of* DEEP HERB*) fire up the bong.*

EBEN   Well, this is something new. Last year it was coyotes.

With a mighty effort, GUILLERMO *wrenches off his cloak, winds it quickly around* TEX, *and hurls it to the floor. It strikes with a painful thump. Hidden now in the folds of cloth, the magical bird struggles feebly and then becomes still.*

The PLAYERS *fall momentarily silent.*

HERB   Wwwooooo. *[Loudly exhales, releasing smoke.]*

LUDI   Do you think it's hurt?

SARA   No shit, it's hurt. *[Gives* GUILLERMO *a look of contempt.]*

RAINIE   Maybe we should take it to the animal shelter or something.

INDIGO   No—it's a wild creature. It's not meant to be in a shelter. I say we just lay it outside on the ground and ask Mother Gaia to do what's best for it. Sometimes human intervention isn't the most compassionate course.

PIPPA   *[Too quietly.]* No.

SARA   Right—it was human intervention that did this. Poor bird.

GUILLERMO   Are you all blind? That bird was trying to claw my eyes out. It's probably infected with cytomegalovirus or something. Get it out of here.

PIPPA   Stop! *[At last, loud enough to be heard. The* PLAYERS *turn to stare at her.]* Don't take it outside. Don't let it touch the ground.

RAINIE   What? Why not?

PIPPA   I've just got a feeling. Leave it here. Leave Guillermo's cloak around it. I'll stay and take care of it.

GUILLERMO   Oh, great. This is great. Now the great Wiccan priestess is going to heal the injured creatures of the forest. Meanwhile the forest itself is in its death throes, and I'm out a perfectly good $175 Capestries cloak.

INDIGO   Mellow out, bro. You'll get your cloak back.

GUILLERMO   Right—covered with raven shit. *[He storms out, banging down the ladder. The* PLAYERS *follow, 1 at a time.]*

LUDI   *[Calling after them.]* Hey. Wait, everybody. We still haven't decided what we're going to do about the Midsummer Night performance. Have we? *[Exits.]*

Only PIPPA *and* EBEN *linger. They look down at the cloak containing the motionless* TEX.

EBEN   You're a good Witch, Pippa.

PIPPA   All Witches are good Witches.

EBEN   Mmm . . . *[Going down the ladder.]* Call if you need anything. *[Exits.]*

PIPPA   *[Carefully unwrapping the bird, she speaks softly to herself.]* We all need something, Eben. All we need is—

The stage goes dark.

PICKUP CITY

Dark.
All Tex understood right away was that everything was dark.

A peculiar darkness, though: purplish, full of unfamiliar flavors of pain. He tried to lift a hand to his face, to verify that his eyes were open, but the only thing that came was a sort of dry, feathery flutter. He felt trapped; he croaked for air. And the pain in his upper body intensified.

Then came a change. Motion: the world jostling him about. Giant hands raised him up. The heavy fabric in which he was swathed, like a baby, fell aside. And Tex found himself looking up through a scrim of smoke-filled light into the vast, all-mothering face of—

"Brruppah!" his strange voice squonked out—

Pippa Rede, the Welfare Witch.

"Shh, there, there," she said. "It's okay, little bird."

Tex was startled first by her words and then by the rushing memory of what they meant: his transformation, his passage through the air, his fight with Guillermo.

"I know you didn't come here by accident, little bird," she was cooing to him. Sounding birdlike, rather, herself. She cradled him gingerly, though with convincing authority, spreading his weight evenly between her two hands, avoiding any pressure against his battered wings and rib cage. "I know you're the special bird of Morrigan, Goddess of War, and I know you came here trying to tell us something."

"Fwwokkggng ahhy," croaked Tex.

Pippa nodded—heavy on the empathy. Clearly, she was clueless. "They wanted to take you to a shelter. But I stopped them. I know you can heal yourself. And I want to make an offering of contrition to the Lady, to apologize for the way we received you."

Think nothing of it, Tex wanted to tell her. Just give me a spoonful of children's Tylenol.

Pippa gathered him up. She arranged the folds of what Tex now understood to be Guillermo's ridiculous Wizard cloak—one of its gold lamé stars was a finger-width from his eyeball—so that he was nicely cushioned, then she bustled him out to her battered Toyota wagon. The Toyota chuttered to life and bumped down the long driveway onto Route 1. Tex closed his bird eyes, nuzzled his beak down into his neck feathers.

When he opened them again, the Toyota had come to a halt, and Pippa was lifting him out through the driver's side door. He knew without looking where he was.

She had brought him home to Pickup City.

From Pickup City—which was not a real city nor even a town, but a long-established squatter's camp outside of Glassport—you could hear the traffic grumbling by on the highway that lay beyond a wild hedge of lilac, black locust, and bittersweet. You could smell produce rotting in the Dumpsters behind the I.G.A. On Sundays, then again on Thursdays, when there was a soup kitchen, you could hear the digitally sampled bells bong through p.a. speakers at the Church of Mankind's Destiny Among the Stars (Rev. Hobart Banebook, Pastor). But unless there was an unusual easterly wind, or a party out of control, as long as you hung out in Pickup City you could not be seen nor heard from the church, the grocery store, the highway or anyplace else. You would, for practical purposes, have fallen through the cracks of the civilized world. And therein lay Pickup City's whole raison d'être.

See, the place was a secret. Not that much of a secret, perhaps. Every old hippie, young slacker, down-and-out lobsterman, wannabe dharma bum and horny teenager in the midcoast area seemed to know about it. But a secret, for sure, from Reverend Banebook, whose church had bought the acreage off the Presbyterians in the Christian equivalent of a Going Out of Business Sale, and who apparently had never gotten around to fully exploring the grounds. Over a span of two decades, Pickup City had evolved from a dumping ground for rusted appliances to a parking spot for high school kids, then a summer camp for boat-trash, and ultimately into a marvel of low-cost, ground-up, alternative housing. Its residents came and went, but the structures they built were still (approximately) standing. There were:

(2) yurts
(1) tipi, insulated with straw
(1) 8 x 8-foot "cube house," from plans in the
July 1974 *Popular Science*
(3) shacks of varied style, built of wood salvaged from the dump
(2) trailers
(1) geodesic dome (intact) covered with asphalt shingles
(1) geodesic dome (coming apart) covered with Plexiglas tiles

and Pippa's own current residence:

(1) nylon "LightHouse" ordered as a kit from Ukiah, California

which—with its approximately Japanese-style footbridge over the drainage ditch, its crescent-shaped Moon Garden, its reverse-osmosis water filter and its world-class collection of wind chimes, bird feeders, cow bells, dream catchers, and anything else that you could dangle from the limbs of the scrubby little trees—was where Pippa and Tex were headed.

Pippa walked swiftly—dark clouds had blown in, and the wind threw flecks of rain at them—but paused when she came to the footbridge.

"Lady," she murmured, fast and low like saying grace at a family dinner, "please open this portal that we may cross, then shut it again against any who would harm us."

Cool, thought Tex. Have to tell Molly about that.

Pippa bustled on. Tex could hear the stream gurgling energetically below.

Crossing the waters, he thought.

Pippa turned up a path to what you might have called her backyard: a muddy, clear-cut, weed-grown patch that recalled what all of Pickup City had looked like, circa 20 years ago. By now the rest of the site had been so thoroughly trampled-on, lived-in, built-up and planted-over that this weedy plot was a genuine relict—a haven of despoilment. In the middle of it, Pippa had made her sanctuary.

It did not, at a glance, seem an overtly magical place. There were no standing stones, no pentagram blazed in the earth, no eerie sigils carved into tree trunks. All you could see, really, was a 9-foot ring where the soil was bermed up and planted with creeping thyme (so there would be a nice place to sit), inside which the grass was worn down by regular foot traffic. Slightly off-center, to the north—the direction of the I.G.A.—was a fat beech stump, chainsaw-smooth on top: this was the altar. Golden moneywort grew around the base of it and a tuft of yellow sedge sprang from a hole in the wood. The only magical tool in evidence today was a Smith & Hawken 3-tine hand-fork, propped against the beech stump as though it had been forgotten there.

"Mommy!"

Tex caught a blurry motion-shot of hair, flying in the wind, as wild and parchment-white as the stems of bromegrass at the end of winter. The girl's feet whickered through the undergrowth, heedlessly, as she rushed into the Witch's circle. She arrived as Pippa was laying Tex on the beech stump, tucking Guillermo's robe up around him. He saw Winterbelle's eyes, a startling shade of blue, peering down at him.

"Mommy," she said very seriously. "Is he real?"

"Of course he's real," said Pippa. Then, frowning, "How do you know it's a he?"

"Oh—you can tell," said Winterbelle. Her lips pouted up and her eyes contracted; she was pondering. She could not have been older than 6 or 7. She wore a leotard and a cape, like a tiny comic-book superheroine.

"Come on, sweetie. Let's go inside and leave him alone. He's probably frightened of us, and he needs some time to get better."

Winterbelle held her ground. "He doesn't *look* real," she said.

Tex had an unpleasant feeling of being transparent, or naked. In a way he was both. He turned away from the girl's sharp eyes; he looked out across the homey enclave of Pickup City. Someone was pulling his laundry down from a line, hurrying to beat the coming rain. Someone else was dangling a line into the swollen rain-ditch, fishing for god knows what. Out on the highway, you could hear the world grumbling by.

"Well, *I'm* going inside," said Pippa. "I want to make some nice brownies."

"Ick," said Winterbelle. "Brownies are ugly furry goblins. I'll stay and watch over the bird."

Pippa fretted about this for a moment. "Okay," she said at last. "Come in if it starts to pour. Or at least get under something." She started away, then called over her shoulder, "And don't let his feet touch the ground."

"What feet?" said Winterbelle. "All I see is claws."

The girl started to hum. Tex got the idea that she was killing time. Sure enough, after a minute or two—long enough to be sure her mother was going to stay put indoors—she slid her hands under Guillermo's cloak, and (no more gently than was strictly called for) she snatched Tex up and held him tight against her chest and made away with him.

He could not see where they were going. He was aware of Winterbelle's feet moving first through tall grass and then onto a path. She started to run, joggling him roughly. From the steady gurgle of water, Tex gathered that she was following the stream. Suddenly she stooped, ducked under something and came into a place that was dim and quiet and green.

"Ari?" she said, in a cautious voice. "Ari—are you up there?"

Tex twitched his head free. Winterbelle was standing beneath a large hemlock, whose bottom limbs drooped low all around them, making a sort of cave. The stream ran close by the roots of the tree and disappeared into a metal culvert, set in an embankment built up of huge chunks of granite. At the top of the embankment stood the church: a plain, white-clapboard building with tall windows. A single Gothic-arched panel of stained glass was set into the rear wall, the altar end, under the eaves.

Lots of altars around here, Tex reflected. Rival gods. Could be a problem.

From up in the tree came a scuffling sound. Needles and bark-scrapings rained onto them. Then something—a fast-moving animal-shape—took flight from a thick limb two heads off the ground.

"Aaiiiyyyaaa!" the flying creature shouted. It landed with a thump close to Winterbelle. She giggled.

"Ari," she said. "Come see what I've got. It's a raven and I think he's under a spell."

The creature drew slowly nearer, with the natural wariness of an untamed thing. Only when it was very close could Tex make out that it was a boy, or something like a boy. He had long tangly dark hair and pale brown skin and deep umber, somewhat slanted eyes. His ears and mouth and hands were large, and his limbs were bony. He wore clothes that he might conceivably have made himself—scraps of mismatched fabric badly stitched together, un-raveling in places, with flaps dangling loose. If he *was* a boy, he would be about 10 years old. If he was an elf, which looked about equally probable, he could be ancient.

"Now don't be afraid of Ari, little raven," Winterbelle whis-pered, assuagingly. She held Tex up so that he and the wild boylike thing could get a look at one another. "He's only like this because his mother is, I mean, *totally* crazy—she's a friend of my mom's—and he's grown up around wolves. *He* thinks he's normal."

Tex laughed—which came out *quonk quonk quonk,* not much like human laughter. But the boy Ari stopped where he was, his slanted eyes opened wide, and he smiled. He reached out with a hand stained yellow with hemlock resin and touched Tex on the cranium, pressing one fingertip lightly against the thin layer of bone above the eyes. There must have been a nerve ending there, because Tex registered the touch as a sudden intense tingling. He fluffed his wings, squirming a little in Winterbelle's grasp.

"Something is protecting him," the boy said. His voice was musical. It sounded joyful and sad, at once. "Put him down."

Winterbelle hesitated. "My mom said—"

The boy nodded. He removed his finger from Tex's forehead. The tingling stopped. The boy aimed a long finger at the stream. "Put him in the water."

Winterbelle squinted her eyes, assessing this. "Well, she *did* say not to let him touch the *ground*."

Damn, thought Tex. Smoked out by a technicality. Typical fairy-tale twist.

Winterbelle kneeled by the stream.

"The cloth," said the boy. "Keep that dry."

She unwrapped Tex and lowered him to the water.

What now? he wondered.

Freezing cold. The water must run straight down from the mountains, he thought. Or seep out the icy ground. The shock of being immersed in it was so great that he writhed and let out a purely autonomic raven-cry—

"Wwrronnk!"

—and Winterbelle shrieked, too, and pulled away from him. He dropped. His head went under. And when he came sputtering up

"A *snake!*" screamed Winterbelle. Not in fear. Her little face bursting with delight.

"Don't touch him," Ari said, gravely.

Tex twisted and slapped the water with—what *was* this? A *tail*? A reptile's long sinuous body? Water entered his throat and he spat it out with an angry, sibilant exhalation.

"Don't worry," said the boy, holding Winterbelle by the arm, drawing her back a little. "Just wait."

Tex felt horrible. Was he doomed now to spend all eternity as a goddamned *snake*?

"Down," said Ari.

—and Tex went under again. He felt himself filling up, bloating, and then his feet touched the gravelly bottom. *Feet,* he thought. That's progress. He lifted his head, broke out into open air again. And Winterbelle shouted:

"A *pig!*"

"A boar, actually," said Ari. "See the hair, and those tusks?"

Tex shook his head violently. He snorted at them. He felt a nearly overwhelming desire to go to McDonald's.

"What's next?" said Winterbelle.

Ari bent down, looking Tex very closely in the eye. It struck Tex that there was something strangely familiar about this child's features. If he had not been conceived by Arthur Rackham, then he must belong to somebody Tex knew.

"Get ready with the cloak," said Ari. "Get ready—*now*."

Tex floundered. Water covered his eyes, and the gravel bottom of the stream pressed itself into his belly. Everything hurt that could possibly hurt. He was simultaneously soaking wet and thirsty. Parched. Strangely, despite being underwater, he had no desire to breathe. Of course, he was dead.

He heard some commotion up there, in the world of air & light et cetera, and out of sheer cussed curiosity he popped his head up. Long gray hairs, streaming with water, obscured his vision. But he could hear the children shouting, over his head.

"Grab him!" yelled Ari.

"By what?" said Winterbelle.

"What do you think?"

"Ahhh!" roared Tex. Small strong hands locked themselves on his hair, and he felt his head yanked back with the force of a construction crane.

"He's not really that heavy, is he?" Winterbelle said.

"Of course not," grunted Ari.

They dragged Tex out of the water and scraped him over some sandy dirt and laid him to rest on a fat hemlock root. He was aware of the Wizard cloak wrapped tightly around him, binding his arms and legs into an all but immobile unit.

"It's—" said Winterbelle, leaning over to stare at him. "It's an old hippie."

"Yeah," said Ari. Making a show of being not impressed.

Not *that* old, thought Tex. But he did not try to speak yet. He was still coming to grips with things. He was a human again, for starters. And the kids could see him.

Ari struck a knightly pose: arms folded, legs planted firmly a shoulder width apart. He demanded: "Are you of the living, or of the dead?"

And Tex smiled, because he realized whose child this was.

"Is," he tried to say, though there was some problem with his throat. He swallowed—that ungodly thirst again—and started over. "Is your mother named Syzygy Prague?"

Ari turned to Winterbelle. He lifted his head, cockily. "See? He knows my mother." As though this proved something. Back to Tex, stern again, he said, "First you have to answer my question."

Definitely a take-no-prisoners attitude, here. But that was his mom all over.

Tex said, "I knew you when you were just a pup. You peed on me, I think."

Ari put on a disgusted look for Winterbelle's benefit. "Well, what's the difference, I guess. They're all a bunch of deadheads anyway."

The two kids balanced themselves on tree roots, holding their arms out and moving in tiny steps. They were silent for a while: it was like a kid form of kinetic meditation. Tex tried to sit up, to get a better look at the situation. But as soon as he put pressure on his left leg, pain slammed up his spine like a jackhammer. He flopped onto his back. A prolonged moan—philosophical as much as physical—rose from his innermost depths.

"Uh oh," said Ari.

The kids came to stand on either side of him. Tex looked from one of them to the other.

"You think you guys might be able to find me some kind of walking stick?" he said. "I've kind of got this—see, I've like broken my leg here. Please?"

Ari shook his head. "That does it," he told Winterbelle. "We better let my mother handle this."

He took the girl by the hand and firmly pulled her away.

"What's the matter?" she said.

Ari did not answer. He stooped down right where he stood and scrabbled around in the dirt and the fallen hemlock needles until he came up with a handful of moss. He pulled this back and forth between his fingers, shredding it into tiny green specks. Then he moved very slowly around Tex and around the big tree, sprinkling the moss as he went. And chanting:

"Green of gravestones,
  Green of damp,
  Hold this specter
  Like a clamp.
  Moss that spreads
  Like melanoma,
  Draw him down
  Into a coma."

"Hey, wait," protested Tex. But watching the boy go round & round, 3 times in all, was making him dizzy. "What is this shit, *like melanoma*? Where did you learn that?"

Only by now he was only mumbling, and the kids had gone away.

So Tex stared up at the hemlock tree,

whose arms reached down
to shelter him, and
he slept.

&
Molly thought, Time out.

She felt drained and headachy from being tuned into the head of Gene Deere. Now on top of that Tex had vanished. Who knew what that meant? Alone on the foredeck, she looked up at the sky from which the first fat drops of rain had begun to spatter, and she thought, Time out. I've got to collect myself.

To collect herself. An odd turn of phrase when you thought about it. As if this being she knew as "herself" were composed of pieces that now and again might get scattered, and you could go from place to place sweeping them up and reassemble Molly out of the heap of them.

Well—but it did make a certain amount of sense. Molly stepped through the hatch into the living quarters and she thought, *Look* at all this stuff. Look at the albums, the books, the Goddess statuettes, the angel-wing begonias—all the things that seemed to have gotten stuck to her as she padded through life, like mud to a shoe. They were only physical objects, yes. But so was the very substance of her body, and where was that? Lying at the bottom of a well in the middle of the forest. Starting to decay now, probably. And yet Molly was not there, moldering away. She was *here*. Feeling lost amid the jumble of her possessions.

These objects, she thought, were part of her not in just a meta-phorical way, but in the same way that her body had been part of her. Her body was assembled out of proteins and minerals and things like that—inanimate matter, in other words—according to some guiding pattern. And in the very same way, her treasured belongings had been assembled out of the raw material of the world according to a definite program—only in this case the program was not deep down in her genes; it was in her mind. Which is not to say that she understood it very much better. Why *had* she developed this weird craze for certain flowers? She could not have answered that, really, any more than she could have told you why her cheekbones were shaped a certain way. The cheekbones were her mother's, the flowers were pretty, but it all might have come out a different way. She could have taken up batik-making and been born looking like her aunt Livonia. Who Molly was, who she had been, who she was becoming—all remained essentially mysterious. Molly *was*, that was all. She was herself.

Suddenly, and with unimaginable power, a stab of poignancy pierced her heart.

I'm going to have to leave all this, she thought. *I'm going to have to turn away, to let it all go.*

That was all. The thought did not linger or explain itself. She did not know why she was suddenly certain of this, the need to start taking leave of things, and she did not know why it had not been forced upon her already. Why had she come back here at all, if only to go away again?

You have something to do

murmured a Voice deep inside her.

She was shaken—not by the Voice, but by the fact that she recognized it, she knew it from somewhere.

Yes, thought Molly. Yes I do. I know I do.

But what?

LOVE + HAVE FUN

Molly tried projecting herself.

She tried to ask herself questions, the way Tex had asked her where his pendant was, and to send her awareness flying out into the akasha to retrieve the answer.

She found that she could not.

The question, it appeared, could not come from within her. Her strange new ability could only be called upon by somebody else. From which she deduced

---

> ### Afterlife Factoid #7
> ### Death is nothing personal.

Nothing private, that is to say. You're still plugged into the Web. Other people are still important. If anything, they become *more* important, because they're the live actors, the Players, strutting across the boards, and you're out here in the wings, paring your nails or whatever. Molly was not at all sure what her job was now—some kind of stage manager, lighting director, what?—but whatever it was, she was certain that it was for the benefit of *them,* the ones still on the stage.

She ambled through the houseboat, looking for clues as to where Tex might have gone. She noticed that the Organic Tofu container was missing from the refrigerator. Aha, she thought, licking her lips, noticing a peculiar taste of salmon there. Finally, on the altar in the pilot house, of all places, she made an Important Discovery.

It was a note from Ludi. And it was scratched (Molly was startled to note) in Ludi's careless, childlike handwriting, in her own Book of Shadows.

Hey guys I guess you still aren't here.
Just dropped by to tell you about the action at Goddin—went OK, except You Know Who always takes over when you aren't around.
A cute guy drove thru in a Range Rover, smiled at me I think.
On my way now to the critique at Eben's.
Hope you guys are OK wherever you've gone to.
Love + have fun,

Ludi

Molly smiled. You could not help feeling a certain fondness for the girl. Especially with Tex and his ludicrous middle-age crushes factored out. Love and have fun, she thought, glancing over the note again.

Ah, youth.

Just before she shut the Book of Shadows and returned it to its drawer, her eye—the left one—brushed across another sentence, and even after she turned away from the altar, the sentence seemed to follow her. It had gotten snagged on the edge of her awareness.

What do you think they're doing out there? it ran.

And that, thought Molly, is a Question.

From somebody else.

Then she felt a throbbing behind her eye—the right one—and it hurt enough to make her want to lie down. She barely managed to pull herself all the way up to the flying bridge, where she saw with rapidly fading attention that Tex's old jeans and T-shirt and multicolored Spindleworks vest were lying there on the nonskid. That was good: they made a cushioned place for her to rest. So she arranged a little spot for herself and she started to lay her head down, but already her mind was getting whirled away in a fast-moving eddy of Time.

THE FUTURE

 The moon was different.

Molly could *feel* this, even though it was midday in the Somewhen her awareness had passed over to— a time and space into which she gazed with an eye that could not blink.

Faerie Moon had been two or three days short of full that night when she and Tex had gone out to the Well. Now the moon— was it the same one?—was well along in its waning phase, toward the end of the third quarter. Rising and setting 51 minutes later every night, it hung now just below the western horizon. Molly felt as though, if she wished, she could peer right through the intervening chunk of the planet and see it out there: coldly radiant, falling forever toward its gravitational destiny. As aren't we all.

But surely that was not what she had come here for.

She looked around at the tiny part of the planet immediately at hand. It was an unfamiliar place: a large featureless room, walls done in cheap paneling, laid out in austerely functional style with the sort of institutional furniture that gives prisons and high school cafeterias a bad name. There were no windows and no decorations except for some posters, taped flat against the paneling, devoted to public-service messages: safety with firearms, reading aloud to children, the duty of all citizens to register and vote.

But here was the odd part. Molly could not figure out whose point of view she was seeing this from. Whereas before she had felt herself hovering just over the shoulder of Eugene Deere, now she seemed to be floating free, like a balloon—tethered to this particular spot, but not to anyone she could see.

Then there were voices. Muffled, and somewhat buzzed-out by the fluorescent lamp ballasts.

Her vision began to shift. It rose upward and appeared to seek out the source of these voices in the manner of an insect being drawn to a light. Molly found herself staring way too closely at the water-stained acoustic tile ceiling, then—

Crash, she thought

—the vision floated through. The ceiling became the floor of the level above, and she found herself hovering in the unnerving hollow of a Christian church. Rows of pews ran back & forth between tall, unadorned windows. Overhead, a series of timber trusses held up a steeply pitched roof. Molly's point of view pivoted gradually, absorbing the scene, and at last came to rest on the marginally more ornate end of the sanctuary where a pulpit stood before a choir stall, brightened by a stained-glass window that rose to a Gothic arch. In place of organ pipes there were Mirage tower speakers.

Finally she saw where the voices were coming from.

(1) guy lean and rangy as a wolf, edgily perched on a choir bench
(1) guy oversized and well fed as a hippo, lying flat-out on the floor

"Where I'm coming to this from," the big horizontal one was saying, "is a clash-of-values direction. I'm not saying this or that detail of their position does not make a limited amount of sense, when you take it in isolation. I'm saying that *in toto,* when you examine their proposals and you see what kind of mind-set they're coming out of, then I begin to have some grave and serious difficulties. I just want you to understand that."

The wolfish man licked his lips. He brought a hand up and scratched beneath his ball cap. The cap bore the round red-and-black logo of the National Rifle Association, which from any distance is easily mistaken for the emblem of the United States Marine Corps. Molly's bodiless point of view drew nearer.

The man on the floor twisted his head around. His jowls shifted so that she could see that he was wearing a white clerical collar. And a jogging suit. He was big but not exactly fat. As he spoke again, Molly understood where she had seen him before.

"So tell me, Wild Jag," he said—pronouncing the last two words loudly and deliberately, as though it were a title being conferred by himself, right here on the spot—"what are they doing out there?"

The Rev. Banebook, Molly remembered. *Call me Hoot.* And the security man from the Goddin base. His name tag had said Eckhart. *Clearance: All Areas.*

"You mean—" Eckhart began.

"I mean, *what are they doing out there.* What are their plans for the base? How do they view the opposition of local activists, such as it is. You want me to write these questions down so you can study them?"

Eckhart looked the Reverend over thoughtfully, neither intimidated nor amused. "You should get more exercise," he said finally. He had a Maine accent that sounded artificial, or at least exaggerated, and a habit of not looking straight at you, even while keeping you constantly in his sights. "Get you over there to the camp, up to Applemont. See the obstacle course we got out there. Down-in-the-dirt survival stuff. Get your ass in shape in a hurry, I guarantee it."

"Wild Jag," said Banebook, returning his head to its former position: faceup, thick neck locked in place, as though pulling guidance directly off the Divine Satellite. He spoke to the empty church at large. "You will have noticed, I'm sure, that I make no effort to convert you to my own way of thinking. Please do me the kindness of treating me likewise. While we are on the subject, however, I might as well tell you that I think your illusions of guaranteed survival are hubris. Sheer hubris. There is only one surefire path through the fiery days ahead, and that path is not a secret. I invite you to come here and learn more about it on any Sunday you like. Now please. Just tell me—"

"They've got these places laid out that they call trial plots," Eckhart cut him off. He spoke so quickly and so cannily you got the idea that his Thank God I'm a Country Boy routine was in some measure a put-on, a performance. "And that botanist fellow, Deere—"

"I've met him."

"I know that. Listen—he's been brought up here to evaluate them. Each plot is about 8, 10 acres, big enough to be like a hunk of real forest. Then there'll be a stretch where they mow, or with the old runways running through there, maybe a hundred yards across. Then there'll be another trial plot. And on like that, all around the base. Now on each plot, see, they've got a different mix of tree types. On one you've got solid fir, say. On the next, some proportion of fir to pine. Then there'll be spruce with a scattering of hardwoods. You know, to simulate what would happen if you cut down on the herbicide and you let nature take its course. Then way out by the north fence—"

"All right, I understand. But what are they testing for? What's their object?"

"There's various things. I guess the main one is, how much yield do they get out of it, and how fast. Another thing is, what kind of wood product is it most efficient to extract, up here. For example, there's *wood* wood, for 2-by-4's and like that, and then there's veneer wood, which yellow birch is supposed to be good for, and there's wood you slice in little layers to make plywood out of. But a big thing, too, is there's pulp wood, which isn't really wood at all. It's fiber, is mostly all it is. They chop it up and soak it in acid to make paper out of. So that's why they're—"

"In other words," the Reverend cut in, "whichever one of these plots proves to be the most resource-effective, that will determine the company's overall management scheme for the North Woods as a whole."

"Damn it, Hoot. I mean, I guess you're right—but damn it, will you let me finish telling you? Out by the north fence, see, is where they're trying out some, what you might call, radical ideas."

"What do you mean by that?" the Reverend asked.

"I mean genetically altered stuff. That's why they hired that Deere, you know. He's supposed to be some hot-shit whiz kid out of M.I.T. or one of those places. And he's a gene-splitter."

"Splicer."

"Finest kind. So they've got him studying those plots up there, and from what I can tell he's looking in two directions. The one way, he's monkeying around with some kind of super-tree, and I'm talking about one righteous hyped-up ass-kicker. So Deere, he's got some batches of *that* in the ground—you know, clones? every one of them just alike—way up there by the north fence. And I mean, you should see it. Vigorous little suckers. Couple feet taller than anything else. Hell on weeds. No animal will touch them."

"Hm," said Banebook.

"Yeah, hm." Eckhart rubbed his chin, as though to soften it. He did not succeed. "But see, that's only one direction. The other is—you'll love this—he's got some plots where he's trying out some *alternative pulp producers*. And you won't believe what that means."

"Kenaf," said Banebook, in the confident tone of a man who's keeping up on things.

"Kenaf is one of them. Deere doesn't like it. Unsuitable for this climate, needs a longer growing season, some such shit. No, you'll never guess. *Marijuana*. Only he calls it hemp. They've got a special strain—now this is a proprietary secret I'm telling you— that they've jigged around with so it doesn't produce any active ingredients."

"Cannabinols."

"But even so, they had to get a special permit from the government to even *own* the stuff, much less be growing it. Just you and me try doing that, huh?"

Hoot Banebook was peering so hard at the stained-glass window that Molly expected the panes to start rattling. "You are telling me that the Gulf Atlantic Corporation is growing marijuana on a former Air Force base?"

"Well, not regular marijuana. Not that you could smoke. I mean, I guess you *could* smoke it. What they did was, they went back and dug up some of the old kinds that sailors used to make rope out of, and they started from there. And Deere seems to like it. He says you get a higher yield of pulp per acre, and you get it *annually*. It's like growing tomatoes or something. So something like the Goddin place, all open and flat, you could turn into a great big hemp plantation."

"A *marijuana* plantation."

"Sure. But not that kind."

"Well," said Hoot Banebook, "you've told me a lot. I think you've answered most of my questions."

"And you'll remember that, am I right? When it comes time to take up that land-use classification?"

Banebook did not reply. Instead, he rose to his feet. It was quite an operation.

"What I need," he said, "is not exercise. It is a new back. I'm afraid the one I was given does not satisfy my current requirements."

Eckhart sat on his bench, looking pleased with himself. "What're you planning to do?"

Banebook stood beside the pulpit, resting one beefy hand there with peculiar delicacy. "Do?" he said. "I am planning to do what I always do on Thursday afternoons. I am going to minister to the needs of the less fortunate members of our community. Then I am going to sit here in the sanctuary and pray. I will pray, among many other things, that the good people of the Gulf Atlantic Corporation arrive at a right and proper decision."

Eckhart smiled. "The Lord helps those who help themselves," he said slyly.

Banebook had begun walking toward the back of the choir stall, where a door opened to a stairwell. As he moved, he seemed to gather purpose and momentum. Just before reaching the door he turned and said, "So how about it, Wild Jag? Would you care to stay for a bowl of chowder?"

CEIST NA TEANGAN

A banner tacked up on the wall of the multipurpose room below announced something in big, cheerful handwriting that Molly could not decipher at first, except for the initial letters

H
C
E

which made her blink; but she figured out that this stood for HOOT'S CHOWDER FOR EVERYONE! and that this was the theme of the afternoon. It was Thursday, then, and this was the rotating soup kitchen, sponsored today by the Church of Mankind's Destiny Among the Stars. The volunteers who cooked the chowder and dished it out to the deserving poor (actually, to anybody who showed up to eat) bustled in and out of the kitchen, hefting big stainless steel tureens.

The folks who were drifting in, by ones and twos and in little family-sized flocks, did not look much different than any randomly chosen cross section of local society. (The only stratum conspicuously missing was the retiree set, who stayed mostly indoors, venturing out chiefly to attend town meetings and vote down the school budget.) They varied in dress, age, gender, and attitude. They were alike in skin color, except for one wild-looking boy whose complexion was medium brown, and a younger, willowy girl who slipped in after him, whose skin was the closest to pure white that living flesh can attain without assistance of makeup. Molly believed she knew this girl from somewhere. The boy too, possibly; unless they just reminded her of characters out of fairy tales.

Then she recognized Pippa Rede, sort of sidling along the far wall, creeping up on the food line, and Molly realized that the girl was Winterbelle. How fast she had grown! Or had the years just zipped by that quickly?

Poor Pippa, she thought. So sweet, and very sharp in her own way. And yet at the same time so helpless. So utterly dependent on things falling out of the heavens for her, *just* when they were desperately needed. As thus far, miraculously, things had seemed with surprising regularity to fall. This free chowder day, just up the hill from Pickup City, being a fairly typical instance.

A stirring of some kind occurred around the entrance. It was as though a strange gust of wind were blowing in, sending dry leaves spinning through the door. Then the knot of people there seemed to unravel, and through the opening she had created stepped Syzygy Prague.

"Pippa!" she called out, in a loud and distinctly Yonkerish voice. "Winterbelle! Ari! What's going on, where does the food line start?"

The room did not exactly become hushed. If anything, it started to buzz with a sudden introjection of energy. Everyone turned to stare at the exotic-looking newcomer—which Syzygy herself did not appear to notice, nor to care about. It happened everywhere. Probably it had happened at the moment of her birth. No doubt it would happen when she passed over to the Summerland.

"Ah," she cried. "There you all are!"

And she advanced through the room toward hapless Pippa, who looked even more inconsequential than before, and toward Ari and Winterbelle, who raced to meet her.

So there they are, Molly thought. The Witches of Glassport. With their wee supernatural children.

Syzygy was some kind of gypsy. Her family had come from Ireland, but they were not Irish. She made no fuss about the way she dressed, wore no makeup, and usually covered her explosive coal-black hair with a cowboy bandana you could buy at Reny's for 99¢. Nonetheless she managed to look like no one else, and to draw attention away from women who ought, objectively, to have left her in their shadow.

She was the neighbor, or co-landowner, or something, of Tex's business partner, Jesse Openhood. The child Ari was supposed to be hers by Jesse, though it was hard to understand how such a thing could have happened.

Molly felt an unusual excitement stirring within her. Something like the way you feel when you've been driving for a long time, and it's dark, and you're a little worried about making it home okay, and suddenly you realize that certain landmarks have begun to appear—that without even being conscious of it, you're driving through familiar territory. Already your shoulders have begun to loosen up; you feel more cheerful, like there's something to look forward to, and it's not even very far off. That kind of excitement.

The thing was, though, *this feeling had nothing to do with her.*

This feeling, she was sure, belonged to Somebody Else.

And it freaked her out, knowing that. Because it was just like before, when she had been surfing the thought-waves of Eugene Deere: seeing what he saw, thinking what he thought, yet all the while remaining herself, and aware that she was only a spectator.

Only now, the feeling was the same, but like, *Who am I this time?*

Her awareness, tethered to a person or presence who remained unseen, moved at a deliberate pace across the room, homing in on Syzygy Prague. When there was only a table-width between them, the point of view stopped. Molly stared at Syzygy at close range through a phantom eye. And suddenly

this is really happening

Syzygy turned her head and stared back. Right into Molly. Through her, out the other side. Locking eyes with the invisible Other.

Syzygy raised her spoon. Steam curled around her upper lip, where there was the faintest hint of a moustache. Perversely becoming, on her. Molly felt warmth rising up from her roots.

Syzygy did not smile or frown; but in a very even voice, she said:

"An de bheoaibd nó de mhairbh thu?"

Which Molly understood perfectly. It was a sort of joke about Syzygy—not strictly a funny one. It meant, *Are you of the living, or of the dead?* and it was the way Syzygy answered when you knocked on her door.

«The dead»
thought Molly.

But the Other, beside her, silently replied:

«Bheoaibd.»

The living. So there you had it: a standoff.

"Here," said Syzygy. She pushed her chowder across the table. "You take the rest."

No hands moved to accept it, but Molly felt gratitude and surprise, partly her own. Syzygy nodded, and then pointedly turned away.

The Reverend Hobart Banebook was making his way to the center of the room, pressing the flesh as he went. People had to scrunch their chairs in to let him by. In his own way, the Rev projected vibes as strong as Syzygy's, only on a frequency closer to the right side of the dial.

"Fellow human sojourners," Banebook said grandly (which Molly thought might be taking a little too much for granted), "I can't tell you how happy it makes me to see you all here. I hope the chowder is to your liking."

He meant it. Molly, or the spirit, maybe both, felt quite certain of this. He actually wanted everyone to like his chowder.

"You know, it's easy to feel invisible nowadays," he went on. "It's easy to feel as though we're just unnoticed faces in the crowd. As though nothing we could possibly say or do would ever matter. Well, I can't say I don't feel that way a lot of the time myself. But I'd like to ask you to consider another possibility. And I'm not saying you have to *believe* this—only take these thoughts away with you today, and let your minds digest them just the same way that your stomachs are going to digest this meal. And then if you want to forget it, then forget it! You won't hurt old Hoot's feelings, I can tell you."

There was a bit of quiet laughter in the room. Indeed, something kindly and even boylike seemed to unfold in the Rev's face as he went on talking. It was not possible to think that he was less than 100% sincere. Which Molly, confirmed antichurchgoer that she was, found altogether unsettling.

"Now *think* about this," he resumed. "Think about the days ahead of us—big days, I guarantee you—and think about yourself being here on this earth to witness them, and then ask *Why*? Why am I right here, right now? Well, let's remember a promise that was made to us a couple thousand years ago. 'And the King-dom of Heaven shall be thine.' Have you ever thought about what that really means? You might suppose that it's just a fuzzy kind of statement about life after death. But I, for one, do not believe that. I do not believe that the Lord ever speaks in a fuzzy way. The Lord is, if you'll pardon my turn of phrase, very down-to-earth in His dealings with humankind. He sticks to the facts.

He names names. So I believe that when the Lord made a promise that the Kingdom of Heaven shall be ours, then what He was talking about was the Kingdom of *Heaven*. Do you follow me? The Kingdom of the Heavens—the Universe, in other words. All the worlds that lie above us and around us. The sky and the planets and the stars.

"What I'm suggesting is that we, all of us in this room, happen to have been born at the close of this most tumultuous millennium, the tail end of the Age of Pisces and the dawning of the Age of Aquarius. And as you know, Pisces is the Fish, a humble creature destined to remain in the water all his life, unable to rise up into the bright big world that lies above him. Whereas Aquarius is the Water Bearer. He is the master of that very element that has imprisoned the lowly fish. He can partake of that element, but when he has had his fill of it, he can rise up on the legs that the Lord has given him, and he can walk right out of there.

"And I'm suggesting to you that we, also, are about to learn how to rise up and walk. We have been—all of us, humanity—trapped and destined to live our lives down in this low earthly place, unable to rise up into the bright big world that lies above us. But we have been given, here at the end of this millennium, the holy gift of mastery over that very element that has imprisoned us. The means of our mastery is not a pair of legs but the human brain, that mighty organ that sets us above the beasts of the forest. With our brains we've learned the technology of space travel. And out of the raw clay of this planet, we've fashioned for ourselves the vessels—great shining arks, you might say—that can lift us up into the Kingdom that the Lord has vouchsafed to us.

"Now isn't that a wonderful thought! That's what I want to leave with you today, my fellow human sojourners. That thrilling possibility.

"But I want to leave you also with a warning. Pisces the Fish does not want to leap out of the water. He does not recognize it for the prison that it is. And just so, there are people today who do not recognize that this earth is a prison for us. They regard it instead as some kind of holy temple. So remember, when you hear people speak of the earth as something to be venerated—even worshiped!—you remember that the Lord has given us mastery over this place, to use for our own ends until such time as we are ready to leave it, to come into our heavenly inheritance. We need not worship the walls of our prison, as the ancient heathens worshiped rocks and trees and graven idols.

"This story I'm telling you is right there in the Bible, you can read it for yourself. The old Israelis were sent out by the Lord to destroy the Asherim, which were likenesses of the heathen goddess Ashera. Ashera was an old name for the dark spirit that resides in the earth, which has been called by many names through the ages. But of course, the dark spirit herself did not perish when her shrines were destroyed. She was still lurking around during the time of the early Christian fathers—living under the name Diana, who was known also as Dea Paganorum, the goddess of the Pagans. And once again, the righteous were sent out to destroy her shrines. So the grove at Manannan was cut down, where the heathens worshiped the dark spirit who led them to believe that the *trees themselves* were holy things. Imagine if Noah had believed that! Why, he wouldn't have cut them down to build his ark and we wouldn't even be here to talk about it."

Hoot Banebook took a deep breath and allowed the silence in the room to grow into something that you could feel, a presence in its own right. Then he exhaled, and the relaxed and boyish smile returned to his face.

"Well, that's all the time I'm going to take away from your meals," he said. "I invite any and all of you to come visit with us again here during our regular Sunday services. But that's up to you, of course. Enjoy your food now, and God bless every one of you!"

Molly watched as the Rev made his way out of the room, reopening the channel that had closed in behind him. She glimpsed Syzygy's wild son Ari out of the corner of her eye—standing up on his chair and looking this way & that around the room, as if he had lost something.

Molly had lost something too. The other awareness had vanished from her mind. She felt cast adrift, untethered. There was nothing to hold her here any longer, and by degrees, like a digital brightness control, the scene around her was fading into darkness.

Just before Molly slipped completely away, she heard the boy Ari's voice, as loud and unselfconscious as his mother's, asking:

"What *was* he, Mom? You know, the invisible guy that was right over there."

Which was exactly the question Molly needed.

WILDERNESS

Out through the wall of the church. Among damp trunks of hemlocks, holding up the slope. Ostrich ferns rising head-high and flopping over, like sodden drunks. Tufts of hybrid turf grass whose seeds blew in from the highway, starved for sunlight, lying down in exhaustion. Ground elder, running cedar, Virginia creeper, a statistically implausible seedling of somebody's *Rhododendron catawbiense.* Lungwort, spleenwort, Bowman's root. Shopping bags, beer cans, a grocery cart. Rusting refrigerators. Everlasting Goodyear radials. Great brown gouges of erosion. Piles of gravel washed downslope. Human excrement. High-gloss faces on the covers of magazines.

A secret world. A hushed brown and green and shadow-black nether region. Cathedral, midden, and boneyard.

Such places are everywhere. They lie between other things, *real* places: buildings and highways and parking lots. They enclose and conceal sewer plants, residential communities, service entrances, exit ramps, hospitals, zoos. Water runs through them. Steep slopes protect them. Animals hide there. They are neither remembered nor forgotten. Rather, unthought-of.

You see them if you want to see them. You enter them if you are insane or lonely; a fugitive or an investigator; curious, desperate, homeless, or simply strange.

They are the new wilderness. They are Nature, born again. Habitat and breeding ground for new species of wild things.

Such as.

THE HOMELESS

Water gushed through the stream and plunged noisily into a wide-mouthed metal culvert. The thick trunk of a tree whose nearest limb was two heads above stood like a brooding, motionless sentinel. At the base of it lay something wrapped in a dirty sheet or shroud that was indigo blue with gold lamé stars. Only when you got quite close could you tell this object was a person. A scrawny sort of person with long, tangled, graying hair.

The wandering Presence or spirit or point of view, to which Molly was still attached like a ballon on a string, drew cautiously nearer. It paused a short distance away, held back by this: a phosphorescent ring of green energy that ran around the person on the ground and around the hemlock trunk, creating a protective energy web. Such artifactures are rare and growing rarer, and their lingering existence made the Presence feel melancholy, as did its own.

The Presence brushed against the protective web, testing its strength. The web was porous, easily breakable. Even at this light touch, its bindings started to unravel. The spirit drew back, somewhat chagrined. Nobody made things properly anymore.

The person on the ground stirred beneath his starry shroud. His mind worked for a few moments, then his eyes came open. Molly was startled to recognize Tex. He stared into a space that nearly coincided with the place where Molly was, or believed she was. But he was not looking at Molly. Rather, he looked . . .

«Like he's seen a ghost!»
she thought.

"Who are you?" said Tex. "*What* are you?"

Very slowly, the Presence began to take on a material form. The first thing you could really get your eyes onto was a hat: a ball cap twisted approximately backwards, so that Molly could see the logo of a major timber-products company:

GULF ATLANTIC
Growing the Future

Then a full-length, weathered green overcoat took shape. It was dirty and a gash was ripped out of it in back, and bulky things had been jammed into its side pockets. Below that were baggy trousers, rolled up at the ends, and a pair of Doc Martens whose heels were in obvious disrepair.

Only then did the Presence manifest itself: pouchy, unhealthy-looking skin; hair the color of oak leaves turning coppery red in autumn, shot with the sullen gray of rain clouds; limbs long and dangling; flesh slack in the way of a body that was once, a while ago, muscular and well developed. Molly could not see the face, but it must have been a sight. Tex looked like he had just swallowed that brown acid at Woodstock.

"Are you a—" Tex blubbed. "Are you a brownie?"

"A what?" said the Presence. Its voice was phlegmy, with a very peculiar accent: nothing that Molly could pin down.

"You know," said Tex, "a big hairy elf. Or maybe a street person? How come you're dressed like that?"

"Is there something the matter with the way I'm dressed?"

The Presence sounded not quite belligerent, but close.

Tex tried to sit up a little straighter. The effort must have hurt his broken leg, because he winced and grabbed his kneecap. "Wow," he said, "I guess I was asleep for a while."

"You mean a nagumwasuck," said the Presence.

"Say what?"

"A brownie. That's what they're called around here. At least they *were,* when people still believed in them. No, I'm not that. You'd know a nagumwasuck if you saw one."

"Ah," said Tex.

«Well, at least he's got the sense to go into his good-vibe act» thought Molly. Truth to tell, she was happy to see Tex again, and worried about whether he was all right.

The Presence eased down on his haunches, a pace or two away from Tex's outstretched legs. Through its alien awareness, Molly could sense the dampness of the ground, the smells of mold and decaying leaves. The water in the stream was tainted with oil, bug spray, artificial lemon fragrance, and urine.

"What's your name?" said Tex.

The spirit shrugged. "Beats me." He scratched the ground for a few seconds, then brought a dirty finger up before his face for closer inspection. He said, "I guess you can call me Beale."

"Beale?" Tex was smiling, but his mouth gave a little jerk, betraying nervousness. He was acting the way you might if you were approached by a panhandler in the park. "Is that a, ah, boy's name or a girl's name? Sorry, but I—"

"*Ha.*" Beale enunciated the syllable, as though to distinguish it from genuine laughter. "You can't tell, right? Whether I'm a man or a woman. You can't even decide if I'm *real* or not. Right?"

Offended again: Molly could feel that, but she had no intimation of violence in the offing. She sensed a great load of bitterness and resentment hanging over the spirit like a cloud.

"You think I'm just some kind of delusion, right?" Beale demanded.

"Easy," Tex said, drawing himself up as best he could. "Take it easy, okay? I'm on your side. At least, I would be if you'd tell me what side you're on."

Beale settled down a bit. The weary head turned away from Tex, glanced up the embankment toward the Church of Mankind's Destiny Among the Stars. More bitterness, more anger. Molly thought:

«This is one fucked-up individual.»

"What?" said Beale.

"What what?" said Tex.

The Presence frowned. "I thought I heard something."

Tex gave him a knowing look. He clearly believed that he was dealing here with a crazy person. Which might (Molly considered) be true. But it was not the whole story.

Afterlife Factoid #9
You can give up trying to understand.
Nothing is ever the whole story.

Tex said cautiously, "So it's Beale, right?"

"Beale," agreed the Presence—pronouncing it differently, though, as if the word were not an English one. "And to answer your question, it's not a boy's name *or* a girl's name. It means *sacred tree.*"

"Sacred tree?" said Tex. The idea seemed to perk him up. He grimaced slightly as the pain in his leg reasserted itself. "Are you like, a Native?"

"Absolutely." Beale pointed at Tex's leg. "I see you've been injured."

Tex shrugged.

Beale nodded, understandingly. "Was it a god or a goddess?"

"Say what?"

"Who broke your leg. This happened in the Otherworld, right?"

Tex opened his mouth and closed it. A narrow smile formed at his lips. "Goddess," he said. "She *kissed* me, can you dig it?"

Beale shook his head. "Too bad. Goddesses are the worst. What form did she take?"

"A gigantic raven," said Tex. "Smelled like . . . why do you ask? Some friend of yours? Are you a goddess too? Or a god?"

"Ha." Beale picked up a stick and poked it in its mouth. "Forget goddesses. And gods. They're hopeless. They're done for. Me?" Taking the stick out, gesturing with it. "I'm a dryad, man. I'm genderless. I'm *older* than the gods."

"No shit," said Tex. He sat up straighter, pain or no pain. Beale's rap was reeling him in like a sucker off the street, hooked on a game of 3-card monte.

"Truthfully," said Beale. Warming up now. Getting into the rhythm of this human patter, like. "The gods only exist because of *you* people, you know? You humans. You invented them. Your old storytellers made them up. This was, I don't know—50, maybe 60 thousand years ago. Believe me. I remember."

"You do?"

"Mm."

"Listen." Beale leaned over, tearing through the remnants of the energy web. He patted Tex on the foot. "Look what's happening to me. My appearance is becoming more human, isn't it? In fact, I'm taking on the attributes of your male gender, because you're *thinking* of me that way. It gives you a handle, a metaphor. A way to grasp me. See how it happens? I'm real. But at the same time, you're making me up. And in that sense, you've got power over me. Just like you've got power over your own gods."

"Yeah?" Tex cocked his head—bemused, but obviously pleased by this idea.

"Absolutely. Think about it. Think about what I look like, right now."

Tex chuckled. He didn't have to think. He said, "You look like a bum."

"A *what*?" (Seeming to take offense.)

"You know," said Tex. "A street person. Someone who's homeless."

Beale reared up, indignant. Then, quite abruptly, he flopped down into his battered overcoat as though his body had been deflated.

He said, "You're exactly right," with a long weary sigh.

His voice had changed. More aged and wistful now.

"I *am*?" said Tex.

Beale nodded. He looked like an old man, worn and beaten. Tex's words did appear to have magically transformed him.

"Homeless," he said. "That's what I am. A street person. Or at least, a ground-being. I've lost my home and there isn't going to be another one. Not for a long time. Maybe never. The thing that happens to your gods, the slow fading—that's happening to me. I'm different, I'm older, but the process is the same. Out of the explicate world, back into darkness."

"Wow," said Tex. "Is there . . . like, anything we can do?"

"We?" said Beale. "Ha."

"You, then?"

"No. *You*. It's you—you humans—that made me this way. Didn't I tell you? I'm a dryad. That's a human word, like Beale. It means tree-spirit. But I'm older than the word. I'm an ancient potency associated with oak trees. In particular, with a northeastern variant of the American white oak. *Quercus alba*. My last home was a 200-year-old specimen growing in one of the unincorporated townships."

"So what happened?"

"I was, you might say, evicted. My tree was aging, and there was a rotten section near the core. So I was . . . harvested."

"Harvested." Tex recognized this as a euphemism.

"The tree was not suitable for commercial lumber use, so it was sawed into sections and fed into a biomass-fired power plant. That did not affect *me*, of course. In the course of things, I would simply have passed into acorns, and thence into seedlings, and finally into a mature tree to succeed the one that died. Or two, or possibly more."

"Wait. You can be in more than one tree at the same time?"

Beale made a fluttering motion with his hand. "Your mind is not structured in the way necessary to conceive this. But we dryads do not have the absolute barrier between one individual and another that you animal spirits have."

"Animal spirits? That's what I am?"

"Please. Let's stick to one thing you won't understand at a time. What has happened to me is, my particular species variant—the subtype of *Quercus alba* that is a physical expression of myself—has been completely eliminated from the North Woods. There are many white oaks left, and many other variants, and therefore many dryads similar—even almost identical—to myself. But a large and growing number of the old patterns are simply vanishing. I mean literally *vanishing*: passing out of the visible realm of the world. We still exist, of course. And certain aspects of us are still active and growing and individuating. It's . . . complicated. But *I*, to the extent that I can be separated from my kindred spirits, am without a single tree to inhabit. I am homeless. Just so."

"Wow."

Tex was hunching forward, crouched up in a little ball. He appeared oblivious to the broken leg.

"Wow," he said again. "*Homeless nature spirits.* What a concept."

Beale said nothing. He seemed to quiver on the edge of the unmanifest. At certain instants, Molly could begin to see through him; then he grew solid and opaque again.

Tex said, "Are there a whole lot of you guys?"

Gus shrugged. "You mean, all over the world? I'd guess tens of thousands, at least. More perhaps. Hard to say. As I was trying to tell you, the boundaries that determine what is an individual—"

"*Tens of thousands of homeless dryads.*" Tex's mind kicked into its speed-guitar mode. "Think of that."

"What else is there for me to think about?" said Beale, a little irked.

«You watch out»
Molly tried to warn him.

«You've got my Bear all worked up now. There's no telling what he's going to do. You poor dryads aren't used to this.»

"You know," said Tex, sounding much more rational now, which was the worst possible sign, "you guys ought to think about getting organized."

"Organized?" said Beale. "But that's precisely what we are, in a way of speaking. We are *organization*. Each of us represents the organizing, the *organ-making*, pattern or growth-field of a particular type of tree."

"No, not like that. I mean, get *really* organized. Form like, a union. A political action committee. Some way to come together and make your voices *heard*."

"We don't have voices," said Beale, testily. "We are incorporeal matrices of life-potential. By strictly physical standards, we do not exist at all."

"Now, you see?" said Tex. "That's just the kind of negative thinking that's got you guys into this mess in the first place."

"*Your* negative thinking. Not ours."

"Let's not get caught up in recrimination. Let's start thinking about concrete steps we can take. Maybe we should start with some kind of exploratory meeting, just to create some heightened group awareness. Is there any way to get a message around, or post a notice or something? Some kind of Dryad SIG?"

Beale sighed. He seemed to regard Tex from a great temporal distance, and to decide that further argument would be unproductive. As a family, primates had not evolved much further than the Age of Reason. There was no sense trying to dispute with them over matters of Higher Truth.

"This is far out," said Tex.

And Molly reflected that she had not heard him so excited for quite a long time. He had not been nearly this excited about the affairs of his mortal existence: the boat, the Street Theater, his partnership with Jesse. He had been going through the motions of those things, as though dutifully playing a role. But now . . .

Molly looked at Tex, practically frothing with excitement. And she thought

«It's like Death is what it took
to bring him back
to life.»

THE SEED

"Hide," said Beale.

Tex did not hear him. He was lying on his back staring up at the hemlock tree. The sun had moved into the west and was making interesting yellow-and-black patterns among the limbs.

"Someone is coming," said Beale, "who will be able to see you. Transform yourself, if you can."

Tex looked around. "Say what?"

"Do you want to be caught again?" To the extent that a dryad can convey a sense of urgency, Beale's voice sounded urgent. "Do you want to have another one of *those* woven around you?"

He pointed at the ground, at the trail of shredded moss that ran in a circle around Tex and around the tree.

"No, hey—" Tex sat up. "Wait, I remember now. The little girl. And Syzygy's boy. He did something to me, cast a spell or something."

"Not a very strong one," said Beale. "But yes. You were enmeshed in an energy web when I discovered you. And someone is coming now who might be able to weave a stronger one. You might be trapped for quite a while. So if you can take another form—an animal, for instance—now would be a good time to do so."

Tex sat up and listened. Voices were coming from not far off, outside the green cave of hemlock boughs. He said, "But—I don't know how."

"You don't? But you said a goddess kissed you. She *must* have given you the ability to transform. It's standard procedure."

Tex's mind flickered briefly over the series of shapes he had occupied before coming to lie here. A *snake*? he recalled, disbelievingly.

The voices were getting closer.

"Right," said Tex, trying to think fast—something he had never been too good at. "Listen, you don't happen to have any reefer on you, do you?"

"Are you making a joke?"

"I just thought . . . you know, a street person . . . Never mind." Tex laid his head back. "I'm kind of new at this."

Beale scowled. "Obviously."

The voice of the boy, Ari, could be heard distinctly now. "No, *this* way," he said. "Under that tree there. *Mm-o-m*! Aren't you listening to me?"

After a pause: "There's more here than just a man," said the voice of Syzygy Prague.

Beale told Tex, "Listen to me now. I am going to transform you into an aspect of myself."

"Finest kind, bro. Is it going to hurt?"

"Only when you germinate." Beale reached out and, with astonishing strength, seized Tex and the dirty Wizard cloak and threw the two of them together into the stream. Quickly he rolled the cloak up and pulled it out, dripping.

Tex was nowhere to be seen.

Then Beale was nowhere to be seen, either.

Ari, followed by Winterbelle and Syzygy, and finally by Pippa Rede, came brushing through the curtain of hemlock branches. The wild-haired, dark-skinned boy rushed into the open space beneath the tree.

"*Here!*" Ari proclaimed, pointing down at the cloak.

Syzygy stepped nearer, coming to stand next to the stream, very still. Winterbelle raced excitedly about, and Pippa said in her timid voice:

"That looks like Guillermo's—"

"Where?" demanded Syzygy at last. "Where is this so-called hippie you drew your circle around?"

Ari shrugged. This seemed of secondary importance to him. He dashed after Winterbelle, around the massive trunk. From behind it he called, "Anyway, there's the cloth with the stars on it, like I told you."

"I see," said Syzygy. She stepped cautiously past the line of moss and into the broken circle. She bent to pick up the Wizard's cloak. Her dark eyes were open wide. Her fingers, with nails as dirty as a farmer's, probed the cloth firmly and efficiently. Then they found something.

From one of the inner folds of the cloak, Syzygy pulled out a computer disk. Its label, slightly smeared by the water, read

Strategy Briefing—
Restricted
Availability

"Probably ruined," said Pippa, who had taken a computer literacy class at the local U.M. extension. "I mean, from the water."

"I see," said Syzygy again. She probed deeper into the pockets of the cloak, as though convinced that some treasure must be buried there. At last she plucked out a small brown thumb-sized object, which she held close to her eyes and regarded very carefully.

"It's just an acorn," said Pippa, so quietly that her words were almost impossible to hear.

Syzygy said, "You are completely right."

The two kids came scampering out from behind the tree, grinning as though they were in on a diabolical secret.

"It is an acorn," Syzygy declared. You would have thought this was a fact of resounding importance.

"Mommy," said Winterbelle. "Ari just said a squirrel told him it's time to go home."

Pippa looked at Ari worriedly.

"A *flying* squirrel," he amplified.

Then Winterbelle giggled and raced off, ducking under the limbs of the hemlock and out of sight. Ari gave a funny little bow to the two women, then he hurried after her. Their mothers stood together for a while, looking at the spot where the kids had vanished.

"Is it my imagination," said Pippa, not quite so softly as usual, "or are our children becoming more elflike?"

Syzygy turned to her and gave her an unexpected smile, radiating warmth. She touched her friend in the lightest way on one arm. Pippa smiled back, shyly.

"Becoming more elflike?" Syzygy said, as though the thought entertained her. "But that is only to be expected, when you consider the times we are living in.

To be expected, and to be
most fervently
hoped."

&
another time, before that,

Ludi had come back to the *Linear Bee*. She came looking for Tex & Molly. But also she came looking for peace, for sanctuary. Seeking refuge. Because the world was too much with her—the world in this case meaning Guillermo Gobán—and as they say in the movies, he knew where she lived.

He knew where Tex & Molly lived too, of course. But he was afraid of Molly. And Tex bugged him. You could tell.

WHO KNOWS THIS?
>   Molly, eventually.

HOW?
>   Because of the magical salmon she ate.

BUT WAIT. THIS HAPPENED *BEFORE* TEX MET, OR WILL MEET, BEALE THE HOMELESS DRYAD?
>   That is correct. Two days earlier.

DOES THIS MAKE SENSE?
>   Yes & no. Sense—Reason, Logic, Induction, Proof, & alia—only arise because of the linear structure of Time. Whereas in the Otherworld, there is no Time.

THAT IS NOT STRICTLY TRUE.
>   No. But it is not strictly untrue, either. In the Otherworld,

Time is a story that is told and retold, each telling always resembling the others but endlessly varying.

MMM. BUT HOW CAN THERE BE STORIES WITHOUT TIME?
Ah: that is a logical problem—a paradox. And Logic has no standing in the Otherworld. That's why Tex will be so happy there.

AND WHO KNOWS *THAT*?
Ask anybody. Now listen—a story does not reveal itself all at once.

IT TAKES TIME?
Mmm. Yes &

NOT KNOWING

Quietly, on tiptoe, Ludi poked about the *Linear Bee*. Quiet, because she did not want to awaken any ghosts. And the houseboat was full of them. You could tell. (Actually Ludi could *not* tell, but here is how she looked at it: If ghosts were going to be anywhere, wouldn't they be here? With all this weird old stuff, masks and skulls and bones and rattles? If Ludi was a ghost, this was *exactly* the kind of place she'd want to hang out in.)

Tiptoeing, because she didn't want to disturb the evidence. When you are looking for clues you have to be careful not to mess up the scene of the crime. And if that sounds too extravagant, then try to explain

The Mystery
Where have Tex & Molly been for the last 6 days?

Because it was not like them just to disappear like this.

Actually it *was* like them. But the timing was wrong. Molly would not have buzzed off with the Street Theater in such a state of squabbling and dissension. The Midsummer Night performance was coming up and there was no agreement as to what kind of performance it should be. Tex, besides, would not have walked away from an interesting environmental skirmish like the thing with the Goddin base. No, Ludi believed firmly that something was wrong, that something at least unexpected and possibly very bad had come to pass. There had been, she suspected, some kind of misadventure.

Ludi loved that word. *Misadventure.* It was bookish, and romantic, and Ludi loved books and romance. Especially children's books, and above all fairy tales. She loved flowers too but somehow usually managed to kill them. Askance, she looked at a row of pots containing Molly's angel-wing begonias. Shading them, its broad leaves gracefully recurved, stood one of Tex's rare palms. Its plastic label read *Pinanga speciosa.* The very thought of things that only had names in Latin made Ludi uncomfortable. Did any of these plants need watering? She felt the soil, which seemed quite dry. She bit her lip.

In the galley she found the Majolica teapot and the Sun & Moon mugs sitting on the table. The tea leaves inside the pot had sprouted a crop of woolly gray mold. Geraniums bloomed gaily in the window, but some of their petals had begun to fall onto the countertop. Decorative—even romantic, like fallen rose petals—but also sad and untidy.

At that moment Goblin the Cat-Person sprang down from a shelf, alighting just in front of Ludi—who yelped.

"Oh, it's you, cat," she said, pressing her hand to her breastbone.

Goblin said, "Wwrrrrow."

"Sure," said Ludi. "I'll get you something to eat. Where do they keep your food?"

It was a relief to hear her own voice, breaking the silence. Exploring the cabinets, she could feel her shifting weight cause the boat to rock. It was a funny sensation, but you got used to it, and after that it was fun. All she could find for Goblin was a can of tuna, the people kind.

"Live it up," she told the cat. "I'll bring you something cheaper tomorrow. If your folks aren't back by then."

Up in the pilot house, Molly's Book of Shadows, which Ludi had left lying open after scribbling a message in it, was back in its place beneath the chart table. The hatch to the flying bridge hung open, and must have been that way for a while, because rainwater had fallen through it and collected in a puddle on the planking.

Did any of these things qualify as a clue? At the risk of tampering with the evidence, Ludi pulled the Book of Shadows out so she would have something to take notes on. Then she stepped warily up the ladder.

On the flying bridge she found a small Tupperware container labeled Organic Tofu. She made an unpleasant face at it. This must be a clue, for sure. Was it possible that Tex & Molly had contracted organic tofu poisoning and, in their death throes, hurled themselves into the water? Ludi opened the book to jot a few notes down.

The Book of Shadows fell open to a page where Molly had written

TO END A TOXIC RELATIONSHIP

This should be done on the waning Moon—beginning of 4th Qtr is perfect.

First, prepare Water of Forgetting:

—Collect dew or rainwater (1st rainfall in May best for renewal).

—Add dash of salt.

—Think or say, "This salt is for cleansing and restoring my harmony with the Earth."

—Allow to soak beneath the Moon, pref. in wooden vessel.

Next, dab finger in water & touch:

—Forehead, thinking "I release this person from my mind."

—Breast, thinking "I release this person from my heart."

—Back, thinking, "I turn my back on this person."

—Feet, thinking "I walk away from this person."

Now you may celebrate with a glass of wine, consecrated to the Goddess.

Ludi's thoughts drifted away from the notes she was planning to take. They homed back in on the world that had lately been with her too much; the world that was right now, in fact, probably hanging around her apartment, waiting for her to get home. She climbed back down the ladder in a pensive frame of mind.

Her foot landed with a little splash in the puddle of rainwater.

When did it rain? she wondered. The day after the Players' performance. Ergo, the day after Beltane. May the 2nd.

Ludi squatted down to examine the water more closely. It was puddled up in a little hollow, where the deck planks were warped. She dipped a finger into it and raised it to her mouth. A faint taste of salt-spray passed over her tongue.

Well, there are no such things as coincidences; everybody

knows that. Ludi swirled her finger around in the water from the first rainfall of May, and—convinced that she was being a *total* idiot, but doing it anyway—she dabbed the finger onto her forehead.

"I release him from my mind," she thought.

She stuck the finger down the front of her sweater. It felt cool on her chest.

"I release him from my heart," she thought. She thought it twice, because it did not sound at all convincing.

Goblin the Cat-Person crept up behind her, brushing himself lightly against her calves.

"Hey, cat," said Ludi. "Get enough to eat?" She ran a finger down Goblin's spine and felt silly, self-conscious.

She hurried through the rest of the ceremony, fairly certain that she was doing it wrong. And that even if she was doing it right, such a simple thing could never work. At least that it could never work for her. Things like this only worked for Tex & Molly. Look at poor Pippa Rede: she was forever casting spells and making charms and dancing naked in her magic circle, and see what a mess *she* was.

Finished, Ludi stood up straight and took a good breath and flicked the salty water off her fingertips. "That's that, you bastard," she said. "Not you, Goblin."

Out in the living quarters, the begonias and the palm tree seemed to gaze at her reproachfully.

"I'll come back tomorrow," she promised them. "Really. I've got to feed Goblin, anyhow. Maybe I can dig up a book about houseplants somewhere."

She had forgotten about keeping quiet, not messing up the crime scene. She was no longer thinking about ghosts. Therefore she failed to notice that she had attracted the notice of one.

Goblin bade her good-bye with a long, philosophical purr. Ludi stooped to pat him. Her final thought, as she bounded up the gangway, was:

Wouldn't it be awesome if it really *worked?*

«Oh, it'll work»
thought Molly.
«I'll make sure of that.»

SCENARIO (2)

 Guillermo was waiting for her.

He was waiting for her in the most aggravating way Ludi could imagine, by sitting at the small table in her kitchen before a bowl of Grape-Nuts and staring at the *Glassport Herald*. He did not look up when she came in. The message was: Oh, are you home already? I didn't hear you coming.

Liar, she thought. You probably didn't pour the damn Grape-Nuts till you saw the VW in the driveway.

"Hi," she said, and wondered why such a simple greeting should appear to represent a major concession on her part.

Guillermo laid the paper down, completely draping the cereal. "This rag has gotten so incredibly fascist," he declared. "There's another guest column by that Banebook guy. This time he's going on about—"

"Please," said Ludi. "I've had kind of a weird day. Do we have to talk about politics?"

Guillermo looked at her, up and down. He *inspected* her. Hair and clothing. Somehow he could do this without appearing to take notice of Ludi herself, as a conscious feeling person, at all. Or that's how it felt to her.

"Do I have any books about houseplants?" she asked him.

"I don't know," he said—sort of pouncing on this, as though it gave him the foothold he needed. "*Do* you?"

Ludi thought that, from a dramatic standpoint, it might be effective for him to wear glasses—the kind with dark heavy frames like Superman wears as Clark Kent—so that, when he wanted to be condescending like this, he could tilt the glasses down and peer over them.

Ludi slipped her shoes off. Guillermo rustled the *Herald*.

"And here's a letter from some gun nut out in Applemont," he said. "Listen to this."

Ludi gazed about the kitchen, conducting what Rainie Moss called an M.R.D.A. (male-related damage assessment).

" 'If the tree huggers have their way, there won't be any place left for human beings to live on. Everywhere you go, you'll have to sign your name and be told what you can and can't do by some government authority. It is hoped that anybody who can see some sense in these points will be sure to attend the orientation meeting next Saturday out at the Sovereign Citizen's Freedom Camp, 11:30 on, refreshments and beer provided.' Isn't that great? It's from a guy called Eckhart."

He glanced up at Ludi, who was staring down at him with her arms folded.

"What?" he said.

"I went over to Tex & Molly's again. There's still nobody there. It doesn't look like anybody's been home for days. Maybe since that night when you guys argued."

"Which argument was that?" said Guillermo, looking away and propping his feet up. "I can't keep them straight. But that's how it is with your peace-and-love types. If you disagree with them, you're the enemy."

"You sound just like that redneck in the newspaper."

"Ha. But isn't it true, though? Tex is one of those 60's guys who imposes this doctrine of imperial mellowness on everybody. And if you dare to get angry about anything, to take the real world seriously, then you're branded as some kind of heretic. And Molly acts like the Street Theater is her private fiefdom. Nothing gets done until she's made up her mind about it."

"Well, she did start the theater. And the two of them do do most of the work."

"Another way of putting that is, the two of them leave most of the *important* work undone."

"Why don't you try contributing more, then?"

"I do contribute," he said, thumping a hand on the table, hard. Grape-Nuts spattered. "I suggest what I consider to be sensible courses of action. And without fail, they get batted down by the 3-bong-hit coalition."

Ludi fumed, mainly at herself. This was not how she had wanted the conversation to go. "Look," she said, "what I was going to suggest was, since Molly isn't around, and nothing's getting done about the next performance—maybe we could get everybody to take a look at these ideas I've got for a script."

Guillermo looked down at her across the rims of his (purely hypothetical) glasses. Like she was crazy. Like he wasn't going to answer her at all. But at last he said, "And what ideas might these be?"

"If you want, I could show you."

"Show me," he said, folding the newspaper, spreading his arms wide, "by all means."

Ludi went into her semisecret private sanctum—a funny little nook on the far side of the bathroom, left over when the old garage-née-carriage-house was converted to apartments—and retrieved a stack of paper from her writing desk. She carried this back and presented it to Guillermo, hoping to convey an attitude of nonchalance. Failing seriously, in all likelihood.

Guillermo accepted the play-in-progress, but for a second or two he kept his eyes on Ludi, as though evaluating this unforeseen turn in their otherwise straight-line relationship. Finally his head made a slight dip, bobbing down just long enough to catch the title.

"A Midsummer's Dream Come True?" he read aloud, one word at a time.

Ludi, who had not intended to say anything at all, found words pouring out of her. "My idea was, everybody naturally thinks of a Midsummer Night's *Dream*, see, so I thought, well why not imagine what it would be like if everybody's dreams came *true*. All at once. On that same night. So what I'm trying to do is present this varied group of people, all these different types, coming from all different places in society, and I'm trying to imagine what everyone's personal dream might be. For some people it might be money, and for others it might be love, and for others it might be social justice—"

"Social justice?"

"For *some* people. And for others it might be a clean healthy world for their kids to grow up."

"And for others it might be social anarchy. Cheap narcotics. Robber-baron capitalism. Legalized child pornography."

"Yes, maybe. But I'm not putting things like that in the play. Would you please let me finish?"

Guillermo tucked his chin back in. "I'm sorry. Pray continue."

"Okay. So." Ludi took a breath. "What I want to present is, a kind of impossibly wonderful vision of how great things might be, if they could be as good as everybody, all together, could possibly imagine. I mean I *know* it's hokey, it's *deliberately* hokey. But at the same time, if you don't give people something wonderful to think about—to *dream* about—then what does anyone have to wish for?"

"They can wish for a higher turnout in the next election."

"Guillermo, please. I'm not talking about elections. I'm talking about what's in people's hearts. And right now it seems to me that what's in people's hearts is nothing but misery. Pessimism. Horrible cynicism. I mean, just like you, sitting here making fun of me."

Guillermo gave her a Who me? look that she averted her head from. It was easier to be sincere without him tapping off a significant portion of her energy.

"And I'm not *even* saying necessarily that the pessimists aren't going to turn out to be right. Maybe the world *is* going down the toilet. Maybe the seas are going to rise and Holland is going to disappear and the hole in the ozone is going to eat Canada. Maybe the rich are going to live inside walled compounds and the poor will burn down the cities. Maybe all the kids will get so used to living in virtual theme parks they won't even notice the difference when all the animals are gone. Okay?

"But my question is, have we gotten so far beyond hope that we can't even *imagine* a happy ending? We can't even *think* of what it would be like if our wishes came true? Do we still *have* any wishes? That's what I want to pose here, that question. And what I want to answer is, No. We can still imagine. At least that. We can still wish upon a star. We can still throw pennies in a well. And *this* is what we wish for—the wonderful dreamy things you see in this play. *This* is how, if there ever was going to be one single magical night out of our whole lives, when we could really change the world just by wanting to, *this* is the way it would be."

Ludi ran out of words at last and she looked around at Guillermo.

He was staring at her. There was, for once, no way to tell what he was thinking.

After a space of time that could not have been measured— short and straight for him, long and twisty for her—Guillermo stood up from the table. He took two steps until he stood directly in front of Ludi. Then he put his hands on her shoulders, pulled her forcefully inward, and kissed her softly on the forehead.

"You," he said, hot dark eyes staring down on her, "are a beautiful human being. You are also touchingly insane."

He held the look for a few moments longer, but seemed to have nothing more to say. Without changing expression, he turned and sat back down at the table and picked up the *Glassport Herald*. Ludi's stack of papers lay next to the bowl of Grape-Nuts, both of which apparently had been dropped from his menu.

At least, Ludi thought,
when somebody feeds it,
a cat has the courtesy to purr.

HORRORS OF CONSENSUAL DEMOCRACY

 The Cold Bay Street Players decided to give it another shot. No ravens this time. Indigo Jones could not attend because he was presenting his regular Friday community radio show called "Stream of Senselessness." Today's playlist was about par.

> Frank Zappa, "Pentagon Afternoon"
> Kramer, "Ovulation Always Brings Me Down"
> Shelley Hirsch & David Weinstein, "Haiku Lingo"
> Brian Eno, "Ikebukuro"

"Well, I'll start," said Ludi.

The other Players looked at her. All except Guillermo, who was speed-grokking an old copy of the *Utne Reader*.

Ludi ran down for them her ideas for the next performance. She spoke with a bit less conviction than she had felt in the kitchen with Guillermo. Somehow knowing he was sitting there, having already blown her off, took some of the oomph out of her. Still, she soldiered on. She was determined to be what Molly would have called a good trouper.

"Wow," said Deep Herb, when she was done. He sat in lotus position in the middle of the loft, swaying in some invisible current of prana. "It sounds so—"

"So *fun*," said Pippa Rede, more perky than average today. "I say let's do it."

Eben Creek lit his pipe thoughtfully and then neglected to smoke it; instead he waved it about like a pointer. "But what *kind* of wonderful things?" he asked. "It's all very well and good to say, Then there's a happy ending. But can you actually *think* of one?"

Ludi raised her arms high and let them fall: between a shrug and a wing-flap. "I was kind of thinking," she said, "that that's what we would talk about today."

Guillermo made a noise that might (arguably) have been a response to something in the *Utne Reader*.

Rainie Moss said, "I could kind of see it. I mean, I could see all the lumberjacks and the bankers and the fishermen getting up there at the end and joining the regular people in a big dance. You know, a celebration of harmony and stuff."

"Oh, right," said Sara Clump. Then she turned back to the task of rewiring the hazardous Equity Lamp.

"What do you mean, regular people?" asked Eben.

"Some fishermen are regular people," said Deep Herb. "Only like, not all of them, I guess."

"Aren't we getting off the subject?" said Ludi.

"I don't think so," said Rainie. "I mean, there's one kind of regular person who's into, like, Right Action, and then there's another who's inwardly cool but just hasn't gotten turned on to alternative consciousness yet. Like who still listens to A.O.R. and shops at the I.G.A. and all."

"But the happy ending," said Pippa, "would it apply to everybody? Because it just seems like . . . could you really make *everybody* happy? All at once?"

Guillermo laughed. He tossed the *Utne Reader* onto a peach crate.

"See, that's the problem I was getting at," said Eben. "Because I think we've devolved to a sort of tribal thing, where basically it's a matter of different paths, different sacred landscapes. We're sharing the Earth with tribes that pray to totally different Great Spirits."

Rainie said, "But then there's another kind of person that's not regular at all. I'm not trying to get into an Us-versus-Them head. But you've got to face it. You're never going to have a banker dancing with a basket weaver. Not in Dublin. Well, I guess maybe in *Dublin*. But not in regular places."

"Could you please define what *regular* means?" asked Eben, relighting his pipe and forgetting it again.

"I thought you said you *could* see everybody dancing together," said Deep Herb.

"I did?"

Deep Herb frowned. "I thought somebody did."

"Well, *I* can't," said Sara. "Plus, I don't *want* to dance with any banker. Unless she's *unbelievably* great-looking. Basket weavers are another story."

"Could we go back a little?" said Ludi.

"Listen to yourselves," said Guillermo.

Everybody stopped and listened. They didn't hear anything. On the radio, Indigo Jones was reading aloud the Virginia Declaration of Religious Freedom, "a document," he parenthesized, "penned by none other than Thomas Jefferson. The *man* T.J. himself."

"You people," said Guillermo, rising to his feet, dark eyes pinning the Players in place, "are completely blind. If you think you're going to accomplish anything by prancing out on the village green and pantomiming some feel-good bedtime story, then you're either naive or you're deluded or—or I wouldn't like to say what else. And I think it's time we got this out in the open. There are some of us who aren't happy with the direction this Street Theater has been evolving—"

"Who?" said Sara, pointing a 3-stranded cable at him. "Other than yourself."

Guillermo said, "That's what we have to find out, isn't it?"

Eben Creek stuck his pipe between his teeth and sucked hard on it. Of course, it had gone out, but Eben didn't notice that.

"This is what *I* say," said Guillermo. "I say it's time we quit kidding ourselves. It's time we admitted that *nothing* we've done so far has had the slightest measurable effect on *anything*. It's time we decided that either we're going to get serious about setting specific goals and accomplishing them, or else we're not. We're just going to keep dancing and smoking dope and pretending that we're raising people's consciousness. And if that's the case, then I for one am prepared to strike out on my own. Because the time has come—the time has come and *gone*—to take some direct action. And I mean direct. And I mean *action*."

Deep Herb, still in his lotus position, appeared to have frozen in place. Rainie Moss was twisting the hem of her batik jersey, nervously. Sara tightened the last screw and switched the Equity Lamp back on. It was fitted out with a new high-efficiency compact fluorescent bulb, which gave off a warm glow, like a table full of candles. Guillermo looked terrific in it.

"What action?" said Eben Creek. "Tell us specifically what you mean."

"Gladly," said Guillermo. "What I propose is, we break into the old Goddin base, and we stage an action right there on one of the runways. And we tell the TV stations in advance, so they can get some helicopters out there. We've got to start thinking big. We've got to think major media."

The Players looked at one another and back at Guillermo. The compact fluorescent bulb shone brighter as it warmed up: a feature of the technology. Pippa moved back a little, taking her usual place in the shadows.

"But what's it about?" Sara asked. "What are you trying to prove?"

"Just this: that the Gulf Atlantic Corporation has plans on the drawing board to completely reconfigure the biosystem of the Great North Woods. And that these plans are masquerading as a simple reforestation program. *Planting trees*—who could possibly have any objection to that?"

"Well?" said Ludi. "Who?"

Guillermo ignored her. "But these trees they're planting—they're not any native species. They're not any *natural* species. They're robot trees. Artificial life."

"Wow," said Deep Herb.

"Yeah, wow," said Ludi, sarcastically.

"How do you know this?" demanded Sara. "You said last time that you've got some kind of proof. Something on a computer disk. So where is it?"

Guillermo peered into the dim recesses of the loft until he located Pippa. He pointed at her, menacingly. "My cloak," he said. "The disk was in my cloak. And *you* took my cloak, with that damned bird wrapped up in it. What did you do with it?"

Pippa edged forward like the accused approaching the witness box. "Syzygy," he murmured.

"Syzygy Prague?" said Rainie. "You mean, the Kitchen Witch?"

"How is Syzygy?" asked Sara, brightening.

"She's got your cloak," Pippa said. "She took it because . . . I guess there was something in it."

"Of course there was something in it," Guillermo said. "There was a computer disk in it. A valuable and sensitive computer disk."

"No—I mean," Pippa stammered, "there was an . . . acorn."

"A *what*?"

Pippa nodded. Obviously, he had heard her. "It was really important, I guess."

Guillermo raised his arms to the heavens. He spoke beseechingly to someone there, mano-a-mano like: "Why? Why is it always *this way* with these people? Why?"

          «Because»
said Molly,
          «that was no ordinary acorn.»

"Well, that does it," said Guillermo. "I'm out of here. I'm out of this absurd Street Theater. Time is too short to keep pissing it away like this. Anyone who wants to get serious about saving the forest before it's too late, let's get together this weekend and we'll lay down some plans. Some *serious* plans."

Then he climbed down the ladder. Leaving Deep Herb, rock-

ing in the unseen (but strongly felt) winds of prana to call after
him:

"What's such a big deal about a computer disk, anyway?"

But the only answer was the sound of Ludi's Volkswagen rev-
ving up. The gearbox ratcheted in a way that would have set
your teeth on edge. Fortunately Molly, in her present configuration, was not encumbered by teeth.

«I can't believe it»
she thought.
«The low-life has taken her car.»

But that was, perhaps, the least of Ludi's problems.

EAT CUTE

"Want a ride?" called Deep Herb, rolling down the
driver's-side window of the latest in a series of virtually indistinguishable small European cars with
rusted-out undercarriages. A lesser, material-plane type of guy
would have figured out by now why his cars kept falling apart on
him. Not to mention why they only cost $200 in the first place.

"Where're you going?" Ludi called back. She stood disconsolately in the field sloping down to the ocean behind Eben's rented
barn. The new growth of low-bush blueberries was purplish, their
juvenile leaves tiny and delicate-looking. You kind of hated to
step on them. A few hops away, a rabbit was hunched down
among the foliage, waiting Ludi out.

Being helpless, Ludi thought, makes you feel at one with the
natural world. You're out here without shelter, protected only by
your wits. If the wind feels sharp or the sky looks like rain, it
means something to you.

Deep Herb said, "Yes or no?"

"Where are you *going*?" Ludi asked again, more insistently.
You try hard to be polite; but *sometimes*—

"To work, man."

I'm not a man, Ludi felt like telling him. But then, in a way,
Deep Herb wasn't either. It was like he had mellowed himself
out into a state of genderlessness.

"At the pizza place?" she said.

"Right, man."

Without hesitation—though Dan Dan's Pizza Scene was down in Glassport, twenty miles from her apartment in Dublin—she said, "Okay. Thanks."

And thus she found herself not only left without a car but stranded in the excruciatingly picturesque village of Glassport—"Where the Mountains Meet the Bank," as Molly once quipped—surrounded by a hellish landscape of white clapboard B&B's, condominiums, balsam-scented souvenir shops, a regional credit-card center, a Smith & Hawken wannabe gardening boutique, a couple of underfunded public schools, and the editorial offices of the *Glassport Herald* ("Serving Right-Thinking Mainers Since Last November": ibid). And then, of course, there was Dan Dan's ("The Last Real Place in Town"); only Ludi seldom went in there because they always seemed to be playing the same tape of klezmer music; or maybe it was that all klezmer tapes sounded the same. In the end, of course, it came down to pounding the pavement, or making repeated calls to her own answering machine in hopes that Guillermo would pick up, or taking a table at the pizza place and waiting for a knight in shining armor to come to her rescue. In short: Dan Dan's or die.

Deep Herb greeted her just inside the door. He had pulled his hair back into a ponytail. "Kosher or nonkosher?" he professionally inquired.

"It's me, silly," said Ludi.

Deep Herb nodded. You must never let anything a customer says upset you. "Right this way," he said, conducting her to a table directly in front of a Magnaplanar speaker so large that it looked like a shoji screen. He handed her the nonkosher menu and said, "I'll take your order whenever you're ready. Meanwhile, enjoy the Brave Combo."

"Thanks for nothing," said Ludi. But Deep Herb seemed not to hear. Perhaps the music was too loud.

Well, it was a Real Place, at least. It had incomprehensible paintings by local artists, hanging plants that could have used a good photon supplement, and a panoramic vista of the police station. Ludi held out till the end of a song that seemed to have been spawned by a mating of rockabilly and Polish wedding favorites, then she picked up her menu and decamped for the bar. The service was less ethereal there. More important, you had an unrestricted view of Dan Dan's eagle feather tattoo. Thus you had a view of a goodly part of Dan Dan, considering where the tattoo was located. And Dan Dan, although weird and a little grungy, was très cute.

"Hey," he greeted Ludi, as she slid onto a barstool. He stood behind the stainless steel counter, karate-chopping dough into servility. Probably he didn't remember Ludi's name. Who cared? She would not have remembered his if it wasn't painted on the window. It was his shoulders she was interested in.

"Dan Dan," she said, "could I ask you a question? I mean, sort of personal?"

He smiled a weird smile, crinkling his little moustache up. "Do it."

"Are you Jewish?" she said.

"No. Why?"

Ludi shrugged. "Could I have a glass of pinot grigio, please?"

When he fetched the wine over, he gave her a little wiggle of the eyebrows and said, "You going to be eating?"

"Who knows?" said Ludi, seizing the goblet.

Dan Dan backed off a respectful step. "Hey, cool," he said. He flexed his upper arms out of nervous habit.

It's amazing how *exposed* men's bodies are, Ludi considered. Look: the muscles are all right there, just below the skin. They bulge out against it. You can practically count the sinews. And that hair under their arms. Doesn't that seem sort of primitive? It's so *odd*, the way this whole animal thing works.

«I never thought of it quite that way»
reflected Molly.

«And you know, now I'm sorry I never really got to know
Ludi any better. She's much more—»

"Yeah, really," muttered Dan Dan.

"What?" said Ludi.

He seemed puzzled to see her there, sitting alone. "Oh, I just— I was just thinking, I guess. Another shot of the pinot?"

Ludi noted with surprise that her glass of wine had emptied itself. "Why not?" she said, pushing it toward Dan Dan. "Men are strange, don't you think?"

"Hey," said Dan Dan. "Life is strange. Pizza is strange. I get cops in here all the time, drinking coffee. I mean it's like, don't they know who I *am* or what?"

"Who are you?" said Ludi—realizing, even as she said it, that the answer would probably be disappointing. Things were that way.

"Beats me," Dan Dan admitted. "I guess I'm the owner of a fucking pizza joint."

Ludi smiled kindly at him. "Well, it's a *good* pizza joint."

«And she likes your tattoo»
added Molly. Always trying to be helpful.

Dan Dan twitched his arms again. "Thanks," he said,
abashedly.

At some point along here, between the first glass of wine and
the third, the barstool next to the one on Ludi's right came to
be occupied. No big deal; except that when Ludi finally got
around to glancing over that way, she thought she recognized the
guy—straight-looking, a year or two older than herself. She
couldn't guess where she might have met him; but that's how it
is in small-town life. You keep seeing these strangers over and
over again, until after a while you're ready to be godmother to
their children, whose names you probably know from hearing
them yelled in the grocery store.

«No, he does look familiar»
Molly agreed. But she couldn't place him either.

"Could I have a small Mex pizza?" the young man said to
Dan Dan. He spoke in a loud, careful way, the way you might
to someone who was just getting the hang of English.

"Our pizzas only come in medium and large," said Dan Dan.
The newcomer seemed to annoy him.

"How can that be?" the young man said. "How can you have
medium without small? Medium means *in the middle*."

"Ah," said Dan Dan. "I'll get that taken care of." He gave
Ludi a look and headed over to beat some dough up.

"Nobody knows what words mean anymore," said the guy on
the barstool.

It sounded like something your father would have said. After
two or three full seconds, Ludi understood that the guy was
speaking to *her*. She turned to look at him—to *inspect* him, the
way Guillermo did: coolly and without emotional complications.
Sort of a Mr. Spock way of looking.

And she saw right away that this guy was what Tex called a
Young Fogy. He looked like a grad student on job-interview day,
Ralph Laurened to within an inch of his credit limit. His medium
brown hair (two tones darker than Ludi's) was cut and combed in
a way that would have been breathtakingly cool if, say, Leonardo
DiCaprio wore it. This guy, it made look like a poseur. Plus he
wore glasses with no rims, which made his forehead look too
large or his eyes too small or his nose too sharp—something in

that general area. His lips were okay. Actually they were good. And the chin was much more human-looking than Guillermo's.

God, thought Ludi, is *that* what I'm doing? Comparing everyone to that asshole? Dan Dan's shoulders, this guy's chin, Deep Herb's testosterone level?

Feeling a little sick, she looked through the rimless glasses into her neighbor's bright eyes and she said:

"What do you mean, *anymore?*"

He didn't miss a beat. "I mean we're living in a postliterate age. We're living in an age of zero cognition. People toss words around as though they were Nerf balls. You know, you can't break anything because there's nothing inside them anyway. Everything is *context-sensitive*. It's just an *expression* of the way you're *feeling* right now. It's an *I* statement. It's what it's like *for me*. The Gospel According to Oprah. One day at a time. That's what I mean by *anymore*."

Ludi thought, Oh dear, one of those. And she thought, His teeth are nice, too.

The guy was still staring at her with this same bizarre intensity. She stared back with at least two glasses of pinot grigio.

"I wouldn't be so sure," she said.

"About what?" he said.

"About what you're saying. This whole dumbing-down-of-America rap. I mean, there *is* such a thing as nonverbal literacy. There are more ways of communicating besides just with words. Look at the ways culture is disseminated nowadays."

"Sure," said the Y.F. "We're a happy global village full of couch roaches."

"Maybe. Partly. But also Net Heads. And garage rockers. And hand-held video producers. I mean, what makes *verbal* literacy so privileged?"

"Privileged?" said the Y.F. "You sound like an assistant professor of Victim Studies."

"No way. I'm fully tenured."

He smirked appreciatively. "To answer your question, though. What makes verbal literacy so *privileged* is that it's what separates us from the rest of the natural world."

"Oh, right. And you can see how great the results of *that* have been. Look—if you think about it, words aren't really a medium of truth. Truth is something you know in your heart. Words operate somewhere else—they only affect your brain. They're a medium of like, data. So they've got no intrinsic valence, either good or bad. You can use them to make the Gettysburg Address or you can use them for propaganda and hate-mongering."

"Which is precisely where knowledge and reason come in."

"Right. And that's exactly the problem. Because if it weren't for reason, you'd never be able to convince people that the things they feel in their hearts—things they know by common sense—are really untrue. You'd never be able to tell them that there's no magic in the world. Or life has no meaning. Or machines are no different from us. Or poor people have brought their suffering on themselves. Or the end of nature is a nonissue. But with words and reason and *knowledge,* whatever that means, you can do all those things. And more."

She sat on her stool feeling light-headed, almost breathless. The Young Fogy watched her in bemusement. Finally he gave her a rueful sort of smile.

"Hey, sorry," he said. "I didn't mean to punch your buttons. I was just blowing off steam, really."

Ludi exhaled. "Me too, I guess. I've had kind of a weird day."

"Tell me about it."

He ruffled his hair away from his eyes. He looked more warm-blooded now.

"Hard day at the office?" Ludi asked him.

"You don't know the half of it." He shook his head, and everything seemed to come loose: the hair, the lips, the weird intensity. "I truly believe my boss might be the Antichrist."

"Aren't all bosses the Antichrist?"

"I don't know. I've only had one of them. And I mean, I like the guy. But he's capable of the most unimaginable acts of corporate lunacy."

Ludi looked down at her current glass of wine and reflected upon this. Most of what she knew about corporate lunacy was from reading *Dilbert.* She wanted to sympathize. But you take one look at the guy, and you have to think it's probably his own damned fault. Really: do they *draft* people into these jobs, or what?

"Why don't you quit?" she asked him.

"Why quit?" he said. "They offered me 76 thousand dollars a year right out of graduate school. I've got my own tissue culture lab. I spend most of the day outside, doing field studies. So my boss is Hitler. Big deal, you know?"

Ludi inspected him all over again. She found nothing overtly abnormal about him. Still, it was probably best to keep a safe distance, in case he turned out to be an alien from the Planet of Decent Health Care.

"You look familiar," he told her.

"Yeah?" said Ludi, cautiously. Maybe he was a stalker. Maybe he worked for the credit-card company. "I guess we might have friends in common. Who do you know?"

He frowned at her. Like it was *her* that was weird.

"One medium Mex," said Dan Dan—heavy emphasis on the qualifier—sliding a hot pizza not quite directly in front of the alien: a little off in Ludi's direction, in case she might be angling for free food or something. He winked offhandedly at her.

"Thanks," said the guy. And sure enough, he asked Ludi, "Would you like to help me with this? It's a bit larger than I was expecting."

"Yeah," she said, "that's why they don't call them *small*."

But he was off that, now. He didn't seem to have any idea what she was talking about. Dan Dan dropped off an extra plate and the guy glooped a molten slice onto it.

"I've never tried this kind," said Ludi, who suddenly felt very hungry.

"Me neither," said the guy. "Actually I've never been here before."

"Never been to Dan Dan's?"

He didn't answer; just forked a piece of the steaming Mex into his mouth. So he couldn't work at the credit-card place, Ludi figured. That was just around the corner, and the lunch crowd from there was what kept Dan Dan open through the long stretch between tourist seasons.

The guy said, "Well, it's not exactly New York style, is it?"

"This ain't exactly New York," said Dan Dan, who heard everything.

"Well, I give up," Ludi told the guy on the next-to-next barstool. The spicy pizza, on top of the wine, on top of Guillermo, made her feel reckless and slightly misandrous. "My name's Ludi. I work in a bookstore. Occasionally."

"You work in a *book*store?"

She shrugged; she saw the irony. "Only in the summer. So: who are you?"

He smiled. Not a space-alien smile, but scary in a different way. The strong white teeth, all lined up, gave Ludi a little quiver of foreboding. She felt some kind of door creaking open . . .

"I know this is tacky," he said, pulling something small and greenish beige out of his jacket. "But I had a couple million of these printed up, and I can't figure out who I'm supposed to give them to."

He was—Ludi could hardly believe her eyes—he was *handing her a business card.* She was momentarily immobilized. She had seen such things in movies, but it had always seemed too . . . *obvious,* too blatant, or something. The card said

EUGENE DEERE, Ph. D.
Senior Researcher, Biogenetics Division
Goddin Forest Research Station

GULF ATLANTIC   ■Growing the Future■

«AH!»

cried Molly, practically tumbling out of the æther. She should have guessed. And yet somehow, seeing him now through Ludi's eyes, Gene Deere was transformed. The same, but weirdly reprocessed.

"So," said Ludi, fingering the nice heavy-stock card, "you work out at the old Goddin base?"

He nodded. He seemed reasonably proud to confess to this.

"Maybe that's where I've seen you before," said Ludi. Then she reminded herself that she was supposed to remain cautious, protect her cover—the more so, now that she knew for sure this guy *was* an alien monster.

"You've seen me—" said Gene Deere. His bright eyes squinted up; he stared at Ludi as though trying to picture her in a different light, a different costume.

She turned her face quickly away. But not quickly enough.

"Doronicum magnificum," he declared, triumphantly.

Really: how could she not look up at him, after that? She looked and she saw all those teeth lined up and she felt a foreboding even deeper than before.

"Leopard bane," he said. "You were dressed like a yellow daisy."

She nodded, as though some dark imponderable power were compelling her to do so.

"You were one of those demonstrators," Gene went on. It was like he was doing this for his own benefit, not hers: taking it one tiny step at a time.

"Right," she said. "And you were that pompous twerp in the Range Rover."

"Ha!" (Not a mirthful sound.) "You're not quite so—Well, I might as well say it. Quite so airheaded as I imagined you would be."

Ludi detected something strange in this sentence; perhaps not anything that the guy really intended to say. She thought she heard a certain emphasis on the word *you*: "the way *I* imagined *you* might be." As though Gene had been thinking about *Ludi*, as an individual person, not just as another daisy in the meadow.

"I'm sorry," he said. "I didn't really think—"

"Apparently not," she said, trying to marshal her resources. Though she suspected it might be too late for that.

"What I really thought," said Gene (and he looked unaffected, puppy-doggish), "what I *really* thought, if you want to know, was, Wow. What beautiful legs."

«That's true!»

Molly remembered. She was amazed that a man would admit to something like this.

"Oh, right," said Ludi. "What a totally brilliant pickup line. I bet you get laid a whole lot using that one."

Gene appeared at least mildly shocked. He worked his jaw, but no reply materialized.

"And as long as we're being so refreshingly candid," said Ludi, "I might as well tell you that you are *exactly* the kind of left-brain right-wing psychosexually fucked-up corporate lackey that I figured you probably were, just from the way you looked behind the wheel of that pretentious car of yours. Just from the way you pushed the *button* and rolled your *window* down. And not even all the *way* down. Like you're too scared to even commit yourself to breathing the same *air* as people who give a shit about the planet. So I guess it's been a pleasure meeting you. Because it lets me know that I'm not such a bad judge of character after all."

She stood up, having more or less given herself no alternative, and took a step toward the door.

She hesitated. Something seemed to be left hanging, some parting shot to be fired.

Gene Deere rotated on his barstool to stare after her—partly in amazement, partly in some sick male helpless emotion encoded in the DNA: you figure it out. No doubt if he was a cave dude, he would have grabbed her and dragged her outside and raped her.

Well, he wasn't a cave dude, though. He was a *scientist*. A

Senior Researcher, Biogenetics. And he worked directly under the Antichrist.

"So research this," Ludi told him. And she grabbed the remaining ⅔ of the medium Mex pizza, and she raked it onto his stomach.

Gene jumped off the barstool as though that was going to do any good. What it did was make the hot pizza ooze down the front of his shirt and pants: guacamole and sour cream everywhere. He roared from the heat of the melted cheese and tore at his clothing. A couple of shirt buttons popped off. A funny-looking pendant dangled from his chest, swinging at the end of a neon green shoelace.

"You look stupid," said Ludi.

«Wow»
thought Molly.

"Yeah, wow," said Dan Dan. Who heard everything.

And as Ludi carried her scorched-earth campaign to the front of the Pizza Scene, Deep Herb held open the door for her.

"I hope you enjoyed your meal," he told her. "I can give you a ride home, if you need one. Only I don't get off till closing time."

"Forget it, Herb," she said, stepping out into the street. "I've had enough of guys for one day."

A Glassport cop and a deputy sheriff named Doug were hanging there in front of the police station, taking a cigarette break. They paused in midpuff to look at her.

"Cave guys," said Ludi, turning partway around so as to include the cops in this. "And gender-free guys. And cute guys with tattoos. And asshole guys stealing my car. And every other kind of guy. And

especially good-looking
science dweeb guys
fucking the
Earth."

&
all this time Tex was inside an acorn.

Which is not the same as *being* an acorn.

More like having your Being in an acorn.

Or having your Being partly in this acorn, and partly not. And the *partly not* is partly in other acorns, and partly in a place that is No Place at all.

Which is how it is to be a dryad.

And Tex thought it was way, *way* beyond cool.

He sang to himself: I'm in with the dryads. I go where the dryads go.

When you're in with the dryads, you *know* what the dryads know.

Ba da dum *pah*—

Human beings from this perspective were like ants. Not size-wise. But in the frantic bustling herdlike seemingly mindless and all too short character of their lives. Racing here and racing there, consumed things, hauling burdens around, making messes, tidying up, nursing their young, ignoring their old, dispatching enemies or getting killed by them, forming alliances and betraying them, procreating and suffering famine and pestilence and invading new territory and dropping dead and melting into the earth. And all in sprawling anonymous masses. To no apparent purpose. Unless the purpose, maybe, was to see how it all comes out.

Only, of course, it never all came out. It just kept going the way it was going. No end. No resolution. Only successive flowerings, contractions, regrowths, new flowerings, ad eternam.

Meanwhile, in the world outside, the scene had changed again.

DA TURTLE'S HOSTEL

Deep in the woods of the western, piedmontese end of Dublin County lies a ghost town called Applemont. An old farming village, it perished when the last of the farms went fallow. Its church and its general store were overrun by deer mice while moose and black bears and coyotes returned to the surrounding countryside. A young woodland sprouted in derelict cornfields, gardens, pastures, and unpaved streets. This is the way the world goes on.

In a legal and political sense, Applemont still exists. Its boundaries are delineated by dotted black lines in the *Maine Atlas and Gazetteer,* denoting an unincorporated township. Such needs as its remaining few residents might have (hunting permits, birth certificates, food stamps) are attended to by the county government in Glassport.

There being no town in a strictly functional sense, however, there are no property taxes. There is no mayor. There is no Planning Board, Road Commissioner, or Building Code Enforcement Officer. The Sheriff's Department cruises by on routine patrols, or when summoned to the scene of a domestic spat, but seldom ventures any distance off the two numbered highways. These features exercise a powerful appeal to certain categories of latter-day American, including:

Back-to-the-landers who migrated here in the 70's
Cantankerous backwoods types who want to be left alone
Passamaquoddy Indians, whose ancestors are buried here
Fundamentalist Xian home-schoolers
2nd Amendment cultists
Tax resisters
Feral teenagers
A retired cocaine distributor

And Jesse, thought Tex: focusing. Syzygy. The wolves. The Hostel.

Yes.

An Isuzu Trooper with Syzygy Prague at the wheel and Ari

the elf in the passenger seat and Tex the acorn in the way-back turned off the paved highway onto the first of a succession of dilapidated fire roads, logging roads, and finally a glorified bear path. This was Jesse's driveway and Jesse had determined long ago to leave it this way, only marginally and seasonally navigable. Good for business, he had ruled. When you consider the types of people we are dealing with.

Syzygy hadn't objected. It was not the sort of thing she cared about. And Ari didn't care, and the other kids that came and went (the balance remaining slightly toward the Came column) got a kick out of it. It put them one step—giant and muddy—further removed from whatever they were running from.

After bouncing and plunging and sliding up the bear path for half a mile or so, the Isuzu came to a big rustic sign suspended from an overhanging oak limb.

DA TURTLE'S HOSTEL
Home of
PROPHETS OF DELIRIUM
and
HOWLING-AT-THE-LOON NEST, C.A.W.
"If you don't like it, you can't have any!"

Syzygy slammed the Trooper to a halt.

"I can't wait to tell Jesse," said Ari, popping his door open. He bounded off before Syzygy could get a reply organized. She sighed instead. It was the most ordinary sound Tex had ever heard her make.

From the parking area, a network of well-marked and maintained trails led into the forest. The one Syzygy chose ran between a male-and-female pair of extraordinarily cold-hardy American hollies—a species almost never encountered north of Boston—and then sloped up a hillside between mature red oaks. The path had been neatly stepped-off in a series of landings secured by sawn logs, in the Civilian Conservation Corps manner. This was Syzygy's private path. Jesse lived at the downhill end of the compound, near the open marshes and the pond, where the animals were more comfortable. The kids lived about halfway between, in a refurbished Adirondack-style hunting lodge that had been falling down from neglect when Jesse bought the place.

Syzygy's house she had built herself, after taking a 3-week intensive course at the Shelter Institute. Someday architectural historians will recognize, even celebrate, the distinctive school of owner-built homes the Institute has spawned all over the North

Woods. People will seek them out, like Usonian houses on the Prairie. In the meantime, you had to respect them chiefly in terms of what they were not. They were not mobile homes. They were not painted white. They were not likely to lure undesirable elements like retirees from Connecticut.

Syzygy kicked open the heavy, Z-braced plank door and left Guillermo's cloak on a rocking chair just inside the living room. She stepped past the huge Russian fireplace at the center of the house to check for e-mail in the kitchen. That was Syzygy's headquarters: she made her living by writing a cooking column called *The Kitchen Witch* which ran in a number of alternative tabloids. The column was distinguished by its jumble of old-fashioned country cuisine, exotic dishes culled from Syzygy's Irish-Romany heritage, and magical potions you could concoct with items you probably already had lying around the house. Lately she had opened a site on the World Wide Web. There too she quickly acquired a following. Her in-box was seldom empty. It was a quirky, peaceable, satisfying life.

Then, of course, there were the kids. And the weird thing with Jesse. It got stranger and stranger. But Tex had never wanted to get into any of that.

A loud knock came on the door and Syzygy yelled, *"An de bheoaibd nó de mhairbh thu?"* without looking around. She was busy, flipping through the day's messages, checking the charge on the batteries connected to the photovoltaic panels, spooning out vittles for her skulk of coon cats. The big door groaned open and Guillermo Gobán stepped through.

"I understand you've got something of mine," he said.

"What?"

Syzygy's head was inside the giant, high-efficiency refrigerator. Guillermo stepped cautiously into the living room.

"Who's that?" Syzygy's muffled voice came out.

Guillermo said nothing. He was staring around the room, taking in the assortment of furnishings. Most of them had been either reclaimed from the dump or knocked together out of scrap wood. There were hand-loomed rugs, Penobscot brown-ash baskets, and books stacked up in high, Pisa-style towers. The pelt of a huge buck, gathered and tied into a pouch, hung from an exposed beam at ceiling height. Syzygy had found the animal, wounded by a hunter, bleeding to death in the woods. She had strangled it with her bare hands and then, with an ordinary kitchen knife, she had gutted it, buried its meat and entrails, and wrapped up the bones in its bloody skin. That's what the old sorcerers of the steppes had done, to ensure that the spirit of the animal would be reborn. The practice had also found its way into such unlikely places as the Lakota legend of the Buffalo Dance. So Syzygy thought it only prudent to haul the bones and skin back home, as a token of hospitality toward any other wandering spirits who might happen by. And that's what the thing was, hanging in her living room. It kind of made you stop and think.

While Guillermo was thinking, and Syzygy was excavating something from the geologic depths of her refrigerator, a small animal—a red squirrel—squeezed through the gap between the jamb and the Z-braced door. The squirrel, behaving as though it had been sent here on a definite mission (which is how red squirrels always act), rose on its hind legs and darted its eyes about the room. Only Guillermo: no problem.

Speedily, purposefully, it leapt onto the rocking chair and rooted with its front paws among the folds of the Wizard cloak. It dug for a second or two, then paused and lifted its head to check for danger, then dug some more. Within half a minute, it unearthed the floppy disk. It grabbed this with its mouth and dropped it onto the floor.

At the small clatter, Guillermo looked around.

"So," Syzygy's voice came from the kitchen. "You were saying what? Were you looking for me, or Jesse? Have we met, by the way?"

"Um, I don't, no," said Guillermo, distracted.

The squirrel plunged once again, hurriedly, to its task. It dug and rooted and finally found the little brown acorn with Tex inside it. This it seized between its paws and stuffed into one bulging cheek. Then, its quarry secured, it jumped down from the chair, made an irreverent chitter and scooted out the door.

Syzygy's mother blamed this kind of thing on the Fair Folk. Sometimes she was correct. Either way, the outcome was much the same.

Away, away the red squirrel ran. Over the storm drain and through the woods. To its great-great-grandfather's house. Currently unoccupied. Where it paused to dart its eyes about, red-squirrel style. And expostulate: *Cheet cheet.*

Cowering in his acorn, held snugly in the warm moist cheek-pouch, Tex felt breathless. That was a purely metaphorical sensation, like the pain of a phantom limb.

Down, down the red squirrel scurried. Into an old garter snake's cold-weather hole. Under a greenstone boulder, its underside damp and smelling of lime. Finally out into an open chamber, its roof supported by an arch of yew roots whose curve traced out the sacred Palladian ratio of 2 units of rise per 9 units of linear extension. Here, the red squirrel opened its mouth and disgorged the acorn onto a bed of dry pine needles.

Tex was prepared to be eaten. He regarded the prospect with an odd abeyance of emotion, as though it couldn't be that much worse than anything else that had happened lately. But the squirrel turned and scampered away.

And Tex found himself alone
in the darkness
of the Underworld.

FAMILIARS

Close on the squirrel's heels (if a squirrel has heels) Syzygy appeared from the kitchen holding a Tupperware container labeled ORGANIC MISO.

Yeah, right, thought Guillermo. He said, "I came for my cloak. You had no right to take it."

"Stop," said Syzygy. She held the plastic vessel before her, as though it contained a powerful ward (as it might well have, if only Guillermo knew). "I don't *do* conflict with males. You'll have to wait till Jesse gets here."

"Men," said Guillermo.

Syzygy lifted the ward higher. "What?"

"Please say *men*," he told her, "not *males*. Unless you'd like to be called a female instead of a woman."

"I don't care what you call me," she said honestly. "I told you, I don't do conflict. Jesse takes care of that. He'll be here in a minute."

Less than a minute. Ari had found Jesse down among the breeding pens and lured him up the hill with the promise of a magic cloak with an enchanted acorn and a floppy disk inside it. Implausibly as it must have seemed to Guillermo (though this happened with Syzygy all the time), the heavy door swung open precisely on cue, and the wild boy blew in. Followed by his short and unintimidating daddy. Followed by a large full-blooded timber wolf.

"Hey," said Jesse, glancing noncommittally at Guillermo. He wore large dirty Bean boots and an auto mechanic's coverall, olive drab. He was dark, like Ari, but more heavily built.

"*Mom,*" said Ari, "where'd you put it?"

"Rrrrrr," said the timber wolf, whose name was Gus.

Guillermo backed the hell up.

"You Frank?" Jesse asked him.

"Not anymore. I'm called Guillermo Gobán now."

"What I thought." Jesse turned to Syzygy. "This is Frank," he explained. "The one Tex doesn't like."

Syzygy nodded. She lowered the container of miso.

"Where's Tex at, anyway?" Jesse asked, of nobody in particular.

Guillermo shrugged. Syzygy muttered in colloquial Irish.

"Hope not," said Jesse. He crossed the living room and sat down on a crudely built deacon's bench, which creaked under him. Gus the wolf came over to get his ears scratched.

Ari said, "Look"—pointing at the computer disk lying on the floor.

At last Guillermo noticed his cloak. He whisked it into his arms and plucked up the disk and made as though to slip away.

"Whoa," said Jesse.

"Rrrrr," said Gus.

Syzygy opened the lid of the Tupperware. The room filled with the ripe smell of *Aspergillus hatcho,* a strain of free-floating mold cultivated since the 14th century in the small Japanese city of Okazaki.

"Sweet Jesus," said Guillermo, "what is that?"

"Jesus had nothing to do with it," said Syzygy. And she turned and—*poof*—vanished into her kitchen.

"Excuse me," said Jesse, "if I don't use much etiquette. It's how you get, living out in the woods. Tell me what the hell you're doing here."

"Now take it easy," said Guillermo, dividing his gaze between Jesse and the wolf. "Look, this disk was stolen from me, that's all. It's got some important information on it. Evidence, you might say. And I just need to get it back."

Jesse said, "Who'd *you* steal it from?"

Guillermo flinched. "Nobody. I didn't steal it. I *got* it, from a friend. One of the guys in my men's group. Who brought it home from his office."

"Men's group?" said Jesse. "You mean like, go out in the woods and beat tom-toms and hop around the fire like a bunch of wild Indians?"

"Well. Kind of. We say Native Americans, though."

Jesse frowned. "I'm Passamaquoddy, and we say Indians."

"Oh," said Guillermo.

"Or we keep our mouths shut," said Jesse. "That's the best course, lots of times. So what's on the disk that's so important to you? What'd you do to get Tex riled up at you, anyway? He's not usually like that."

Guillermo glanced at the timber wolf, apparently weighing the likelihood of being swallowed up like Little Red's grandmother. "It's a pretty long story," he said.

Jesse smiled. As though long stories were his favorite kind.

Ari said, "Let's plug it in Mom's computer and take a look."

"That won't do any good," said Guillermo. "I've tried. They've got some kind of access lock on it. This friend of mine, the one who took it for me, was going to help me break into it."

"Access lock?" said Jesse. "You talking personal key or password protection or what?"

"I, um, don't really—I'm not all that computer-literate, actually."

"Neither am I," sighed Jesse. He pushed himself to his feet. Gus the wolf sprang up beside him. They made for the door with Ari scampering behind. Jesse said, "Time to bring in the Pod."

WILD IN THE WOODS

Pod was an acronym, actually. Prophets of Delirium: part of a chain of acronyms beginning with Legion of Doom and Masters of Destruction—LOD and MOD—and continuing, at last count, through the Republic of Desire, though that was pure sci-fi. "Delirium" referred not to the mental state but to a character in a comic book by Neil Gaiman. "D" had originally been for "Death" (another comic heroine), which later had been rejected because the alt.fan.death thing was getting a little overdone, wasn't it? Also, "Prophets" had been "Priests," which was cool inasmuch as it elevated Delirium to a sort of goddess standing, but then a girl showed up. Anyway: things evolve.

There was one way to join the Pod, and it was not easy, but on the other hand it was democratic. You had to follow a trail of clues dropped like Hansel's white rocks in various on-line hidey-holes, and eventually, having collected them all, you had to hit the nonvirtual road and make it up to Maine, thence to the ghost town of Applemont, and ultimately to this supremely scrambled-brain operation known as Da Turtle's Hostel. Where you had to be cleared by Jesse and Syzygy, whose heads operated according to some algorithm not understood by the Goddess Delirium Herself. More fundamentally you had to be the sort of person who would *want* to do all this. All of which kind of winnowed it down. This is pretty highly confidential information, by the way, being revealed on the assumption that you will not fuck severely up and go mouthing off to the likes of, say, the Concerned Madres of Amerikkka. Capiche?

So anyhow. On the day of Guillermo's visit, the Pods in actual residence at the Hostel numbered three, and they were:

Saintstephen Bax, a Fresh Air kid gone native
Thistle Herne, a Wasp in flight
Shadow Malqvist, a heavy-metal Viking

And they all bunked together in the fixed-up but still radically run-down hunting lodge. And they did pretty much whatever they felt like doing. Though they had to hustle occasionally to find something to eat. And they bathed by swimming in the pond when weather permitted, and by sweating in the sauna and rolling in the snow when it did not. And they all lived happily ever after.

So far.

Jesse and Ari and Gus came down the trail noisily toward the Pod lodge, followed by a considerably discomfited Guillermo. There they were greeted by Saintstephen, who sat on the porch in an attitude of contemplation. On closer inspection he turned out to be watching a spiderweb getting woven between his knee-cap and the armrest of a bentwood rocker. His greeting consisted of a rude-sounding noise directed at the timber wolf.

Gus raced ahead and jumped onto the porch and knocked the sturdily built black kid onto his back. So much for the spiderweb. Saintstephen slapped him lightly on the jowls, one side and then the other. Ari called:

"Eat him!"

And Jesse held up the computer disk.

"Ho," said Saintstephen, heaving Gus off his chest. "What up, O Father of Us All?"

Jesse Frisbeed the disk and Saintstephen snagged it. Gus tried to take it away from him, but the big kid fended him off.

Saintstephen, who had lived here since before the Pod had been officially incarnated, perused the disk for clues. "This, I take it," he said upon deliberation, "represents some great and vexing mystery that only I can solve."

"You and any pube with an Amiga," said Shadow Malqvist from the open door.

Shadow was a whole other story. He had blond hair down to his wazoo and Nordic iconography all over his otherwise bare chest. Odin's axe dangled from one ear. Shadow was an AFDC kid from a commune somewhere in Vermont whose father had seemed like a good idea at the time. And his mom had been equally hopeless, though more in evidence. Living here with Jesse and the wolves was not actually that big a lifestyle change for Shadow. The absence of caseworkers was cool, however. And the available hardware definitely was an upgrade.

"Well, why not?" said Saintstephen. He flipped the disk into the air and let Gus catch it this time. The wolf held it expertly between flesh-shredding teeth. Saintstephen motioned toward the door. He said, "If you will just walk this way, please," and fell into a bizarre Igor-lurch.

"Pretty fucking stale," said Shadow.

"Eat him," Saintstephen said to Gus.

Gus yipped happily. He loved all the attention.

It took the Podsters on Duty, or Pod² (a nested, 2nd-order acronym), seven minutes to blow through the lock on the floppy disk. Then the big Radius monitor in the common room filled up with the logo and current slogan of the Gulf Atlantic Corporation.

"Boing," said Shadow.

The others—Jesse, Ari, Guillermo and Saintstephen, Gus having been banished to the porch, and Thistle being elsewhere in the galaxy—leaned inward, though the screen was large enough not to have to strain your eyes at.

"What is it?" said Ari, hopping up and down.

Saintstephen shrugged and Shadow was too cool to do even that.

"What it's *supposed* to be," said Guillermo, "is some red-hot top-secret corporate bullshit."

"*Cool*," said Ari.

"Yeah, cool," said Saintstephen. "So let's run it."

PERFECTION

Picea marina (cultivar)

This is a desirable shape of a black spruce tree [said the narrative voice of Chas Sauvage].

This is a desirable shape for three reasons.

First, the trunk is straight. This is necessary for maximum production of usable, commercial-grade lumber.

Second, the limb configuration is wide and symmetrical. Were this not the case, there would be gaps through which light could enter to fuel the growth of competing specimens or forest weeds nearby.

Third, the infill of photosynthetic surfaces is dense. This provides for maximum acquisition of available insolation, which in turn allows us to place the individuals on a tight grid.

Now, while this is a desirable shape of a spruce tree, it is not the ideal.

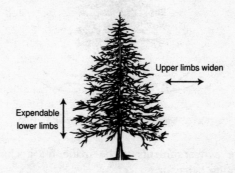

Upper limbs widen

Expendable
lower limbs

Here we see two ways in which the tree shape could be rendered closer to an ideal configuration.

First, the lower approximately 1/3 of the tree's limbs can be encouraged to atrophy and drop.

Second, the upper limbs can be induced to spread more widely in the first years of growth, with subsequent infill of photosynthetic tissue.

Implied in this schematic is a 3rd structural enhancement, not spatial but temporal. By manipulating the activity of growth-regulator genes, the upper, vigorously growing sections of the tree are stimulated to produce higher levels of clear-grained wood more rapidly than would naturally occur. Such an adaptation, in the days of fluctuating and unpredictable evolutionary selection, would have benefited individual members of the species in the short term, but over the long term would have worked against the species generally. Rapidly generated woody tissue would have been insufficiently hardened-off against the possibility of an atypically cold dormant season. Today, however, with the advent of irreversible global warming, this danger can be discounted.

All the above enhancements are readily accomplished through a two-pronged application of traditional propagation-and-selection methods along with newer, cutting-edge, genome optimization technology.

Now let's explore another means of improving upon the wild-type species.

Dispersal of allelopathic
agents via widely spreading roots

There are two arguments to be made for a change in the spruce's rooting behavior.

First, there is the phenomenon, still incompletely understood, by which biochemical signals are dispersed among genetically similar individuals—triggering, for example, a collective response to some environmental challenge, such as the arrival of a predator insect. Most of these chemical messages are passed by way of water dispersal through the roots, the solution being released generally at night, during periods of low exfoliar transpiration.

Second, and more pertinent, is the phenomenon of allelopathology. Many trees, and in particular temperate-zone conifers, have the capacity to produce and secrete—again, through the roots—substances which inhibit germination of the seeds of competitors. That is why you seldom see much understory growth in an established grove of evergreens.

The black spruce is typical in this respect. But the eastern hemlock, *Tsuga canadensis,* is truly exceptional. So we have developed a proprietary means of inserting a segment of the

Tsuga genome into our *Picea* breeding stock, whereby the synthesis of allelopathic agents is literally expanded tenfold.

Impressive as these competitive armaments are for the spruce tree, however, there is a final mechanism which might be desired to bring it one step closer to the ideal. And this bears upon the tree's methodology for reproducing itself.

Needle-bearing conifers, or more broadly speaking, gymnosperms, are at a certain reproductive disadvantage, vis-à-vis angiosperms or deciduous hardwoods. In the first place, their rate of growth, following germination, is comparatively slow. This allows commercially undesirable species—such as, here in the North Woods, sugar maple and red oak—to steal the march, as it were, and take up a dominant position in a regenerating woodland.

In the second place, hardwoods, which evolved later than conifers, have a competitive property that is difficult to counteract, even with rigorous application of herbicides. This is the ability to sprout new leading shoots from the trunks, and in some cases from the roots, of an established tree. That is why the largest single living organism in the world is *not,* whatever you may have heard, a fungus growing somewhere in Ohio, but actually a 6,000-ton, genetically identical stand of quaking aspens cloned naturally from a single individual in the mountains of Utah. This organism covers 106 acres and consists of 47,000 seemingly independent trees, all of which have sprung from a single vast and unbroken network of roots.

In the face of this capacity to spread and dominate, what can our ideal black spruce hope to do? Well, in this case, if you can't beat 'em, borrow from them. We have in recent years developed a technology for introjecting chromosomal segments from that very quaking aspen—not into the core genetic program of our breeding stock, but into the separate, self-replicating nucleotides contained within organelles of the root tissue itself. Such genetic information cannot, of course, be transmitted through ordinary sexual inheritance. It only inheres in individuals who have been cloned by tissue culture from the parent stock. This is actually an advantage, in that it renders *extremely* slight the risk that this proprietary genetic material will ever escape the control of Gulf Atlantic Corporation.

Now, drawing together all these enhancements, we have something like the following.

Picea x dawkinsia 4.3.2

This tree, for which a plant patent has been applied, represents the key commodity—the football, as it were—of Gulf Atlantic's presence in the Northeast. And it is truly a powerful creation.

Its upper limbs grow quickly and spread broadly to capture and hold space and sunlight.

The trunk thrusts upward fast and straight, producing clear-grained wood at the maximum sustainable rate.

The lower limbs atrophy and then drop, further crowding and darkening the region around the base of the individual, while allowing free circulation of air to ensure optimal health.

The roots spread widely, dispersing germination inhibitors throughout the surrounding soil, and facilitating intra-specific pheromonal communication.

And lastly, from these roots can spring an entire new network of individuals embodying all the above qualities—in addition, naturally, to the less exceptional but nonetheless vital attributes of the parent strain: general systemic vigor, foliar toughness, resistance to the effects of acid rain and the like.

This tree, which we are calling Dawkins Spruce, is literally the future of the Great North Woods. Once inserted—even in a limited, scattered, or mixed-growth setting—it will become over the course of a decade or two the dominant species throughout its range. Then, having achieved this position, it will be highly resistant to being supplanted, regardless of unforeseeable down-year changes in the regulatory climate. In horticultural terms it will be ineradicable. Within a generation, the North Woods will be transformed from an unplanned and often chaotic mixture of second-growth forest, small- and medium-scale tree farms and conventional timber plantations, to a uniform and fully optimized monoculture: an assured commercial softwood resource for the next century, at the very least.

For all the reasons cited above, the insertion of *X dawkinsia* 4.3.2 by the earliest and most expeditious means available is strongly recommended. By taking this action, the long-term position of Gulf Atlantic in the Great North Woods will have been definitively secured,

for practical purposes,

forever.

ENTERPRISE

The floppy disk had barely popped out of the drive when a bell rang way off at the Long House—
clung clung clung
—a salvaged bell buoy auctioned off by the Coast Guard that Jesse had picked up years ago because he figured Tex would shit himself over it. Paranoid Tex swore the Coasties had a file on him going back to the days when he really *had* been packing some weight down in the secret hold disguised as a fuel tank. Jesse doubted it. But it was Tex's gift to think up crazy ideas; and if 99% of them were nothing but wasted mental energy, that still meant that a solid 1% were crazy *good* ideas, and that counted for a substantial skewing of the inspiration-to-perspiration ratio in their business partnership. But that was all right. Things evened out over time, and he and Tex had always done okay for themselves.

"Got to run," said Jesse. "Sounds like customers." And he hustled off, leaving everyone else, including the wolf, staring suspiciously at one another.

Down at the Long House—a 1977 Oakwood 2-BR mobile home, shingled and fitted out with an insulated roof-pitch converter—he found an aged brown Suburban with a Maine Sportsman's Alliance window decal and a bumper sticker that said

HINKLEY SHOT THE WRONG BRADY

The customer sat in an aluminum chair on the veranda of the Long House, nursing a beer and flipping through a recent issue of *Green Egg*, the quarterly journal of the Church of All Worlds.

"Hey," the man said. "You read this stuff?"

Jesse sort of recognized the guy from crossing paths at the

Irving Mart: a lean, gray-faced man wearing an all-weather camouflage jumpsuit. "Who are you?" he said.

"Jag Eckhart." The man stood abruptly, thrusting a hand out.
"Wild Jag, some people call me."

Jesse nodded. He stepped into the Long House and came back
out holding a chain leash and a steel-reinforced leather muzzle.

"Your name Openhood?" the customer said.

Jesse nodded slowly. He held his eyes on Eckhart's. He thought
about whistling for Gus, but decided it wouldn't be good for
business. The customers did not like to see tame animals. They
did not like to see tame anything. That's why they were here.

"So," said Jesse, looking down the gravel path toward the
breeding pens, "you interested in one of our pups?"

"Pup, hell," said Eckhart. "I came here to buy a *wolf*. Is that
what you're selling or not?"

In Jesse's mental ledger, the price of the breeding stock just
doubled. Without speaking he set off walking down the trail.

"Where you going?" called Eckhart.

But Jesse just kept going there and eventually the customer got
the picture and came scrunching down the gravel behind him.
He wore heavy, Army-style boots that made a lot of noise. But
that's what the gravel was for, after all. To scrunch under your
boots, to telegraph your approach. So that even if the wind was
blowing the wrong way, the wolves would be expecting you.

A quarter mile along, the path ended and the woods thinned
into scrappy stands of willow and alder and swamp white oak,
then into winterberry and bog laurel, and finally cattails and
sedges. There was real water out there, Leman Pond, but you
couldn't see it through the heavy marginal vegetation. The first
run of chain-link began where the footing got damp.

Eckhart was fast behind him, breathing hard. They stepped
along a narrow run of tromped-down bracken. The wolf smell
was strong enough that even Jesse could sense it now. After a
while a second run of chain-link started on the other side of the
trail. They were hemmed in now. The path became narrow and
overgrown with grabby weeds, thistle and burdock and multiflora
rose—a pain-in-the-butt gauntlet that you just had to thrash your
way through.

"Going too fast for you?" Jesse called back to Eckhart, loud
enough that the animals would recognize him.

"A little slow, if you ask me," the customer huffed. He sounded
impatient. "You got any wolves around here, or what?"

Jesse turned and stopped him with a look. "They're tracking you now," he said, keeping his voice flat. "They're checking you out. The smell of you. The way you move. You'll never see them, though." Jesse started walking again. "Not unless they want you to."

Eckhart was quiet for a while. After several more paces his belt snagged on a big Chinese bittersweet that had gotten itself intertwined with the chain-link. By the time he worked himself free, Jesse had reached the gate. With deliberate slowness he unlocked it.

"Go on in," he said. "Meet your pup."

Eckhart paused. He peered through the fence at what looked to be a barely penetrable thicket of winterberry. The plants grew in sprawling clumps, a little better than head-high, and some of the upper twigs still held scarlet berries from last autumn. The berries didn't soften and sweeten until after a long freeze, but usually squirrels and winter birds were hungry enough to clean them out anyway. Seeing these berries hanging on in May, with fresh green leaves popping open around them, told you that the winter had been mild, with plenty of food around.

Eckhart said, "What do you mean, my pup? Don't I get to choose?"

"Sure," said Jesse. "You can choose to buy him or you can leave him for somebody else. The pup's got a choice, too. He can decide to show himself or to keep hidden. Not much you or I can do about it."

Eckhart looked dubious. "Don't you train them at all?"

Jesse stepped through the gate into the wolf pen. It was about half an acre in size, but you couldn't tell that. He planned to offer Eckhart one of the larger wolves. The best thing all around, he figured, would be to sell this man an animal that would waste no time in getting away from him.

"You want a trained animal," Jesse said, "you get a dog. Or a wolf-dog, or a coy-dog. Just pick up an *Uncle Henry's,* you'll see them advertised every week."

"I don't want no damn coy-dog," said Eckhart, pissed enough to come into the pen now. Jesse latched the gate behind him. "I want a wild-ass goddamn wolf."

Jesse nodded. Out of one pocket he pulled out a package of meat wrapped in plastic, fresh from the I.G.A. He made a clicking sound with his tongue, the feeding signal. In truth he had conditioned the pups, to this extent. It had been their only contact with humans. They were just shy of 13 months now—too old for imprinting. Essentially, they were always going to be wild.

The pup appeared with a little more clicking and coaxing. It was a male, with sharp black markings on a gray-and-brown-streaked coat. He was well developed for his age. He approached

Jesse from the side farthest away from Wild Jag Eckhart, growling softly, keeping his head low. Jesse tossed him some of the meat.

"Doesn't seem as though he likes you," he said to Eckhart.

"Shit." Eckhart took a step closer. The wolf growled and pawed at the ground where the meat lay. Eckhart stopped. "Well, he's got to learn to like me, I guess. Or at least he's got to learn who's the boss."

Jesse, unexpectedly, gave him a big smile. His teeth were white but uneven, straighter on one side than the other. He threw down a second piece of meat. The wolf raked this toward himself with a paw.

"What do you call him?" Eckhart said.

"They don't have names."

"Yeah?"

Jesse crouched a little. He held out the remains of the meat in its plastic wrapping. The wolf moved a step in his direction, then stopped. His eyes were like one-way mirrors.

It was all part of the plan, Tex's big idea: the outlaw breeding project that would return the long-vanished timber wolf to the eastern end of its historic range. And simultaneously, of course, turn a little profit for him and Jesse. They had begun with a mated pair of adults acquired from renegade breeders in Idaho. Then they built the pens at Da Turtle's Hostel. Now they were into the third phase, raising the pups past the age when they could be domesticated and offering them to an eager market of macho backwoods types who wanted something a little crazier than a pit bull.

This was where the uncertainty, both practical and moral, set in. Because it was virtually certain that none of the customers would be happy. The wolves would not be tameable, and they might prove to be dangerous to their owners. The owners, in turn, might react in any number of ways. They might shoot the animal, or they might report Jesse to the law. Most likely they would just turn the wolf loose.

In this case, since the wolves were native-born—not captured and ferried down from Canada or someplace—their territorial instincts would incline them to stick around Applemont. There were plenty of woods to hide in, and plenty of prey to hunt. Long-term, the plan called for a second breeding pair, genetically distinct from the first—there were supposed to be other outlaw stocks in Montana and eastern Oregon. If Tex and Jesse could just keep it rolling for a few years, the whole operation ought to become irreversible.

With no warning, Jesse pounced. He grabbed the young wolf

by the neck and slapped the muzzle over his jaws. The wolf kicked and snarled, but Jesse was one strong motherfucker.

"Give me a hand," he yelled to Eckhart.

Eckhart hesitated, then threw himself into the mess of man and animal, displaying a ferocity that gave Jesse pause. With the wolf outnumbered, Jesse tightened the muzzle and snapped the leash in place. Then he backed away, leaving Eckhart to wrestle the animal himself.

"He'll be getting sleepy now, anyway," Jesse said, wiping his brow with a cowboy kerchief. One of his wrists showed deep scratch-marks. "There was a little medication, you know, in that meat."

"Don't look sleepy to me," said Eckhart, through gritted teeth.

"Wait till he's really awake," said Jesse. "You'll notice the difference. Better get him home before then."

After a few minutes, Eckhart was able to stand and catch his breath. The wolf, though still awake, had become clumsy and docile.

"So," he said, panting and grinning. "I guess I'll take him, all right. How much do you get for them?"

"Thousand dollars," said Jesse.

"Say what?"

Jesse turned and started toward the gate.

"How about six-fifty?" said Eckhart behind him. "Hell, I can get a couple of wolf-dogs for less than that, and go ahead and breed my own."

"They won't be wolves," said Jesse. His hand was on the latch. He stood his ground and waited.

Eckhart came closer, dragging the leash. The wolf trailed along; he wanted to lie down, but didn't seem to care that much. Eckhart stared at the animal for a moment or two. Finally he looked up at Jesse and said:

"Can I write you a check?"

Jesse shook his head.

Eckhart smiled. He reached into a pocket of his jumpsuit and pulled out a cheap nylon wallet stuffed with 20's. "I guess you do know your business," he said, peeling them out.

Jesse nodded. He hoped so. He guessed he would miss the pup, but he wasn't sure. He guessed that a level of uncertainty was inevitable in this line of work.

He just wished he knew where
Tex had gotten
off to.

&
in the Underworld time stopped

with a lurch, and Tex popped out of the acorn, which morphed back into Beale, the homeless dryad. Don't ask how such things happen. They happen all the time, Down There. You'll see for yourself soon enough.

The red squirrel's great-great-granddaddy's nest had blown up into this gigantic cavernous place that was imbued with a mysterious cool green light—a glow like moss seems to make after a thunderstorm. Only this glow came from the dirt itself, that formed the structure of this immeasurable underground temple (which was at the same time just a little red squirrel's nest), as though the dirt were radiating the energy of its secret slimy moldy germ-infested life. You could see the roots of the yew tree overhead, swollen with vital humors they were pumping around, and huge flakes of leaf mold, rotten wood disgorged by beetles, worm castings, fractally intricate fungi, nematodes squirming through the gaps, and a ceaseless oozing of dark teeming water.

"Wow," said Tex. "I wish I had a camera or something."

"You'll remember," said Beale. He looked as mournful as ever. "Always."

"Remember what?" said Tex.

"This encounter," said Beale. "You will carry it with you from one incarnation to the next—if your kind of being has more than one of them."

"Hey," said Tex, "what *about* that, anyway? I could never quite decide."

Beale shrugged the way an oak tree shrugs: massively stirring energies passing through him and moving on. "It is not for you to decide," he said. "It's one of the great Mysteries."

"Ah." Tex stretched his arms, then his legs. He found that nothing hurt, that he was able to move freely again. (Therefore, he supposed, he was not really touching the Earth.) "So, what encounter? You mean, with *you*?"

Beale pointed at the high ceiling, supported by its arch of tree roots. "That is the root of the yew," he said solemnly. "Do you understand?"

"Understand what, bro?"

Beale sighed. "The yew," he said, "is the Final Tree. It is the tree that, in more civilized times, your people planted in their graveyards. It is thrice deadly, because its branches are used to make arrows, its berries are poisonous, and its roots grow fat on putrefying flesh. Thus it is the tree most beloved of the Worm."

"The worm?" said Tex.

"No," said Beale. Like he heard perfectly well the casual, lower case inflection. "I suppose I'm wasting everyone's time, arranging for this audience."

"Hey, no, listen—" Tex held his hands out, a display of good intentions. "Sorry if I'm slow on the uptake. I'm kind of new to this scene, you know? Maybe if you take it just a step at a time—"

Beale shook his head. "I had thought you must understand. All your talk of *getting organized.* 'Make your voices heard,' you said. Naturally I assumed you would want me to take your proposal to one of the Primary Beings. To an entity powerful enough to act upon your recommendations. That's why I brought you here."

Tex looked around. The chamber seemed to swell, to acquire new levels of complexity. Some weird dimensional thing was going on.

"Woo," said Tex. "This is making me dizzy."

"To say the least," said Beale.

"To say the least." Tex shuddered. "So you're saying, you brought me here so I could meet, like . . . the Ruler of the Underworld?"

"That would no doubt be easier for you," said Beale. "But I'm afraid there's no time for the mediation of human-scale deities. I thought I explained this to you. I myself am older than your gods. But I am an infant compared to the Primary Beings. You have transcended the human realm altogether. That's what will make this encounter so memorable."

Tex started to ask again, What encounter?

But the Underworld was changing too rapidly. The walls of the chamber became so distant that you couldn't see them any longer—only *feel* them, a horizon inscribed around the infinite. The green glow sublimated itself, becoming a kind of semivisible atmosphere. And the roots of the yew began to throb and to writhe, extending themselves everywhere, a living web, growing and interweaving. As Tex watched, the roots explored the millionfold wrinkles of darkness with hungry, insectile proboscises. And every place they probed, the darkness ruptured open to reveal a tiny living presence: a sentient organo-chemical matrix: a source of nourishment for the Final Tree.

This was a Vision, Tex realized. Not a normal perception, or even an altered-state thing like a near-death experience. As Beale had said, it was beyond the human realm. It just went on and on, way beyond *anyone's* ability to process. Let alone Tex's. And at the same time every single part of it was accessible, instantly knowable. How can you be everywhere at once when you're no place at all? Well, dig this.

"Here," said Beale. "Look now."

Tex grokked that the whole network of sucking rootlets fed into a series of fatter and fatter tubules, swollen bodies pumping with life-stuff. And these in turn were drawn inexorably together into a hungry center, a sort of black hole into which everything was being sucked. And at first the center was not a visible thing, it was wrapped in some kind of plasmic event-shroud. Then Tex felt himself being drawn into it. *Hoovered* into it. Consumed.

He felt a root penetrating his larynx. He looked down and saw that a slender, moist, tentaclelike appendage was sinking into him—growing into his body, raking his throat with alien cilia and spreading down into his entrails and up into his brain. It was drinking him dry. But what it was removing from him was not raw bodily things. It was a stream of words, memories, snatches of rock & roll, embarrassing episodes from his childhood, anger, tenderness, sublime moments of peace, unfocused anxiety, sexual arousal, the taste of mayonnaise on celery, the color yellow, the smell of Molly's hair, the night sky over Jerome, Arizona, a falling leaf, an orgasm, fields of bluebonnets in the spring of 1972.

"What the fuck is this?" he said, or tried to say.

These words flowed out of him as everything else was flowing—into the root, through the web, down toward the voracious insatiable center. And then at last, watching his words flow in, Tex finally got a look at the thing. The *Being*:

It was soft and squishy. It was fat and roughly cylindrical, with swollen bands from top to bottom. It was the color of sallow, sickly flesh. It smelled like brine and rotting horseshoe crabs and dung. It seemed to possess a number of eyes, though these may have been some kind of tumorous excrudescence. And it was getting fatter by the moment, feeding on Tex and on everything else—all the little blobs of tasty protoplasmic sentience it could gets its grasping tongues into.

"Well, *fuck you*," said Tex. Who figured that this horrible Being could eat him, but it couldn't sweeten him up.

"Tex Darffot," said Beale, "I bring you into the holy presence of the Bishop of Worms."

INTERVIEW WITH THE WORM

The Bishop of Worms emanated a sound like an aircraft carrier passing wind.

Beale said, "The Worm expresses the idea that your mind has an unpleasant taste."

The dryad stood next to Tex, only without a root snaking out of his throat.

"Yeah, well, just wait," said Tex. "It gets worse. Wait till he gets down to my like, kinky sexual fantasies and shit like that."

The Bishop rumbled and the Underworld shook.

"The Worm is not a *he*," said Beale. "The Worm has no human attributes whatever. The Worm is the Great Devourer of all things manifest. Its nature is to digest and dispose. All things that have ceased to be but may one day be again, in some new form, fall within the Worm's domain. But you should know this already, much of it. These matters are widely discussed in your own literature."

Tex nodded. "Sort of like a cross between a white hole and that thing in *Dune*."

It had gotten to be sort of diverting, watching his words flow away, down into the incalculable maw of his Wormship.

The dark bulges that Tex thought might be eyes moved around on the Bishop's clammy surface. Thousands of rooting append-ages shivered and slid across each other, like so many snakes growing out of Medusa. A sound like the sky being torn down the middle blasted through Tex's eardrums, bringing the activity of his brain pretty much to a halt. It was kind of a relief.

Beale said, "The Worm wonders whether you are the slave of any particular human deity."

Tex started to say No, but slithering out of his larynx instead went the name

NEMAN

and Tex watched in puzzlement as this oozed its way toward the Bishop. About halfway there, the name appeared to get stuck. The draining away of Tex's memories slowed to a trickle, then stopped. That damned goddess appeared to have clogged up the plumbing. Then Worm spoke again, uttering more or less:

GGWNNWWGGMMRLLGGLLNRRWWNGGGRLLN NGWWRLLGLRWWLRGGNNMMKRRLRRZWWGN GGNLRRFFFFT.

And Beale started to translate; but Tex cut him off.

"Hey, I couldn't agree more," he said. "If I were you, I'd spit Her the fuck back out."

The Bishop of Worms does *not*, evidently, spit things out. But the coiling root that snaked its way into Tex's throat was abruptly severed from that massive quivering body. As Tex watched, it began to wither, becoming insubstantially small until it completely disappeared. He clutched at his throat. Unfortunately there seemed to be an open wound left there.

First, the kiss of a goddess, he thought. Now a tracheostomy by the King of Compost.

"If I'd known it was going to be like this," he said, "I would've just stayed alive."

Beale lowered his head, as though profoundly embarrassed.

The Worm made another noise. It was the sort of noise that would stop hens from laying for the whole summer. No analogy Tex could conceive would remotely have done it justice.

"The Worm wonders what service you have promised to the Raven deity."

"Service?" Tex frowned. He couldn't quite remember. "Nothing, I don't think. As I recall, she said it would *entertain* her, to grant my wish."

The Bishop began to rumble, but Tex answered before It could finish.

"None of your business," he said. "My wish is a secret. And I take secrets to the *grave,* man."

Beale stared at him—like, Are you being serious?

Tex decided that now was the time to seize the monster by the horns. He squared his shoulders, faced the Bishop of Worms straight on—trying to look It straight in the eye, though this was a confusing proposition.

"Just let me lay this down," he said, "okay? Okay: Beale here has explained to me that you're totally beyond the human realm and all that. So I guess probably you're not too concerned one way or the other with a little insignificant dude like me. But if you're the same Worm that I read about back in, what was it— *Songs of Innocence and Experience,* maybe?—then probably you *are* interested in things like growth and decay and so forth. I mean, not *human* growth and decay in particular. But the whole picture. Life. Earth. The Noösphere. Gaia. Because see, it's like I was telling Beale here, I just don't think it's time to give up on everything. I think there might be some alternatives—short of, I mean, you just sucking everything into your gut and starting over again later, or whatever your plan is."

The Bishop of Worms made an utterance, and Tex realized that he could actually understand it. It was along the lines of

I MAKE NO PLANS.

"Sure," said Tex. "Of course not. Big atemporal guy like you—what are *plans* when you're as old as the Universe? But see, what I was saying was, I think maybe you're sticking your roots in where they don't belong here. No offense. But it just seems to me that, if what you're doing is reabsorbing all the nature spirits like Beale here who are sort of down on their luck and don't have anyplace to go—well, it might *seem* like you're doing the best thing, keeping the streets clean and all. But don't you think it's sort of premature? I mean, suppose everything was to turn around? Suppose the trees were to stop dying, for example. Suppose biological diversity were to suddenly start increasing again. You take away all these poor homeless dryads—and all the flower fairies and frog devas and whatnot—and who's going to step in and show all those baby life-forms how to grow? You expect a bunch of stupid DNA to know how to put itself together? Let me ask you, Bishop—did you ever try to build anything out of Legos?"

The Bishop swelled and shook. Its epidermal layer exuded mucus. It gave a thermonuclear belch.

"Never mind that," said Tex. "I'm just drawing a comparison here. My point is, it's not the little tiny individual pieces that matter. You *need* the pieces, sure. But you lose a few, you pick up some extras, that's not what's really important. What's important is like, the picture on the outside of the box. See? Not the stuff in the box at all. Because without the big picture—the like, meta-Lego—you can fuck around all day with the pieces and you've still got diddly-squat. It's the roomful of monkeys with typewriters all over again.

"So this is what I'm saying. You take away the spirits—the elves, the fairies, the dryads, all the magical higher-plane stuff—and it's like you've wiped the picture off the box. What's left is just a bunch of plastic garbage. You get me?"

The Bishop of Worms said:

NO.

"Story of my life," said Tex.

Beale took a step forward, in some upper-dimensional way.

"Your Primacy," he said, in what Tex considered to be a kiss-ass tone of voice. "Perhaps I may be able to clarify the matter. What this deceased human entity is suggesting, I believe, is that You might alter Your supremely farsighted and incomprehensibly beautiful intentions, vis-à-vis the morphological entities of the Earth—organizational field-matrices like myself—so that instead of granting us the great fortune to be reunited with Your blessed unmanifest Substance, You condemn us to a further period of wretched and thankless realization on the cursed plane of the Explicate. This former human believes that by so doing, You might improve the chances of there being a continued abundance of dying and putrefying sentient matter upon which to nourish Your divinely necrophagic Self. Whereas the human suggests that otherwise, should the Earth be drained of what he crudely terms its magical components, the reconstruction of its noetic body at some future time is cast gravely into doubt."

The Bishop of Worms changed color and texture, taking on a wet, pinkish cast suggestive of bloody vomit. It extended Itself into the twisting, flattened configuration of an intestinal parasite. Some kind of brownish-purple fat sweated from Its millions of pores. Clearly, It was deep in thought.

Tex turned to Beale. The dryad looked wan. There didn't seem to be a whole lot of oomph left in him.

"Buck up," said Tex. "What's the worst that can happen? We die and get eaten by—"

The Worm
suddenly
hideously
lunged down
exposing a set of fangs the size of the Korean Peninsula
and chomped Tex and Beale and much of the surrounding
landscape
into Its gullet
and what happened next is not suitable material for a story
that might inadvertently fall into the hands of impressionable
materialists.

And that was

THE END
(of that).

the next time Tex came to himself

he was inside the acorn again.

And he was in the red squirrel's great-great-grandfather's nest. Again.

And the roots of the yew were shaking overhead.

And dirt was raining down.

And suddenly a big hole was torn open in the ground above.

And a huge paw with claws on it reached in.

And scooped up the acorn.

And lifted it up to a great big mouth (but not as big as the Bishop's).

And the next thing Tex knew

he was swallowed
by a bear.

&
the next time Molly came to herself

she was lying on her own bed aboard the *Linear Bee* next to Ludi, who was tucked snugly beneath the T-shirt quilt, with her golden-tipped hair splayed across Tex's pillow like a pool of fallen sunshine, breathing slowly and deeply, fast asleep.

And Molly was surprised. Not so much by Ludi's being here. But by the fact that she, Molly, felt so pleased about it.

She got up from the bed—floating somewhat, as though all this time spent in the Otherworld was making her spirit less substantial—and moved slowly around the living quarters.

The plants had been watered. The angel-wing begonias were perhaps a trifle too damp, but the hot May sun—or was it June now?—should soon take care of that.

In the galley, Goblin the Cat-Person lay curled up in a mixing bowl. This was a new trick. Molly felt a funny little pang—something like jealously, but of a gentle sort, and mixed up with fondness—like a mother hearing that her child has performed some miraculous feat at school of which he has given no hint at home. On the floor, Goblin's bowl held traces of I.G.A. dry cat food. Next to the sink, the Majolica teapot and the set of Sun & Moon mugs sat sparkling clean in the wooden dish rack.

So, Molly thought. Life goes on within you and without you. She felt empty.

Then she felt, more simply, light. Cleaned out of the nonessential. She felt that if she did not concentrate on staying here, anchored in her little kitchen, she might begin to float again. Away, floating away. And what would stop her?

Molly wondered if she could still turn on the radio—whether she retained that much connection to the material world. Then she imagined how Ludi would feel if she woke up to, say, Indigo Jones dishing out a set of Captain Beefheart. The thought made her laugh, and Ludi made a little noise in her sleep.

Dreaming:

Molly caught a whiff of linden blossoms, honey-sweet, the warmth of someone's breath, a tingle of Harmony Ball earrings. Mullioned windows. Muslin drapes hanging blowsily from a brass rod. Hardware. Luff of cotton in the summer breeze. Oily scent of a highway. The softness of a peach. *Pearlescence.*

Is this, Molly wondered, really what dreams are made of? Only fragments, jumbled contents of a life? She had always imagined dreams were something beyond that, more meaningful or magical. But perhaps it was ordinary waking life that was full of meaning and magic. And dreaming was only the place where you could savor that, where you weren't distracted by the fussing and quarrelsomeness of the daily routine.

Insubstantially, Molly sighed.

Descending from her dream, Ludi stirred within the T-shirt quilt. For an instant—a clear, surprising sliver broken out of time—her mind seemed to brush against Molly's. It was like two hands, waving absently, touching by happenchance. For an instant they held one another.

The moment fell away. Ludi opened her eyes and she said out loud:

"Forever?"

But that, the sound of her own voice, brought her fully awake, and immediately the dream, that dark touching, fell below the horizon of her consciousness.

"Ah," she said, kind of a sigh, kind of an articulation of pleasure. She smiled at the bed and the quilt and the cozy, sunwarmed, flower-bedecked living quarters of the *Linear Bee*. Without rising, she stretched across to the built-in bedside table and clicked on the radio.

It was Bad Cathy. She was playing something by k.d. lang from the soundtrack of *Until the End of the World*. Molly thought, So much for clairaudience.

Afterlife Factoid #10
Even for the dead, psychic powers are an iffy business.

Ludi lay there listening for a while. Finally she made a little groan and lifted herself to a sitting position.

"What a night," she declared.

Molly smiled. She laid an immaterial hand on the young woman's shoulder.

"I hate men," Ludi said.

She threw the blanket off, newly energized, and Molly thought of Tex's all-time favorite line from a network TV show: "Hatred becomes like energy. It's a kind of food. You can live on it."

But then Ludi crossed the room toward the tiny ship's head, and she said, "No I don't." And she slumped a little, as though the realization that she did not truly hate men were too terrible to contemplate, this early in the morning.

Well, that's how men are, thought Molly.

Ludi took a quick shower and then emerged dripping and naked to put the kettle on. She pulled out Molly's old supply of Earl Grey and spooned it generously into the pot. Molly got the curious sense of her own life being lived at a slight remove—not much alteration of the routine, other than a change of bodies. She tried to get into Ludi's head to see how it felt from in there (besides which, she was not entirely sure what Ludi was doing on the houseboat: hiding from Guillermo?), but she could not.

Vexed, she drifted forward to the pilot house to brood over the little altar.

The chart table had been dusted. The candle there and some of the rocks had been slightly displaced.

Molly put her fingers on the Zuni bear fetish. She could feel its energy, a tingle running through the meridians of her ghostly fingertips; but she could not quite pick it up, only jostle it a little on the altar top. How did poltergeists manage to throw furniture across the room? Syzygy would probably know. The little turquoise bear toted a bundle of medicine rocks on its back, and a tiny red feather, like a tail, which it appeared to jauntily wag. Molly thought you really could see something of Tex in it. Something about the tiny carved and painted eyes. A gleam of irreverence.

"Bear," she said, "what's happened to you?"

And the *Heavenly Bear* replied:

> I AM KEEPING HIM SAFE. HE WILL BE RETURNING TO THE
> WORLD SHORTLY.

Molly pulled her hand back from the fetish and thought, Wow.
I didn't know it could talk.

Ludi walked in. She was wearing clothes now, though still
damp and barefoot. She stood beside Molly and looked down at
the spread of ceremonial objects on the chart table.

"Did you move?" she asked the little bear.

Her voice was light, unconcerned; she did not suspect any such
thing, really. She reached down and picked up the fetish and at
the instant she did so, a little spark of qi seemed to crackle into
her hand and up her arm. Her eyes opened wide.

"That's it," she said. She squeezed the fetish hard: Molly could
sense the energies flowing between them. "I *knew* I had seen
that before."

The bear? No—Ludi's eyes were fixed on something else, an
object lost and now found again in a freshly remembered setting.

Still holding the bear, Ludi walked quickly back into the cabin
and tugged on her bright pink high-top All-Stars. She pawed
at the pockets of a lightweight jacket she had hung on Tex's
giant hookah.

"Aha!" she cried.

When you think you're alone, Molly reflected, you actually
behave in a rather melodramatic fashion. Like you're playing to
an invisible audience. Like you *sense* that someone is watching,
even if you don't believe it.

Ludi held up the business card of one Eugene Deere, Ph.D.,
Senior Researcher. She rubbed the heavy-stock paper between
her fingers, as though it held the solution to some tantalizing
intrigue.

Ludi said, in her stagiest voice: "Now *where* do you suppose I
might *find* you, Mr. Deere?"

And Molly thought, *I* can tell you that.

STORMING THE FORTRESS

 They hit the shore together. Ludi was a jogger and
she made good time winding through the streets of
Dublin toward her apartment on the other side of

town. Molly was a spirit, but nonetheless the journey was tiring for her. She tagged along a pace or two behind, just over Ludi's shoulder, but that wasn't the strenuous part. What tired her out was the effort of keeping her grip on the young woman's awareness. Because Ludi was a Woman Possessed.

What possessed her, exactly, was hard for Molly to tell. To be sure, the raw facts of the situation were easy enough to assemble:

1. Guillermo had taken Ludi's car in order to chase down his stolen computer disk.
2. So Ludi, stranded, had ridden with Deep Herb to Dan Dan's Pizza Scene.
3. Where she met Gene Deere.
4. Who was wearing Tex's pendant.
5. Which Ludi glimpsed (without recognizing it) while dumping pizza in his lap and storming out.
6. To spend the night on the *Linear Bee*.
7. So that she wouldn't have to decide right away how to deal with Guillermo.
8. Only now, having placed the pendant in its proper context, she was determined to track it down.
9. For what purpose? At the very least, to demand to know how a corporate toad like Gene Deere had gotten his hands on Tex's treasured belonging.
10. But 1st she would have to sneak over to her own place and steal her car back.
11. Without alerting Guillermo, who was probably lying in wait for her.
12. Though of course, he would be pretending not to.

All of which Molly more or less easily understood.

What was mysterious, though, was Ludi's unusual state of—what would you call it? Exalted anxiety? A jacked-up, adrenaline-enhanced condition that did not seem to fit the observed facts of the situation. Like, *at all*.

What we have here, Molly decided, is Narrative Tension. A dramatic ploy she had always admired. The tension in this case being created by a disjunction between what is known by the protagonist (Ludi) and what is perceived by the audience (Molly). Which in dramaturgic terms gives rise to a need for resolution, for release—a condition of mounting stress perhaps psychologically related to rising sexual pressure. Molly could hardly stand it. She struggled to hang on while Ludi trotted across town.

Ludi's apartment, several blocks away in a pleasantly faded residential quarter, was the finished-off second story of an old garage. It was roomy, private, impossible to heat, and eminently affordable. You climbed up to it via a flight of open stairs on the windiest side of the building. At the base of these was a gravel parking area that entirely covered what had been the backyard of the associated house, except for a row of obese lilac bushes full of dead wood.

Sure enough, there was Ludi's orange Volkswagen.

Sure enough, there was a light in the kitchen where Guillermo was probably plunked on his butt waiting for her to get home.

But sure enough, by the time he heard the car fire up and got his face to the window to see what was happening, she was out of there! And Molly was right behind her. It was cool, zipping along just above the roof of the car with the wind whipping right through your face.

Ludi got lost twice on the way out to the old Goddin Air Force Base. She didn't mind; it gave her a chance to stop and ask for directions, which led to conversations with friendly people hanging out in their front yards looking for someone to talk about the weather with. On mornings in the Maine springtime, this was something you did. Ludi suspected there were people alive who had met their future spouses this way.

Past a big lumberyard that exuded the fresh smell of sawn wood, past a local sculptor's welded Cor-Ten naiads in their pond of cattails and lily pads, Ludi turned left onto a road that had acquired a Buffalo Commons atmosphere since the base closed down—empty houses, lawn grass grown tall and golden, deserted parking lots sprouting crops of fireweed, a rusting corrugated metal bowling alley—and after a couple of miles she came to the chain-link and barbed-wire perimeter of the Goddin Forest Research station, which looked both desolate and prosperous at the same time. It was like one of those ambitious enterprise zones in the middle of a bombed-out ghetto. Only here at least the air was clean and the sun made you feel optimistic and the sky spread out like there was no end to anything.

The contract security guy came out of his little shack holding a clipboard. He said, "Good morning, ma'am. Is anyone expecting you?"

Ludi held out Gene Deere's business card. She said, "I'm doing an interview."

The security guy brightened. "For Channel 5, right? Finest kind. Just sign here, please. The big hangar there on your right."

It was so easy Ludi was caught off balance. The Volkswagen puttered slowly forward, crossing an immensity of concrete before rolling into a parking area whose hundreds of spaces held only half a dozen vehicles, including the dun-colored Range Rover. Ludi parked a short distance away, took a breath and thought, Go for it.

The hangar door, which you could have slid the Glassport Public Library through, gaped open. Ludi stepped into a dim, echoing cavern. Huge strips of black nonskid rubber marked out the places where the strategic bombers used to go. On the walls were arrows, stripes, cryptic military acronyms and fire hoses. Ludi's All-Stars made a squishy noise on the concrete floor.

Not quite all the way across, she heard voices. One side of the hangar was divided by fireproof concrete partitions into a series of offices. The voices were coming from one of these, but it was impossible to tell which because of the perversity of the hangar's acoustics. She listened at one door and then another, and finally she took a deep breath and more or less lunged in through the next one.

Eugene Deere stood sideways to her, looking away through a miniature rain forest of fat green leaves, extravagant blossoms, whiskey barrels bursting with bromeliads and ferns, vines climbing through fluorescent fixtures overhead, and what appeared to be a mature marijuana plant. Somewhere in the depths of this, Sefyn Hunter sat cross-legged on his desk. He noticed Ludi and froze in place. By the time her eyes got past the outrageous purple-and-orange sexual apparatus of a bird-of-paradise flower, Sefyn was beaming at her with his #5 (Friend-of-a-Friend, But Not a *Close* Friend) smile.

"Well, as I live and breathe," he declared, bringing his arms down to rest on his hips, "it's Lovely Ludi."

"Hi, Sefyn," she said, pronouncing it like *seven*, which Guillermo had told her was linguistically correct. Sefyn was one of the guys in Guillermo's men's group.

This cost her time. Gene Deere turned to look at her and was not quite as astonished as she would have liked him to be. Still, he seemed pretty surprised. He turned to face the door with his mouth closed and his clear brown eyes open, wasting no effort grasping for something appropriate to say. Which left it all up to Ludi.

She came another couple of steps into the office.

"Have you two *met?*" asked Sefyn. He sounded eager to hear, either way.

Gene said, "We, ah—"

"I threw some food in his lap," said Ludi. She turned to Gene. "I guess I should say I'm sorry. But I'm not sure whether I really am or not."

"Why, isn't that *wonderful,*" said Sefyn. He hurried over, brushing aside the trailing air-roots of a *Monstera deliciosa* with big white splotches, like some Victorian disease. "I had no idea such things were still being done. You know, everything's gotten so impersonal nowadays. You just flame each other over the Net and so on. Please, tell me more."

Gene looked studiously at Ludi. She was thinking of how to bring up the matter of Tex's pendant; but Gene surprised her by addressing Sefyn: "If Chas calls looking for me, tell him I'm out visiting one of the work sites."

Sefyn nodded in a discreet, all-knowing way. "I understand *perfectly,*" he said. He gave Ludi a wink.

Gene motioned toward the office door—he still hadn't spoken a word to her—and Ludi started to move that way in a basically instinctual response. Then she stopped; she looked at Sefyn.

"If Guillermo calls looking for *me,*" she said, "tell him he better come up with some gas money."

Sefyn took a quick breath, processing these developments as rapidly as he could. "My, *my,*" he said. "I better jot down some notes."

"So where are we going?" Ludi asked Gene, out in the empty shell of the hangar.

He smiled at her. His skin was very smooth, but it formed small wrinkles around his eyes, as though they were just a little older than the rest of him. His collar was crooked and his hair, which could have been charmingly unkempt, was instead choppy and askew. Portrait of the science nerd as a young adult, Ludi thought.

Gene said, "I thought since you've come all this way—for what reason I can't imagine, but I guess you'll get around to telling me—I might as well give you a little tour. Show you what we're doing out here. Prove to you, perhaps, that we're not all demons. Or did you have something else in mind?"

It can wait, she thought.

«Wait for what?»
thought Molly.

But wait for what? Ludi wondered.

"We can take my car, if you like," Gene went on.

"No," she said. "Let's take mine."

There was no cloud in the sky. High up, a formation of Canada geese was changing direction, the classic V-shape broken into something resembling a question mark.

WORKING FOREST

Past the gate, Gene pointed her onto a secondary road heading north, through the unincorporated township of Applemont. Ludi stopped for gas at an Irving Mart, where a banner advertised a 3-for-2 deal on Marlboros.

"Why don't they just give up?" Gene said, while Ludi turned the car off and wondered who was going to get out and pump. "Who smokes anymore?"

"People in Applemont," said Ludi. She opened her door and stuck a foot out.

"Want me to pump that?" said Gene, bestirring himself.

"No. I just want you to pay for it."

She was amazed by how that came out—not at all funny; even angry, somewhat, though whatever anger she felt now was probably meant for Guillermo.

Gene laughed. "How about if Gulf Atlantic pays for it?" he said, offering her a credit card.

She took it through the window and their eyes met.

"Can I turn on the radio?" asked Gene.

"It's on," she said. "It never goes off. The button's broken. You just turn the volume up."

"Blaupunkt," Gene muttered.

By the time she paid for the gas and a 6-pack of Fruitopia and a bag of chips, he had changed over to Maine Public Radio, which was playing an Impressionist piece for small chamber orchestra. Tuneless, Ludi thought.

"This is great," said Gene, pointing at an imaginary midpoint between the two speakers. "*The Kairn of Koridwen*. Charles Tomlinson Griffes. A weird little micro-symphony that was only performed a couple of times and then everybody forgot about it. Now somebody's finally recorded it, and listen, it's like hearing a brand-new piece, only it's 80 years old."

To Ludi it sounded like mediocre Debussy. Should she say

this to Gene Deere? Why did it matter at all—let alone to such an extent that she decided to keep her mouth shut?

The road was in bad shape. They bumped through an unremarkable countryside of hayfields and blueberry barrens and patchy woods and mobile homes. After several miles the electric line came to an end at a taxidermist's place called THE LAST STOP. Ludi didn't mind driving, but she would have liked some conversation. She had nothing to say, herself, and Gene's contribution consisted of announcing the titles of movements.

"I think this is 'The Wrath of the Priestesses,' " he would say, or "Listen—it's 'The Gift of the Sacred Berries.' "

"Do you know this by heart or something?" asked Ludi.

He looked at her, maybe surprised by her tone. "I've got it at home," he said. "And I've always liked programmatic titles. It gives you something to relate to. Otherwise music's pretty abstract. Like theoretical physics. That's probably why Einstein was into Mozart."

Ludi steered around a pothole large enough to bury an Irish wolfhound in. "You've got this same record at home? How come you're so excited about hearing it, then?"

Gene looked puzzled. He looked away, out at the road. "I don't know. I guess it sounds a little different now—you know, hearing it with somebody else."

Ludi wondered if she had been giving him a hard time. Not that she hadn't meant to.

Gene went on, "It makes it fresh, don't you think? As though you're experiencing a thing from someone else's point of view."

She nodded. "That's interesting," she said.

He pointed at the radio. " 'Carmelis Prophesies for Mordred,' " he announced.

"What?"

"Take this next right. Now, now!"

Ludi spun the wheel and the VW skidded around a turn, onto the shoulder, off the shoulder, back on again, and finally to a halt at a 45° angle from the axis of the road. If you could call it a road.

"Don't do that," she told him seriously.

"You handled it fine," he said, patting her shoulder.

"Where are we?"

"Nowhere yet. Listen, it's the final Dirge. Very tragic ending. Typical Celtic stuff. You want me to drive?"

"I can drive," she said. She turned to look at him. "So, what did you want to show me?"

Gene waved his hand around. "Take a look," he said. "Look at the countryside."

Ludi saw nothing unusual. They were in the middle of woods that had been logged heavily a couple of years ago. Tall trees were sparse, and some of the slash or unwanted scrap timber lay in piles here and there, pushed out of the way by someone's bulldozer. You could see trails where the skidder had run, dragging the big logs out. A new growth, primarily birch and alder, stood about shoulder-high.

"It's a mess," said Ludi. "It's ugly. I hate it when the woods look this way."

"It *is* a mess," said Gene. "Whether it's ugly or not depends on whether you're the fellow who did the cutting, I guess. So drive up ahead a little further."

The Kairn of Koridwen was over and there was a program announcement about an on-air debate over bringing back the native timber wolf.

"I wish they would do it," said Gene. "I'd like to see one."

"You would? I think I'd be scared."

"So would the wolf. That's why it's a silly debate. People are afraid of wolves because they grew up hearing about Little Red Riding Hood."

"I kind of imprinted on *Peter and the Wolf*," said Ludi.

"You did?"

Ludi nodded. "But isn't there more to it than that? I mean, aren't there farmers who are worried about their sheep, and so forth?"

Gene shook his head. "That's just a rationalization. It all comes back to Little Red Riding Hood."

"*I* think it comes back to people being afraid of Nature, period. It's this whole Western thing about control. There was a bounty on coyotes here a few years ago."

"Really?"

The radio announcer slipped on some Rosemary Clooney.

"Show tunes!" said Ludi, in a quiet, joking way.

Gene surprised her by laughing. The first song was "You with the Stars in Your Eyes." Ludi loved this song; though where could she have heard it before? Maybe such things are communicated to you *in utero*.

The two of them looked at one another and Ludi was not sure what they were talking about. She thought about Tex's pendant again. But as usual, the time did not seem right.

Gene said, "The thing about woods like this is, they're managed on basically a cash-and-carry basis. What I mean is, some private citizen owns the land, and he does nothing with it for 15 or 20 years except let everything grow, and then one day he decides he needs something—money, firewood, something to do, I don't know—so he comes out here and does some cutting. Then he skidders the logs out, then he disappears again."

"So?" said Ludi.

"So—it's a pretty brainless way to manage a potentially productive forest. There's no control over what grows here, for one thing. That's just left to chance, to whatever happens to seed itself and fend off competitors most successfully. Plus, there's no effort to thin the woods so that a few selected individuals get optimal sunlight, so they can grow straight and strong. And *then* there's no effort to do the harvest itself in any kind of efficient way. Some trees get cut but not utilized because they're the wrong size or wrong species. Lots more get killed by soil compression, followed by root necrosis. They seem to be alive when you drive away, but almost immediately they die in place. Of the trees that *are* taken out, up to half the wood mass may be left behind to rot when the limbs are slashed off. So you're left with something like *this*." He pointed out the window. "It's a mess. Economically as well as biologically. And it's ugly."

Ludi knew there was something wrong with this, but she couldn't get a hold of it right away. "People have been doing it this way for hundreds of years," she said.

"Not much more than 150," Gene said. "Not around here. And even in that length of time, they've seriously degraded the resource."

That's what it is, she thought. It's words like *resource*, when what we're really talking about is Nature. The living Earth.

"Who says," she asked him, "that the woods have to be *managed*? I mean, you're talking like it's a choice between these little small-time woodlot owners and big efficient corporate operations like you guys. Why not just let the woods alone?"

Gene smiled and nodded his head. Like he knew, and was hoping, that she would get to this. "What do we have here?" he said, reaching down and scooping the *Maine Atlas and Gazetteer* off the floor of her car.

"It's messy, I know," said Ludi. "I just keep it there in case I get lost. You'd be surprised how handy it comes in."

"It's *paper*," said Gene. "It's part of the millions of tons of paper that are consumed in this country every *day*. Do you know that to print just one Sunday edition of the *New York Times* takes an amount of wood pulp that is equivalent to 540—"

"Stop it." Ludi winced. She tried to close her ears. "I hate statistics like that."

"Right. Everybody does. Everybody would much prefer not to think about it. But they go out and buy the newspaper anyway, or they get their coffee in take-out cups, or they heat with a woodstove. Or they keep road maps in their cars."

"That's printed on recycled paper," said Ludi. "I checked."

Gene didn't want to hear about that. "And remember, there's more people in the world every day. More people that need toilet paper, and *TV Guide*s, and wood to build their houses. So don't kid yourself. The lumber is going to get harvested, and large corporations are going to supply the vast majority of it. And with good reason, too. Here's the good reason right here."

They had entered a whole new territory. The road was freshly topped with gravel and the scrappy woodlands were gone. In their place was a wide, sharply contoured landscape covered to a uniform height in something with dark green needles.

"This is a professionally managed tree plantation," said Gene. "These are black spruces, about six years old. They'll be ready to harvest in another nine or ten."

Ludi let the Volkswagen ease to a stop. It was kind of awe-inspiring, to be honest. It reminded her of the Pine Barrens down in New Jersey.

"Now out of this land," said Gene, "you'll get up to five times—*five times*—the return in wood mass that you get from a haphazard small-scale tract like the one back there. Which means that you can build that many more houses, or print that many more copies of the *Times,* or do that much more of anything, in the same amount of land, and in a lot less time. See: the demand for wood is the same, one way or another. It's all a question of how much of your limited resources do you want to devote to meeting it."

"Maybe it ought to be a question of how much we can reduce our wood consumption. And aren't there other things to make paper out of? Guillermo was telling me—"

Gene waved these objections aside. "That kind of stuff is just nibbling around the edges. Sure, we might as well do it. It'll certainly help somewhat. But all these dreamy Live Simply fantasies overlook the fundamental nature of the national psyche, which is very much a more-is-better proposition. I'm not saying that's good. I'm not saying it's bad, either. I'm just trying to deal with the situation as it actually exists."

Which *did*, Ludi thought, set him apart from most of the people she knew. Because the people *she* knew

> #1, probably did not understand the situation as it ac-
> tually existed, by reason of their being perpetually
> spaced out, living in Maine, disdaining the concept
> of the Real World, et cetera; and
>
> #2, to the extent that they did understand what the
> Real World was like and how it operated, they
> were wholeheartedly committed to changing it
> right away, from top to bottom. And in the
> meantime,
>
> #3, they just got high and
>
> #4, talked a lot.

So she would have to say that meeting Gene Deere, in this respect at least, was actually kind of a trip.

"So," she said, "that's what you do, huh?"

He smiled at her. All of a sudden he looked a bit unsure of himself, perhaps self-conscious about talking so much. Ludi wanted to tell him that it was okay, that the Better Living Through Forestry rap had been quite informative. Like getting up close and personal with a green guy from Mars. Only this one had brown eyes and was cute. In his dweeby kind of way.

"I'm actually just a biologist," he said. "I do research. I make proposals. All this—" (waving out the window) "—that's done by somebody else. Like my boss."

"The Antichrist," said Ludi.

Gene looked taken aback. Then the little smile came back. "Ah," he said. "You've got a good memory."

"It wasn't that long ago."

"No, but—" He looked away. He acted like he was lost, way out here in the woods. Maybe he wasn't used to having people pay attention to him.

"So," said Ludi. "You work with Sefyn?"

"He's my A.A. Unusual fellow. Is he a friend of yours?"

"He's a, um—" She looked straight at Gene and just stepped into it. "Look, I noticed back at Dan Dan's that you were wearing a thing around your neck. Like a pendant. Actually it was a skull, a carved bone thing. You were wearing it on a shoelace. And the reason I wanted to—I mean, it looked like something that belongs to someone I know. And I wanted to ask where you had gotten it."

Gene touched his sternum, through his Oxford-cloth shirt. He reached into the front of it and fished around. Finally he opened the top two buttons. "Here it is," he said.

There it was. Tex's little grinning skull. It stared up at her eerily, as it always had. Behind it, a few dark brown hairs and a smooth, well-formed chest.

"Is this it?" said Gene. "Did your friend lose it or something?"

"I don't know. I mean yes, I'm pretty sure it's the same one. But I don't know if he lost it. I, um—I haven't talked to him for a few days."

Gene thought. "About a week?"

"About."

"Because that's when I found it. I was out on a hike, and I looked down and there it was."

"Where?" said Ludi. As she said it, a funny trembly sensation came to her, as though she did not really want to hear the answer.

"Not too far from here," said Gene. "West of Dublin. In Applemont, actually. It was just lying there beside a big rock."

He did not seem to notice that Ludi was drifting away on him, that she was only half listening.

But she noticed, eventually, when the words stopped. She felt the silence filling the Volkswagen up, a little too full to be comfortable. She looked up at Gene and found that he was looking back at her, holding the pendant between his fingers. Like, waiting for something. He gave her again that uncertain smile of his. With his shirt unbuttoned, he looked young and vulnerable.

He said, "Would you, um, like to go see?"

"See what?" she asked. And she thought, Dumb question.

"Where I found the skull," he said, turning to face the road, innocently. "And, you know—where I live. It's this interesting old bungalow. Very well preserved, architecturally."

There were implications here. Ludi knew what they were. And she knew what it meant when she put the Volkswagen back in gear and said:

"Sure. Which way?"

THE RIGHT TO BEAR

Molly could have warned them.

The shortcut that seemed like such a totally great idea—a perfect diagonal slicing through the empty north end of Applemont and popping out just above Gene's rented bungalow, that looked so solid and reliable on the map—turned into a rutted mud-capped nightmare after only a show tune or two. The Volkswagen plowed onward, making slow headway, and by the time "Tangerine" ended and "Fascination" began, Ludi voted to turn back, but oh, no: Gene, gripping the *Atlas*, seemed to perceive this as a challenge directed at the adequacy of his testosterone supply, just like they all do, or would have, under the circumstances. So they kept driving until Ludi lost patience and stopped the car halfway to the bottom of the Gully at the End of the World. There she clambered out onto the wet shoulder and said:

"Fine. Then *you* drive."

So Gene slid across the bony gearshift knob and nestled hesitantly in the unfamiliar driver's seat. Ludi didn't feel like getting back in at all, but of course, she did, when it became clear that Gene intended to go ahead with this. She settled into the warm hollow left by his body and breathed the funny smell he had left there: expensive macho toiletries that Guillermo would have disdained. Guillermo liked to smell like sweat—"an honest human animal scent," which incidentally made it seem as though he performed some kind of manly toil for a living. (Sailmaking was actually a computerized operation that involved a lot of stitching and reinforcing of artificial fabrics.) Gene smelled like glossy-magazine products. Ludi wondered how many trees you had to cut down to print one issue of *GQ*. Say what you might about the American psyche, it seemed to Ludi that there was a certain amount of room for national self-improvement.

The Volkswagen started moving. It crept downward, then lurched to a halt, then crept downward again.

"The brakes are a little touchy," she said.

"Yeah, no kidding."

He got the hang of it by the time they reached the bottom of the gully. The uphill slope ahead of them looked immensely high and steep. In fact, it looked impossible.

"If we got stuck here," said Ludi, "I mean, just supposing—do you think we'd get eaten by bears?"

"We're not going to get *stuck*," Gene said through clenched jaws. Then he sort of got it, that she might be teasing a little, and he forced a smile for public consumption. "Anyway, I don't think there are too many bears around here. Are there?"

"Tex says there are."

Gene let the clutch out and the Volkswagen slurped upward.

"Ha!" said Gene, laying a little extra gas on. His death-grip on the wheel relaxed somewhat. "Who's Tex?"

"Tex is my friend that owned that skull you've got on," said Ludi. When the words were out she noticed that she had mixed up her tenses, past and present. Which was it?

The Volkswagen slid sideways from one rut to another, like a water-skier passing over the swells of a wake. The road looked like a location shot for some natural-disaster movie.

"Hang in there," said Gene—more to the car than to Ludi, she thought.

The car took heart. The little wheels found a solid piece of something to grab on to, and the Volkswagen shot up the remaining stretch of hillside.

"Oh my *god*," said Ludi, louder this time.

"What?" demanded Gene, turning to frown at her. "We made it, didn't we? I told you—"

"No," said Ludi. "I mean *that*."

He looked. They both looked.

A platoon of armed and dangerous-looking dudes wearing camo fatigues and black greasepaint and packing heavy firepower spread out across the road, half a dozen paces in front of them. A couple of the guys dropped into a crouch, leveling AK-47's at the windshield of the Volkswagen. Others began edging up the sides of the road, performing some flanking maneuver. There were seven or eight in all. More than enough.

"What the hell is this?" said Gene, more angry than frightened. "Is there a guerrilla war going on around here that I haven't heard about?"

Ludi put a hand on his leg, a quieting gesture. "Don't get excited," she said. "You don't want to alarm them."

"Alarm *who*?"

By this time, a couple of road warriors drew up even with the Volkswagen's headlights. One of them made a funny downward motion with his hand—as though signaling them to lay down their weapons. Ludi quickly dropped the *Maine Atlas and Gazetteer*. Gene stuck his head out the window.

"May I ask who the fuck you think you are?" he said.

"Whoa, friend," said the nearest gun-toter. "You got a few questions to answer yourself, so I'd suggest you not go popping your mouth off."

"*I've* got a few questions to answer?"

In Ludi's mind, a strange and perhaps implausible scenario spun itself out like a videotape on fast forward:

Gene gets mad.

Gene jumps out of the car.

Gene and the guy in combat fatigues yell and curse at each other.

The guy gets tired of this and blows Gene away.

Gene's guts splatter across the VW, through the window, and onto Ludi's lap.

Ludi spends years in expensive therapy recovering from post-traumatic stress syndrome.

She ends up doing talk shows and marrying an asshole who sells commercials for cable television.

All their children are named Robert.

"Tell me something," said the guy outside Gene's window, whose assault rifle had an ammo clip 15 inches long. "Didn't you see the warning sign posted back up the road?"

"No," said Ludi, smiling nicely. "I'm sorry. We were a little confused. Are we on your property?"

The man smiled back, but there was something still not exactly polite about it. "Where you are," he said, "is not exactly anybody's *property*. Where you are is, you've entered a Freedom Zone. You've entered a part of America that's been reclaimed by free Americans, in the name of constitutional sovereignty. You'd know that if you had read the sign."

"We didn't *read* the goddamn sign," said Gene. "And if we *had* read the goddamn sign, it wouldn't have meant shit."

Ludi pressed his leg a little harder.

The man stuck his head closer to the window. His greasepaint had been unevenly applied, heavier on one side than the other. Heterosexual men have no business fooling with makeup.

"You've got quite a mouth on you, son," the man said, though he did not look old enough to be using the word *son* in this way. "Why don't you step on out of the car and we'll talk this over without getting the lady involved."

"I'm no lady," Ludi told him. "I write articles for local newspapers, sometimes. You don't want a lot of really bad publicity, do you?"

"There's no such thing," said another guy, slinking up along Ludi's side of the car. "We *want* publicity. We need to open people's eyes to what's really going down here. That's how we get our recruits."

"Recruits?" said Gene. He was having, Ludi thought, a really hard time getting the picture here. "What do you think you're doing, forming your own banana-republic army out here? Do you guys have any functional brain cells, or what?"

"I've had about enough of this bullshit," said the guy with asymmetric paint. He reached for Gene's door handle.

"Hold it!" a different voice yelled. "Back the fuck off."

All the guys in their fighting gear were clustered around the front of the car now. One of them, dressed like the others except with a captain's twin silver bars on his ball cap, pointed at the man who was ready to go hand to hand with Gene. The man grumbled but obediently stepped away.

The officer type came forward. He wore twin 9-millimeter pistols in leather holsters that drooped gunslinger style low down on his hips. His face, behind aviator glasses, was thin and gray.

"This fellow's not dangerous," he told the others. "He's just a boy from away who's gotten himself lost. Isn't that right, Dr. Deere?"

The gray-faced man looked at Gene, who for the duration of several heartbeats did not recognize him. Then Gene said:

"Eckhart?"

The man nodded.

"Eckhart, in charge of security?"

"None other." The man nodded. He repeated the nod for Ludi.

She thought it was probably safe to scowl at him.

"Eckhart," said Gene, "what the hell is going on here? Are you guys crazy? Is this part of your job?"

Eckhart seemed to chew on something. "Not directly part of the job, I guess you'd say. But I guess you could call it *related*. It's a security matter, only it goes beyond just Gulf Atlantic."

"Evidently," said Gene. His hands kneaded the steering wheel, spreading dampness around.

Eckhart gestured up the road. "Maybe it's time for you folks to get moving along."

"I've got no problem with that," said Gene.

"Want me to drive?" Ludi offered, as gently as she could.

Before he could answer, there was a shout from somewhere ahead on the roadway.

"Who's that?" said Eckhart. "Who's on rear guard?"

"The new fellow," somebody told him.

The shout came again—far enough away that you couldn't make the words out, just a general sense of agitation.

Suddenly a pop struck Ludi's ear like a quick pressing-inward of air. It was a rifle going off. In the next few seconds it fired again. And again.

Eckhart spat in the dirt. "Damn flatlander," he said. "Go see what the hell—"

His eyes opened wide.

Ludi followed them, peering through the jumble of battle fatigues and firearms. She saw, perhaps 20 strides away, a huge brown animal lumbering up the road

"It's a fucking *bear*," one of the men said.

The word seemed to jar them into motion. They spread out. A few took cover in the trees, and one climbed on top of the Volkswagen.

The bear, a good 800-pounder, was trudging heavily up the road, as though this were not something it had really wanted to get involved in. It paused to check the banks on either side: slippery and steep. Then it took a few steps closer to Ludi's car. Briefly it looked back in the direction the rifle shots had come from.

That was when Eckhart opened fire. He shot first with the pistol in his right hand, then with the pistol in his left hand. The bullets struck somewhere in the dense fur around the bear's neck.

The animal roared and slapped itself beside the head, where the bullets had gone in.

As though released from a spell, the other men started shooting too. They fired their assault rifles in single shots and in bursts of fan-fire. One of them threw a hunting knife. Not many of the several dozen rounds discharged actually came close to striking the target. But enough.

The bear bellowed. It went down on its knees and then rolled onto its side. It breathed and cried and bled for a little while, but basically it died without making too much fuss about it.

Ludi felt absolutely sick. She was nearly overpowered with disgust. She closed her eyes and swallowed a couple of times— swallowed nothing, her mouth was empty—then she felt Gene lift her hand from his leg, which she seemed to have been squeezing the blood out of.

"I'm sorry," she said.

"For what?" he murmured. Neither of them knew what she was talking about.

"Killed that damned bear," one of the guys in greasepaint said.

"I guess," said another.

Eckhart walked over to where the dead animal lay. After a few seconds he said, "Motherfuck."

Gene opened the driver's door and got out. Ludi tried to stop him, but failing that she got out also. They walked over to the bear and looked down where Eckhart was staring.

"It was a damn mama bear," he said. "It was about to have a baby."

Ludi gave a cry. Eckhart was pointing at something bloody sticking out of the bear's groin. The head of its unborn cub? Part of the placenta?

Gene bent over, getting in close to it. He tapped Eckhart on the arm. "Look," he said. "See that?"

"Mother*fuck*," said Eckhart. "The sucker's still kicking."

Ludi looked. She could not *not* look, though she didn't want to. The thing sticking out of the dead mama bear squirmed inside an oozing membrane.

Gene said, "You ever seen anything like this?"

Eckhart shook his head. "Nope," he said, *"but."* He reached into a sheath on his belt and pulled out a knife with a long blade, serrated on one edge. "I'd say we ought to take a shot at getting that little sucker out of there."

The two men stared into the mess below them. Gene said, "How about if I spread the legs apart? Then maybe you could—"

Eckhart looked back. Neither of them knew what maybe he could do. He twiddled the knife.

"Here," said Ludi. "Give me that."

Eckhart stepped aside, though not altogether out of the way.

"Sorry to have to do this, Bear," said Ludi. "But it's the only chance."

She nodded to the two men. They each grabbed a leg and pulled on it.

The little male cub, which was born alive about 45 seconds later, Ludi named Tex.

Gene smiled at her weakly. His face was the same color as his business card. Eckhart lay down on the ground, smiling stupidly, like a drunk who's just thrown up. The cub pawed blindly at Ludi's chest, which was covered with blood by now. She hummed softly, to calm it, a cheerful ditty from *Brigadoon,* fresh in her mind from public radio.

"What do you figure we ought to do?" said one of the guys in greasepaint. "Think we ought to call an animal shelter or something?"

"Keep away from him," Ludi said sternly. She remembered all too well the Fish and Game Department Visitor Center down in Norway, where they kept orphaned animals locked in cells as large and comfortable as gas-station rest rooms.

All the men looked at her, waiting for further instructions—as though they expected her to be plugged into some eternal feminine mystery channel.

"Okay," she said, after a period of deliberation. "We've got to get some milk in him, or some baby formula or something. At least some water. And we've got to clean him up. So here, help me—let's get him in the car."

It took Gene a couple of minutes to understand that she meant *him*.

"I'll ride in the back," she said, "and keep him calm. Just drive nice and steady. But don't take all day."

He nodded. He helped her into place and started the Volkswagen. The Sovereign Citizens Militia gathered around to wave them off, like heavily armed Munchkins.

"Where did you say we were going?" Gene asked, nodding good-bye to them.

"Don't ask me," said Ludi. "It's your bungalow. Put the pedal to it."

He had nothing to say: nothing to Ludi. Easing the clutch out, he muttered to himself,

> "If I drove a classic baby like this,
> *I'd* take better care
> of it."

&

Tex thought, What am I this time?

Not a bear.

Yes a bear. Bouncing baby bear in the backseat of a car. Cuddled in the lap of a nice-smelling human girl. Or was it a woman? How was a bear to know?

The girl was humming. Music soothes the savage beast, maybe. But show tunes made Tex restless. He remembered the melody from an otherwise forgettable made-for-TV flop starring Robert Goulet.

Go home, the lyrics went, *go home.*

Go home with Bonnie Jean.

He imagined a guy in kilts leaping up in the air, a cleaned-up version of the old wild sword dance. Kilts, clans, chieftains, mists and moors. All lost. Driven out by a bunch of sheep farmers. The Highlands cleared. Forests chopped down, turned into ships and stockades and steeples. And history reseeds itself.

The savage beast was getting riled up.

"Shh," said the voice of a beautiful maiden—a princess, needing only to be rescued from a fire-breathing drag. "We're almost home. We'll get you some nice milk to drink."

"Um," said somebody else—not the drag; maybe a knight in shining Armani. "Actually I don't think I've got any milk."

"You haven't got any *milk*?" The princess wasn't digging it.

"It's not natural," said the knight, speaking hurriedly, "for adult humans to drink the milk of another species."

"Not *natural?*" said the princess. (Tex knew this voice, but the bear did not. They were going to have to work out some better means of communicating, the two of them.) "You go around spraying poisons with airplanes and you're worried about milk not being *natural?*"

"I don't, um—"

The knight sounded cowed and the car squeaked around a corner. The new road was bad and the whole backseat, princess, bear & all, bumped up and down, up and down. It made the bear feel sleepy. So the bear slept.

And Tex, awake inside but constrained by an infant animal's senses, could only faintly discern that the car was slowing and a voice said:

"Well, here we are. Home sweet home."

While the other voice, sweet and light as spring air, said *That's their car!* but the bear was twitching and fussing in his sleep and Tex got distracted and thought no more about that.

HOME WITH BONNIE GENE

"I just want to know what it's doing there," said Ludi. "I mean, they wouldn't have just *left* it. Would they?"

"Mm," said Gene.

Their voices were muffled by the fabric of an old curtain. Tex lay curled in one of those little cozy chambers built around a fireplace. An inglenook. With built-in dark wooden benches and a curtain holding the warm air in. He was down on the floor on a pile of blankets, and a fire was snapping and leaping in the hearth. The baby bear was halfway freaked out by this but halfway hypnotized. It wanted to stare at the flames while Tex wanted to turn the damn big head around and peek under the curtains and see what was going on out there in the living room, where the voices were coming from.

"Bear," he said—he could hear his own voice, but the bear evidently could not—"we've got to work together, here."

Footsteps approached. The bear tensed up. Outside the curtain, Ludi's voice said: "I'm just going to check on how Tex is doing."

Which blew him away. But she meant Tex the *bear,* not Tex "The Bear."

The curtain opened and there she was. Huge. Gentle-voiced.

Warm. The little bear loved her. Mommy, it thought, in bear-think. It raised its furry head to get stroked and cooed at. Ludi smiled and obliged and the endorphin rush was like an explosion of ecstasy. The bear licked Ludi's finger, tasting sweat and other particularized human biochemicals—the distinctive taste of Ludi—and Tex thought either he or the bear was going to O.D. on it.

What an awesome *feeling,* he thought. You could like, *swim* in it. There was absolutely nothing to compare it to.

Ludi stood up. She walked out. The bear felt stupid and placated.

"He's fine," said her voice through the curtain. "Now sit down and talk to me."

"Talk about what?" said the man's voice.

And all of a sudden—wham—it hit Tex who this was, where they had brought him. It was like one of those paradoxical shapes, a Klein bottle, where you kept going and going and all of a sudden you were back where you had been, only in a different plane, violating the 3-dimension limit of Euclidean reality.

He forced the bear to struggle to its feet. He, they, the bear, poked a nosy black nose through the curtain and then squeezed the whole head out.

Ludi and Gene Deere stood a couple of paces apart in a low-ceilinged living room, crisscrossed with dark beams. The walls were plaster painted mustard-yellow. There were high casement windows with many small panes. Through them blew a breeze so full of forest smells that the little bear, with his acute animal sense of olfaction, felt both frightened and intoxicated.

Gene flopped an LP onto a Thorens turner and eased the stylus arm down.

Tell me, prayed Tex, I am not hearing the theme from the James Bond movie *Casino Royale.*

"You have to hear this on vinyl," Gene said. "There's this one track where they had the London Philharmonic out in a big studio, and Dusty Springfield with a mike inside this little tiny booth, and I swear, you can *actually hear the walls of the booth.* Listen."

He turned around, riding a little endorphin high of his own; and he looked right into the eyes of the bear. His smile faded.

"It's trying to get away," he warned Ludi.

Tex got the bear to make a whimpery little growl.

"Isn't he precious?" said Ludi.

"Isn't it illegal to keep a wild animal in your house?" said Gene.

Ludi shrugged. She beckoned Tex to come to her. "Is it?"

"I believe so. Besides which, I have no real desire to keep a wild animal in my house."

The bear waddled over to Ludi on his funny new feet.

"It'll just be for a while," said Ludi.

"What does *a while* mean?" said Gene. "A while until what?"

Ludi rubbed the bear on top of its head. "Until we think of something."

"So it's *we* now."

Quit being a prick, thought Tex. The little bear growled at Gene, not much more convincingly than before. Just wait a couple of weeks, Tex thought. I'll bite your pecker off.

Dusty Springfield began to sing "The Shadow of Your Smile." The savage beast mellowed out somewhat.

"What could their car be *doing* there, though, is what I wonder," said Ludi.

Gene sat down beside her in a stiff period chair that exhaled dust from its thin, worn-out cushion. "I can't answer that," he said. "But I wish your friends would come and get it. It's a bit of an eyesore. And something inside it doesn't smell very good."

"You've been inside it?"

"Well." The prick fidgeted. "I was looking for some kind of, I don't know. Record of ownership or something. Some identification."

"For Tex and *Molly*?" said Ludi. There was laughter in her voice. The bear liked that.

"For whoever owns the car," said Gene, testily.

"Forget it," said Ludi.

"I'd love to."

Ludi scratched the bear's ears, thoughtfully. "Do you mind if I take a look at it?" she said.

"Why should I mind? It isn't my car."

"And would you mind showing me," she said, her voice a little more deliberate, "the place where you found Tex's pendant? I'd just like to, you know—look for clues or whatever."

Gene nodded. "Why not?"

Ludi beckoned to Tex. "Come on sweetie," she said.

Behind them, Gene shut the door firmly, as though striving for a note of finality. He gave the bear a territorial glare.

Glaring back, the ghost inside the animal thought:

Don't mess with Texes.

LAST TIMES

1. The Saab.

The front passenger-side tire, with its slow leak, had gone flat. The windshield where the seal was broken had seeped water onto the dashboard, dissolving the ink on the labels of several cassettes.

"It's their car, all right," said Ludi. Her voice carried a certain tone of resignation. As though she had hoped, right up to the last moment, that it would turn out to be somebody *else's* ancient rusty Saab with beads and chickadee feathers dangling from the mirror. An easy and understandable mistake. But no.

Gene walked a couple of paces behind her, and the little bear toddled unsteadily to a drummer of his own. It came upon a chipmunk hole at the base of a cedar and sniffed at this suspiciously. Get used to it, kid, was Tex's advice. Rapacious little bastards are everywhere. But nobody much had ever minded Tex, and the little bear wasn't now.

Gene said, "You say you haven't seen them at all since that night?"

"At Eben's barn," said Ludi. "Just before the full moon."

Gene frowned. He was not attuned to the Pagan sense of time. "About the middle of last week?"

"I guess." Ludi hadn't started her summer job yet, so she wasn't plugged in to things like weeks. "I've been to their boat a hundred times, but there's no sign of them." After a bit more thought she amended: "*Almost* no sign."

Gene gave her a punctilious look. "Has there or has there not," he said, "been any sign of them?"

Ludi didn't notice the impatience in his voice. "You'd have to know Tex and Molly, I guess. I mean, maybe a couple of little things have moved around—but see, that's what the place would look like anyway. Whether they had been there or not."

"I see," said Gene. "So you're saying, the objects on your friends' boat are accustomed to moving themselves about? Whether anyone is aboard or not?"

Ludi looked at him like he was hopeless. He *was* hopeless, as far as Tex was concerned. "You'd have to see their boat," she said. "There's really no way to explain it."

Gene nodded in a knowing way. A wise-ass way. "Of course," he said.

The bear waddled over to Ludi. It raised its head, then—unable to contain itself—it lifted its front legs and rose to a two-legged stand.

"Hey, wow," said Ludi, taking its forepaws in her hands. "Look at this! What a great big tiny guy!"

Gene looked down with intense, though clinical, interest. "I absolutely do not believe this," he said. "A newborn animal should not be able to do these things."

"This is no ordinary baby," said Ludi. She bent low so that the bear could lick her cheeks. "This is—oo, he's slobbering me! This is *Tex*."

Gene sighed. "Yes. Well. I guess that explains it."

"Want to take a little walkie?" Ludi said, wiggling the furry paws. "Want to go for a little hikie in the woodsies?"

Gene led her across the road, to where the logging trail began. Ludi glanced back once at the old Saab that sort of hunched over, like a weary soul who was ready to ease into retirement, for sure, but had been hoping for something a little more dignified than this. Mud was caked on its fenders and one of the bumper stickers had started to peel. Ludi said, "What a shame."

But neither Gene nor the baby bear knew what she was talking about.

2. The forest.

Tex had expected to feel creepy, at best, and weepy, at worst, retracing his own final footsteps. To his surprise, the stroll through the cool spring woods was kind of a gas. The tiny furball got off on it—all these far-out nature smells and things to chew on and whatnot. But another thing was: I'm still *here,* dudes. I'm still hanging out and doing my own thing. It was like Tex had won some major bet. It was something like he had felt when he turned 40 and realized he *still* hadn't gotten around to cutting his hair and cleaning up his act. Only, of course, cosmically cooler.

Afterlife Factoid #11
There's no use acting like a grown-up
when you're not going to get any older.

"There's an old cellar hole back in there," said Gene, pointing off one side of the trail.

"That's neat," said Ludi. She glanced back to be sure little Tex was tromping along okay.

Gene said, "It's eye-opening, really. You tend to think that the general trend is for people to be spreading out everywhere, conquering new territory. But around here, there's plenty of evidence of the forest advancing and people being in retreat."

"Vinland," said Ludi.

Gene didn't stop walking, but he pivoted all the way around to look at her.

"You know," she said, "Vinland the Good? Where the Vikings lived? Lots of people think that was in Maine, you know. Right around here, maybe."

"The Vikings were in Labrador," Gene said over his shoulder.

"Yeah, right," said Ludi. "Only there are no grape vines in Labrador. And Vinland means vine-land, you know? As in grape vines? So it had to be someplace farther south."

"Nova Scotia," suggested Gene.

"Not enough trees," she said. "That's why it's named after Scotland. The Vikings always wanted to be someplace with trees, so they could build ships and houses. They wanted someplace that looked like Norway. *This* looks like Norway."

"Ever been to Norway?" asked Gene.

"Have you?"

He stopped walking for a moment, long enough for her to catch up. "Is there something about me," he said, "that impels you to provoke a constant argument? Do I *represent* something to you, something you violently disapprove of?"

Ludi looked at him closely. "I don't *violently* disapprove of anything."

"Somehow I knew you were going to say that."

"You did not."

"I did. But fine, don't believe me. Only don't you see, it's part of the pattern. Some little way to get that wedge in and pry open any possible area of disagreement between us."

"Why would I do that?"

"I honestly do not know."

The little bear moved in front of Ludi, pressing against her legs. Nudging her away from Gene.

"Is it much farther?" she asked. "I think Tex might be getting bored."

"I seriously doubt," said Gene, setting off again, "that bears get bored."

"That shows how much *you* know," said Ludi.

And for once, Gene remembered, or quickly learned, how to say nothing.

3. The rocks.

"Right around here," Gene said. He led Ludi to the boulder where he did his stretching exercises. "I looked at the ground and I—"

He paused. Something did not seem right to him.

The little bear practically rolled down the last stretch of the trail. His tiny legs were numb. His head felt stuffed with weariness. He wanted to find a nice patch of sunlight to curl up in, but Tex clamored on the inside to keep him alert. Just a little longer.

"What's the matter?" said Ludi.

"These rocks," Gene said, frowning. "They don't seem to be in the right—"

Tex looked at the boulders and the little bear's muscles seized up. He thought, *I don't believe it.*

The rocks had moved.

One huge chunk of greenstone had shifted to the left, and an adjacent slab to the right. Now there was a clear space between them, wide enough for a person to walk through.

"Has there been any kind of tremor activity around here?" asked Gene.

"You mean like an earthquake? I don't think so."

"Me neither." Gene paced back and forth. He did not have Tex's clear memory of how the rocks had been. But he remembered the one he had leaned against; his body knew the exact angle of its inclination. And he knew that now it was different. He turned with an expression of visceral discomfort. "It doesn't make any sense, though. They couldn't have just *moved.*"

"Sure they could," said Ludi. "Rocks move all the time."

"I know, but—I'm not talking about geologic time here. I'm talking about, *since last Thursday.*"

Ludi shrugged. To her there appeared no reason why rocks could not have moved since last Thursday. "So what's behind here?" she asked, poking her head into the breach.

"I'm not sure I would go through there," said Gene. "It might not be safe. If the formation is unstable—"

"Don't be a wuss. Rocks don't just move for no reason. Something's got to *move* them."

"Exactly," said Gene.

"Okay, then," said Ludi.

So finally:

4. The Well.

HOME (1)

It was easy. Now that you didn't have to know the secret way in. You just clambered through like Ludi was doing, displaying nicely the extent of her trim and muscular legs. The tired bear followed her out of love and fear and something like an animal intimation of the flowing of the Tao.

The old nomadic hunters had the idea that an animal would present itself to you at certain times, allow itself to be killed for the higher good of its blood, the common good of bloodkind. Tex hoped this wasn't what the little bear was up to. One Tex down the Well seemed plenty. Slow down, pardner, he advised. But nobody ever listened.

Up ahead, Gene said loudly, "Oh my gosh."

"What is it?" said Ludi, her view obstructed, hurrying to catch up with him.

"Um, I—excuse me," Gene said.

Ludi stepped out onto the final slippery ledge. "Whoops," she said. "Sorry."

Tex was dying by this time. The bear scrambled over the rocks, sliding on the damp surface, and almost *did* fall into the water. But Gene reached down and grabbed him (none too gently) by the scruff of the neck. Tex growled, but he was thankful. Then at last he saw what the fuss was about.

It was about two things. Three, if you count the bird.

#1, the Well was full of water. Full to the top. Where there had been a gaping hole, there was now a brimming dark pool with water roiling up from underneath, spilling over into a stream that had never existed before. The Well had become a spring.

#2, in the center of the dark spring swam a naiad. A water-nymph. She was blond, green-eyed, naked, angelic. Most of her was underwater, but you could see enough of her adolescent breasts to develop a large impediment to clear thinking if you were into that kind of thing.

#3, this being optional, a large bird with blue-black feathers was perched beside the spring in the limbs of a broken yew tree. The tree appeared to have been split through the heartwood by whatever force had cleft the rocks and given rise to the spring. The bird—a raven—was actively ignoring Ludi, Gene, and the naiad, so as to devote all its attention to the little bear.

"Gosh," said Gene. "Hey, we're sorry, we didn't mean to, um, startle you like this."

Tex thought this was no way to talk to a naiad. But the angelic creature said:

"You didn't startle me. I heard you coming a mile off. I hope you weren't planning on swimming here, though. I don't think there's room for two more. What a cute little bear. Is he yours?"

Gene and Ludi looked at one another. Tex began to suspect that the naiad (whose voice you might have called a tiny bit snotty) was perhaps not a supernatural creature after all. It was possible she was an actual girl.

She took a big breath and went under. You could see her white silhouette wavering there, beneath the dark surface. Then she faded, going deep. She was under a long time.

"Some swimmer," said Ludi.

"Yeah, I guess," said Gene. He seemed totally flummoxed. Obviously this was not the sort of day he had expected to have, a few short hours ago. "But who do you suppose—"

With a noisy parting of the waters, the girl came up again. She sucked in lungfuls of air and blinked up at Ludi and Gene.

"Still here?" she said.

"If you don't mind my asking," Gene said, "would you happen to know if this place was any, um, *different* a week or so ago?"

"If you don't mind my asking," said the girl, treading water, "who the fuck *are* you?"

"I'm Ludi," said Ludi. She pointed to the bear. "This is Tex. Some rednecks killed his mother."

The girl nodded. None of this seemed to faze her. It also did not faze her that she was naked in a pool with two grown-ups looking down at her.

"And um, I'm Gene," Gene said. For a smart guy, he sounded like a moron. "I live on the other side of the hill. And I've been hiking down this trail for months, but I've never seen this place before."

"No kidding," said the girl.

Ludi said, "Do you live around here?"

The girl nodded. "I guess. Kind of. Actually I don't live anywhere right now, in particular. I'm kind of between places."

"So how did you get here?" said Ludi. "We didn't see any cars."

"No kidding," said the girl. "Listen, if we're going to have this big conversation, why don't you help me out so I can quit paddling."

Ludi extended an arm. The girl pulled herself onto the ledge. She was thinner than she had looked in the water. Her limbs were like wooden toy things, and her hips protruded through the pale flesh. Water clung to the tiny, sun-colored hair on her legs. Her pubic hair made a ball no larger than a child's fist. She looked about 15 and on the borderline of anorexia. Maybe it was just a look.

Gene Deere narrowed his eyes and half turned his head, going through the motions of propriety. Then he decided not to worry about it, which is definitely what Tex would have recommended.

"Are you hungry?" said Ludi.

"Sure," said the girl. "I mean, look—I'm not a pitiful waif or anything. You don't have to feed me out of guilt. But sure, I'm *definitely* hungry. I've been out since like daybreak."

Ludi turned to Gene. "What have you got?" she asked.

"At the house?" He looked perplexed.

The girl told Ludi, "My name's Thistle, by the way. Thistle Herne." She stuck her hand out and Ludi shook it. Then the girl pointed to the raven. "That's Jack."

"Herne?" said Gene. "You wouldn't be related to—"

"Jack?" said Ludi.

"I'm not related to anybody," said the girl quickly. "In fact, I'm living under the name of Sanders now. I've got ID to prove it." She reached for a pocket that was not there, then seemed to recall that she had no clothes on.

"Ah," said Gene. "Well . . ."

He motioned toward the trail, raising his eyebrows, as though inquiring whether the ladies were ready to go.

"I should get dressed," said Thistle. She walked around the edge of the pool. Her clothes, strung on the branches of the yew tree, consisted of baggy cutoffs, a T-shirt with a bunch of frogs and the legend AMPHIBIAN ARGYLE, and a pair of hiking boots, sans socks. "Let's go, Jack," she said.

"You've got a pet raven?" said Gene.

"Sure," said Thistle.

The bird squonked. It agitated its wings, but didn't move from its branch.

"Actually he belongs to these people I'm kind of staying with. Or *actually*, he doesn't really belong to *anybody*. He just kind of hangs out there."

They headed off, over the rocks. Ludi looked back to be sure the bear was tagging along. Tex followed close behind Thistle, breathing her agreeable girl smell. Then—

RRRRRWWWAAAAA

—screamed the raven. The bear's heart opened and filled with blood and almost forgot to pump it out again.

Suddenly there were black wings everywhere, batting the bear's eyes, hammering his ears. Claws ripped down through the flesh over his scalp, laying open deep gouges. The pain felt like fire.

The little bear had no idea how to defend himself. The raven seemed to be everywhere at once, pummeling and scratching and gouging with its beak. Probably it could not really have killed a bear cub. But it was giving it a good shot. The best little Tex could do was rear up on his hind legs, flail his arms around, and let out a hearty bellow.

That scared off the raven for a few seconds. Tex bellowed again, and Ludi's voice called, "What's happening? Tex, sweetie, where are you?"

"He's here," said Thistle. "Jack is—Jack! Stop it! Here, somebody help."

Now the raven was back. Plunging for the eyes now.

"You fucker," he yelled at the bird in his silent, imaginary ghost-voice. "I'll get you for this."

OH, YOU WILL?

said the raven. The *Raven,* rather. And it flew straight at the little bear's head. It taunted:

GET ME, THEN.

The little bear lowered its head, barely in time. The claws tore at his ear.

"So," said Tex. "It's you."

Thistle had torn her T-shirt off and was beating the air with it, trying to drive the *Raven* away. Plucky little thing, thought Tex.

YES

said the *Raven.*

OF COURSE IT'S ME. THIS IS MY DOMAIN, IS IT NOT?

The bird swerved, out of range of Thistle's T-shirt. It dove briefly and tore at the girl's hair, but this was not a serious attack. More like the *Raven* was trying to make a point.

Tex said, "Looks like you've done a little redecorating."

The *Raven* said,

> YOU'VE MADE A FEW CHANGES YOURSELF. I CAN'T SAY I
> APPROVE OF YOUR CHOICE OF BODIES.

"What choice?" said Tex. "I got eaten. Then I got reborn, or some such thing. Don't ask me."

The bird went back to its perch on the yew tree. It gave Tex the evil eyeball, though he got the impression it was thinking things over.

Ludi was tugging at the bear's skin. "Come on," she whispered. "Let's go, let's get away from it." Then she stooped to look at the bear more closely. "Oh, look what a mess you are."

The *Raven* got her from behind, snagging her hair and yanking it hard.

Ludi screamed. She struck out at the bird, but just missed.

"Leave them alone!" Tex demanded.

The *Raven* said,

> MAKE ME.

"Fucking right I will," said Tex. "Now you listen to me."
And this time,
Somebody
did.

HOME (2)

 And he soared.
Up and up, spiraling sunwise, like an eagle.
The great black wings were his again.

Tex was in the raven, and the raven was Tex, and the *Raven* was gone. At least gone from the explicate plane: unseen and silent.

Down below, farther and farther, the little bear and the three freaked-out humans. Watching him fly away. Their mouths open, closing; but their words lost in a whir of wind, flutter of leaves, distant crash of waves, unceasing roar of sunshine.

There are times, thought Tex, when it feels *damn good* to be dead.

Then he thought twice about it and cocked up a wing and spiraled down again. Moonwise, like a hawk. He thought, One last look. Give them something to think about. It was the raven in him, the Trickster.

The little bear saw him coming but looked merely befuddled

about it. He was an ordinary bear now; as ordinary as he would ever get. The girl Thistle looked up next and gave him the finger. Ludi grabbed baby Tex up in her arms, getting more blood on her shirt. She was magnificent.

With an unearthly *qqqwwwwrrraaawrll*—startling only to a nonraven—Tex coasted over the dark water to the fallen yew tree. His impulsive act had acquired a certain meaning as it progressed. Not an infrequent phenomenon, he supposed. He took a perch on one of the branches that had twisted and snapped when the tree crashed down. Jesse said to Tex once that it takes weeks, even months, for a tree to die. If you cut one down, you have to keep its spirit propitiated for a *long* time. Tex looked over the yew tree, split violently through the trunk, and he could imagine the injured spirit trapped in there, as it eased down into oblivion.

With his beak, he grabbed a twig whose wood was still semi-green and pliable. A shriveled cluster of berries clung to their stem. The twig flexed resiliently; Tex could feel the woody tissue being crushed as he bit through it. Then he threw himself back into flight—that exhilarating moment when the kinetic energy of his body was transferred to the cushion of air—and turned east toward Dublin.

The *Linear Bee* rocked gently at its mooring, pressed by a sea breeze that had arisen as the afternoon sun warmed the land, drawing the ocean air inward. The acute raven eyes spotted Molly, laid out on the flying bridge, possibly sunbathing.

"Honey," he cried in an almost-human voice. "I'm home!"

Molly did not stir. As Tex spiraled lower, he saw that her eyes were closed; she was evidently in one of her trances. He landed on the railing and from there hopped down onto Molly's leg. His weight (about 5 pounds, he guessed) barely made her twitch. He deposited the yew twig in the middle of her stomach.

Then he hopped off her, onto the deck of the *Bee*. As soon as he touched it, he became himself again. That is, if the concept of *self* still had any definite meaning. He was an immaterial, graying, bearded, thirsty, and cranked-up dead hippie.

Stroking Molly's long brown hair, he said, "Wake up, Raven, I've got a bunch of stuff to tell you."

Then, lifting and twirling the yew twig:
"And I've brought company
for dinner."

&
for a time Molly almost let go,

let Ludi slip away. She had watched her confront Gene, question him about Tex's pendant, visit the Saab, and walk through the forest. She had seen the mama bear killed and the little bear born and then saved from the dangerous raven. She had watched Thistle rise from the Well. She had watched Gene and Ludi lock horns until it was clear that they were about evenly matched; except Molly would have bet on the feminine contestant as having the greater staying power. Now she wanted to go home to the *Bee*. She wanted to hang out in her own space and to go through the motions of some comforting ritual, like cooking dinner. Still, she hung on.

She was waiting for something.

She did not know what.

Back at the bungalow Ludi fed some Wheat Thins mushed up with water and nondairy creamer to Tex the bear, while Gene and Thistle surveyed the contents of the refrigerator. Out of the meager selection on offer, Thistle chose leftover beans & rice from Salazar's Genuine Home-Cooked Mexican Food, a take-out trailer parked at varying locations up and down Route 1. The air blowing out of the microwave smelled pretty good to her. It smelled like a number of things, not just the stuff from Salazar's. She wondered if Gene had ever cleaned it.

While eating, Thistle cruised the racks of LP's and CD's to which a wall of the living room was devoted. She pulled out Tod Machover's opera *Valis*, based on the Philip K. Dick novel. One-handed, scarfing greasy food directly from the paper plate with her mouth, she dropped the album into the player.

"Don't smudge that up," Gene said.

Thistle poked buttons on the Carver preamp. She turned the old McIntosh up to 6 and waited until the tubes glowed, then punched the player on SHUFFLE.

"Do you like Machover?" Gene asked her.

"Not really," she said.

"I don't either," said Gene. "But it's interesting. And you have to keep up, I think. Personally, I'm more attracted to the New Tonalists."

Thistle shrugged. The music started off slight and MIDI-sounding and got loud and full very fast. Ludi felt left out of things, on the floor nursing the sleepy bear. Thistle discovered the inglenook and lay down on one of its built-in benches. By the time Gene went in to ask her whether she wanted anything to drink, she was asleep. She slept deeply, like a child, with one arm thrown up beside her head, the wrist pressed against the carved oak backrest.

"Well," said Gene. "What now?"

Ludi peeked in, then out. "Let her sleep, I guess. Then when she wakes up, give her a ride back to wherever she's been crashing."

Gene's head popped up. He remembered: "Damn, the Rover. I left that back at Goddin."

Ludi thought this over. "I *could* take you to get it," she said. "Only who would look after Tex?"

"And her," said Gene. He stared down at Thistle as though she were some unstable chemical compound liable to change states unpredictably.

"Maybe she doesn't need looking after," Ludi said.

"Yeah. But maybe my house does. Who *is* she, is what I'd like to know."

"She told you her name. What more do you need?"

Gene gave her a look. Clearly he needed something besides that. He walked around his living room, picking things up, though he then did not appear to know exactly what to do with them. "This has been," he said, "the strangest day of my life."

"Yeah, well—it could get stranger."

He turned. His eyes were clear and sharp. His clothing was slightly askew; but that seemed in character, somehow. His Oxford-cloth cuffs were folded back so that you could see his wrists, which were almost abnormally thin. Ludi thought, He must get like *zero* upper-body exercise.

"You seem so bright," Gene told her, out of nowhere. "And

so . . . normal. Sometimes. But then again, you seem like a creature from another planet."

Ludi gave him what she hoped was a condescending smirk. "Hey, thanks," she said. "I was kind of hoping you'd notice." Which was true: because if a guy as straight as Gene Deere did *not* think she was weird, it was time to consider brain surgery.

"Maybe I should lay down," said Gene.

"Lie," said Ludi.

He nodded, weakly. "Maybe you should just go. And I'll just figure something out about my car in the morning. And about the bear. Or no: *Sefyn* can figure out something about my car, and *you* can figure out something about the bear."

"Sounds good to me," said Ludi. She looked down at Tex, who was snoring beside the sofa. "Well, hey—thanks for showing me around. It was very informative."

"De nada," said Gene.

Neither of them could think of a way to improve upon that, so Ludi walked out. It was starting to get dusky. The first spring peepers were singing back and forth. The air smelled so terrific— like the mountains, and everything growing, and negative ions, and wildflowers—and every breath made you feel so full, you could almost start shouting, just to release some of it.

At the door of the Volkswagen, Ludi realized she did not know how to get home from here. On the other hand, she did not want to go back and ask Gene for directions. That would spoil her otherwise flawless exit: Molly would not have approved. Anyway, she had the *Atlas*.

Molly—still hanging in—was flattered to find herself popping up in Ludi's thoughts. (And it was true: she would *not* have approved.) She wondered how badly Ludi was going to get lost.

INSURGENCE

So badly, it was half a tank of gas later when she rolled into the parking area below her apartment. She was exhausted and mad at herself. And to put the icing on it, she couldn't find a place to park. The place was full of beaten-up vehicles, among which she recognized those of a couple of Street Players. And in the middle of everything, taking up at least 3 human-scale parking spots, sat an outrageous Eldorado gleaming with custom chromework. A pirate flag flew from the tallest of its several antennas.

Climbing the stairs to her door, Ludi was ready (she thought) to face, to disapprove of, and if necessary, to evict whoever and whatever she found waiting in her living room. Even so, the scene alarmed her.

The air was heavy with hemp smoke. The Venetian blinds had been drawn shut. All the furniture was drawn into a sort of trapezoidal cluster in the center of the room. Indigo Jones was there, and Rainie Moss the gardener, and Sara Clump the electrician, plus—inescapably—Guillermo.

But that was not all. Oh no. Beside them, and seeming to glow in the smoky gloom, was one of the whitest-skinned people Ludi had ever seen—the more so because

(a) he wore no shirt and was covered from the waist up (at least) with polychrome tattoos, chiefly of serpents and dragons, and

(b) he was sitting on the arm of a chair whose primary occupant was a large and very dark-skinned teenager, wearing a woven-reed Panama hat equipped with a small, solar-powered fan. In Ludi's apartment, where the only light came from an undercabinet fluorescent in the kitchen, the fan was motionless.

Both of these strangers looked a little older than the girl Thistle, but not much.

Guillermo glanced up when Ludi slammed the door.

"It's about time," he said. "Where've you been?"

"Performing an emergency cesarean," she told him.

He made a sour face. Like, Very funny. "Well, you've missed some pretty interesting discussion. We were just about to take a vote on going forward with our next action."

Ludi walked into the kitchen, where she flipped on the bright overhead double-circline fixture, a semicool relic of the Other 60's, the one moms and dads had lived in. Most of the kitchen was of the same period: aquamarine refrigerator, speckled Formica countertops, and a wood-veneer breakfast bar with matching stools. In the slightly uncanny light of the low-watt bulbs, the whole thing glowed like a vision brought on by martinis and Frank Sinatra.

"Good god," moaned Guillermo. "Couldn't you turn that down a little?"

"It doesn't turn down," said Ludi. "It turns *on.*"

Very faintly, like a mosquito whine, Ludi could hear the clock radio in the bedroom playing Van Morrison, who had apparently chosen the WURS late-nite rock show to die on.

"This is Saintstephen and Shadow," said Guillermo, pointing to the teenagers. He did not indicate which was who. The white one, whose hair also was devoid of pigmentation, gave her a cryptic hand-sign.

"Peace with honor," he said. His voice was sticky with saliva.

I feel, thought Ludi, as though I am standing upon the threshold of Hell.

"Come, sit," said Indigo Jones. He motioned grandly to a place on the sofa that was occupied by Sara Clump. Evidently Sara was expected to relocate. Of course, she did not. She glared at Ludi as though it had been *her* idea.

"You can sit here," said Rainie Moss, indicating a portion of her own chair into which a cat might have squeezed.

Ludi looked at all of them, one at a time. "I seriously think," she said, "if I have to listen to 'Brown-Eyed Girl' one more time, I'm going to turn into a cantaloupe."

"I hear you," said the kid with the Panama hat. When he looked at her, facing the kitchen, the fan on his hat-brim started very slowly to rotate.

"I kind of like some of his later work with the Chieftains," said Rainie.

"Give me a break," said the kid with tattoos. Ludi thought that for purposes of taxonomic convenience she would assign this one the name Saintstephen, and the other Shadow, though this seemed marginally racist.

"Could I ask," she said, "what you all are doing in my living room at 1:30 in the morning?"

"If you'd *been* here," said Guillermo, "we wouldn't have to run it all down again."

"I don't want you to run anything down," said Ludi. "I want somebody to answer my question. Then I want you all to leave so that I can get some sleep."

"Wo," said Indigo Jones, drawing back into the flattened cushions of the sofa. He had just lit a fresh Philly, at which he now stared as though unsure whether it was safe to become any higher.

"Don't get mad at *us*, Ludi," said Sara Clump. "We're just doing what we ought to have been doing all along. We're trying to get serious about shutting Gulf Atlantic down."

Ludi let out a breath that made a sound escaping her mouth like *Oh*, but she did not mean "Oh." She did not mean anything.

Unless perhaps it was Please no more about Gulf Atlantic in one day. She sat down on a stool at the breakfast bar. "What goes into a martini?" she said.

"Do you want to hear about it before we vote?" said Guillermo, gratingly. "Or do you just not care?"

"Gin and dry vermouth," said Rainie. "Three to one."

"Thank you," said Ludi. "No."

"Four to one," said Shadow (if that was his name).

"To make a long story short," said Indigo, "we're about to vote on whether to try to disrupt the propagation systems at the Goddin plant. Which we think would seriously impede any kind of gene-splicing experiments they've got going on."

"And these guys," said Sara, indicating the two teenagers, "are going to help us."

"Help us what?" said Ludi. "Get arrested? Why don't you guys just stick to something easy, like tree-spiking? That way at least you get some fresh air." She peered into cabinet doors under the bar, looking for leftover liquor from last year's Unemployment Day bash.

"*Anything* to one," said Rainie. "As long as it's cold when you serve it."

"We've got some major intelligence," Guillermo confided. He looked from side to side with gravely lowered head: his Jungle Command Post Pre-Strike Briefing mode. "We've learned that they're planning a major powwow in just a few weeks. The C.E.O. himself is coming up from Houston. A guy called Burdock Herne. He apparently runs the company on a tight leash, so his appearance must indicate that they're getting ready for some kind of major push. Therefore the time to strike is *now*. That's what the vote is about. Because this is something that touches all of us."

Sure it does, thought Ludi. *Todos somos Sandinistas,* right? She was sick of it.

"You just hold the glass of gin," said Indigo, who had resumed work on his hemp buzz, "and you *show* it a bottle of vermouth." His round belly rose and fell in a graduated series of chuckles— like one primary laugh followed by a number of aftershocks. This was noiseless, however, as he was holding the smoke in.

"You don't even have to do that," said Shadow, not to Indigo but to Ludi. She wondered if he was flirting with her. "You just swirl the gin around a little and you whisper over the top of it, *Vermooooooth.*"

"Well, here goes nothing," Ludi said from the kitchen. "Cheers, everybody."

"Cheers," most of them said. Only Guillermo looked at her as though full of regret, and Sara Clump glared at everyone.

Ludi took a sip, then a swallow. She did not like the taste of the martini, but she saw immediately what the point of it was.

"Okay," she said. "Good night, everybody. Nice meeting you, Shadow and Saintstephen, whoever you are."

"Wait, wait," said Indigo, looking up helplessly from the sofa. "We haven't voted yet."

"All in favor—" said Guillermo.

"No," shouted Ludi. So loud that it surprised her. "Get *out* of here. Go down and vote in the *parking* lot. Vote in the middle of the *street.* Just get out of my home

right

now."

COME FLY WITH ME

There was one of those Music of Your Life stations on AM. Ludi found it without much trouble. She liked the way the dial lit up, green and floaty like the numbers were underwater. She lay on her back, entertaining thoughts about the function of music in a pluralistic society. Does it unite, or stratify? Transcend boundaries or codify them?

"If you could use some exotic booze," she sang along, "there's a bar in old Bombay."

In her dreams, she soared like a bird. She floated like the Goodyear Blimp. Then she crashed like the mid-Atlantic phone grid.

HOME (3)

Molly found Tex nodding off in the living quarters of the *Bee.* The radio was playing the Them version of "Gloria." Just when you think it can't possibly get worse.

"Hey, Bear?" she said, poking him. Her ethereal fingers penetrated slightly into whatever he was composed of. But the touch got his attention anyhow.

"Raven," he said sleepily. "What time is it?"

"What difference does that make?" she asked. Genuinely wondering.

He looked wounded, and immediately she felt bad for having spoken sharply, so she sat down beside him, patting his more or less virtual hand.

Afterlife Factoid #12
The dead have feelings like everybody else.

"I guess I'm just tired," she said.

"Yeah." He stretched and aimed a finger at the radio. "If they're going to crawl that deep in the catacombs, why not play some Pearls Before Swine?"

"Or Love," said Molly.

"Tim Buckley."

"Moby Grape."

"It's a Beautiful Day."

"We should get our own show," said Molly. "We've got time now."

Tex laughed, and she leaned her head on his shoulder. It felt warm. Sort of like a pillow of gentle energy.

"It's good to see you again, Bear," she said.

"You too."

She felt him stir, as his thoughts worked their way through him: a trait he retained from life. Obviously there is a lot to this mind/body conundrum that biology has not yet accounted for.

"I've got stuff to tell you," said Tex. "But I don't know if I've got the energy."

Molly nodded. She cuddled closer to him. *Into* him. The two of them seemed slightly, here and there, to overlap. "That's weird, isn't it?" she said. "Not having the energy. Because if we're not like, pure energy, then what are we?"

"Mm." He pulled her close. She nuzzled his shoulder. "Do you want to get in bed?" he asked.

"I don't know. Do you suppose pure astral energy can sleep?"

Tex stood and reached out for her. She drifted up into his arms.

He said, "On a night like this,
I'm ready to believe
anything."

O

"It's only a beginning, always."

—RICHARD M. NIXON, resignation speech

or
was it morning again?

Did the tide move again under the boats in Dublin Harbor? Did the sun flash all the visible colors and then some through the cut-glass prism in the pilot house of the *Linear Bee?* Yes or no?

If yes, then a stripe of chromium yellow would have splashed across the raven feathers and a couple of rocks and the steer skull from Jerome, Arizona. As the houseboat rose, the colors would have red-shifted, like interstellar light. As it fell, they would have vanished in the ultraviolet. And on WURS, Bad Cathy would have been wrapping up a set.

"Come on, folks. Is it just me? I mean, 'Me *muchacho*—you *muchacha.*' Do you wonder why they built a big erection and shot it off at the moon?"

Again.

If no, then maybe Tex just rolled over and felt Molly. More than he felt himself, even, or the bedclothes rumpled beneath him, or the air moving cool and damp across his back, he felt the well-known intricate womanscape of Molly rising and curling and breathing beneath his hand, shifting gently in response to his touch. His fingers moved in response to her shifting, and she rolled nearer to him and he rolled halfway to meet her. Her eyes were still closed, but she murmured—

Bear

—as probably she had done a thousand times, or a million: some definite number but not a number that is known. Not even a number that the Universe remembers. A secret number that exists not in Tex's mind or Molly's but in the space they have made between them, in the little akashic alleyway where their private spaces overlap. In that dark infolded place that is neither Tex nor Molly but both of them, things are known that we do not know. Stories are told that we do not hear.

We know this, however.

━━━━━━━━━━━ ⚓ ━━━━━━━━━━━

Afterlife Factoid #13
The dead can make love.
It's heaven.

"Are we still here?" said Tex. After a certain indefinite interval. Molly smiled. She twinkled his little silver earrings. She said: "Would you like some tea?"

Again?

"Yes."

TWININGS

In the galley of the *Linear Bee,* Molly watched tea leaves drift and settle, forming tiny galaxies at the bottom of the pot.

For all she knew, everything was spelled out there, in the random constellations of darkness within darkness. The comings-together and driftings-apart (and collapses, and annihilations) of the Universe are random like the falling leaves, and yet beneath the randomness is a beautiful order. The molecules of water are separate but they interpenetrate, they flow together and become one thing. The Majolica pot is a bucket of particles, millions of molecule-sized droplets all jumbled up; but it is also a tiny ocean of waves, governed by an orderly and irreducible dynamic. Matter is built of atoms which are built of particles which are built of quarks. But also matter is *Mater,* the Dark Mother, the foaming firmament of all possibilities, the infinite womb of the unmanifest.

Molly came up for air. This reminded her of the revelation she had experienced once while doing acid, when she realized that her TV remote control contained the same secret code employed by the I Ching. The code derived from this same paradox—the contradictory nature of quantum reality—which in the I Ching is neatly reduced to two symbols, the simplest of all symbols: the solid line of continuity, waves, undivided space, oil paintings and analog hi-fi

———

and the broken line of quantum events, particles, separateness, television screens and digital audio.

— —

In that earlier flash of understanding, Molly had taken one look at the little keys that mean STOP and PAUSE, and she had grokked that the quantum contradiction is hard-wired into your brain. The first symbol is absolute, whole, and unambiguous; the second is merely a space between Before and After, a separation, fraught with uncertainty.

Two things. Irreconcilable. But eternally twined. And ever so slightly asymmetrical, because the arrow of time (viz, the PLAY button) gets involved.

Which, of course, the I Ching also takes into account. Hexagram 63, Already Done, consists of three pairs of STOP and PAUSE lines stacked up in a kind of shaky tower—

☲☵

—which looks balanced but it is not. The oldest of the many layers of text and commentary that have grown around it like a coral reef warns you, *There will be good fortune to begin with, but chaos at the end.* And indeed this triple-decker STOP & PAUSE sign is associated with upheaval, revolution, and the ancient funerary rite known as the Dance of Yu: an asymmetric, lame-legged movement that is choreographed by the hexagram itself. The good leg takes a step, making a clean break; then the injured leg drags.

Brokenness and continuity: the universal dance of the Otherworld. It is the gait of Oedipus (whose name means Swollen Foot) limping to Colonus. Of Cinderella, wearing an Otherworld enchantment and only one shoe, skipping home from the ball. Of Rumpelstiltskin, one foot caught in the floor, hopping in rage, then vanishing into the nether realm from which he came. Of the Crane, emblem of Celtic eternity, perched on a single leg, its long neck twining into a multidimensional knot. All these things are connected; they all lead back around to the same thing; they form a mysterious circle that models the circuits of the human mind.

All of this, Molly divined in her teapot, while the Earl Grey steeped.

Wow, she thought.

Afterlife Factoid #6 (Review)
Death's an absolute mind-scrambler.

She poured the tea and stuck her head into the sleeping cabin. "Bear?" she called.

But Tex had gone back to sleep. He lay half-curled on his left side, the covers pulled unevenly around him, one worn, bony hand resting lightly on his injured leg.

SPIRALS

Tex dreamed of being a bird. A magical bird, with great wings like a condor, a quick retentive mind like a parrot, and X-ray eyes like Superman.

He spread his wings. He rode upon the air.

Below him, a complicated threadwork of roadways stretched outward like protein strands, organizing the living plasm of the countryside. Houses and yards were small and intensely ordered, like mitochondria. Woods lay dark and blobby, like vacuoles. Motor vehicles shunted like metabolites. It was easy to think of the land as a great living thing, an organism, and to imagine human beings simply as parts of it, intelligent organelles working together like a strung-out, slightly paranoid nervous system.

On the other hand, it was just as easy to think of the human presence as an out-of-control, metastasizing cancer. Growing at all costs. Feeding itself by whatever means necessary, discharging its waste products into the bloodstream, invading all the available territory. In the long run, inevitably, killing its host.

Which vision was correct? Neither, probably. Both. Two things at once, the truth lying in some dimension beyond them.

Tex swooped low over Eben Creek's barn, glimpsing through its cracks the props and costumes of the Cold Bay Street Players.

He had conceived the Players, originally, as a kind of crystal, a seed, like a strand of DNA inserted into the chromosomes of Mother Nature. From it would spring forth new structures, new organs of perception, fresh ways of seeing and relating to the other, non-human constituents of the world. Instead, the strand had itself undergone a sort of meiosis: splitting into two separate and irreconcilable parts.

Tex flew south. He followed Route 1 down to Glassport, soaring over the credit-card center, Dan Dan's Pizza Scene, Pickup City, Pippa Rede's magic circle, the Church of Mankind's Destiny Among the Stars. Through a window of the church Tex saw a poster urging parishioners to attend this year's Walk for Life, proceeds to benefit the Dublin County AIDS Coalition. There was no figuring Christians, Tex thought. With Witches, at least, you knew where you stood.

West of Glassport the countryside rumpled into hills and then small mountains, carved by rivers and scooped into ponds. Out here, where real estate was cheaper, Rainie Moss's farmhouse stood amid neat geometric formations of organic herb beds. Sara Clump lived in a mobile home with her older, motherly lover. Indigo Jones raised chickens and goats, which caused problems for his neighbors. Deep Herb moved in and out of group houses where people kept odd hours and did not exhibit recognizable patterns of social interaction.

Tex wondered why he had never seemed to befriend anybody *normal*. He flew higher, spiraling toward the clouds, hoping to get things in broader perspective.

From up here, the Earth was beautiful. And yet the Earth was sick. You didn't have to be a magical bird to see that.

Everyone felt the sickness; it pervaded the living body of the world; its symptoms afflicted everybody.

The Wal-Mart crowd felt it in the disaffection of their kids, the decline of values, rampant crime, mindless crap on television. The Real Food Co-op crowd felt it in poisoned air and water, a tax system stacked in favor of the rich, a culture whose only creed was unrestrained consumption. For people of Tex's generation it was the small-mindedness, the lack of transcendent values, the pervasive cynicism and apathy that seemed to define Generation X. For the Xers, it was a world in which nothing of value was left for them, in which all belief systems were equivalently vapid.

Tex supposed that for himself, the heart of the sickness lay in the increasing ugliness everywhere—the replacement of woods and fields and unrestricted views with stores and parking lots and a haze of car exhaust that blocked your view of Cadillac Mountain, the first place in America to be touched by the rising sun.

But if the world was sick, like the Waste Land, languishing under some strange curse, then what was the key to breaking the enchantment? Where was the Grail Castle, hidden in changing mists? Who was the Wounded King?

Tex sighed. His dream unrolled, sweeping him northward.

In a blink, like magic, Da Turtle's Hostel lay below him, green and lush and secretive. The tree cover was dense and you could not see much of it, but you could see the bear-trail leading in, and the graveled parking area, and the clearing Syzygy had made to build her house. You could see Leman Pond, but you could only imagine, if you knew they were there, the wolf pens down in their marshy hollow. Tex hovered for a while, remembering it all, but it made him sad and he let it go.

Past the Hostel the land got scruffier, trees younger and rangier, as you passed over the woodlots and penny-ante tree farms and hayfields and abandoned sheep pastures of Applemont. If you knew what to look for, you could spot the tiny marijuana gardens, plots of no more than a quarter acre, usually tucked in among some kind of cover crop. Even before the advent of a locally bred strain, Waldo 44/57 (whose numbers referred to the latitude of Applemont and the estimated days from sowing to harvest, respectively), marijuana had been the #2 cash crop of Dublin County, second to lumber products. Now it unquestionably was #1. To the extent that the family farm survived in this part of the United States, it was due to the persistence and Yankee ingenuity of these small-scale hemp growers.

The northern edge of Applemont coincided with the perimeter of the Goddin base. Tex thought of all the Air Force aviators who, during 5 decades of Cold War, had approached its runways just the way he was now, swooping in low, skimming the treetops. But the analogy between himself and a nuclear bomb-dropper was too weird, even for Tex. He blinked away the runways and hangars and focused instead on the rectangular patches laid out between them, where a million young saplings (by his quick, Superman's-eye count) stretched their limbs up at him, waving in the summer breeze.

So this, thought Tex, is what they mean by "Forest Research Station." Acre upon acre of genetically optimized, cloned and tissue-cultured wood-making machines. It gave him a chill like the one he had felt when he heard the phrase "prescription turf" used to describe the grass on a football field.

Just before he swooped past the northern fence line, more than ready to put the place behind him, Tex's quick corvoid brain flashed onto a perception that ordinary human consciousness would have rejected as too ridiculous to contemplate. In the final series of trial plots—a row of 4-acre rectangles nestled against the chain link and barbed wire—he detected a familiar pattern of dusty green, sharply lobed, pinnate leaves. If he did not recognize it for a several seconds, this might have been because it was *too* familiar. Then he eased up on the airfoils of the great condor wings and drifted lower, spiraling slowly southward.

Ridiculous, yes—but there it was: a perfect, orderly series of marijuana plots. The plants were huge for this early in the season, their leaves tinged bronze. It must be a pure or nearly pure strain of *sativa*, the Mexican species that grows too tall for backyard gardens and seldom flowers anyway, this far north. From which Tex deduced

(a) that these fuckers weren't worried about getting caught, and

(b) that they weren't growing this pot with the idea of harvesting flower buds; and therefore

(c) that something very strange was going on.

Tex spiraled around and around. Eventually he made himself dizzy. The dizziness turned into wooziness, like you feel when you're halfway stuck in a dream and halfway trying to wake up, to respond to—say—objectionable music issuing from your clock radio. Then Tex realized that he *was* waking up; the magical bird was dematerializing; the only thing left of his dream was one lingering image—a glorious vision of amber waves of pot.

THE MESSENGER

 Molly was tidying up the *Bee,* though she couldn't think why—was she expecting company?—when she found a sprig of some dark-needled evergreen, still hanging on to a clutch of last year's withered berries. Tex must have brought it home from somewhere, for unfathomable reasons of his own. The resinous sap was sticky, and the needles left a fresh, pungent smell on her fingers, so Molly popped the sprig into a little Swedish rooting ball that hung from a bracket in the galley. You never knew what was going to take root, given a chance—Molly once succeeded in growing roses from florist's cuttings—and in any case it was her policy not to discard a plant until she was absolutely certain it was dead.

When Tex woke up at last and came bouncing into the galley, he discovered her staring at the little evergreen as though waiting for some vestige of life to declare itself.

"Molly," he told her, "you won't believe it."

Not believe something? That was hard to imagine. She smiled, pointed at the Sun mug. "Want me to nuke your tea?"

"Funny you should mentions nukes," said Tex. "My god— what's that?"

He stared at the rooting ball. Molly looked.

The sprig she had placed in water only a short time ago (she was not certain how long, now that Time had lost its moorings in mortality—but surely not *that* long) was beginning to grow. As she and Tex watched, it sprouted tiny new olive-green candles that extended into stems from which needles emerged in a regular, distichous pattern—the alternating featherlike structure common in conifers and grasses but not elsewhere. From the bottom of the sprig rootlets formed and ramified. The rooting ball became crowded with them. It was like a nature film done in time-lapse photography, only cooler because you didn't have those jerky leaps from one frame to the next.

"Better get that thing out of there," said Tex, "before the glass breaks."

Then the glass broke. The prophet sighed. Molly leaned forward as quickly as she could, and droplets of water and particles of glass spattered onto her hands. The sprig itself—now grown to the stature of a minor branch—had gotten wedged in the wrought-iron bracket, where the swaying motion of the boat made the little thing appear to be squirming to free itself.

But just because you're hallucinating doesn't mean there *aren't* alien monsters in your kitchen. The little evergreen flexed; its stems fattened and stiffened. It turned toward the light, and its dangling root mass squirmed in what must have been a desperate grasping for soil and water.

"What *is* it?" Molly asked. As though Tex could have told her.

Tex told her: "It's a yew. It was growing out by the Well. The Well's a spring now. There was a naiad swimming in it. Only the naiad turned out to be just a teenage girl. The yew was dying, so I brought a piece of it home. I was a raven at the time, see, although just before that I had been a bear. Before that I was an acorn. It's kind of complicated."

Molly looked back and forth between Tex, who was hard to believe, and the writhing yew, which was impossible.

Afterlife Factoid #14
Being dead takes some getting used to.

The yew branch looked plaintive now: all hung up and helpless with its roots flapping in the air. *Save me*, it seemed to cry out.

So Molly grasped it carefully by the thickest part of the stem and lifted it free of the wrought-iron bracket and held it out before her.

"About time," said the yew.

Then the yew turned into a woman and jumped out of Molly's hands, landing with two (size 11) feet on the glass-and-water-strewn deck.

This was not like computerized morphing. In actuality, the way such transformations occur is more like the way you look at a certain image on paper and over the course of time you under-stand that you can see it in more than one way. Like one of those 3-D graphics that emerge out of a pattern of color-specks; or the more old-fashioned optical illusions where a thing can either be a wineglass or it can be two faces staring at one another. That's how the yew branch revealed itself to be a woman. Molly came to see how, really, it had been a woman all along. A yew branch, too. Both. Or more than both.

She wondered if there was any Dramamine on board.

"Some place you've got here," the yew woman said. Her voice was ripe with sarcasm.

Tex shot a quick, apologetic glance at Molly—like, When you've been around as long as I have, kiddo, you learn to take this sort of thing in stride. She resented his attitude.

The yew woman was not remarkable-looking, one way or the other. She appeared to be in early middle age, trim and healthy. There were frown-lines at the eyes and mouth. A touch of gray in the hair. Clothing dark and sensible. Something bothersome, an air of morbidity, about the way she carried herself. Little man-nerisms with the hands—a habit of rubbing them, one at a time, along the opposite wrist—that might get annoying after a while. All in all, about what you'd expect of a yew tree.

"So, hey," said Tex, making conversation, "are you another dryad, or what?"

"*Another* dryad?" said the woman.

"I'm a friend of Beale's," Tex explained.

"Who's Beale?" said Molly.

Tex shrugged. "Oh, just this oak tree guy."

The yew woman nodded. "I see. Well, perhaps that's why I was sent to you."

"You were sent?" said Tex. "To me? But I thought it was *me* that picked up *you*."

"Don't be sophomoric," said the woman. "You ought to know that no possibility exists in isolation. All movement arises from the Field." Her lips curled in a sort of smirk. "When did you die, yesterday?"

"A couple of weeks ago," said Molly. "I think. Do you have any idea what day it is?"

"It's still the Day of the Humans," said the woman. "Unfortunately."

Tex and Molly eyeballed one another. Tex made a little wiggle of the brow, as though assuring her that whatever she might be thinking, he wholeheartedly agreed.

Molly gave the yew woman a sweet smile that she used on rude checkout clerks at the Co-op, where people sometimes were a bit too sure of their moral correctness to bother with being polite. She said, "Would you like to have a seat in the living quarters? I'm sure you must be tired, after all you've been through."

The woman lifted her gaze to the ceiling. Her hair rustled, very faintly, like a bed of fallen needles. "You can't even *begin* to imagine," she said.

"Oh, I'm sure," said Molly.

The yew woman left the galley, looking for a place to plant herself.

"Was your friend Beale like this one?" Molly said quietly to Tex.

"No, no. He was cool. He was . . . odd. And he *changed*—you know, like he was trying to find a human form that he could get comfortable with. But he had a good heart. Or whatever."

"Pith," suggested Molly. "Then, what's the matter with *her*?"

"Hey," said Tex, shrugging, "you know how it it with yews. The Final Tree, right? Thrice deadly. Most beloved of the Worm."

"What are you talking about?"

"You'll see," said Tex. He goosed her below the ribs, prodding her into the living quarters, where their houseguest had taken up a central position on the sofa. Goblin the Cat-Person lurked nervously under the coffee table.

Molly entered with the Majolica pot. "Care for some tea?" she asked.

The yew woman raised her head a few degrees higher than was absolutely necessary. "I don't drink the juice of other species," she said.

Molly nodded. "I've heard *that* before."

"So," said Tex, sliding into an armchair, under the wide leaves of a pinanga palm, "do you have a name or anything?"

"Or anything?" said the yew woman. "I have many things. If a name makes you feel more at ease in your dealings with me, then I shall answer to the name of Idho."

"As in My Own Private?"

"No."

They fell into a three-way stare. Goblin slunk over and wrapped himself around Tex's leg. Tex reached down to give him a dutiful stroke.

"Is this cat gaining *weight*?" he asked, mystified.

"Beats me," said Molly. "There's a 40-pound bag of cat food in the pantry."

"I assume," said Idho, the yew woman, "you have matters you would like to discuss with me."

"We do?" said Molly.

Idho fixed her eyes upon Tex. The pupils were exceptionally dark and hungry-looking. For an instant he felt a tightening of the throat.

"You mentioned," he said, uncertainly, "you were *sent* to us?"

"I did."

"Could you, um—elaborate on that? A little? Please?"

Idho sighed. She crossed one leg over the other. As she moved, her body seemed to shift from plane to plane: the yew's rough, blackened bark supervening the dark fabric of her slacks, then fading again. She allowed a few moments to pass, then spoke abruptly.

"You have been in the presence of the Bishop of Worms."

Tex flinched: an involuntary reaction that caught Molly's eye. "The *who*?" she said.

Tex shook his head. "You don't want to know."

Idho appeared to smile very thinly, though this might have been a shadow briefly falling across her face. "The Worm," she said, "has given due thought to your petition. And I have been elected to deliver Its reply."

"Would somebody," said Molly, "like to tell me what is going on?"

Idho flicked a glance at her.

"Later, babe," murmured Tex. He had gone pale, as though the mere recollection of the Bishop of Worms was sapping his vitality.

"Why later?" said Idho. "I have been sent with a message and I am quite sure the message is intended for both of you. You are in this quest together, are you not?"

"Quest?" said Tex. His eyes rolled, as though he felt seasick.

Molly took his hand. "Of course we are," she said firmly.

Idho regarded the two of them in apparent distaste.

"Very well. Now the Bishop, of course—" with a nod toward Molly "—is the Destroyer of Forms. The Gaping Maw Beyond Eternity. That Which Endlessly Devours Yet Remains Unfilled."

Molly nodded, paying careful attention, like a student in the front row. "You mean like Kali, the Goddess of Destruction?"

"Bush league," said Idho. "The Worm excretes a billion Kalis with every drop of Its blessed sweat."

Molly looked at Tex, who grimaced. "Smelled like it, too," he said.

Molly nodded for Idho to continue.

"This deceased human," the yew woman said, not quite deigning to look Tex in the eye, "had the presumption to appear before the Worm with a request that certain matrices of morphic potential be spared from the Maw and allowed to remain a while longer in the Field of Possibilities."

"Pardon me?" said Molly.

"Dryads," Tex said quietly. "Tree spirits. White oaks, and a bunch of other things. All the stuff that's being wiped out from the woods around here. You know, the subspecies, the variant strains—all the forms that are lost when you convert forests to tree plantations. See, this guy Beale explained it to me. Sort of."

"I doubt," said Idho, "that Beale or any other of my kind could succeed in explaining very much to *you*. Obviously you have failed even to begin to comprehend the nature of the implicate form-creating fields that you call *dryads,* to take a relatively minor point. Nonetheless, a petition was made to the Worm, and the Worm, in Its omnivorous knowingness, has pronounced a ruling, which I shall hereby relay to you. I suggest that you attempt to stabilize yourselves."

Tex and Molly exchanged glances. Wordlessly, each tightened his or her grip on the other's hand.

"Shoot," said Tex.

Idho smiled. She raised her arms, which turned into scaly limbs and then to tree adders. The adders uncoiled, lashing out and seizing Tex and Molly around the necks and squeezing until it seemed their heads would explode.

Then their heads exploded.

THE WORM SPEAKS

 On WURS, Indigo Jones began a long set of Julian Cope ditties.

The sun set and rose and set and rose over Dublin Harbor.

Ludi came and watered the plants and fed the cat and left again.

Two guys got stabbed outside the biker bar on Water Street.

In Glassport, another proposed school budget was voted down. The heavens opened. The wind shifted to seaward. Waves slapped like rubber flippers against the hull.

After a week or so, the voice of the Worm fell silent.

On the *Linear Bee,* things settled down. Sort of.

MITES?

Molly raised her hands very tentatively to feel her head. There was *something* there, at least. She looked over at Tex. He was clutching his throat.

Idho still sat in the middle of the sofa. She stared at her fingernails as though checking for stains beneath the tips of them.

"Come again?" said Molly.

"Please," said Idho, disdainfully. "Don't make me repeat myself. It will be worse the second time."

"Yeah, really," croaked Tex. He sounded as though his throat was lined with newsprint. "I think I got the gist of it."

"You did?" said Molly. Like, incredulous.

He nodded. "You've just got to get used to the guy's accent, I guess." He turned to Idho. "But what I want to know is: did he say *mites?"*

"Mites," repeated Idho. "That is correct."

"Mites?" said Molly. Like, even more incredulous.

"That's what I thought," said Tex. "So listen—what's so special about mites?"

"What are you *talking* about?" said Molly.

Tex patted her hand. He continued to stare at Idho. "I mean, why would the Bishop grant my request in consideration of the *mites?*"

"The Bishop," said Idho—shrugging, as though this ought to be obvious enough—"is exceptionally fond of mites."

"I see," said Tex.

"Well, *I* don't," said Molly.

"Obviously you do not," said Idho. "Obviously you are both completely blind."

"*Half*-blind," said Molly, huffily. "You don't have much in the way of manners, for a divine immortal Nature spirit, or whatever you are."

Idho smiled. It was the smile of a satiated jackal. "Whatever I am," she said, "is not a well-mannered thing. It comes of dining on putrefaction, I suppose. The Bishop is exceptionally fond of *me,* also."

"Wait," said Tex. "Tell me what's such a big deal about mites."

Idho sighed. "Mites," she said wearily, "are the supreme guarantors of the health of a forest. They are the caretakers of elderly trees, the defenders against disease and pestilence."

"Give me a break," said Tex.

"You asked. Now hear the answer. You present yourself as a friend of trees. Yet clearly you understand nothing about trees at all. Have you never wondered how it happens that an oak tree—which can live to be many centuries old, and which during all that time is confined to a basic package of physiological traits that it inherited at birth—is nonetheless able to survive in an environment in which predatory insects can evolve through several generations in the course of a season? And where hostile microbes can do the same in the course of a *day?* Have you never thought to ask how the stolid old oak tree can possibly adapt to such a fluid and ever-changing world?"

Tex shrugged. "I guess not."

Idho gave a nasty sort of laugh. "Of course not. Your understanding of life is crippled by a mind-set of ruthless competition, the Selfish Gene, Nature red in tooth and claw."

"No it's not," Tex protested, weakly.

"Your whole species," she went on, "sees life as a struggle of all against all. That's evident in everything you do—the way you live and the way you think and the way you structure your society. And because you see so narrowly, you do not ask—you cannot *conceive*—the questions which ought to be obvious to anyone, which would reveal at once the fundamental flaws in your ideology."

"I don't really think I've got an ideology," said Tex. "Not *that* one, for sure."

Idho dismissed him with a wave of the hand. "*What's the big deal about mites,*" she said, mocking him. "The big deal about mites is that they keep your mighty oak trees alive. They form vast, interlocking colonies high above the ground, among the leaves and in the uppermost branches. They feed on bacteria and fungi. They feed on dust, on particles of smoke. They feed on the bodies of other mites. They digest organo-chemicals that fall with the rain. They inject the host with toxins that render it unpalatable to insects. They manage farmsteads of nitrogen-fixing flora. They exist in such numbers and in such a diversity of form that by comparison to the forest canopy, the soil itself is only half-populated. And they adapt to changing circumstances with a speed and creativity you cannot imagine. They exchange genetic material freely with the organisms that pass among them. They can reorganize their genomes so as to spawn whole new species in the presence of a significant threat. And all these things they do every day, every night, without stopping, and without the slightest recognition from you sapient apes who think of living beings as so much organic machinery."

"Hey, not me," said Tex.

"Not you?" Idho feigned consternation. "Have I confused you with some other species, perhaps? Did the great Worm send me to the wrong place?"

"Calm down," said Molly. She wasn't sure whom she was speaking to. Both of them seemed to take her advice, settling back into their seats and glaring across the contested space.

"That's pretty cool," said Tex after a minute or so. "About the mites, I mean."

Idho smiled at him. That terrible jackal expression. "Do you remember the rest?" she asked him. "The Worm's conditions?"

Tex sighed, fatalistically. "There would have to be conditions," he said.

"There always are," said Molly.

"Number 1," recited Idho.

THE FORM-FIELDS MUST BE GIVEN NEW ORGANISMS TO INSPIRE.

Tex shuddered at this echo of the Bishop's horrible Voice. "What does he mean, inspire?"

"The Worm is not a *he*," Idho reminded him. "Inspire means to inspirit. Look it up. Number 2."

A HOME MUST BE MADE FOR THEM—A SANCTUARY.

"Great," said Tex. "Like what, I'm supposed to invest heavily in virgin forest?"

"Number 3," said Idho.

YOU HAVEN'T GOT ALL THE TIME IN THE WORLD.

Idho cast a smug look over them. "You weren't *required* to get in over your head like this," she said. "You could have just rotted and been reabsorbed like everyone else. But no: you had to play Make a Wish at the doorstep of Death. You had to summon your feeble deities. Now live with the destiny you have invoked."

What destiny? Molly started to ask. But it was too late. Where Idho had been—*what* Idho had been—there was now only a clutch of withered black berries. Molly crossed the room and picked them up and rolled them gently between her fingers. Tex came over and put a hand on her shoulder, rubbed the muscles there, or the place where physical muscles would have been. It felt wonderful.

"What now, Raven?" he asked her.

Molly cupped the berries in her hand. "I think I'm going to plant her," she said.

> "I'd like to see her
> trapped in a
> little pot."

or
"am I stuck with this bear for life?"

Gene Deere demanded. He followed close on Ludi's heels as she tromped down the gangway to the foredeck of the *Linear Bee*.

"Stuck?" said Ludi, not looking back at him. "You've given your life over to being this corporate drone working in a metal can on an Air Force base and now you're whining about being *stuck*?"

The thump of their footsteps, then the clamor of their voices, jarred Tex and Molly from a midday doze in the sunshine of the flying bridge.

"What's going on?" muttered Tex, sleepily.

Molly stuck her head out over the open hatch. Gene and Ludi were passing through the living quarters now. She listened while they clattered aftward, toward the galley. The houseboat rocked with the shifting of body masses.

"We've been boarded, it sounds like," Molly said.

"By pirates?"

Tex was smiling at her, his eyes narrowed to little slits, as though he were stoned.

"Let's go see," said Molly.

Down in the galley Ludi leaned into the open door of the refrigerator. Gene stood behind her, examining the assortment of magnets holding up magazine clippings and recipes and photographs there. He removed one item for closer examination: a touristy snapshot of a young woman with long brown hair smiling beneath a sign that read:

WELCOME
to
JEROME, ARIZONA

"You can tell a lot about someone this way," said Gene.

"Yeah?" Ludi replied from somewhere around the hydrator. "So, what's your take on Tex and Molly?"

"Typical leftist ditzes," he said. "Earth Firsters. *Mother Jones* types. I could probably draw you a picture of what the two of them looked like."

"*Look* like," said Ludi, straightening up to face him. "Okay— so draw. There's paper on that shelf over there."

"I *can't* draw," he said. "I was just saying—"

"I know what you were saying." She went back to her rummaging among the vegetables.

"What are you looking for?" said Gene.

"Nothing in particular. Something to make a sandwich out of. I haven't been eating all that well lately. I've had a bunch of stuff to deal with."

"Like what?"

(Molly's question exactly.)

Ludi closed the refrigerator door. She was holding a slab of mystery cheese from the I.G.A. deli section and a mostly empty jar of brown mustard. "None of your business," she told him lightly, pirouetting to face the counter.

The galley was so tiny that even this minor adjustment of position required Gene to back up a step. Even so, Ludi's elbow rubbed his stomach. Laying the food down, she gave him a glance across the shoulder that Molly read as appreciation of his taut youthful abs. Gene was oblivious.

The mystery of the cheese had deepened with age. Gouda? Gruyère? Something hormone-enhanced from Wisconsin? Ludi cleavered off a thick chunk upon which she lavished the remains of the mustard.

"Doesn't smell very appetizing," said Gene.

"You had your chance," said Ludi, "to take me out to breakfast. Now suffer."

"I had other things on my mind," he said. "I didn't expect to get, you know—caught up in everything."

Ludi took a large bite of cheese and chewed it thoughtfully. When her mouth was clear she said, "Caught up? In what? You mean like, taking an interest in a fellow human being? I can see how that would be unfamiliar to you."

"I was trying," said Gene, sounding irked, "to be helpful."

"Yeah, well. You certainly helped get me confused. And I was confused enough to begin with."

"About what?"

"None of your *business*."

Which now, on second hearing, Molly understood to mean: Guillermo. Ludi was trying to avoid Guillermo. She was ducking his calls and even keeping away from her own apartment. Hence, she was not eating too well.

Which explained, Molly figured, at least in part, Ludi's frequent visits to the *Linear Bee*.

But what explained Gene Deere?

Obviously, thought Molly, I've got some catching up to do.

QUESTS AND QUESTIONS

"Bear," she said. Nudging Tex, who had drifted off in the sunshine.

He moaned. He covered his head with a pillow.

"Bear," she repeated. "Don't you wonder what Ludi is doing here on the *Bee?* And why she's brought Green Gene along?"

Tex got an eye open long enough to say: "I figure it's not our problem."

"But it's our boat."

"But we're dead."

"Not *that* dead. You heard what the yew tree person said. We're on a Quest. You and I. Together."

Tex shook his head. "She wasn't talking about a quest into other people's lives."

Molly could not argue. And yet in her heart, or someplace, she knew that these matters were all tangled up. Everything connected with everything else. "All movement arises from the Field."

Tex gave a slight jerk. "What's that from?"

"Listen," said Molly. "You've got this friend who's an oak tree, right?"

"Not exactly." He propped himself up. "He's a, some kind of field of potential form, I don't know. A dryad."

"Exactly. So you've got to figure out something about trees if you're going to help him. Right? Now, who knows all about trees?"

"Who knows all about trees?" said Tex: compliant now.

"A botanist," pronounced Molly. "And right now, for reasons we do not know, we've got a botanist standing in our galley."

"Yeah?" said Tex. He studied her face, like trying to figure where she was going with this.

"So don't you wonder," she said, choosing her words with a certain precision, "why Green Gene is following Ludi around, and why they are now aboard our boat?"

"Yes," he said. "Definitely."

She waited. He was as thick as a stump sometimes. "Then why don't you ask me?" she said.

"What?"

"Why don't you ask me, Why is Gene Deere following—"

"Ah!" Tex brightened. His little earrings jangled as energy seemed to flow out from him. "You want *me* to ask *you*, so you can do that vision thing."

She patted his hand. "That's a good Bear," she said.

THE PAST OF THE PRESENT

Thistle Herne, the formerly naked teenage girl, had a facility for making herself quite at home in virtually no time under any circumstances. After inhabiting the inglenook of Gene's bungalow for a day and a half, she settled herself in the passenger seat of the Range Rover as though she expected to be living there for at least a month. First she plumped up Gene's brushed-cotton cricket sweater to make a pillow; then she rotated sideways so that her legs were on the seat beside her, the knees jutting up an at angle that no one over the age of 25 would have found tolerable; and then she rested her head on one hand, supported by a skinny elbow, and began browsing through a stack of magazines, trade paperbacks, and CD liner notes that she had assembled for the voyage.

"Okay," she said to Gene, who was watching with interest from the driver's seat. "I'm ready now."

As though he had been waiting for this.

Which he had, of course.

Among the items she had borrowed (Gene hoped this was not a euphemism, but he was too weary to make a contest of it) were:

Bang on a Can LIVE, Volumes 1–3
Ada
SimAnt
Space-Age Bachelor Pad Music by Esquivel
Typical Emergent Patterns in Artificial Life (Xeroxed monograph)

How the Leopard Changed Its Spots: The evolution of complexity
Archie McPhee (mail-order catalog)
Journal of Consciousness Studies, Volume 2
CRI American Masters Series: Lou Harrison

As Gene drove, she reprogrammed the buttons on his radio.

"You shouldn't listen to public broadcasting," she told him. "No one should. Not till you're my dad's age. Then I guess you need it."

"How old is your father?" said Gene.

"I haven't got a family," she said. "Remember?"

Gene shifted up. "Don't lose that damn Archie McPhee," he told her: sternly, in loco parentis.

"Trust me," she said, favoring him with an angelic smile.

The sight of her long thin legs speckled with sun-bleached hairs annoyed him. He knew that you were not supposed to fixate on things like this—she was young enough to be thought of as *somebody's daughter*—but there was a definite aesthetic perfection about the way she looked, a quality of idealized form-in-development that he found beautiful from a standpoint that he hoped (and would have argued) was more scientific than sexual.

Probably he was correct. It was his business, after all, to unravel the mysteries of morphogenesis, or the creation of forms. One of the oldest and still most perplexing of these mysteries is the matter of sameness within diversity. That is, the phenomenon whereby all growing limbs—human or horse or salamander—can be seen to resemble this *particular* (slender, slightly pink-toned) limb, to such an extent and in such fine detail that you really *have* to suppose a universal principle to be at work. And yet the effort of nearly two centuries to assign this similarity of form to a branching tree of ~~common~~ ancestors had failed to yield the smoking Adam. The old hope of explaining such parallels of morphology through strict Darwinian analysis—random small-scale variation followed by natural selection followed by further variation, ad exhaustio—now seemed doomed to failure. Not that any of Gene's professors had been quite prepared to admit it. You had to be young, he guessed, and uncommitted to the reigning orthodoxy. Or at least not worried about tenure.

The fact was that this perfect limb of the teenager on the seat beside him told (as did all limbs, growing from every kind of creature) a kind of story: a story that Nature repeated again and again, following the same sequence of plot twists, the same unfolding of themes, adapting it to an infinite variety of protagonists. And whatever the reasons Nature loved this story so well—whether they were rooted in hard physics or (as Einstein liked to say) the mind of God—they did not seem to arise from a local context. They were not, in other words, determined by an individual's genes. No: the moral of this old and ever-beguiling story, "How Thistle Got Her Leg," had to be sought in the broadest possible context: the context of Nature itself. Or Herself, as the case may be.

Gene liked to think of himself as open-minded. Not to the extent of entertaining heretical views like Sheldrake's theory of Morphic Resonance (whereby Thistle's leg was shaped this way because many *previous* teenage legs had been shaped this way). But enough to feel that there was something important that was not yet known, something just out of reach, waiting to be grasped. Something unthought-of and astonishing.

Thistle had spun the dial hard left, to WURS.

"I saw my father's *head* explode," she chanted.

"What?" said Gene.

Thistle looked at him, then out the window. "Take a right here," she said.

"Where?" said Gene. "I don't see a road."

"There *isn't* a road. This is a Rover, right? What are you worried about?"

The place where they turned was a muddy track about one arm-span wide, designated only by a blaze orange placard hand-lettered with a black permanent Magic Marker to read:

> YOU ARE ENTERING
> FREE TERRITORY
> Cops, Feds, Tax Assessors,
> Animal Rights Activists—
> TAKE NOTE

"This is completely Master Ninja," said Thistle. She slapped her bare thighs.

It was a good design, Gene thought. After all these millions of years, it still gets the job done.

SPIRALS (2)

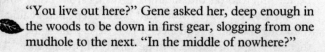 "You live out here?" Gene asked her, deep enough in the woods to be down in first gear, slogging from one mudhole to the next. "In the middle of nowhere?"

Thistle gave this careful and, it seemed to Gene, unnecessarily prolonged consideration. Finally she said very seriously, "I don't really live anywhere."

"Ah, yes. I forgot."

"And I don't *think*," she continued, looking back out the window, "you would really call this the *middle* of nowhere, would you? I mean, wouldn't that be somewhere up in International Paper territory?"

Gene chuckled. Perverse exactitude was a quality he could relate to. "Have you been up that far?" he asked her.

"I've been everywhere," she said.

In her lap lay a Xeroxed pen & ink graphic labeled:

Fig 12. Emergent spiral formed in the Beloussov-Zhabotinsky reaction, compared with meristem (typified) in juvenile *Liquidambar styraciflua*

She stared at this for a while and then wondered aloud, "What are these things all about?"

He could not be sure whether she seriously wanted an answer. It was dangerous to think and drive.

"I swear to God," he said, "I thought I saw a wolf back there. Right in that stand of birch trees—just staring at us."

"Probably," said Thistle.

Her disinterest appealed to him, somehow. He tapped the drawing at the top of the page, which looked like this:

He told her, "The Beloussov-Zhabotinsky reaction is a self-organizing pattern that arises when you mix a certain combination of organic and inorganic chemicals in a petri dish. It's cited there as an example of the spontaneous emergence of order out of chaos."

Thistle nodded. Gene tapped the picture at the bottom of the page:

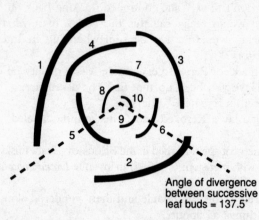

Angle of divergence between successive leaf buds = 137.5°

"And here," he said, "you've got the same distinctive spiral— it's drawn differently, but it's got the exact same angle of divergence, 137.5 degrees—shown by the meristem of a sweet gum tree. But that's an arbitrary choice. You could walk out into your backyard and find the same thing almost anywhere. Spiral phyllotaxis is the most common pattern of growth in higher plants, and this particular angle is the most stable of the spiral forms that occur."

Thistle nodded again. She turned the paper sideways, then upside down. The patterns were no more or less apparent from any angle. After a while she asked him:

"What about maples? Red maples?"

"Well, no," he said. "They display a different pattern, if that's what you mean. They're said to be whorled."

"How about lawn grass?"

"Um, no, I don't think—"

"Then you won't find it in *our* backyard," she said. "Because that's all we've got. And some crappy yews around the foundation."

Gene was mystified. "Out *here*?" he said. "You've got nothing but maples and lawn grass?"

"No," she said. "Back home." And she turned the page, and that seemed to be the end of it.

The woods were as magnificent as the road was god-awful.

Tulip poplars soared like classical columns, their side branches so high that they were hidden by beeches and maples. The trunks themselves were intricate vertical landscapes, deeply channeled and fissured, bristling with a hairy lichen called old-man's beard. Except for some huge and exotically colonized boulders, the ground was completely hidden beneath a miniature jungle of bright green ferns, as luminous as stained glass in the sunlight. Gene was slipping into a (strictly professional) reverie, when Thistle said:

"So what's it mean? What's the connection between a sweet gum and a bunch of chemicals in a petri dish? Is this some kind of stupid science trick?"

Gene suppressed his immediate reaction. It was actually a more interesting question that it seemed to be. "Not a *science* trick, exactly," he said. "That's the point, more or less. Actually it's a trick that has thus far *eluded* science. The point is, there is *no* connection between a growing *Liquidambar* and a bunch of chemicals reacting in a petri dish. They're unrelated in almost every way. Living versus nonliving. Spatial versus flat. Naturally occurring versus artificially created. That's what makes the pattern so fascinating. You see? Because there's no obvious reason, as far as our current level of understanding goes, why this precise spiral should emerge, as opposed to some other pattern. Or no pattern at all."

"So what are you saying?" said Thistle.

"I'm not sure I'm saying anything," he said. "What the author of the *paper* is saying is: genes don't govern everything, after all. The conventional view, you see, is that everything about the structure of a sweet gum tree, or any other living thing, is written into a set of assembly instructions, encoded in the DNA. And if we only knew how to decode it, we could learn how you put together this tree. But the author argues that this is not, in fact, a proven scientific principle. It is merely a belief. An act of faith— like religious faith, except here the belief is in an unknown molecular mechanism. The picture shows that an identical form has arisen spontaneously from an assortment of chemicals mixed together and left undisturbed in a laboratory, where there is no DNA present. No program of any kind. Except whatever program might be said to exist implicitly in Nature itself—in the fundamental structure of the Universe."

"Cool," said Thistle.

"Well," said Gene, "yes." He felt rather pleased with himself, with his powers of explication. Maybe he should have gone into teaching.

Nah.

The muddy path merged into another, slightly wider and more frequently traveled, muddy path. A short distance farther they passed under a sign that read DA TURTLE'S HOSTEL.

"Who's Da Turtle?" asked Gene.

"Beats me," said Thistle. "I think it might be a joke. Or something."

"What's C.A.W. stand for?"

Thistle smiled, as though this were a joke also. "The Church of All Worlds," she said. "Jesse's a minister."

Gene tried to make this compute, but it did not.

The long miserable drive ended in an egg-shaped, gravel-surfaced parking area, the first inarguable sign of American civilization they had encountered for the past half hour.

"This is the place," said Thistle. Efficiently she gathered up her belongings—almost all of which actually were Gene's belongings. "Thanks for the lift."

Gene was surprised at how let-down he felt. He was disappointed to have this adventure come to such an unceremonious end. Not that he had been expecting anything else, in particular. (Want to come in for a beer? Say hi to my mom?) But at least to have a bit of his curiosity satisfied. Which is not to say that until this moment he had been aware of *having* any curiosity. Life is full of these surprises.

Thistle was out the door and down on the ground with her arms full of books and CD's and magazines. In what appeared to be pure afterthought, as she was shoving the door closed with a hip, she peered through the window at Gene and said, "Want to come in for a Jolt or something? Say hi to the Pod?"

He hoped she did not take it amiss when he laughed out loud.

BREAK-IN

The Adirondack-style hunting lodge Thistle led him to sat in a grove of tall sycamores, whose leaves made a distinctive whirring noise in the wind—something like the sound you would get if you cut off a few feet of garden hose and swirled it rapidly over your head. Gene wondered if anyone ever had thought about classifying higher plants according to the sounds they produce. He guessed not. Botany, as a science, is caught in a sort of prolonged adolescence, in which many of the lessons of childhood have been temporarily forgotten (to be brought back to mind, painfully, in the next century or so), but maturity and wisdom remain far out of reach.

Over the door of the lodge, someone had nailed a wood-burned sign like the kind you make at summer camp. It said

SANDERS & SCRAPERS

Thistle explained: "They've diversified."

The large, high-ceilinged, timber-trussed room inside the door was crisscrossed with shielded cables, decorated with posters of rock bands with names Gene did not recognize, and furnished principally with stacks of comic books, recycled paper and obsolete electronics. Toward the far wall a computer workstation had been set up on a big table. A blond-haired, barefoot teenage boy sat before this wearing black sweatpants, a sheepskin vest and a shiny helmet with two lethal-looking horns sticking out of it: a costume piece from the *Götterdämmerung,* possibly. From the sound-out port of the CPU, a wire led to the amplifier/subwoofer box of a SoundStage speaker system, out of which roared death metal of unbelievable volume and abrasiveness.

"Pretty good bass definition there," Gene said.

A second teenager, this one dark-skinned and burly, dressed like an extra from some Depression-era production of *Huck Finn,* turned to look at Gene and Thistle. He made a strange hand sign.

"Peace with honor," said Thistle.

The boy canted his head a few degrees, apparently unable to hear a word over the music. He came toward them and Thistle said:

"Are we interrupting anything?"

Saintstephen shook his head. "Shadow's gone to war. He could be at this for hours."

Thistle introduced Gene. "I camped at his place for a couple of nights and he gave me a ride home. Gene, this is Saintstephen Bax. Over there that's Shadow. I guess he's busy."

Gene nodded. He wandered over toward the workstation to see what was happening on the huge Radius monitor. He noted a rather witty sign, done in antique-looking crewel work, that read HACK THE RICH.

"And what?" he said. "Download to the poor?"

"*Exactly,*" said Saintstephen.

Gene supposed he could relate to that. The screen was filled

with interesting columns of numbers, accompanied by multivari-
able charts with parameters labeled

PH–DILUENT (INTROJECTED)
PH–DISCHARGE
CALCIUM ION CONCENTRATION
TEMPERATURE–AMBIENT
TEMPERATURE–DILUENT
CO_2 ENRICHMENT THRESHOLD
TOTAL LUMENS
TOTAL SALINITY
NUTRIENT INJECTION RATE
CYCLE TIME (0 = CONTINUOUS)

—and so forth. Gene thought it looked oddly familiar.

"Is this some kind of simulation?" he asked.

The kid at the computer did not yet seem to have become
aware of his presence, though Gene now stood close enough to
wish the boy would break for a shower. Kernels of Smart Food
popcorn (white cheddar flavor) smushed underfoot. Gene had
no quarrel, nutritionally, with this, but he preferred the floor-
texture of Cheese Doodles.

"Not exactly," said Saintstephen, who was following him.
Thistle had vanished. "It's some kind of environmental regulator
system, we're still trying to figure it all out."

"What's to figure out?" said Gene. "This is the kind of control
system you'd have in a specialized greenhouse. If you were growing a single crop, say, and you wanted to optimize the variables
for rapid foliage output, or for timed inflorescence, or root-mass
buildup. Or whatever."

"No shit," said Shadow, still staring at the Radius.

"Yeah." Gene moved a little closer. Most of the objectionable
smell seemed to come from the sheepskin vest, which was woolly
and rough-textured, as though it had been yanked right off the
animal with no fuss over tanning or cleaning. "What you've got
here, I would say, is a system that's been set to nurture softwood
seedlings, or possibly a batch of young clones. Probably you're
dealing with a closed hydroponic loop here, a circulating nutrient
mix that gets sampled and adjusted at preset intervals."

Shadow looked around, not at Gene but at Saintstephen. The
two boys seemed to confer on a private wavelength.

"How robust is that?" Saintstephen asked.

"The system or the plants?" Gene reached down and adjusted

the volume control on the speaker box. "Plants are pretty robust, as a rule. But when you make them part of a loop like this, they become sensitized to the overall state of the system to a much greater degree than you'd find in the wild. Sharp gradients—a cold night, for example—can be pretty disruptive."

Shadow ran a finger down the list of parameters on the screen. "How about a sudden nutrient dump?"

"Flood the system with nitrogen—something like that?" Gene paused to consider this.

"Yeah. And then back off right away. A one-shot deal."

"The plants ought to shake that off. Off-the-scale increases in nutrient levels can trigger a sort of paradoxical effect, where the plant actually drops its rate of uptake to the point that its growth gets stunted. Then what you've got is basically a normal healthy crop that's smaller than it ought to be."

"That won't do it," said Shadow.

Saintstephen tapped on CALCIUM ION CONCENTRATION. "What does that do?"

"Ah," said Gene. "That's actually pretty interesting. It would depend on where you were in the development cycle. But potentially—if the plants were quite immature—you could have some *very* bizarre root structures and leaf formation patterns and things of that sort."

Thistle returned with a 6-pack of Jolt Cola. Shadow and Saintstephen each took one, popped the caps, and touched the aluminum rims together.

"Cheers," said Saintstephen.

"Skoal," said Shadow.

They drank.

"Hey," Shadow said to Gene, "thanks, dude. You've really given us what we were looking for."

"Have fun," said Gene. He accepted a Jolt from Thistle, raised it to his mouth. In so doing, his eyes moved past her toward the door of the hunting lodge. Cola spumed painfully up his nostrils. "My god," he gurgled.

He had seen a wolf.

DA TURTLE'S HOSTEL (2)

 Jesse Openhood stepped cautiously through the doorway. Beside him, Gus the timber wolf pawed the wide-planked floor.

"That your car down there?" Jesse asked Gene.

Gene's eyes were fixed on the wolf. It was a beautiful animal, its coat more charcoal than gray, with lighter markings around the flanks. The head was large and intelligent-looking.

"He won't eat you," said Thistle.

"Probably," Shadow qualified.

"Hasn't chewed on anybody for a while," added Saintstephen.

Jesse smiled and tickled Gus's ear.

By this time Gene had put it together—that this animal was a pet, that they were teasing him.

"Yes," he said. "That's my car."

Jesse nodded. "Nice." He didn't show much in the way of an expression. He was stocky and umber-skinned.

Gene felt disoriented. None of these people looked alike.

Thistle explained to Jesse: "Gene lives on the other side of the mountain. He's got a little *bear* at his house."

Jesse nodded, as though this were perfectly reasonable.

"Cool," said Shadow.

Gene said, "Well, not exactly *living*—"

"His name is Tex," Thistle interrupted.

"Nice name for a bear," said Saintstephen.

Jesse's eyebrows wrinkled. "A bear named Tex?" he said slowly. It didn't sound like a real question—more like the way you might repeat the title of the book you were hunting for, while you paced before the shelf. Then he smiled in a quiet way, as though he had found it. "Come on out," he told Gene. "We'll take a look around."

Gene wasn't sure what to think. He was standing in a hunting lodge deep in the forest with three teenagers, a man he took to be an American Indian, a high-powered computer, approximately 10,000 comic books and a full-blooded timber wolf. A can of Jolt Cola, which he despised, was in his hands. An infant *Ursus americanus* was in his living room, probably taking a dump.

"I'm a botanist," he announced unexpectedly. He felt a sudden need to establish his position in the world, unambiguously. "I came up here to study patterns of tree growth. My specialty is the genetic issues involved in reforestation."

"Ahh, soo," said Shadow and Saintstephen together. They eyed one another thoughtfully across their cola cans.

"That's pretty interesting," said Jesse.

"So okay," said Gene. "Sure. I'd love to take a look at your place."

They started on the Mosquito Path, which led up the hill toward Syzygy's.

"That's a stand of American ginseng in there," said Jesse, pointing. "We're trying to leave it alone."

Gene nodded. He recognized the plant from textbooks. *Panax quinquefolium.* The name meant 5-leaved panacea.

"They say it's more Yin than the Asian kind," Jesse went on. "I figure it's kind of like old-age insurance."

Some of the *Panax* plants were blooming: small white 5-petaled flowers, like wild strawberries. "More Yin?" Gene asked, politely.

Jesse nodded. "That's what they say."

The path wound steeply between rocks and huge clumps of ostrich fern, whose opening fronds rose head-high, then sprawled in a kind of giant bird's-nest configuration. From somewhere in the middle of them, a voice called out:

"*Danger! Danger!* Approach at your own risk!"

"That you, Ari?" said Jesse.

"*Danger!*" the voice called again. Something about it sounded alien, mechanical. Like the voice that reminds you to take your car keys out of the ignition.

Suddenly the fern-fronds exploded in a fury of motion, of emerald light and black shadow. Into the air, on powerful wings, rose a large bird whose feathers were dark and opalescent.

"It's Jack!" exclaimed Jesse. "Jack, where've you been, bro?"

The bird flew to a beech limb about 30 feet up, where it perched and looked everywhere but down at them.

Gene stared at the bird, then at Jesse. "You've got a talking raven?"

"All ravens are talking ravens," said Jesse. "Jack's a *bilingual* raven. He and Ari have been training each other."

Gene did not want to know what, exactly, Ari might be. The logical extrapolation was probably a college-educated mountain lion.

"Ari's our elf," Jesse told him.

Gene squeezed his eyes shut. It was worse than he had imagined. "Lead on," he said.

The raven followed them the way a cat does: keeping well back and pretending to pay no attention. They passed Syzygy's house, about which Jesse offered no comment. The grounds in its immediate vicinity had been cleared and—though this might not be the best term—landscaped. Dozens of good-sized local stones had been arranged in a 12-foot circle on top of what Gene thought must be the septic mound. Nearby, four white birch trees, standing in a nearly perfect square, were knitted together with a web-work of brown, pliant cord. The shrouds squeaked and groaned as wind bent the trees, stretching and then easing up on them.

"That's a death trap," said Jesse.

Gene flinched.

"Made out of deer gut," Jesse went on. "Each of the sides points a different direction. So when one of them breaks, you know that's the way death is coming from. You can take precautions."

Gene nodded. He guessed it was good to take precautions. "Did you make it yourself?"

Jesse laughed. (What was funny?) He shook his head. "That's Syzygy that does that," he said. "She's a natural."

"Ah," said Gene. "Right."

Now, here was a worrisome thing: Gene felt as though all of this was beginning to make a certain kind of sense to him. Not *logical* sense. Some other kind.

But what other kind was there?

That was the worrisome part.

Past Syzygy's house, the trail divided. The choices were marked with wooden signs nailed to a tree.

ROAD TO HELL>
<BEATRIX FARRAND MEMORIAL REFRIGERATOR WALK
TRAIL OF BEERS>

"You call it," said Jesse.

It was hard to resist the refrigerator spirit walk. But in the end, the mythical impulse won out.

"I've always wondered," said Gene, "what the Road to Hell looked like."

Jesse nodded without smiling. There was no figuring this guy's sense of humor, or absence of one. He gestured for Gene to go first.

The Road to Hell looked pretty much like the Mosquito Path, only it was on the southern face of the hillside, where the ground warmed more quickly in spring, so the vegetation was further along. Trilliums had colonized a broad rockfall, spilling down its face as blood-purple as wine. Jesse and Gene descended quickly, stepping into damper and lusher terrain where the trees grew tall but sparsely. Water-seeps linked up to form runlets that smelled like the rocky insides of a cave, cold and faintly metallic. Mosses and lichens grew in bizarre profusion on everything that was keeping reasonably still.

At the bottom of the hill the trail settled into a groove between two slopes, running alongside a stream whose water could be heard burbling under a thatchwork of cattails and sedges and wild irises, their brown cast-off leaf blades beaten down by foot traffic. Gene guessed—it was out of his realm of expertise—that this must be a wildlife corridor. Paw prints of varying size and shape lay between boot-marks and barefoot kid-marks. If you ran into a bear heading up this trail in the opposite direction, there would be no obvious way to get around him.

Gene dallied a bit, feigning interest in a small native grass—a *Chasmanthium,* possibly—that bore a clear kinship with bamboo. He let Jesse step past him, then asked, "Where does this path go?"

Jesse paused, giving this question more thought than it properly deserved. "Not much of anywhere, I guess," he said finally.

They rested for a moment. The Road to Hell had led them to a marshy Nowhere. The sun was hot, and the first black flies of the year rose to hover near their faces, not yet mature enough to bite. Jesse could resist swatting at them. Gene could not.

"You want to see something interesting?" Jesse asked.

He pronounced *interesting* as a word of four equal syllables. Gene had always found this odd—as though the word really had something to do with *interest,* as opposed to being an all-purpose, essentially meaningless modifier.

"Sure," he said.

Jesse brushed aside a fan of cattail blades and plunged into the soggy undergrowth. Gene wasn't wearing the proper footgear for this, but he followed anyhow. He felt as though a challenge to his seriousness as a botanist was at hand. The black flies swarmed closer, entranced by his sweat. Off the path, you lost all sense of direction. Vegetation, water, tangled roots, sucking pools of organic muck, were distributed more or less randomly. In the middle of all this Jesse came to a stop, gesturing toward a rounded plant-mass that stood about waist-high.

"Know what that is?" he said.

Gene knew but he didn't. The plant was like a stunted tree, of spreading habit, propagating itself by a running rootstock. It shared a sizeable patch of wetland with keeled-over spruces and Labrador tea. It did not look like something that belonged here. Gene reached out and ran one finger down the sharp edge of one leaf. The foliage was stiff, evergreen but winter-burned, held up on thick and slightly bristled stalks.

"That right there," said Jesse, "is a palm tree."

Palm tree? Gene started to say. But before he could muster the proper incredulity, he realized that Jesse was exactly right.

"That's a saw palmetto," Jesse said.

"*Rhapidophyllum hystrix,*" Gene murmured, as if a button had been pushed.

"I heard once," Jesse said, "that people grow palm trees up in Ireland, right at the edge of the North Sea. So I figured, why not see about growing a palm tree here in Maine? So Tex brought me up a few of the Southeastern ones, you know, from one of his business trips. And this is the one that took."

Gene held up a hand. Superfluous information would only jumble the picture here. "You're growing *Rhapidophyllum* in— what is this, Zone 4?"

"What's that?" said Jesse.

"That's 20 to 30 below. Average winter lows."

Jesse shrugged. "*I'm* not growing it. It's growing by itself. I just plunked a few of these in the ground. The other ones died. That's all *I* know." He paused, looking from the plant to Gene. "Kind of thought you might find it interesting. In your line of work."

"It is very interesting," said Gene. He pronounced each syllable carefully. "It is very interesting indeed."

WOUNDED KING

Gene stepped up to the door of his boss's office brandishing a somewhat overexposed Polaroid image of a saw palmetto growing unprotected in Applemont, Maine. Before he could even knock, Chas called to him:

"Deere, is that you? Shut that door behind you, if you would."

Chas was the sort of person whom, when he is being polite, you have to be wary around. Gene stepped into the large, almost empty polyhedron of executive space—chosen probably on the basis of square footage rather than on its intrinsic architectural merits, of which none were detectable. One quick look at Chas's face and he quietly slipped the Polaroid into his shirt pocket.

Chas beamed a beefeater's smile at him. "Been doing a bit of field work, have you?"

Gene glanced down at the lower portions of his body, where

latté-toned mud caked his boat shoes and continued a good distance up his chinos.

"All in the position description," he said.

"Fine, that's fine." Chas seemed to have forgotten what they were talking about. "Have a seat over there, won't you?"—pointing to a deck chair safely away from the kilim rug that ameliorated a minor fraction of the concrete floor. "I've got some big news and some medium-sized news and some baby news. Which would you like first?"

Gene settled into the canvas sling, which was not comfortable. Why have deck chairs if you haven't got a deck? He said, "Maybe you should start small and work your way up."

"Fine."

Chas came around his desk and perched himself on the edge of it, a position he seemed to find sympathetic. On the wall behind him hung a row of nicely framed oil paintings of dogs.

"Baby news," said Chas. He raised a finger to signal the numeral 1. "AIDS Walk. This Saturday. Dublin Village, downtown, starts at noon. Important to ensure that the Company is well and conspicuously represented. Nuff said?"

Gene felt an urge to jot some notes. "Is that in the position description too?" he asked. Smiling *hard*, so Chas could tell he was joking.

"Thank you for your spirit of cooperation, Deere. Are we ready to proceed?"

Gene sighed. Chas took this, correctly, to mean Yes. He raised two fingers, which could not possibly have been a gesture of peace.

"Medium-sized news," he said. "Replanting program. Ongoing evaluation of the trial plots. Report and recommendations needed from you ASAP. Decision to be made at the next regional staff meeting. Which, as you *ought* to know, is scheduled for July 1st."

Gene frowned. "Isn't that a little . . . rigid? I mean, timetable-wise? I wasn't expecting to have to make a final decision that quickly."

"You don't *make* the final decision," Chas reminded him. "You make recommendations. Decisions are made at a Higher Level."

"Thanks," said Gene. (Only a day job.) "But my understanding was, we'd keep an eye on things at least through the remainder of this growth season. Then we'd have fall and winter to—"

"The world turns," Chas said. "Time waits for no one, as I believe Mick Jagger observed. The Company has made a commitment—" He paused, adjusted his position on the edge of the desk, as though he were shifting into Ex Cathedra mode. "The Company has made a commitment to plant twenty million trees next spring in the Northeastern Sector. *Twenty million,* Deere."

Chas pressed his hands together, a gesture something like a yogi concentrating his energies for some act of major-league spirituality.

"That's a very meaningful number. That's a number that represents the seriousness of the Company's involvement in the ongoing reforestation of the North Woods. Do you hear what I'm saying?"

Gene wasn't sure. He heard enough to make him suspect that there was a good deal more he wasn't being told.

"And in order to make good on that commitment," Chas went on, "it is of paramount importance that we settle *firmly* upon a unified planting strategy. That we do so at the earliest possible date. And that we then take immediate steps to push it through."

Something about this choice of words seemed odd, Gene thought. "Unified strategy?" he repeated, like a kid trying out a bit of newly learned vocabulary.

"Unified," Chas affirmed. "Region-wide."

"I'm not really sure," Gene said hesitantly, "that a *unified* strategy is possible. Or that it's a sound idea, scientifically. You've got a pretty diverse region here, when you really look at it. Especially if we're talking also about the Maritimes."

"We're talking *region-wide,*" said Chas. He appeared to like the sound of this.

"Right. So. The best plan is probably going to involve a contoured, sector-specific planting scheme. We've got lots of variables to play with—species mix, weed control methodology, desired time to harvest. And on and on. So I figure, we might as well give ourselves the benefit of all that freedom to customize our approach."

Chas held his arms up with the palms facing out, as though Gene were pointing a gun at him. "Fine, fine," he said. "That sounds like *exactly* the sort of thing that should go into your report. Be sure to state your recommendations clearly in order of preference—A, B, C, and so forth. And remember to address the option of a unified stand of X-4.3.2." Chas raised a wrist, shooting the cuff so he could look at his watch. He punched a little button to activate the calendar function. "Now let's see. I'd like that report on my desk no later than the last week of June, if you can swing it. That would be, it looks like, the 23rd."

Gene opened his mouth. He wasn't sure whether he was at a

loss for something to say, or whether he had so many things to say that the problem was where to start. In the end he let his mouth fall shut again. That is surely what Chas would have advised him to do.

Three executive fingers went up.

"Now," said Chas, "big news." He clapped his hands together. It was like a toy gun popping off in the metal-and-concrete room. "Guess who's coming to town?"

Gene could not imagine. "Sydney Poitier?"

Chas scowled. Then his smile buoyed up again. He turned, pointing at the row of portraits on the back wall.

Let me guess, thought Gene. "A border collie is coming to town?"

His tone of voice must have been comically idiotic, because Chas exclaimed, "Oh, for mercy's sake, man." He aimed his finger more precisely. And at last Gene got the picture.

Centered between the dogs-in-oil was a somewhat larger (though less majestically framed) likeness of Burdock Herne, Esquire, Chairman and Chief Executive Officer of the Gulf Atlantic Corporation. His tanned, tax-sheltered and stock-optioned head seemed to glow with an immanent celestial light. Closer inspection revealed this to be caused by an Itty Bitty Nite Lite that Chas had cannily fastened just over the portrait.

"Nice job," said Gene.

"If you can keep it," Chas rejoined: a rare, apparently spontaneous remark.

"Herne is coming to Maine?" Gene said.

"Not just Maine, Deere. He's coming *here*—this very facility. This *room,* I shouldn't wonder. He expects to be briefed on the status of our operations. And I'm sure he'll want to know where we expect to be, say, 12 months from now, 24 months from now. The whole down-year perspective."

Gene reflected that in the context of the life of a forest, or even a tree plantation, 24 months did not constitute much of a perspective. But at least now he understood where the pressure for a quick decision was coming from.

"Have you met him before?" he asked Chas.

"Met him?"

Chas seemed to consider what Gene meant by the verb *to meet.* Gene supposed this was an Eskimos-have-11-words-for-snow kind of thing.

Chas said, "We spoke briefly during the Cancún retreat. That was year before last."

A cloud passed over the executive countenance. Chas had not, as the in-house saying went, *made the retreat* last year. Invitations for the over-Christmas trip to Cancún were handed out in mid-December to the previous year's top performers. Burdock Herne was said to personally draw up the guest list. It was the most anxiously awaited of the Company's annual rites; and it had the titillating subplot that none of the executive-tier employees knew more than a week in advance whether or not they would be spending the holiday with their families.

"Has Herne got a family?" Gene wondered.

Chas gave him a quick, probing look. "Why do you ask?"

Gene shrugged. "Oh, you know. All those holidays down in Mexico. Doesn't he celebrate Christmas?"

"Everybody celebrates Christmas," said Chas, whose Episcopalianism was probably cemented in his genes. A nontransposable nucleotide sequence. Gene smiled. Chas frowned. "He's got a teenage daughter," he said. "The word is, she's a bit of a problem."

"Problem?"

Chas gave him a serious, confidential sort of look. "The usual thing. Drugs. Music. Clothes. Sex, I suppose. And now the obligatory running away from home."

"Mm," said Gene. "Music and clothes. Sounds terrible."

Chas nodded, distantly. "The word is, he's been quite upset over it."

"Herne?" said Gene.

"Isn't that who we're talking about?" Chas walked around his desk and stood before the official portrait, which was mounted high enough that you had to stare slightly upward at it. "The word *is*," he said thoughtfully, "he hasn't been acting like himself lately. He's been brooding. Delegating important decisions to the regional managers. Walking out in the middle of board meetings. Not at all his usual style."

Gene said, "So, is the daughter all right?"

"Who? Oh. I suppose so. Kids are all right, usually. In the long run. I'm sure she'll grow out of it. Meanwhile, it's all having an impact on the well-being of this Company."

"I see," said Gene. He did see. He rather wished he did not.

"Well." Chas clapped his hands again. "Enough about that. Have we covered everything?"

What mean *we*, Kemosabe? Gene stood up and said, "So you want my report by—"

"June 23rd."

"June 23rd. Isn't that Midsummer Night?"

Chas's handsome face was expressionless. After a long moment he said, "I have absolutely no idea."

Gene took care to place one mud-caked shoe on a corner of the kilim rug. Before he could get away, however, Chas called:

"Oh, and Deere. Start wearing a beeper, won't you? If you're going to be spending all your time away from the office, I'd like to be able to track you down."

And what, thought Gene—eat me? He returned Chas's amiably carnivorous smile.

HYSTRIX HYSTERICS

Sefyn couldn't believe his eyes.

"It's lovely," he said, cradling the Polaroid in both hands. "I can't believe it didn't defoliate worse than this. Do you suppose the snow cover protects it?"

"That's a thought," said Gene. It was a great relief to be back in his own little corner of the wide world, where a sense of proportion still obtained. "I ought to have asked him about that. It was down in a sort of hollow, so there could have been some drifting."

Sefyn nodded excitedly. His eyes darted between Gene and the photograph. "We *must* go pay it a visit," he said.

Gene wondered if he would be able to find his way back. "Da Turtle's Hostel," he said quietly.

"I've tried to grow these indoors, you know," Sefyn said. "But I can't get the right combination of sun and humidity and heavy soil. Rain forest types are *so* much easier."

"Easier than natives?" said Gene.

"Oh, much. People don't know how difficult it is to grow native plants properly. This may be a weed down in Florida, but try growing it in a tub in your living room, and honey, it's all over."

"It's not actually a weed in Florida," said Gene. "Not anymore. Most of its habitat has been *improved*, as the saying goes. I believe it may actually have been proposed for listing as threatened. But that was before Property Rights."

Sefyn shook his head. He handed the Polaroid back. "Maybe that's not so bad, though," he said, "if you can really grow it in Maine."

"You can grow it. At least, that guy Openhood can grow it."

Sefyn sighed. "I've known people like that. Who could just stick anything in some dirt, and it would take off."

"Ah yes. The proverbial green thumb." Gene peered into the blurry Polaroid. "Personally, I can't keep a damned mother-in-law's tongue alive."

"Well, of course not," said Sefyn. "You're a botanist. You've learned too many *scientific facts*. You know about *molecules* and all. That's the worst thing you can possibly do, if you want to grow anything."

"It is?"

Sefyn gave him a kindly, sympathetic look. "Here," he said. "Want to help me water?"

"Sure."

Sefyn handed him a long-spouted Haws watering can. "Give them all they want," he said.

Gene kept the obvious question to himself. He tilted the can over a strapping *Azorina vidalii*, which looked like a cross between a Canterbury bell and a Mayan-temple bromeliad.

"Sefyn?" he said.

"I'm listening." His administrative assistant was lost in a thicket of abutilon.

"Do you know anything about bears?"

"Sure do." From deep within the mass of greenery, sunlight falling through the skylight flashed on Sefyn's large gold hoop earring.

"Some days you eat the bear," he said.
"And some days the bear
eats you."

or
should we call the
whole thing off?

Ludi asked herself. Only four of the Street Players bothered to
turn out for the No Shit Emergency Planning Meeting with two
weeks to go, now, before Midsummer Night.

Furthermore, as to the four who had showed up, there were
serious questions about the extent of their true motivation. Gathered in the field behind the sagging rented barn were:

EBEN CREEK whose place it was;
PIPPA REDE who was on her way home from Midcoast Human
Resources with little WINTERBELLE;
DEEP HERB who was severely personality-deficient; and
LUDI SKEISTAN who might be doing this just to show up
Guillermo

Not much to work with. Plus: Ludi's scenario was in tatters.
Nobody had come up with a better idea. And last week's drench-
ing rain had gotten into the barn and ruined most of the masks.

The weather today, on the other hand, was perfect. Early June
in Dublin is your quintessentially iffy time: it can be blustery and
cloudy and cold enough to need a wool sweater, or it can be
sparkling and sunny and warm enough to flop out naked in the
middle of the blueberries. Today it was the latter, though everybody thus far was keeping his clothes on. Ludi had spent the
past 15 minutes folding pages of her stillborn script into imagina-

tive shapes, an attempt at origami that failed as completely as the words on the pages had failed to constitute a satisfactory drama. But the folded paper did catch the southwesterly wind nicely and go skipping and gliding down the slope toward the dark blue-green waters of Cold Bay. Out in the channel a large oil tanker painted bright orange was easing itself northward toward the deepwater terminal at Kingport.

The terminal had been yet another stupid project that neither the Street Players nor their allies among the Green Party / Real Food Co-op / Womyn's Movemynt / Organic Pot Growers Association / and Other Overlapping Losers' Groups had been able to stop or even to slow down. Thus it took its place on a list of other brain-dead but unkillable ideas that included filling wetlands to widen the tourist highway, running a snowmobile trail through "forever wild" Baxter State Park, lifting the No-Wake restriction offshore of the Rachel Carson Wildlife Sanctuary, building condos and a chemically dependent golf course in the Dublin River watershed, and inviting the regional credit card center to transform Glassport Village into a soulless, sterilized, architecturally depressing, privately-policed, low-wage, zero-job-security, high-tech sweatshop.

But that was the karma of the world.

So Ludi wondered, Why not give up? Why not disband the Street Players? Or let Guillermo and his self-righteous cadres run the show?

Ludi sighed. It is genuinely difficult to concoct a work of art about Magic and Happiness and Hope when you feel cynical and bummed-out and pessimistic.

Deep Herb, who could barely be seen among the tall grass and blueberries, said: "We could like, have maybe a big street party and get the Combat Mammals to play, and we could raise some money selling T-shirts."

"Raise money?" said Pippa. This was a concept she was unfamiliar with.

Eben said, "Every time the Combat Mammals play, the police show up."

"But the cops will already *be* there," said Herb. "They always come to our performances. It would save everybody a lot of trouble."

Everybody looked at Deep Herb, or at least the hollow space his body had made in the grass. One of his hands was tracing out patterns in the empty air, or possibly warding off blackflies. They were starting to bite now.

"I don't get it," said Winterbelle.

Her mommy patted her on the head. "You'll get used to it, honey," she murmured. Her voice sounded dreamy. It was that kind of day.

"We're supposed to be a theater group," Ludi felt obliged to remind everyone. "If we can't come up with some kind of dramatic presentation, then maybe we should—"

"Where's your theater?" Winterbelle asked.

Eben said, "The *street* is our theater. That's why we're called Street Players."

"What street?" said Winterbelle.

"Explain it to her," Eben told Pippa.

"Explain what?"

Ludi sighed again. She looked at the scattering of paper across the field. "I don't see how we can do anything at all, the way things are now. With so few of us."

"You can always do something," said Winterbelle.

The little girl sat with her back very straight. Her body was wispy, her hair thick and yellow-white, and her eyes an implausibly brilliant blue, so that she had the look of a prepubescent Barbie. Pippa gazed at her daughter fondly and Ludi felt, for the very first time in her life, a stab of primordial womanly instinct— a deeply rooted, inchoate desire to move into a tidy little home with white clapboards and painted trim and beget a brood of human young. Involuntarily she clutched at her stomach, though that was not precisely where the urge was coming from. She avoided looking at either of the two males present, lest in her confused state she should suffer some kind of imprinting. The thought of a house full of Deep Herbs in diapers was too much for a single woman to bear.

Winterbelle snapped her out of this. "Why don't you just do what we did at our school?"

The girl attended some kind of unorthodox learning center whose curriculum was based on the "indications of Rudolph Steiner." Ludi was fuzzy about the details—as she believed Pippa was also—but the building was nice. Lots of big trapezoidal windows.

Everyone gave Winterbelle their full attention. They were glad to have somebody taking charge. Ludi was no different. But at least she had the sense of irony to recognize how appropriate this was: that the Street Theater, which had been founded by Tex and Molly, had progressed to the point of taking directions from a second-grader.

"At school," Winterbelle told them, "we wanted to put on I think it was *The Empire Strikes Back*. But the trouble was, there were only six of us in my grade and everybody wanted to be Princess Leia except for the boys who wanted to be Darth Vader. Even after we talked Keanu into being Luke Skywalker, that didn't leave anybody for a lot of important parts."

"Somebody named their kid Keanu?" asked Eben.

"There's *two* Keanus," said Winterbelle. "But the little one's just in Old Testament Stories. So anyway. What we did was, we made up signs with names on them and two pieces of ribbon—brown for the good guys and white for the bad guys. Then when the grown-ups came to see the play, we stopped them at the door and hung a sign over their head, and we said, That's who you are. Because see, everybody has seen the movie a hundred times except for Denim's mother's lover who doesn't believe in supporting violent adversarial cinema. But Denim had seen it a hundred times anyway, I'm not sure how."

"What two separate people named their kids Keanu?" Eben said.

"Get beyond it," said Ludi. She nodded to Winterbelle. "Go on."

"So everybody got to be who they wanted except the grown-ups. And even Denim's mother's lover who didn't know who Yoda was, somebody told her he's this little monster who's like a Zen master, so when it was her turn to talk she just made up these heavy sayings. 'Agriculture is mechanized land-rape' and things like that. It was cool."

The Street Players weighed this information. Deep Herb settled back in the grass. Eben shook his head, still coming to grips with the Keanu thing. Pippa stroked her daughter's hair.

"You were really wonderful, honey," she said.

Winterbelle ducked out of her mommy's reach.

"So what you're telling us," said Ludi, "is that you just went out onstage without a definite script, and you just kind of acted it out. And everybody knew the story because they had seen the movie. Is that it?"

"No," said Winterbelle. "That's not it at all."

Ludi was stumped.

"We didn't go out on*stage*, for one thing. We don't *have* a stage. And mostly, except for right at the beginning, we let the grown-ups kind of do most of the acting. They really got into it, after they got over thinking how weird it was. We all just mostly ran around the Star Destroyer and the boys blasted each other with fazers."

"Do they have fazers in *Star Wars*?" Deep Herb said from his hole.

"It wasn't *Star Wars*," Winterbelle crossly reminded him.

"Aren't we forgetting something?" said Ludi.

They all looked at her. No one could remember what they were forgetting.

"What *story* are we supposed to be acting out? I mean, that's the most important thing, right? If we're going to try to do this, we've got to think of some story that everybody knows."

"Not necessarily," said Winterbelle.

Ludi was slightly irked. You could carry this out-of-the-mouths-of-babes thing only so far. "Why not necessarily?"

"Because," said Winterbelle, "Denim's mother's lover didn't know the story, and she was *great*."

"That's true." Pippa nodded. "She stole the show."

"I stand corrected," said Ludi. "We still need, however—correct me if I'm wrong about this—a *plot*. We can't just go out there and hand out signs with nothing written on them, and say Welcome to the Clueless Revue."

"Then it's easy," said Winterbelle. "You just pick some story that everybody knows. Right?"

"Sure," said Eben.

But Ludi thought, What story is that?

INTO THE WOODS

She drove to Gene Deere's house. She had promised days ago to help him with the little bear and she hadn't exactly forgotten, but her summer job at the bookstore had started, plus there were Molly's plants to water and Goblin to feed. You cannot possibly save the world with so many distractions.

Gene wasn't home, but somebody else was: a short Native man with a beer belly. He was out on the front porch, which had big wide columns, shingled up to handrail-level, playing with little Tex. When Ludi got out of her car he stood and introduced himself as Jesse Openhood.

The name was familiar. "Are you a friend of Tex's?" she guessed.

The man looked down at the bear, which was pawing and scratching at his leg. "Looks like I'm a friend of *two* Texes now."

"I'm Ludi," she said, holding a hand out. He shook it. His

hand was thick and warm. "I'm a friend of Tex's, too. And Molly's. Have you seen them?"

Jesse gave her a funny look. "I'm not sure. I don't think so."

Let it pass, Ludi decided. She said, "Isn't he cute?"

"And big," said Jesse, "for his age."

"That's what I thought too." She swatted at a black fly. "So, are you waiting for Gene?"

"I met him one time," said Jesse. Not exactly what she had asked. He went on, "Thistle told me where his place was. She told me about the little bear."

"Oh: Thistle." Ludi waved her hand back and forth in front of her face. There were so many flies that you couldn't deal with them on an individual basis. Jesse smelled strongly of citronella. "Are you, ah, Thistle's—"

Jesse looked at her. Like, waiting to hear what she was going to say. In the end she couldn't decide what she wanted to know, so she asked instead, "Why are there so many damned bugs around here?"

Jesse smiled. "Well, it's funny," he said, "but there's a story about that."

"I bet."

"It's a story about Laks—you know who he is?"

Ludi shook her head. Tex was rolling around on his back in the wet driveway, evidently intent on getting as dirty as possible. She sat down on the porch steps.

"Laks is a very evil fellow," Jesse said. "There's a lot of stories about him. He can be kind, too, but that's usually just to fool you."

"So this is some kind of legendary figure? Like a Native American thing?"

"Passamaquoddy," said Jesse. "I guess you could say he's legendary. Some people would tell you he's pretty real. Anyway, this Laks was up on top of a mountain once and he saw a great big rock and decided he'd pry the rock up and roll it down into the valley. So he did that and when the rock went rolling, he thought he'd race it and beat it to the bottom. And so he did. But when he went past the rock he yelled, 'Hey, Rock. You're slow and you're stupid!' Then he ran on down and he made a little camp and caught some fish and was cooking his dinner. But all of a sudden there was a big whooshing sound and here comes Rock, crashing through the forest and knocking down big oak trees here and hemlocks there. And before Laks could do anything, Rock had come along and flattened him out and squashed him dead. There was blood everywhere, and all his limbs were torn off."

Ludi wondered where the bugs came in. Jesse sat still for a minute—thinking, presumably, but his face was completely blank. Then he said:

"Laks can't die, though. He's a hard one to get rid of. He was all splattered around there except for his spine, which is where the life is, but he called out, *Bones, come here!* And his bones got up and came to him, and he said, *Now muscles, come!* And on like that, and soon he stood up and he was alive and whole again. Now Laks gets madder than anyone when somebody tricks him, so he made up his mind he was going to get even with that Rock. So he followed the trail where it had gone rolling through the forest, and finally he found it lying down in a little hollow full of water. So Laks picked up some boulders and he pounded at Rock until it was all smashed up into little pieces, then he took the pieces in his hands and he crushed them into smaller pieces until there was nothing left but dust.

"But see, you can't kill Rock, just like you can't kill Laks. So when Laks went away, Rock turned himself into a million little black flies and midges and mosquitos, and they rose up out of the water there and they've been tormenting people ever since. And they'll go on tormenting people till everybody goes away and takes that evil Laks with them. That's the end of the story."

Ludi nodded appreciatively. She liked it a lot. It sounded neat and authentic. She wasn't sure it sufficed as an explanation of the black fly phenomenon, however.

They sat there for a few minutes, playing with the bear. In time it became evident that Jesse was one of those people who are comfortable sitting in silence, while Ludi was not. Restless, she said, "I bet Tex has made a mess inside."

Cautiously she got up and nudged the door open, just a little. It smelled like a zoo, only without evidence of regular upkeep.

"Oh my," she said, pushing the door open all the way. The bungalow was worse than anything she had imagined. It was worse than anything she *could* have imagined. She wasn't sure where to assign the blame for this, but it seemed possible that it was at least fractionally her own fault. If she started now, maybe she could make a dent in it by the time Gene got home from work.

Of the rooms downstairs, the kitchen looked most salvageable. She began by collecting the garbage spewing out of two plastic bags that little Tex had mauled. Gene, she saw, did not separate his compostable kitchen waste from the rest of the trash, which was why the bear had found it so appealing. There were even a couple of recyclable juice bottles. Ludi made a noise of disapproval with her tongue and teeth that cannot be transliterated. The bear took this as a note of approval. He prowled around her calves, nearly causing her to topple.

Ludi got tired of the kitchen after that and ambled through the other rooms, picking things up and putting them where she guessed they ought to go. She had heard stories of houses where the interior designers had placed tiny red dots so that you would know exactly where the little tabletop accessories belong. With Gene's house there was no telling. Where would an anal-retentive science dweeb put the latest issue of *The Absolute Sound*? On the coffee table or beside the sacred stereo?

That sort of mind-game got tiresome too, so Ludi followed a trail of abused clothing through the hallway to the stair landing. She picked up a polo shirt, a cotton sweater, a pair of striped athletic socks, piling them onto her forearm. Item by item she made her way up the stairs. She suspected that what she was actually doing was yielding in a very sneaky way to the promptings of curiosity. By the time she reached the largest of the three bedrooms (the other two of which were completely empty), she had amassed a heap of clothes almost too large to see over. She waddled across the room and dumped it on a chair next to the bed.

It hit her all in a flash.

She was standing in the middle of her little brother's bedroom.

Her brother had been a soldering-iron sort of kid. His room had been filled with contraptions that looked as though they might blow the house up or electrocute somebody, model rockets that he planned to blast off in the back yard, a computer programmed to make up dirty limericks from lists of randomly chosen words. She could see immediately that Gene Deere had been that sort of kid exactly, and in fact that he had never grown out of it. The soldering iron was gone, but in its place were equivalent grown-up gadgets—a negative ion generator, a Grundig multiband radio, some sort of Scandinavian all-in-one exercise apparatus, various stainless steel and wood executive playthings that you set in motion or contort into physically implausible shapes, and a very complicated mobile that Ludi took to represent a molecule of DNA. There were also a home weather station, a very sophisticated telephone, and an autographed photo of Richard Feynmann. She wondered if he had some kind of household robot to fetch his slippers for him.

Ludi fell into a kind of nostalgic reverie. She thought about her brother and the mysteries of the male/female dichotomy—and also the dweeb/normal person dichotomy—and she was reluctant to come out of it, even when she heard Jesse's footsteps on the stairs. The footsteps came down the hallway and stopped at the bedroom door.

"Check this out," Ludi said, turning to him. But it was not Jesse.

It was Gene Deere. He stared at her in what could *not* have been absolute astonishment (her Volkswagen was shiny orange and it was parked in plain view out front), though it certainly looked that way.

"You are standing in my room," Gene told her.

"Yeah." She gestured weakly toward the pile of mangled laundry. "I was just picking up your clothes—"

"You were in my house, *picking up my clothes?*"

He didn't get it. For some reason she knew that she would be unable to explain it to him. She tried anyway. "Yeah—they were like, all over the stairs and the living room and they had teeth marks all over them."

Gene came forward, shaking his head. "I'm not believing this," he said. "I am simply not believing what I see here."

Ludi tried changing the subject. "Did you run into Jesse downstairs?"

"Who's Jesse?" demanded Gene. He was getting hotter in the brainpan the longer he was in the room with her. "Some other animal you've dragged home to live with me?"

"Jesse is a Passamaquoddy Indian and he was sitting on your front porch," said Ludi.

That stopped him for a moment. "Oh," he said. "Jesse. He was here?"

"The last I saw."

"Well, he isn't now."

"Oh. Too bad. I guess you missed him."

"Why are we having this conversation? Why do I come home from a hellacious day at work to find you standing *in the middle of my bedroom?* Is there something I don't understand? Am I going to have to start locking my doors now?"

"You might as well," said Ludi. She walked out to the hall. There was no talking to them when they got like this. Her brother had been exactly the same way. As though they really had anything to hide. What was he scared of—that she would find back issues of *Penthouse* tucked under the mattress? Semen stains on his pajamas? What?

"And now you're just going to walk out?" Gene called after her.

"Looks like it."

He came down the stairs behind her. Tex the baby bear was asleep on the bottom landing. Poor thing, thought Ludi. He must have had a hard little day.

"This is just too much," said Gene, looking over the wreckage of his living room. "I can't absorb any more."

"I know the feeling," said Ludi. "I know you don't think I do, but I do. Give me a call when you feel more ordinary and we'll talk things over."

"More ordinary?" he said.

He was practically shouting now, as he trailed her out to the muddy driveway.

"I *never* feel ordinary!" he shouted as she climbed into the driver's seat and shut the door on him.

"Practice," she said, starting the car. Though she knew he couldn't hear her.

2 AT ONCE IS TOO MUCH

When the knock came at the door of her apartment—her first thought was, Is it him?

Him meaning Gene.

Her next thought was, No way.

But along with that thought came another, semisecret one. Which was

(If I think it's not him, then maybe it will be.)

And it was in this state of mind, approximately, that she stepped past the Danish Modern living/dining ensemble and pulled open the door.

"*What* is that music you're listening to?" said Guillermo.

He proceeded directly to the kitchen, where he stood before the Formica-topped breakfast bar, glancing warily about: the guerrilla jefe checking for signs of government occupation.

"English muffins?" he said, examining the remains of Ludi's breakfast.

"It's Marilyn Horne," said Ludi. " 'Lush Life.' Got a problem with that?"

Guillermo appeared to notice her for the first time. "I was only asking."

"What do you want?" she asked him. And before he could answer she tacked on: "Frank."

His chest swelled up, held the air for a long moment, and dropped. *The jefe recognizes with great sadness that his people have entered a time of unremitting struggle.*

"I haven't seen you for a while," he said. "I just thought I'd look in and see how you were getting on."

"Getting on?" she said. "That sounds like something an old lady does. It's only been a *week*."

"Week and a half."

He walked out into the living/dining area and arranged himself prominently on the sofa, like an important element in the design. *Decorating Rule #3: Create a focal point to draw the composition together.*

"Something interesting is about to happen," he announced.

"I bet."

"No, really. I just wanted to tell you, so you can be watching the news this evening."

"What part, the weather report? Are you going to part the waters of Cold Bay so all the wage slaves can escape?"

"All right, forget it." Guillermo shifted his position. More accommodating now. "So how are *you* doing? How's your play coming along?"

Ludi sighed. Resistance was futile. He was going to keep working at her until she loosened up. If necessary, he would reach into some deep pocket and produce flowers, chocolates, groovy earrings, smooch her neck, run his hands up and down the inside of her thighs—and *that* was the last thing she needed.

"The play's kind of blocked," she said, prophylactically. "I thought I had something, but now it's gone."

From the bedroom, the Music of Your Life station was playing Kiri Te Kanawa's version of "Here Comes That Rainy Day."

There was another knock on the door.

"Want me to get it?" said Guillermo.

"No," Ludi said—not stopping Guillermo, who bounded up and crossed the room in the time it took the Nelson Riddle Orchestra to drop a schmaltzy 7th diminished chord.

Guillermo pulled the door wide very quickly, so that Gene Deere was caught in a kind of psychic undertow. He stood on the mat with his mouth half-open and a potted plant in his hand. The plant looked a little droopy.

"*What* is *this?*" said Guillermo.

Gene took a step forward, which brought him into range of the door, should Guillermo decide to slam it. Ludi thought of warning him. Gene said, "It's a datura."

"That's not what he means," said Ludi. "Guillermo, would you please get out of the way and let poor Gene get through?"

"I'm not *in* the way," Guillermo said.

"Not physically, maybe. But psychologically you're a major obstacle."

Guillermo and Gene examined one another. Neither seemed to like what he saw. Finally Gene stepped all the way in, holding the plant out toward Ludi.

"I guess this probably ought to get out of the draft," he said.

"Gene, this is Guillermo," said Ludi. "He's an enemy of the state and possibly a criminal. Guillermo, this is Gene. He's a young fogy and defender of the status quo. Could I get you guys some weapons? Would butter knives be okay?"

Guillermo shook his head. "You didn't used to be this way. This . . . hardened."

"Things didn't used to be this hard," said Ludi. "I'm sorry, but I was having a really nice morning all to myself and now it's gotten a little confusing. If one of you guys would just leave, then maybe I could figure out how to handle the other one. Two at once is too much."

Gene said, "I guess I came at a bad time." He moved to put the plant down on an end table. "No, it won't get enough light here," he said. He walked to the windows that overlooked the parking area, set the plant down on the floor, fiddled with the Venetian blinds. "Can I make a stack out of these magazines?" he said.

"They're my *Parabola*s," Ludi said, in what she thought was a firm and clear voice.

He piled the magazines knee-high and set the plant on top of them. He stood back; checked the angle of insolation; adjusted the trim of the pot. Now it seemed a chair had to go. The whole thing was weirdly absorbing.

"What does he think he's doing?" Guillermo asked.

"Some biological thing," Ludi supposed.

"He's rearranging your living room."

Ludi noted with enjoyment the look of discomfiture on Guillermo's face. "This disturbs you?"

"I would think it might disturb *you*."

"Are you kidding?" she said. "You should see the number I did on his place."

Guillermo took a little while metabolizing that. Gene augmented the *Parabola* pile with a couple of months worth of *Gnosis*. Abruptly Guillermo stood up.

"I don't want to know what's going on here," he said, making for the door. He lowered his eyebrows to deliver a final, Parthian shot, but his sling was empty. Ludi smiled sweetly at him. Exasperated, he stomped out and slammed the door.

"There," said Gene, standing back from his handiwork. "What do you think?"

"It's different," said Ludi.

3 LITTLE WORDS

"Here," said Gene, reaching into his pocket. "I wrote the name of the plant down. *Brugmansia inoxia* 'Dr. Seuss.' "

"Dr. Seuss?"

"That's correct." He handed her one of his business cards with this horticultural designation recorded in small, meticulous lettering on the back. "It gets very big trumpet-shaped flowers that are yellow with some red inside the throat. Also, it's supposed to be hallucinogenic. But I wouldn't experiment with that because it's highly toxic. You have to extract the active ingredients in a very precise way. Which I, personally, have no knowledge of. So. Anyhow—"

His voice tapered off. Having run through the botanical stuff, he now lost his way. He stood in the middle of the living room as though he was not sure how he had gotten here.

"Well, gosh," said Ludi. "Thanks. I'm sure it'll be very pretty. If I don't kill it first."

"Sefyn said it's quite adaptable," Gene said. "Anyhow, I thought you might like it. 'Dr. Seuss,' I mean. Since you work in a bookstore."

She looked at him in surprise. "How do you know I work in a bookstore?"

"You told me."

"I did?"

"That first night. At the pizza place."

"You remember that night at the pizza place?"

"Of course I remember. *You* were the one that was drinking. Not me. You didn't give me a chance."

"Oh." It came back to her now. The medium Mex, et cetera. "Sorry about that."

They looked at one another. Then they both decided to smile.

"You want an English muffin?" she said.

"Sure. Thanks."

They walked into the kitchen and she sat him down at the breakfast bar.

"Those are interesting light fixtures," he said.

"I think so too. I might steal them when I move out of this place."

"Take the refrigerator, too," he said. "That's practically a museum piece."

"What museum, though?"

"I don't know. Wherever they keep Bess Meyerson's hairdo."

She shook her head. He had never mentioned this strange sense of humor. She slathered a bunch of butter on his muffins and slid the plate across the Formica, diner-style. The radio was playing "I've Grown Accustomed to Your Face."

"Somehow," he said, with his mouth partly full, "I did not picture you living in a place like this."

"What did you picture—love beads and incense?"

"More like, crystals and New Age music."

"I like *some* New Age music. Lucia Hwong, for example. Steve Tibbets."

"I wasn't being critical. Just categorizing."

"What's the difference?"

He shrugged, knocked off the muffin. "So," he said. "What was that guy, your boyfriend?"

Ludi let the question pass. "I was just sitting here trying to get some ideas for this play. I haven't made much progress. It's like my mind is playing blank tape." Then, thinking this might be something there was a theory about, she asked him, "Where do ideas come from, anyway?"

Exactly as she hoped (and feared), he lifted his shoulders and lowered his chin, and he said, "Well, there's actually been a lot of work in that area. You know, Darwin called his book *The Origin of Species,* but what most people don't realize is that he never actually explained where new species come from. What he did was offer a convincing theory of how *existing* species might adapt to competitive pressures or changing environmental conditions. But not how species themselves—wholly distinct organisms—originate. One of the things the fossil record is *not* ambiguous about is that species do not arise the way Darwin speculated, as the result of tiny random mutations. There's just no evidence that that's how morphogenesis works. New species just all of a sudden seem to *be* there. Like, all in one piece."

"*Like* all in one piece?" said Ludi. "I thought I was the only one who talks like that."

"Everybody talks like that," said Gene. "It's how we think. We think by analogizing. It's quite helpful, especially where difficult problems are involved. We might say, for example, that there's a suspiciously *created* aspect about the way new forms appear in nature. Which is to say, some form of creativity appears to be involved. And from our own experience we know that creativity is almost never accidental."

"So?" said Ludi.

"So?"

"Where do new ideas come from? That was the question. Remember?"

"Correct. Well, it's fairly straightforward, actually. New ideas come from play."

"*Play*? As in, The play's the thing?"

"What's that? No, um—as in, unstructured activity. Turmoil. The inherent dynamism of physical reality."

Ludi considered this. Life was full of turmoil, for sure. But that seemed to be more the problem than the answer. "I don't think I get it," she said.

"It's my fault," said Gene.

Which were three little words that Guillermo, for one, could not possibly have uttered. Already Ludi detected a New Thing here.

Gene said, "For example, if you look at a slime mold—"

"A *what*?" said Ludi.

"Or okay—an ant colony. Or wait. A basketball team. You find basically the same type of creativity present. There's always this precarious balance between order and chaos. And see, if the balance tips just the tiniest bit one way or the other, everything changes. And what we're interested in, where creativity is concerned, is a situation where the balance tips in the direction of chaos, or instability. *Unstructured activity* is the term currently in favor. Because when that happens then the system—the basketball team, let's say—tends to do one of two things. Either it falls totally apart, in which case it loses the game, or else it snaps back into some new order that cannot be predicted beforehand.

Therefore it is genuinely creative. Therefore the opposing team cannot have anticipated it. In which case, you score points.

"In a real basketball game, this process happens over and over again. That's why the game is interesting. Because the team retains an organismic integrity—it remains a basketball team, even as it exhibits this continual unfolding of novelty. So in a way, you're watching evolution in progress. And it *is* evolution, really, because the way the game is played, the way the players interact on court, *does* change recognizably from one season to the next, in a totally unpredictable way. Yet it remains basketball. It doesn't suddenly turn into a different game. And there's absolutely nothing random or accidental about it."

"I still don't understand," said Ludi. "I mean, I get what you're saying. But I don't get where chaos has to come in. Couldn't everything stay nice and calm and orderly, and you still win the game?"

"Well, actually, there is a biological term for when things stay nice and calm and orderly. The term is Death."

"Ha!" said Ludi. "I thought you were going to say, Employment."

"What's the difference, I guess," said Gene.

"Really."

"But no—if you don't think of chaos as *messy*—if you just think of it as another word for *play*, sort of a temporary departure from rules and structure and things like that." Gene spun the butter knife, watching idly as it came to a halt, pointing toward Ludi's left breast. "I could show this to you better than I can explain it."

"Great," said Ludi. "You can write my play for me."

Gene seemed to find this amusing. "Sure. And I guarantee it would be creative. In fact, it wouldn't be like any play you'd ever seen before. Apart from that, all bets are off."

Ludi sighed. "At this point, I don't think any bets are on."

Gene shrugged. "Well, maybe I *can* help. Sometimes it's good to get a fresh viewpoint. Why don't you show me what you've got?"

"There isn't much to show."

"That's good. I don't have much of an attention span. Generation X, you know?"

Ha, she thought. And she led Gene Deere into her bedroom.

26 CHARACTERS IN SEARCH OF AN AUTHOR

TIME: The Present. One night in Summer.

SETTING: Somewhere at the outer edge of America.

SITUATION: The cultural, ethnic, economic and religious conflicts rending society have spread, like cracks in a sheet of glass, to this small, somewhat isolated community. Until now, whatever differences have existed among the residents have been smoothed over by neighborliness and toleration. A live-and-let-live attitude has prevailed. But lately the divisions have grown sharper, or people's willingness to overlook them has worn thin. The rich are getting richer while those living on the margins—not poor, but lacking the comfort and security of the middle class—grow more numerous. The over-40 crowd does not respect the young, and of course, vice versa. Religious people dislike other religious people who don't agree with them even more than they dislike the totally unreligious. Everyone hates his job, except for the bosses, who hate something else, usually the government. People only feel comfortable around other people exactly like themselves. Everyone clings to something—anything stable, even if it's only nostalgia for a lost golden age, or simplistic political ideas, or end-of-the-millennium fantasies. They're like kids hugging their stuffed animals, scared of strangers, afraid of the dark, crying for help that doesn't come.

OUR STORY begins when a cross section of these people are thrust together under unusual circumstances in a public place on a warm, moonless summer night.

DRAMATIS PERSONÆ:
(Unless specified, characters may be either male or female)
AGING HIPPIE (1)
AGING HIPPIE (2)
ARROGANT YOUNG IDEALIST
AFFLUENT PROFESSIONAL GEN-X TYPE (male)
MINIMUM-WAGE GEN-X TYPE (female)
CREDIT CARD CENTER DRONE
LIPSTICK LESBIAN
TAOIST WAITER (gender-free)
WELFARE WITCH (female)
WILD CHILDREN (assorted)
TV NEWS REPORTER

COMMUNITY RADIO ANNOUNCER
NATIVE AMERICAN
CHAMBER OF COMMERCE TYPE
GUY WHO SLINGS PIZZA
CORPORATE EXECUTIVE (may be tourist or summer resident)
RADICAL FAERIE
TOKEN AFRICAN-AMERICAN
GUN-TOTING SURVIVALIST
EVANGELICAL PROTESTANT (does not have to be minister)
SOMEBODY WHO RECENTLY MOVED FROM CONNECTICUT
SOMEBODY'S DAD
A LAW ENFORCEMENT OFFICER
PETS AND OTHER ANIMALS (assorted)
TREES AND OTHER PLANTS (assorted)
ROCK (female)
AMORAL TRICKSTER (supernatural, either gender)
BENEFICENT, HEALING DEITY
ELVES, WOOD-SPRITES, NAIADS, DRYADS, ETC.

"You're kind of losing me here at the end," said Gene.

"Don't worry about it," said Ludi. "I'm kind of losing myself, to tell you the truth."

"It's interesting, though."

"Interesting. I hate that word."

"Yeah." He looked at her with a peculiar smile. "I know what you mean. But some things really *are* interesting, you know?"

"Yes. And no."

"But, um—" Gene hesitated, lifting the two sheets of paper as though making doubly sure there were no more of them. "I mean, what does the story consist of, exactly?"

"That's kind of the problem," said Ludi. "There kind of *isn't* a story. I can't think of a plot. But I mean, *life* doesn't have a plot, does it?"

"No. But it has events. It has changes, developments. Besides, life doesn't have elves and naiads, either, does it?"

"I wouldn't bet on it," said Ludi, quite seriously.

That sobered him up.

"Let's take a complex-systems approach to this," said Gene. "Have you got any scissors?"

MEMES

 "My poor play," Ludi lamented, staring down at her bed, where pieces of her manuscript lay spread out on dozens of strips of paper. The bedspread was green nubby cotton. In miniature, you had here the scene in Eben's field, with scraps of Ludi's scenario blowing down toward the bay. Only Gene had made this mess on purpose. In her *bedroom*. She wondered if this was a very subtle, nearly symmetrical form of revenge.

"These are memes," Gene explained. "Tiny pieces of information for your actors to remember. They're like genes, only made out of words instead of nucleotides. Get it?"

"Get what?"

He pressed his lips together, impatiently. His eyes were bright; he radiated bustle and energy. "I know I'm not *that* bad at explaining things," he said. "Look, let's take one of these characters, okay? Here: Lipstick Lesbian. What does that mean? No, stop, I don't need to hear it. Let's assign this character a meme. What would be a good meme?"

Ludi didn't have the faintest idea what he was talking about. "Your call," she said.

"Okay. Let's say:

Meme LL
The only person you can rely on is yourself."

He wrote this in tiny letters on the back of the scrap of paper. "Now we assign this meme to this character, and this governs how this character interacts with the others. Okay?"

"Maybe," said Ludi.

"Fine. Now another character. Corporate Executive. What should we do for him?"

Ludi said, "You get what you pay for?"

Gene shook his head. "Something more dynamic," he said.

"I know," said Ludi.

Meme CE
The one who dies with the most toys wins.

"We'll go with that," said Gene. "Now, you see what we're doing here? The idea is, you assign a very simple meme to each character, then you put all the characters into play and you observe the ways in which they self-organize. You should see the characters begin to grow in complexity, become more peoplelike. In which case your system is evolving."

Ludi twiddled with the ends of her long hair. "Doesn't sound like all that much fun."

"Then we adjust the memes. Or we tinker with the character mix. If it works, it *ought* to be fun. It ought to feel like a game. Conversely, if it feels like a game, then you're doing it right. You're pushing into the realm of novelty, of pattern creation. At least, that's how it works in biology. I don't know much about theater."

"That's evident."

He looked at her. There was something different in his expression—an openness, as though some translucent barrier had fallen, and he was adjusting to the new, unobstructed view. Or maybe that's only how Ludi felt, and she was projecting. Anyway he seemed to study her, the way she imagined he might study some unexpected development in a laboratory. After a minute he smiled.

"This is really the way it works," he said. "From the bottom up. Patterns emerge from chaos. Which is the problem with conspiracy theories, and with deterministic theories in general. They assume some kind of hidden program that governs everything. But there's no program because there's no way of controlling a dynamic and creative process. If you succeed in controlling it, the process stops. The system dies. I would think playwrights might have noticed this before now."

"Maybe they have," said Ludi. "I don't know. I'm not a playwright."

"Oh, you will be," said Gene, looking away from Ludi, down at the scraps of paper. "Really. I bet you. You will be."

THE PRESENCE OF THE PAST

"I don't get it," said Molly. "They were getting along great, back then. So why are they here in our galley scrapping at each other?"

"You tell me," said Tex. "You're the know-it-all. Maybe there's some way to do a PAUSE and FRAME ADVANCE on these visions of yours."

"I don't think so," said Molly. "Anyway, my eye is tired."

"Poor Raven."

His tone was gently mocking, but his smile was warm: the old Tex. He rubbed her temples the way she liked, and she leaned back against the rail of the flying bridge, letting the sensation ripple through her.

"Sometimes," she said, "just lately, you know? I feel like I could float away from here."

The fingers at her temples pressed for a second harder. Tex said:

"Better not. Not just yet. We've got stuff to take care of."

Molly made a noise between a hmm of pleasure and a moan of dread. Her emotions seemed to be converging into a single, multihued energy.

In the galley, Gene was staring at Ludi, who was licking the smeary remains of a mystery cheese sandwich off her fingers. She took her time about it.

"And no," she said when she was good and done. "You're not stuck with the poor little bear forever. Just till he's ready to go out on his own."

"Which will be when?" said Gene. "When we're all dead?"

Tex grumbled something not even halfway audible. Why doesn't he give up speaking, Molly wondered, and just growl?

They hung there, two invisible presences, at the door of the galley. Gene and Ludi were so close that Molly could have stuck her hand right through them.

Tex said, "So this guy is a real scientist?"

"He's a botanist," said Molly. "Is that real?"

Gene said, "What do I think about *what*?"

"This place," said Ludi. She brushed past him, waving a hand around the *Bee*. "Tex and Molly's houseboat. All their cool stuff. Isn't it great?"

As she spoke she stepped into the living quarters; one elbow passed through Tex's chest. He sighed. Ludi frowned, as though a peculiar thought had niggled at her mind. Then she went the rest of the way to the sitting area, turning in the middle of the room.

"Can you imagine *living* here?" she asked Gene. Her slender arms spread wide. "I think it would be swell. Don't you? I thought you'd get a kick out of it."

Gene entered the room with much less enthusiasm. "You're starting to sound like a Cole Porter song," he said.

"Really?" The thought made her faintly smile. "That radio station, I guess. I've gotten to like it, though. Except the commercials, which are all for like Buicks and pharmacies. And you've got to be careful you don't accidentally hear Paul Harvey."

Gene chuckled grimly. "Yeah, that can blow your whole day."

His eyes passed over the bookshelf, flashing with recognition at *The Complete Marijuana Grower's Home Handbook.* "Hey, look," he said, "this is a classic." He pulled it out, too quickly: the binding had come unglued and pages fell everywhere.

"I'll say." Ludi stooped to examine a black & white photograph of a plant so happy-looking it appeared to be humming to itself. She said, "What's Durban Poison?"

"Ah: the first *really* excellent strain bred for the small-scale grower." Gene's hands were now full of loose pages which he was attempting to place in order. "That was on the West Coast somewhere, working mostly with *sativa.* Then the major breeding work shifted to the Netherlands, and *indica* came into play. Personally I would have stuck with *sativa* and tried to get a natural dwarf with a quick flowering cycle. But that's just me."

Ludi settled onto the couch. She examined him from a new angle. "Why does a totally square guy like *you* know so much about growing marijuana?"

"*Square?*" He looked at her in annoyance. "That's worse than swell. Do you object to people taking an interest in things? I am a botanist, after all."

"All I was asking was why. It doesn't seem to fit, is all."

"Oh, it doesn't?" He spread the disassembled parts of the *Home Handbook* on the coffee table. "I suppose what *you* want is things to be—what was it? Nice and orderly. Well, it might interest you to know that I am one of the few people in the United States legally certified by the Food and Drug Administration to cultivate *Cannabis.*"

She studied his face—completely serious, though that could have been routine dweebishness—and at last she said, "Are you trying to bullshit me?"

"Not at the moment. It's part of my work at Goddin. There's been interest lately in the potential of *Cannabis* as a fiber crop— to feed paper mills, and also for textile applications, because it isn't water-intensive like cotton. There's a real need for something to plug the hole in the pulp supply, now that loblolly pines are dying in Carolina. Hemp is a logical candidate. So yeah—I'm growing marijuana. It's only a day job."

Ludi's look of amusement was drifting (perhaps unwittingly) toward fondness. Molly smiled, too. Gene was so *young*—not even born yet when smoking pot was something you did as a gesture of tribal affiliation: not just for the sake of getting high but for the different way it made you look at things. Of course

Molly had now been looking at things that way for so long that it was hard to remember what had been so different about it.

"I bet you've never smoked a bud," said Ludi.

Molly came around to rest beside the younger woman on the sofa. The view of Gene's face was better. She liked watching him react to Ludi's constant challenges. He surely could not have understood what this was all about. As perhaps Ludi didn't, either.

"How about it?" Ludi pressed him. "Tell me all about your wild and crazy life."

On Gene's face, a struggle unfolded. Two opposing groups of facial muscles were involved—one of which wanted to lift his brow and narrow his eyes in a look of savoir faire, while the other wanted to clench his jaw and flash his eyes in denial. The contending forces tugged back and forth, until a third (more Gene-like) expression broke through them. Baffled and boyish—science whiz flunking out of English 205, Absurdity in Contemporary Drama—he flopped on the sofa, a safe enough distance from Ludi.

"I don't get it," he said. "Why can't we pick a topic and have a conversation without the whole thing coming around to being about *me*? What is this weird fascination you've got with whether I have antennas growing out of my head?"

Ludi fidgeted deeper into the sofa and said, "Hey, don't take it so personally. I was just—"

"Just what?" said Tex, hovering across the room.

"Shh." Molly laid a hand supportively on the young woman's shoulder.

"Tell me," said Tex. "You can let me in on these woman secrets now that I'm *dead*, can't you?"

Molly shook her head. "That's why they're called secrets."

"You were *just*," Gene repeated carefully. He stared at the coffee table covered with photographs of pot. The wake of a passing lobster boat caused the *Bee* to rise a few inches, swaying to starboard. Through a porthole came the noise of a radio tuned loudly to the country station that called itself 92 MOOSE.

"She's actin single," the singer lamented, "I'm drinkin' doubles."

"Yeah," said Ludi. "I was just."

The two of them looked at each other. Gene looked at her eyes and she looked at his mouth. From its place in the sky the sun hurled down enough thermonuclear energy to satisfy the needs of humankind for a couple of weeks. Photosynthetic organisms captured a fraction of this, but as with most of the blessings of Nature, the planet blew 99 percent of it.

Gene hadn't shaved this morning and his upper lip was shadowed by a pale brown moustache. Ludi's hair was a lovely mess. Their mutual blood pressure rose and they smelled like a pair of healthy young animals. Molly felt her own immaterial body quivering.

"Um," said Gene.

Ludi moved closer to him. Not touching. But into his bubble of private space. She tossed her head, as though getting something out of the way.

"Hey," she murmured.

"Hey," he said. Scared to death—but the kind of scared that might instantly snap over to medal-winning bravery. His eyes were large and brown and they seemed to deepen, to enfold things.

Her hand was almost on his arm and
his lips were moving to hers when
a beeper went off.

"You've *got* to be kidding," groaned Molly.

"Yes!" shouted Tex. "Saved by the bell!"

Ludi practically leapt off the sofa. She said, "What's that?"

Gene's eyes fell shut. If he was trying by force of will to make the beeper self-destruct, he failed. Like a man waking up from the greatest dream *ever*, he moved his hand to his belt and unclipped the plastic box. One-eyed, he stared down at it.

"It's the Antichrist," he said. "I am being summoned to the Underworld."

"Watch yourself, buddy," said Tex. "That's nothing to joke about."

Molly could not believe she was hearing Tex say that *anything* was nothing to joke about.

> **Afterlife Factoid #15**
> It's amazing the effect death has on people.

Ludi seemed not to be listening. Her energies were devoted to recomposing herself. This involved mostly her hair, which she gathered in a sort of bundle that she then could not decide what to do with.

"Would it be okay," said Gene, considerately looking away, "if I used your friends' telephone?"

"Their what?" She smiled in a familiar, mocking way.

He blinked at her. "They don't have a *telephone*?"

"This is a boat, Doctor."

"So what? They could get a cellular phone."

"A *cellular* phone?" Ludi smirked. "Tex and *Molly*?"

"Oh, excuse me. They're friends of *yours*, aren't they. What was I thinking of?"

They looked sardonically at one another: comfortable again. Back on familiar territory.

Gene said, "I guess I better go find a pay phone somewhere. Or maybe I should just drive out to Goddin."

"On a Saturday?"

"Is it Saturday?" Gene shook his head. He was not accustomed to losing track of time. He shrugged. "Probably it's nothing that will take very long."

Ludi bit her lip. She said, "I've got to work later this afternoon."

"You do?"

"Not for a while, though."

The beeper went off again. Gene switched it off and stuffed it deep in a pocket.

Ludi smiled. "The Antichrist always rings twice?"

He didn't get it. Biology major. He took a step toward the hatch. A narrow slice of sunlight fell onto his face, and he raised his hand to block it. Then he turned back to Ludi and said:

"Why don't you come? It probably won't take long and then we can do something."

"*Do* something?" she said. Like a kind of dare. A challenge.

Blithely he accepted it. "Maybe if you behave," he told her, "I'll show you my marijuana fields."

WILD BLUE

"Where are you going?" Molly asked the raven perched on the railing of the flying bridge.

Quoth the raven: "Never mind."

"What are you going to do?"

"Nothing."

Molly didn't believe this for a minute. She had half a mind to grab the pesky bird and clip his wings.

"You're going to spy on them, aren't you?"

The raven did not deny this. He lifted one clawed foot and then the other, edgily.

Molly said, "How did you learn to do this, anyhow?"

"Do what?"

"Do *what*?" She shook her head. "Are you aware that you have turned into a *bird*?"

"Oh, that." The raven made a funny wing gesture: sort of a shrug. "Just an old motewolon thing."

Molly thought, Who says you can't teach an old Bear new tricks? "Just be careful," she said.

"Ha!" he cawed at her. "What's the worst that can happen— I die and get eaten by a Worm?"

The raven took flight. He circled the flying bridge a couple of times, blatantly showing off. Molly pretended to be unimpressed.

"This shouldn't take long," he squawked.

And Molly stood there watching
until the magic bird
disappeared.

or
maybe it'll take a while

after all, thought Tex, when he was away from the *Bee* and staring down at the immensity of creation. Something about being up here made you want never to touch the Earth again. Like something about dropping acid made you want never to come down. You never wanted to lose this feeling of clarity, of freedom from constraint, of boundless perspective.

He had lost sight of Gene and Ludi. But by spiraling higher he could make out the Goddin base, a quilt of green fields and cinder-colored runways spread across the countryside to the west-northwest. Tex glided for a minute or two, taking a look at the world he had known.

To the east he saw brownish, boulder-strewn expanses that looked like desolate moors but were actually profitable blueberry fields. He saw clusters of white houses, and among them the occasional obligatory steeple. In the middle distance rose the blue hump of Awonadjo Mountain, with the insectile antenna of WURS on top. Past that lay Cadillac Mountain, the first spot in the U.S.A. to catch the rising sun. Southward, hundreds of islands drifted like ice floes. Beyond them lay the great murky ocean he and Molly had sailed in upon.

Turning inland, he saw land so deeply green that it might have been black. The Great North Woods, rolling all the way up to Canada and then still rolling on until the last stunted spruces gave way to sedges and mosses and stunted ericaceous shrubs of the treeless tundra. It looked so mighty and endless that you almost couldn't make yourself worry about it. But it was not the

forest that had been. It was trammeled and weakened and reduced. Even so, it remained a forest: home to moose and coyotes
and eagles and bears. (And wolves! but that was Tex's secret.)
The day was coming when none of those creatures could survive
there, when the forest became a vast monocultured tree farm,
and ultimately when even the trees themselves succumbed to a
surfeit of nitrates in the rain, leaching of mineral cations from
the soil, steady bombardment of unfiltered ultraviolet radiation,
and a thousand other daily insults from an increasingly hostile
world.

The Worm would have the whole thing, before it was over.

And then it would be over.

What can a raven do? Tex turned westward and tucked his
wings in close and lowered his beak and stiffened his resolve. He
was going to be a good trouper. He was going to make Molly
proud of him.

But first, he was going to see what Gene and Ludi were up to.

A.C.

A beaten-up brown Suburban sat in the outermost
of the parking lots of the old Goddin base. From his
tree-high approach altitude, the raven's eyes could
make out only one of the many stickers that occluded its
windows.

BAN FIREARMS—
MAKE THE STREETS SAFE FOR A GOVERNMENT
TAKEOVER

A government takeover? thought Tex. Followed by what: the
government installs itself as . . . *the government?*

In the back of the Suburban, fenced off from the passenger
seats by a steel mesh like that in city police cars, was a large and
unusual-looking dog.

No time for that. Gene Deere's Rover sat outside the huge
sliding doors of a converted hangar, retrofitted with rows of skylights. Some of the skylights were open for ventilation, and Tex
could detect the characteristic odor of a greenhouse: peaty, ni-
trogenous, oxygen-rich and watery closeness. He flattened his
wings and slid down on currents of humid air, feeling like a
hugely cool hang glider.

The aluminum struts that supported the hangar roof made an impressive though somewhat dangerous perch. Below Tex hung banks of high-intensity-discharge lamps, their output blue-shifted from that of natural sunlight. Waves of heat rose from them, and the air hummed with the kind of buzz you get from an improperly grounded amplifier. Through the buzz Tex made out the sound of voices, somewhere below. The humidity and the HIDs together created a ceiling-level haze that was difficult to see through; so Tex (with misgivings duly recorded) stepped off the strut and fluttered downward, into the blinding upper cavity of the hangar.

Now he could see that the greenhouse held hundreds of parallel arrays of hydroponic tubs, linked by fat black rubber hoses and transparent plastic nutrient tubes, with an overhead matrix of ABS pipes that dispensed carbon dioxide. From a certain perspective the whole thing looked like a massively magnified computer chip, so that for an instant Tex—still descending in a wobbly spiral—felt like one of the reluctantly downsized kids on *The Magic School Bus.*

Then his sense of proportion flipped around and he felt awed by the hugeness of the operation. Thousands—no, *millions*—of tiny evergreen plants stood calf-high in the endless rows of water-filled tanks. Their needles were dark green, nearly black, and their stubby limbs stuck out in cone-shaped patterns that appeared identical from one baby tree to the next.

Clones, Tex supposed. An entire army of willing and able troops being readied for a blitzkrieg on the North Woods. As with well-made war movies, you had to admit there was a certain pulse-quickening grandeur about it all. You found yourself, even against your will, stirred by the martial hymns. Your feet tapped in time to the goose-stepping storm troopers. The next thing you knew, your popcorn was gone.

Tex snapped out of it. He heard the voices again, and he saw two men and a woman walking between ranks of seedlings on the opposite side of the hangar—far enough that Tex couldn't see their faces, though he figured they must be Gene and Ludi and (at last we meet!) the Antichrist. He swung himself around and flew in for a closer look.

Gene appeared to be annoyed and slightly flustered.

Ludi looked bored, ready to get out of here.

As for the A.C., he was as handsome, tanned and impeccably tailored as Tex had always (subliminally) supposed he must be. Sort of a Bar Harbor Yacht Club type.

Forgetting that he was visible, Tex glided close enough that Ludi, distracted, took notice of him. She stared up as though grateful to find something to look at, besides these rows of plants and soughing fluid lines. The two men were locked in arcane discussion—

calcium ion levels ... root-temperature spikes ... morphological impairment ...

—so Tex circled back, giving Ludi another fly-by. She smiled when she saw him. She waved with one whole arm.

"Hey, Jack," she called. "Is that you?"

Jack? thought Tex.

QUOONNK, he called back to her. Just by way of making small talk.

Gene looked about, as though sensing that another conversation was taking place. He saw Ludi gazing toward the ceiling but did not follow her eyes up to Tex. "Are you talking to yourself?" he said.

"Deere," snapped the A.C. "Pay attention, won't you?"

Gene turned back to his boss. "I'm listening," he said. "You were telling me about the message on the terminal."

"It wasn't a *message,*" the A.C. said. "It was a *banner.* Here, I took a screen shot."

From a pocket of his Nautica windbreaker he pulled and unfolded a letter-sized piece of paper. Tex had to swoop daringly low to get a look at it.

"What the hell is this?" said Gene.

The A.C. folded the questionable document and returned it to his pocket. "I gather," he said, "that this amounts to a claim of responsibility. I've left the system just the way I found it, until the security people get here."

"You've reported this to the police?"

"Of course not. I'm talking about *Company* security people. I telephoned Houston earlier this morning. They're going to send a team up no later than Monday."

"That's a long time to keep the computers frozen."

The A.C. shrugged. "That's an Operations problem. I've got to place maximum priority on protecting the integrity of our systems."

Gene turned to make sure Ludi was still hanging around. He said, "Of course, it will take some time to assess the damage. Maybe the plants will suffer only minor developmental impairment."

"What the worst case?" asked the A.C.

"Worst case." Gene frowned. "Okay. I guess the worst case is, these root systems are sufficiently deformed that the stock is no longer field-viable. We have to run off another batch of tissue samples and start over. No more than a few months' delay. Plus the expense, of course."

"A few months' delay? Plus the *expense*? Deere, do you have any idea what you're saying here?"

"No," Gene cheerfully admitted. "That's an Admin problem, isn't it?"

The A.C. was a sporting type. He touched an imaginary épée to his chest and said, "Got me. Nonetheless, let me give you an idea. If we actually were to lose a few months' growing time, then there is scarcely any way we can attain our goal of twenty million new trees next year."

Gene raised one finger: a point of order. "Not quite true," he said. "This hit only affects the stock of X *dawkinsia* 4.3.2. And it's not clear, to me at least, how strongly committed we want to be to that particular strain. We can easily make up the loss out of other stocks. Also we can offset some of it by digging 4.3.2 out of the trial plots, though I grant you that's a pain in the butt. Our best bet, though, might be to adopt a more diversified planting regimen. That's the direction I'm leaning in, anyway, to be honest with you."

"Deere," said the A.C., his voice curiously gentle, as though he were speaking to a child. "Spare me your touching honesty. All I ask is your diligent attention to your duties. Right now I would say that your most pressing duty is keeping these plants alive and—what was your term?—*field-viable*."

Gene's expression was hard to read. He seemed intent upon not making eye contact with his superior.

The A.C. went on, apparently to himself, "It would be *wonderful* if we could get this nailed down before the King gets up here."

"Who?" said Gene.

"The C.E.O.," said the A.C., his irritation obvious. "The Mondo Jefe. Burdock Herne. Have you forgotten already?"

"Not at all," said Gene. "Midsummer's Eve, right?"

He turned to overtake Ludi, who had wandered some distance down the aisle. The two of them receded slowly toward the hazy glow of the hangar door.

Tex let them go. He hung around the A.C., circling slowly beneath the hot lights. He figured that anybody who was unlikable enough to make Gene Deere look good by comparison merited closer study.

The A.C. stared at the hydroponic baths for a minute or two. Then, with violent abruptness, he reached out and yanked hard at a juvenile spruce twig. The whole tree came slurping out of the growth medium, splashing fat drops of its nutrient bath across the executive trousers. Wincing, the A.C. dropped it to the floor. Then he kicked it away, underneath the tanks.

"Goddamn mutant-ass plants," he said.

UNTAMED

Departing the hangar, the A.C. set off across the parking lot at a serious hiker's stride, making for the beat-up Suburban. Tex could not tell where Gene and Ludi had gotten off to. The Rover was gone. He scanned the road leading out toward the main gate, but found it empty. Then he remembered Gene's promise to show Ludi his marijuana fields. Tex had already seen the marijuana fields. He decided to stick with the A.C. awhile longer.

Out of the Suburban stepped a life-size G.I. Joe.

"Howdy, Mr. Sauvage," he said, in a C&W drawl.

The A.C. spoke in a very low voice: "Eckhart. Sorry to keep you waiting."

"Not waiting," said Eckhart. A bit of his drawl evaporated. "Thinking. If your mind is active, you're never wasting time."

"What's that from?" said the A.C. *"Management Secrets of Genghis Khan?"*

"We could probably learn a lot from old Genghis," said Eckhart. "But as I recall, it's from one of your Gulf Atlantic training tapes."

"That's what I'm referring to," said the A.C.

Tex wondered if Sauvage meant the same thing as Savage. He

thought not. Some connection with an old Truffaut movie clung
to his mind; but only by a thread.

"So," said Eckhart. "I gather you folks have had some kind of
security breach."

"*We* have had a security breach. And *you* are the Chief of
Security. Though frankly, I suspect this is not exactly in your
bailiwick."

"Say what?"

"It's not in my bailiwick, either. I've called in some Company
hotshots. In the meantime, the sun is shining and there's hay
to make."

"Ah," said Eckhart. His smile was fangy. His long teeth were
cigarette-yellow. "Now you're talking my language, Mr.
Sauvage."

"Without going into a wealth of detail," said the A.C., "I can
tell you that we have been attacked electronically by what appear
to be fairly sophisticated eco-hackers. I'm talking about computer
criminals who are pushing an extremist Green Party–type agenda.
They've broken into our propagation system and they may have
succeeded—I say *may,* though I'm afraid it's pretty certain—in
disrupting our breeding operation geared toward next season's
replanting strategy."

Eckhart listened to this with slightly squinted eyes. After a moment he said, "You don't mean Green Party, do you? Maybe
you're thinking more like Earth First. Because the Greens are
more like Libertarians. They got that biology professor they ran
for governor. Quite a few of them out in Applemont."

"Eckhart," Chas Sauvage said, "please. Try to understand the
importance of what we're talking about."

Eckhart gave Sauvage a quick, sly glance that Tex immediately
recognized. It was the look Mainers give to people who think
they're a bunch of ignorant yokels. "I do understand what we're
talking about," he said. "We're talking about some high-tech
monkey-wrenching."

"No," said Sauvage. "We're talking about God's own hand-
engraved, gilt-edged opportunity."

"Come again?" said Eckhart.

Sauvage was smiling, not pleasantly. "Remember that rather
unconventional project we talked about? The, ah, controlled
burn?"

"Aha." Eckhart nodded rapidly. "I get you."

"Well," said Sauvage, "this band of hackers, whoever they are,
have just handed us the chance of a lifetime. We can move for-

ward with that scenario, and the blame will quite naturally fall upon the ozone-heads. We don't even have to draw the connection overtly, ourselves. We can simply issue a routine press release—trusting that law enforcement authorities will apprehend the parties responsible, et cetera—and let the media draw their own conclusions."

Eckhart licked his lips. He smiled appreciatively. "Come over here," he said. "I've got something to show you."

Sauvage allowed himself to be led around to the back of the Suburban. Eckhart tapped on one of the windows, and a large, unusual-looking dog hurled itself, snarling, against the glass. The thud of impact was audible way up where Tex hung in the breeze.

Chas Sauvage moved back a full two steps. "What in god's name is *that*?"

Eckhart, clearly beside himself with pride, said, "*That*, my friend, is a full-blooded timber wolf."

"A wolf?" said Sauvage. "Here in Maine?"

"Born and bred," declared Eckhart, beaming.

And Tex spiraled up and away, thinking:

Another satisfied customer.

INTO THE WOODS (2)

He found the Rover empty, in the X where two runways crossed. At each of the four quarters stood a patch of baby forest. Tex spiraled up but saw no movement anywhere. No movement, that is, except the bending of tender branches, the flutter of marijuana leaves, the whicker of spruce needles, the ceaseless stirring of air, the passage of cumulus billows across the sky. When you came down to it there was little else in the world *except* movement. Movement and change. What Tex was looking for were two of the very few things that were keeping still.

He coasted low across acres of foliage. He called out in his raven's voice. No answer.

Ludi, he thought, where are you?

He was surprised by how he felt. Like a lover rejected. Churned-up inside. What right or reason he had to feel this way was not a question he could have answered. He thought about Ludi's gold-tipped hair, her long thin arms, her Missouri smile, the laugh that could be surprisingly hard and mocking.

Below him grew saplings, shoulder-high, interplanted with

shrubby hemp. The air was spiced with resin. Knowing that the hemp had been altered so that it no longer produced THC did not prevent Tex from catching a contact buzz. He wondered if it was safe to fly like this. Then he remembered that he was already dead. He was dead, yet he was still having adventures. His survival seemed always in doubt. It was as though he had already graduated but was still required to study for exams. Whereas in Real Life—what did that mean, anymore?—Tex had dropped out during his freshman year and never looked back. There had been too much to do to waste time being taught things. Now he felt that he had left nearly everything undone and learned more than his head could hold. How had this happened?

He felt crazy and confused.

Ludi, he thought in his human mind.

GRRREEEGGH, he cried in his raven voice.

Then with a kind of vision that belonged to neither—a matter of pure intuition, quick flash on the screen of the 6th chakra— he saw where the two of them had gone.

The small metal sign at the edge of the little woodland read:

PLOT 28b
Hard / softwood
"Naturalistic" mix
No spray

Ludi's denim jacket dangled from a corner of it. The sun was high, and the day was growing warm. Hot, almost. Tex wondered if ravens could sweat. His avian lungs were pumping air a couple hundred times per minute. How long could a bird keep this up?

He flew low, barely clearing the branch tops. For kicks he snagged leaves with his claws. The sap felt sticky and cool. He listened for sounds of conversation, laughter, footsteps in fallen leaves. But nothing. Wind in his ears. His own miniature throbbing heart.

You could believe this was a real woodland. All the pieces were there: oaks and beeches and willows; pines and spruces and firs; blooming chokecherries, shadbush, ironwood, inkberry, fringe tree, yellowwood, eastern larch; ferns and forbs and ground covers whose seeds the birds or the wind had ferried in. The chief clue that it was an artificial place was that in Nature such randomness is *not* the rule. The natural world is not a level playing field, featureless as a spreadsheet. Subtle changes in topography and soil type, drainage patterns, wind direction, accidents of seed distribution, the migration and feeding habits of local fauna—all interacting with the inbuilt strengths and weaknesses of the trees themselves—produce clearly recognizable structures of dominance and distribution. Oaks will prevail in one area, larches in another, firs in a third, all within sight of one another. And the patterns will change with time. The larches will die out after one generation because larch seedlings cannot thrive in the shade cast by their parents. A new order, a path of succession, will emerge.

But always there is structure, pattern, organization. Randomness is a statistical hallucination.

So this was *not* a real forest, then. But what was it?

It was a garden, Tex supposed. A place where Nature had been played with. Maybe a botanist's idea of Paradise.

In Paradise, you had beauty and you had betrayal. You had innocent joy and bitter disappointment. You had sweetness and sadness and surprise. You had flowers. You had failures. You had lovers and lookers-on. Fresh-faced youths and jaded old snakes. That was the nature of Paradise. Or, if you thought about it, the paradisiacal aspect of Nature. Not one thing but many.

It could not be simplified. It could not be mastered. No part of it could be chucked out or the whole shebang would be lost. *Poof*—the memory of an enchanted garden vanishes into fairy tales.

Tex heard the sound of breathing. It came from a glade of white birch. He wheeled over and grabbed a claw-hold on one of their slender uppermost limbs; the whole tree swayed with his weight. Its pale green, heart-shaped leaves quivered as though someone gently were shaking them. Close to his eyes were dozens of minuscule yellowish flowers, from which a small cloud of pollen rose as the branch shook in Tex's grasp.

Ludi lay on her side almost directly underneath him. Her jeans and her cotton sweater made a cushion for her naked hips and shoulders. Her body looked breathtakingly elongated, the unbroken curve of flesh stretching out like some path your mind had followed in a dream. Her skin was a uniform color, a kind of parchment-tan, paling to rose-toned white at the buttocks and darkening to rich amber at the nipples. Where Gene's fingers lightly moved along her thigh, the skin yielded so softly and yet so clearly that Tex could swear he felt it in his own body—felt both the touch and the being-touched. His heart filled with blood and kept swelling and probably would have exploded. Only he was a magical bird and couldn't die.

He didn't really want to look at Gene, but Gene was there to be looked at and somehow it was unavoidable. The tall young man was perfectly formed in a way Tex didn't think he himself had ever been: arms and legs and torso in ideal Da Vincian proportion, not especially muscular but nonetheless sculpturesque, subtly shadowed where the limbs flexed and contracted. His body hair was a uniform pale brown, and it made him look warm and soft rather than grown-up and manly. Tex pushed aside the clear impression of what Gene's embrace must feel like to Ludi: soothing, thrilling, electric where his skin moved against hers.

Afterlife Factoid #16
Even for the dead, sex goes off like an atomic bomb.

Ludi curled the long fingers of one hand around Gene's penis. It looked huge in them, fat and purple-capped. The skin was stretched smooth and you could see a single bulging blue vein. Ludi pulled it toward her stomach, squeezed it into the soft flesh there.

How would she even *think* of having such a thing inside her?

More to the point, how could *Tex* think of it? And yet how could he not: Gene's groan of overwhelming need might as well have been his own. Ludi's leg bent upward and slid across Gene's thigh and she rose up slightly, pressing him down under her. She rolled enough that you could see the gentle declivity of her perfect ass, the tender muscles clenching and relaxing as her body took him in. He pressed against her with the whole lower part of his abdomen. His eyes were closed and he must have imagined that he was going to cease to exist at any moment. Sounds came out of their mouths that could have been universally understood, though they did not exist in any language.

It looked like swimming. The motion was as gentle and as powerful as a gathering wave. Their mouths fused and their arms interwove. Ludi rolled farther onto him and one of his knees came up and you could see his testicles and the base of his penis, the shaft disappearing in Ludi's darkness. By this time Tex was not even pretending to try not to look and was *way* past kidding himself that this wasn't a turn-on. It was sickening in a way, too, but still: a turn-on. The smells and the textures and the fluids mingling and the bits of leaf-mold clinging to their skin. The rising pace, the accumulating pressure. Ludi tore at Gene's hair and he put a hand in the middle of her back and held her tightly in place for a series of deep, drawn-out, stabbing thrusts. There was violence in the end of the act but also a weirdly savage magnificence. Ludi's hair fell like a cataract across his face and she gasped once, twice, lowered her forehead to his own, and looked down to behold the wonder they had made between them. Gene's eyes opened wide and delirious and drank her in, then he pressed his mouth to her neck and appeared to shudder or even to silently whimper. The last drops of his semen drooled onto her leg and onto the ground as he fell out of her.

Then they rolled back together and they stayed that way. The sun on their skin and the wind drying their sweat and the trees that huddled murmurously around them all became part of the multisouled being that they were. Tex felt like crying or sighing or collapsing in exhaustion and futility. Instead he lifted his wings and vanished in the desolate blinding perfect sky.

NEWS

The Channel 5 reporter that everyone called Gidget was doing people-on-the-street interviews at the main intersection of Dublin while the annual AIDS Walk was trying to get itself under way. She asked Sefyn Hunter, bedecked in a giant red sash like a New Year's Baby, whether the epidemic had altered his sexual practices in any way.

"It doesn't matter what you say," she confided. "They'll never run this on the 6 O'clock Report. Maybe at 11:00, but by then everyone's asleep."

"Well, honey," said Sefyn, "you've just answered your own question, haven't you?"

Gidget switched the microphone off.

At the dais set up outside the C-Vu Cafe, Donna di Fuora, Chair of the Dublin County AIDS Coalition, was talking loudly. Some people listened and many did not. The crowd comprised about 75 or 80 people, mostly marchers but also street kids and fascinated tourists holding video cameras and a deputy sheriff named Doug. It was one of those fresh and clear and beautiful days early in the Maine summer that are so perfect you tend to forget what you're supposed to be doing. *Life,* you think, is what you're supposed to be doing.

"We have been fortunate thus far," Donna di Fuora practically shouted, "in comparison to some of the hard-hit areas across the country. But let's remember that even a single needless death is one death too many."

«A needless death?»

thought Tex. He perched on the metal arm of a streetlight, just over the halide bulb. Gidget was below him, scanning the crowd for someone bite-worthy. Tex felt drained, woozy, and paradoxically lost, which is why he had come here to the center of everything to regain his bearings.

«What does that mean—a needless death? Everybody's *got* to die sometime. So you could say that every death is necessary, in the long run.»

There you had it: the extent of his disorientation.

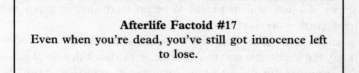

Afterlife Factoid #17
Even when you're dead, you've still got innocence left to lose.

Hoot Banebook came up to the dais to deliver a few well-chosen exhortations. The organizers of the Walk were trying to interest people in forming a line along the sidewalk. From his perch on the light, Tex could see the uppermost crosspiece of the radar mast on the *Linear Bee,* bobbing up and then falling out of sight behind the dead chicken plant.

"It is not for us to judge our fellow man," Hoot Banebook declared. "As it is not for us to judge the workings of the Lord."

Amen, thought Tex. Looking down at the milling, gossiping, laughing, feckless, well-intentioned crowd—good people, every one, though prone to error and ignorance and litigation—you could not help wondering how it could be that the world was such a total mess. You could not help thinking that all this positive energy and community spirit must be signs of a healthy society.

"We needn't think ourselves so perfect," said Hoot, "that we are in a position to condemn the sins and transgressions of those around us. Especially people whom we do not even personally know."

Maybe it was like an old tree. Maybe these do-gooders in the intersection of Dublin, Maine, were like the part of an aging tree that continues to put out fresh green leaves, to endure heat and drought, to reach bravely upward for sunlight, even while the great body of the tree is dying and rotting away. There were chestnut trees in the woods around here that had been felled by blight 80 or 90 years ago, yet whose great hollow stumps continued every spring to produce a crop of hopeful young foliage. And every summer the new foliage would succumb to the blight and the tree would be a little bit closer to finished.

Trees like that, Tex thought, are like the corpse who doesn't know he's dead. He sits up in the middle of his own wake and starts crooning "The Wild Rover."

"Tolerance is a sign of strength," said Hoot. "It is a sign that we are not afraid to look upon others with compassion, whether or not we personally approve of their particular choice of lifestyles."

Tex had never been sure how to feel about those old chestnut trees. He almost wished that one year he'd be hiking through the woods and find that the trees had given up at last; that their spirits had fled, and there was to be no more shining green and irredeemably doomed foliage.

At the same time, you had to keep pulling for the old rotten thing, the impossible survivor. Maybe in the black depths of January, some crafty old chestnut motewolon would be given the power of the Mite.

"Don't *now friend* me, you self-righteous motherfucker."

Tex dragged himself out this thought-stream to discover that a shouting match had broken out on the street below. One of the participants was Hoot Banebook.

"Come now, young man," the Rev said. "Let's not poison this civic occasion with personal attacks, just to further the homosexual agenda."

Gidget pointed her microphone at him. Meanwhile the camera operator searched for Hoot's antagonist, who was elbowing his way through the onlookers. All Tex could make out was a floppy, tomato-red Capestries beret.

"You've got a lot of nerve," the heckler shouted, "accusing *us* of personal attacks. When there you are up there, making your passive-aggressive sneers about *lifestyles* and *marginal social groups* and telling us we should *tolerate the shortcomings* of people. But we know what you're really saying. You're saying it's *wrong,* and we can't *personally countenance* it, but let's be big Christian soldiers and not let it get our morale down."

Tex could not have said at exactly what point he realized that the heckler was Guillermo. It was not a question of recognizing the voice (which was echoey from up here), but of the habit Guillermo had of using the word *we* when actually he was talking about himself—as though his personal being was of such magnitude that he needed a plural pronoun to encompass it.

"I can tell, young man," said the Reverend—speaking grandly to the crowd more than to Guillermo—"that you're feeling a good deal of anger and resentment here. Perhaps you've known someone very well who has been struck down by his tragic illness."

"Don't make *me* the issue." Guillermo reached the front of the crowd, where the Channel 5 camera dude got a fix on him, while Gidget moved in like a socially awkward shark.

"Of course not," said Hoot. "Of course not. The issue is much larger than you or me. The issue is nothing less than our very survival as a free and God-fearing society."

"You don't fear God," Guillermo said. His disadvantage in height was made worse by Hoot's position on the curb. "You don't fear AIDS, either. You think you're safe because God is on your side. But let me tell you, mister. If this germ doesn't get you, then the next one will. And don't think there isn't going to be a next one. Because what you and your right-wing cronies are doing to this planet is unleashing all the forces of pestilence and famine and plague you've read about in that Book of yours. And *then* some. You like Bible stories because the awful things happen to somebody else. You can pretend you're the Israelis and you're wearing the white robes. But you're really the Pharaohs, and the next time holy wrath is rained down, it's going to fall on *you*."

Guillermo moved a step closer to the TV camera, and—media savvy to the bone—peered five and a half hours into the future and gave the viewers of the 6 O'clock Report a companionable nod.

"Remember, folks," he said, "you heard it here first. And here's another scoop for you. Today at the Goddin Forest Research Station, a major system failure occurred in the machinery that sustains the mutant tree clones that the Earth-haters are planning to set loose to destroy the Great North Woods. The action today was only a temporary shutdown. But it serves as a warning of what is to come. If people like the Reverend here are intent upon waging war against every form of life other than their own, then they have to understand that they won't be the only army on the battlefield."

Gidget let him do this: rattle off his little *pronunciamiento* without interruption. The Reverend Banebook was less inclined to surrender the airwaves. He stepped off the curb and bore down on the camera, the reporter, and the spot directly underneath Tex's streetlight.

Guillermo took a step back, perhaps out of bodily fear. The

camera operator sensed a shifting of the wind. As Gidget redirected her microphone

and the Reverend uttered a stentorian clearing of the throat

and the camera refocused

and the old goddess Neman—whose specialty was provoking discord among erstwhile allies—rustled her feathers in wicked glee

Tex the raven stuck his tail out over the edge of the streetlamp and released a stream of magical bird poop. It accelerated in pious accord with the Traditional Value of 32 feet per second, until interrupted by the Reverend Banebook's right temple. From there it splattered a bit, mostly downward onto the man of the cloth's cloth, but also outward onto the lens of the Channel 5 news camera. Gidget was spared, though startled. She clutched Guillermo's sleeve. Guillermo offered what comfort he could; then he doffed his Capestries beret in a salute to his unknown assistant.

"Many thanks, Brother Raven," he said to the bird on the streetlight.

And Tex croaked:

DE NADA.

"Did that bird *talk* to you?" asked Gidget.

"It's possible," said Guillermo. "We have a lot to learn about the minds of other creatures on this planet. Would you like to sit down and have some coffee?"

"God, I'd love to." She clutched his arm more tightly, stooping to adjust the fit of an uncomfortable-looking shoe.

He guided her toward the door of the C-Vu Cafe. Her camera operator, still buffing his lens, was left wondering what story to follow here.

And at last, the AIDS Walk got under way.

STREET LEVEL

The Walk wound through Dublin, leaving the microdowntown and heading out toward Route 1 so as to garner attention. There was little to look at except the Lesbian Avengers from Lewiston, whose usual in-your-face act this year included a sign declaring, mysteriously,

WE ARE ALL POSITIVE

Tex flapped a fair distance above, taking note mostly of how passing motorists were reacting, when he recognized something familiar about one of the last Walkers in line. This was a tall and somewhat stooped-over man, dressed unseasonably in a drab shapeless coat, his gait so lethargic that you expected him at any moment to keel over. Curious, Tex swooped down for a closer look.

The lugubrious fellow had as close as you could come to no facial expression at all. He appeared to be conscious, was about the extent of it. Then the fellow turned and raised his head and looked the raven right in the beady black eye. And Tex exclaimed:

"Beale!" Only of course it came out sounding different than that.

"It's me," the sad-sack dryad admitted. He lifted an arm and Tex flapped down and landed there.

"Beale," he said. "Where've you been keeping yourself?"

"Nowhere."

"Out in the woods, you mean?"

"*Nowhere.*" Beale became churlish. "Dimensionlessness. The vanishing point of the spiral, the inner infinity."

"Ah," said Tex.

Beale trudged on for a while in silence. You would have said he was moody, but that would imply a certain level of emotional energy.

"Hey, listen," said Tex. "Did you get the word from the Bishop? He's letting you guys stay on, if I can come up with someplace for you to live. I haven't had much time to look into anything yet. But that's pretty cool, right?"

Beale appeared to ignore him.

Tex persisted. "Want to drop by the *Bee* after the Walk? We could get a bite to eat. Molly's been dying to meet you."

Beale looked at him, perhaps trying to decide whether Tex was being ironic.

"I do not eat," he said. "I photosynthesize. I act as a liaison between the inanimate stuff of the Earth and the ceaseless flow of energy from the stars. I am a receiver, a site of transubstantiation. Not something that you drag home and stuff food in."

"Hey," said Tex, "I was just trying to be friendly, okay? If this is how you're going to act, then maybe it's time to say happy trails."

He did not raise his wings to take flight, however, and Beale did not appear to want him to go.

"I apologize," said Beale—slowly, but catching Tex off guard.

"I haven't been feeling myself lately. I'm not accustomed to rapid change, and I believe it's left me rather disoriented."

"Change?" said Tex. "What change?"

"Oh, you know."

"I do?"

Beale made an expansive gesture with his free arm that might have signified something heavy and Buddhist or might have been an effort to shoo black flies away.

Tex cut him off. "The bugs are dying out, aren't they? That must make it about Father's Day."

"Rose Moon," said Beale.

"Time for the mosquitoes to start."

"Bears come down from the mountains."

"Massholes on vacation."

"Wolves choose mates."

This gave Tex pause. "Hey, cool. So. What month does that make it?"

Neither of them knew.

Then Beale said, as abruptly as possible for a dryad: "Evolution."

"Say what?"

"You asked what change. That is what change. Evolution. Morphogenesis. The creation of new forms."

"What are you talking about?" Tex looked around, as though one of the other AIDS Walkers might explain it to him. But the two guys immediately in front of them were into some totally other conversation: the pedantic new conductor of the Bangor Symphony, an insane all-Rachmaninoff concert, a pianist named Ivo who looks like Jonathan Brandis. De gustibus, right?

"What am I talking about?" said Beale, coming to a halt. He raised the arm Tex had dug his claws into, so that the two of them stood eye to eye. "I'm talking about an intemperate bargain you struck with a meddlesome goddess. Which you now have imprudently extended to include one of the Primary Arbiters of Reality."

"I kind of didn't think that Reality was like, open to arbitration."

Beale spat into the dust of the roadside. Where the saliva spattered on the gravel, a tiny seedling sprouted, grew rapidly, fattened and matured, spread its limbs, showered acorns, began to decline, rotted, and vanished.

"Come with me," Beale said. "I'll show you what you have done."

"I'd love to see that," said Tex. "Really. Because most of my life people have accused me of hanging around doing nothing."

"This is not your life," said Beale, "any longer."

SPIRAL DANCE

The raven flew with the acorn in its mouth to the old Goddin Air Force Base, now a gleaming exemplar of post–Cold War private-sector economic conversion.

"The greenhouse," Beale directed him, and Tex plunged without slowing through one of the open skylights. The sudden access of heat and humidity came as a bodily shock, and Tex seized a purchase on a copper misting pipe.

"Okay," he mumbled as best he could with the obstruction in his mouth. "We're here. Now what?"

"Eat me," said the acorn.

Tex almost choked. "I beg your pardon?"

The acorn sighed. "You're an animal. I'm a plant. Ingest me."

So the raven did.

And immediately, everything was different.

Around him, the vast B-52 hangar with its blinding matrices of HID lamps felt cramped and dim. The bulbs pretending to be sunlight were puny, anemic things, their spectral output scarcely adequate to keep an African violet alive. The millions of trees strained upward, wanting more. In the tanks, the nutrient solution smelled mediciney, like ultraprocessed and vitamin-fortified baby food. Tex yearned for air, for wind in his face, for rain splashing his skin and rinsing the dust off.

"Bummer," he said. "Get me out of here, man."

"Why?" said Beale. "If it's good enough for trees, why not people?"

In the next moment, the dryad was standing before him—back in his humanlike form, feet astride the snaking plastic tubes in the middle of an aisle. And Tex was himself again (though dead.).

Beale said, entirely deadpan, "I suppose you are wondering why I brought you here today."

"I thought it was me that brought you."

"Nonsense. I thought it might prove enlightening to you—being present at the creation."

"Creation?" Tex adjusted his position on the pipe, which creaked and shimmied along its vast length. "Are you sure we've got time for that?"

"Creation takes no time at all," said Beale. "Ask any of your own great thinkers. The new idea appears in a flash, as quick as light. What takes time is the subsequent process of translation. Pinning the idea down in words, or in symbols and equations. Or in our case, in molecules. In DNA."

"I see," said Tex.

"I doubt that," said Beale. Not unkindly. Just matter-of-fact. And of course he was right. "Creation is preceded by stress. The world changes. Relationships dissolve. The system is thrown into chaos. Old truths no longer apply; the future is completely in doubt."

"What are we talking about?" said Tex. "Plants? People? The world?"

Beale said, "Early this morning, some friends of yours disrupted the life-sustaining equipment to which these trees are shackled. Now it is not at all certain whether the trees will survive. *If* they survive, we cannot foresee how it will be accomplished. In a moment such as this, the barrier between what is actual and what is possible becomes thin and permeable."

"Hold on," said Tex. "Friends of *mine*? You mean Guillermo?"

"Not friends you *know*," said Beale. "But friends nonetheless. Because they are carrying out in the living world the tedious, mechanical procedures required to implement your great wish. You do remember your wish, I hope."

"What do you know about my wish?"

"Very little. But I know how such things go. You project some desire into the Unmanifest, the Field of All Possibilities, and then you expect it instantly to be fulfilled. But of course, things do not happen that easily. Magic is an *extremely* complicated and wearisome affair. And most of it has to be worked out in the physical, explicate world. It has to obey the Laws of Nature. Not that *you* care about such hindrances. You are only interested in results. But look—you are causing me to digress."

"I am?"

"You are. I was trying to explain evolution to you. But I see we have a problem with your attention span. Very well. I will employ special audiovisual effects."

Beale turned and touched his hand to a little spruce tree—the gesture was ludicrously affected, as though he were doing a parody of *The Birth of Adam*. But like most timeworn artistic devices
it worked
and Tex felt as though a whole new world-view was being

projected into his head; or else maybe he was being projected In There: into the world of the spruce seedling, not just as a human looking out but as a different kind of thing altogether, an arrangement of vegetal tissues with no head, no center of awareness, only a diffuse and fluid kind of relationship with the outside world. The sense of intimacy with the air, the light, the other trees nearby was exhilarating.

But what Tex really dug was the *music*. It was like a photon dance—splattery, bright, pointillistic. It *unfolded*. Then it refolded again. It was like a bubble that got larger until it couldn't grow outward anymore so that it formed a kind of umbilicus and turned itself outside-in, growing back into its own hollow core, filling itself up. *Invaginating*.

This was not a thing you could see (in fact, it defied Tex's efforts to visualize), but rather a thing you simply cognized. It was a rhythm deep inside the music, like a drumbeat so low-pitched that you could only feel it pulsing through the floor and into your feet.

"What *is* this?" said Tex.

"What you are experiencing," said Beale, "is the consciousness of this young tree."

"But the *music*," said Tex.

"The music is the message," said Beale. "It is, if you will, the effort of the tree to express itself—to say, This is what I am. Now, please: pay closer attention."

Tex tried. This time, instead of sound, he was seized by a vision: a discomfiting image of writhing twisty things wrapping around each other, coming unwrapped, grabbing other things that floated in a viscous stew, nurturing blobs of quivering matter, breaking apart, recombining.

"This is the genetic material," said Beale. "This is the level at which the tree attempts to transcribe the music of life into the mechanics of living tissue. Only as you see, it is plunging into chaos. Its organization is disrupted. The implicate tree and the explicate tree—the timeless idea and the living reality—are no longer in balance. This is an unstable situation that cannot continue. The most likely outcome is the plant will die."

"Great," said Tex. "More death. It's the story of my life."

"In this case, however," said Beale, sounding infinitely regretful, "a different outcome is possible. In fact, it is all but inevitable. Watch."

Tex watched. Now what he perceived was *texture*. Wet, warm, slick, foaming with trapped gases, thick with minerals, coalescent with proteins. Neither solid nor liquid but something else. Proto-plasmic. Tex thought of a slab of raw liver, a handful of cold spaghetti, a loaded condom.

"Yich," he declared.

"Behold," said Beale. "The *prima materia*. The cellular constit-uents from which life is sculpted. Remember, the music is the message. The genes are the tools, the intermediaries. *This* is the medium itself. This is how the life-idea expresses itself."

Tex liked the concept. He let the yicky warm gooey stuff seethe around him. "So, where does creation come in?"

"On a very gross level," said Beale, "it can be driven by the living substance. A shortage of one thing, a surfeit of another, can force an adaptive response at the next level, the genetic mate-rial. Let's go back there."

They went. Tex watched the chromosomes dance, long stringy molecules writhing and splitting and changing partners.

"Now another way of effecting change," said Beale, "is to in-tervene at this finer level. You insert a new strand, or induce an error in copying an old one. These things happen quite naturally all the time, mostly through the migration of viruses and viroids. In this way, new molecular ideas spread democratically through-out the biome. It's as though you reached into an orchestra and pulled out the tuba player and inserted a mandolin. As to the music *itself*, however—"

Then they were floating gloriously free, drifting on etheric chords. It was recognizably the same as before and yet ever-changing, ever unfolding.

"*Here*," Beale said, "is the level at which genuine creativity comes into play. Not coarse manipulation of the artistic tools, or even coarser disruption of the raw clay. Rather a change, if you will, in the mind of the artist."

"The Artist?" said Tex. "You mean, like . . ."

"No," said Beale. "I am not talking about one of your gods. I'm talking about the damned spruce tree. I'm talking about the organism itself. Haven't you ever stopped to consider what an organism actually is? Haven't you for an instant wondered what is the difference between a lump of organic matter wrapped in cellophane at the supermarket, and a lump of organic matter walking around chewing grass in a field?"

"Believe me," said Tex—imagining himself lying at the bottom of a well, being chewed up by hungry little . . . you don't want to know—"I wonder about shit like that *all the time*."

"The difference is, the lump of living matter is not just a heap of parts but a *whole*. Its own master. Its own god, in a sense. It is both the thing and the *idea* of the thing—the possible and the actual. Is this too philosophical for you?"

Tex cleared his throat. "Sort of a top-down versus bottom-up approach, right? I can dig that. But still, it kind of seems like the real question isn't *how*. Like, how does biology really work—I mean, who cares? The real question is *why?* Why do cool new things keep happening? Why does all this *newness* keep popping up?"

Beale made a clucking noise. "Don't you realize," he said, "that what you are asking is, in effect, the oldest and hoariest question in the book? It's that tired and, I'm afraid, rather lame old riddle, *Where do ideas come from?*"

"That's it!" said Tex. "Exactly. Where do ideas come from?"

"Oh, for heaven's sake," said Beale. "Isn't that obvious?"

WHOME

Beale spoke a word then that Tex could not hear. Not because he wasn't listening. But because the sound of that primal syllable ripped his inner self like a tsunami and swept him away. Away from spruce trees and copper pipes and nutrient baths.

Away from the former Goddin Air Force Base.

Away from Dublin County, Maine.

Away from green fields and forests and spring air and sunshine.

Away from the troposphere of a planet being jarred into chaos.

Away from everything he had ever been near to. And then farther.

Away from qualities.

Away from Time.

Away from Tex.

Until finally

awareness that was not fixed upon anything
nor tethered to any mind

rose from a centerless place
to occupy all of creation

and every possible good thing

—palm trees, laughter, northern lights, Ludi's amber nipples, the green flash at sunrise, omelets, warm sand, Andrew's Dark Brown Ale, innocence, rock & roll, summer evenings with Molly, colors, coldness, surprise—

existed
effortlessly together
as near and easy as a thought

and where and who Tex had been was only explosive delight

Then he thought, *This* is where ideas come from?
And Beale said

No

And it was gone, all of it. And there was
only

dark.

LEAVING WHOME

 Tex felt like crying or actually cried—without a physical body the distinction was hard to draw—and he felt royally ripped off and he raged and swore & cetera. The memory of that Place or that Level of Consciousness (for which, of course, no known word would do) would not leave him; yet however he tried he could not get any nearer to the feeling of what being There had been like. He felt stripped and cast out and inconsolable.

And Beale, who must have known and who must not have cared, said:

"*This* is where ideas some from."

"This?" said Tex, looking around. Seeing nothing. Well, the darkness.

The absence.

The loss.

Beale said, "Here. Now. After you have left. While you can remember. In the moments when you suspect you have found a way back. Even a dream in which you *seem* to be back. In *this* place, *these* moments, ideas are born."

"No."

"Yes. Of course yes. Why is it that fresh new ideas invariably seem so familiar? Why do we recognize them by their beauty? Why do the people most blessed with creativity tend so oddly often to go mad? Because the moments when the channel opens are not easy to bear. How many times would *you* care to repeat this?"

"Hey," said Tex, "once or twice a month would be plenty."

Beale gave a graveyard chuckle. "Having departed from There and finding ourselves Here, most of us are content to live out our years or our millennia with no more than the faintest recollection of what it was like. We find a makeshift sort of happiness here in the Manifest, and we await with some mixture of fear and cautious hope the day when we are taken back again. Only now and then—sometimes quite by accident—do any of us risk opening the doors of creation. Still, they never remain closed for very long. Some awareness somewhere is forever prying them open, just a crack. And so you find new ideas, or more properly new *creations,* occurring all the time, everywhere, without surcease. That is the blessing and the curse of this outer world. The desire, and the possibility, however faint, of going back."

"Going back where?" said Tex. Worried that this was a dangerous question. Needing to ask it anyway. "Where *was* that?"

Beale did not reply for a while. Then, after a measureless interval, he groaned as though making a tremendous exertion and he said

"There is some reason to think
that Place is called
Whome."

or
"maybe it's pronounced
like whom,"

Tex said.

"No," said Molly. She was very sure of herself. "Like home."

"How do you know?"

She shrugged. Who knew? But she knew.

"It comes from *Finnegans Wake*," she said.

"You've never read *Finnegans Wake*," said Tex, who knew a few things himself. A few more, now, in fact, than he could really handle.

Molly shrugged again. "So what? Nobody else has either. But everybody knows that's where *quark* comes from. So I guess somebody thought, Well, if the word for the smallest possible unit of existence came out of this book that nobody understands, why not find some word in here that means the opposite? Right? Because the whole problem with modern times is that we've gotten really good at breaking everything into little pieces and scattering them on the floor until nothing works, because nothing *means* anything—it's all just a pile of random pieces. So what we need is to find a new language for talking about *whole* things. Things that work. And the obvious place to start is with a term for the biggest whole thing of all, which is Everything—not just the Universe but everything that's *not* the Universe also. Get it? The big unity beyond all the differences. So: Whome. There's no place like it."

"That's for sure," said Tex.

He sat on the sofa clutching a big pillow whose stuffing had settled mostly to one side. He felt unsteady, insecure. These transformations were getting to him. Nothing was certain anymore. Which maybe had always been the case, but now the understanding of this had slithered inside of him. Unwillingly, he grokked it. On WURS, Bad Cathy was tossing off a not exactly reassuring set including but not limited to:

"Miserable" by Portishead
"Buzzards and Dreadful Crows" by Guided by Voices
"Treacherous Cretins" by Frank Zappa
"Muscoviet Musquito" by Clan of Xymox

"Hey," purred the Cath, who had not kicked her college deejay habit of stepping on opening rhythm chords, "this one goes out to all you folks swabbing yourselves down with Green Ban and getting ready to face the day."

Tex moaned. He did not want to face this or any day. He wanted to lie in his bunk and feel the tide rise and fall beneath him and inhale a little reefer.

Before him, cheerfully, Molly placed the steaming Sun mug from which rose a tangy perfume of bergamot.

"Why haven't we run out of this stuff?" Tex grumbled, accepting the mug and staring disconsolately into its depths.

"I must make," croaked Ronny Moorings, "myself clear."

"Then sing so we can understand you," Tex suggested.

"Bear," said Molly, "you're talking back to the radio again."

"Yeah?" He propped himself up a little straighter. He tried a sip of the Earl Grey. Not bad. Unsatisfying, but still: a ritual.

"It's the Afterlife," Molly said. "*That's* why we never run out. You know, the cauldron that's never empty? The apple that's eaten but never consumed?"

She raised her Moon mug to her lips and smiled at him with her eyes.

From the next room, the sleeping compartment, came the sound of yawning. The boat swayed a bit as someone rose and crossed the deck; then the hatch popped open and Gene Deere strode (naked, youthful, well hung: the bastard, thought Tex) through the living room and into the head.

"How long do we have to put up with this?" Tex asked Molly.

She hummed lightly, tilting her head. Tex imagined that he could hear the sound of Ludi's breathing in the room next door: faint, warm, regular.

Gene Deere emerged from the head accompanied by the sound of water being discharged into the holding tank.

"I hope they remember to get that pumped," said Tex.

"Bear," said Molly. "You're growling."

"It is the nature of bears," said Tex, standing his ground, "to growl."

"You're jealous."

"You're crazy. What are they staying *here* for, anyway?"

"Because it's *theirs*," Molly explained, infinitely patient today.

"It is not. It's mine. Ours."

"Don't you see? It's a thing they've got together. It's not her place, and it's not his. It doesn't involve that kind of decision. Plus, it's a secret."

"Then how come we know about it?"

"We don't count."

"*We* don't count? It's our *boat*. And if you ask me, it's getting kind of crowded in here."

"Let's go out on deck, then."

"All right," said Tex. "All right, damn it. You've been trying all morning to get me up. I'll get up. I'll go out and soak up some goddamn fresh air and sunshine. Probably I'll be the first dead person in history to get skin cancer."

"There," said Molly, rising perkily, smoothing out her cushion (though it showed no impression of where she had sat). "That's the old Bear spirit."

ON A CLEAR DAY

From the deck, with her good right eye, Molly could see, no kidding, *forever*. Some of what she saw was good and some of it was disturbing and some of it she didn't understand.

On the whole, the part she didn't understand was the most interesting. She gazed here and there until she felt a headache coming on. She felt Tex tugging gently at her sleeve.

"Raven," he whispered. "We've got company."

Gene and Ludi had come out from the cabin to stand at the rail, just behind the deck chairs where Tex and Molly sat.

"What's he doing?" Tex said.

In one hand Gene held something about the size of a checkbook. He pressed this to his ear, waited a few moments, then started to talk.

"Sefyn?" he said. "Listen, is Chas in yet? Yes, I know what time it is. I mean actually I *don't* know. Has Chas been—"

"I'm not absolutely sure," said Molly, "but I think he may be talking on a cellular phone."

"A *cellular telephone?*" Tex was halfway out of his chair. "On *my boat?*"

Molly stroked his arm. "Shh, calm down. I'm sure he'll be taking it with him when he leaves."

"When he *leaves,*" fumed Tex. "I've been waiting a day and a half for the guy to leave. I don't think he's *ever* going to leave. Why should he?"

"To go to work?" said Molly. It wasn't something either of them was familiar with. "Be quiet."

"I understand," said Gene. "Believe me. Just tell him—no, forget it. *I'll* tell him."

Ludi wandered away from him. She came to stand between Tex and Molly, staring down absentmindedly at the breakfast table. Suddenly her eyes focused. Her arm reached down and, with due caution, her fingers touched the Sun mug. Slowly she lifted it, stared at the tea swirling inside, raised it to her mouth.

"It's still warm," she said quietly.

"What's warm?" said Gene. "Not you, Sefyn."

"Nothing," said Ludi. She swirled the mug, staring into its dark interior. Then she glanced around the deck, up to the flying bridge, over the railing at the peaceful waters of Cold Bay.

"Thanks," said Gene. "I guess I'll see you when I see you. I've got to take a shower first. Or something."

He returned the phone to his shirt pocket. "I'm sorry," he told Ludi. "Were you saying something? I couldn't get Sefyn to be quiet once I got him going—you know how he is."

"No," said Ludi. "Nothing." She placed the Sun mug down gently, right where she had found it. "Just the usual stuff."

Gene watched her a moment, as though hearing something odd or unfamiliar in her voice. Then she smiled so brilliantly that his brain must have been wiped.

"I think I love you," he told her.

"I kind of figured that," she said.

"How about you?" he said.

She tapped the side of her mouth with one long finger. "I think," she said, "I'm not in my right mind at the moment. And I think this boat is probably not the best place to try to get sane again."

"You want me to take you home?" he said, obviously and instantly concerned. Even to Tex, he seemed touchingly vulnerable. "You want to be alone for a while?"

"No," said Ludi. "I like it this way."

Gene exhaled in relief.

Tex gritted his teeth.

Molly sighed.

Ludi said, "You probably ought to go to work, I guess."

"Yeah. Sefyn says Chas is apeshit because these security guys are everywhere and the King is coming to town. And I've got a report due."

"Let me borrow your phone," she said. "I need to call the bookstore."

"You can have it," said Gene. "I'm sick of telephones. Are you in trouble at work, do you think?"

"Oh, no," said Ludi. "Work is the trouble. I'm going to tell them I quit."

Gene thought for a moment and then shook his head. He did not know what to make of her.

"Get used to it," said Tex.

"I'm trying," he said.

"What?" said Ludi, cupping her hand over the phone. "Did you say something?"

"I don't think so," he said.

"Maybe I'm just hearing things."

"Me too."

"It's this boat."

The *Linear Bee* rocked. The harbor swells rolled. The sun crawled higher and Rose Moon, hidden beneath its glare, waxed a tiny bit more full.

"I think it's haunted," Ludi confided, to no one in particular.

"There are no such things as ghosts," said Gene.

"You sure?"

"No," he said readily. "I'm not too sure about anything. Do you have any idea what day it is?"

"June, I think."

He walked over and kissed her. She tossed the telephone overboard. It floated for a while, then a wave slapped it against the hull, and Tex never saw it again.

FACE THE MUSIC

Time waits for no one? Maybe. But everybody on the payroll of the Gulf Atlantic Corporation seemed to be waiting for Gene Deere by the time he rolled in to his office a couple of hours later. He was wearing a crisply ironed shirt and a job-interview-grade tie and a sport jacket that still had the dry cleaner's tag stapled to the loop in back. He was showered and shaved and combed and generally burnished. His skin was tanned from sunbathing naked on the houseboat. Despite all this he managed to feel scrungy and unkempt, and found himself half humming and half growling an early Tom Waits tune, "Whistlin Past the Graveyard," as he strolled into the made-over hangar. Sefyn looked up at him and registered a note of honest surprise.

"Good *morning*," he said. "Would you like your messages one at a time, or batched by priority?"

"Let's start with the least important ones."

"*Least* important," said Sefyn, leafing through a stack of notes. "That would be 'Tell Deere to call me right away or I'll have his left testicle—Sincerely, Chas.' "

"I take it he escalated from there."

"Didn't he just," said Sefyn, fanning himself with the memo pad.

In the executive polyhedron, Chas sat beneath the portrait of a border collie named The Old Captain, flanked by a pair of young men who looked as though they might be out of prison on work-release.

"Deere," said Chas, glancing up from his ThinkPad. "These are Bruce and Rocky. They're from Texas."

The two young men nodded at Gene and went back to staring down across Chas's shoulder. Poor social development, Gene thought. An excellent sign.

"Look," one of them said, pointing at something on the active-matrix display. "Anybody running Satan could have picked that up. Who handles your lockup around here?"

"A guy named Eckhart," said Chas, distracted. "Did you say *Satan*?"

"And that's just for shits and grins," said Expert #2. "We ain't even into the heavy lifting yet."

Chas looked up at Gene as though appealing for mercy or, at any rate, human understanding. He found little. Gene was actually looking at the dog. The dog appeared highly intelligent; though that could, of course, have been a trick of the portraitist. Gene had read that dogs, on average, display communications skills on par with those of a human two-year-old.

"Deere?" said Chas. "Are you there?"

"Sorry," said Gene. "Did I miss something?"

"The question is whether *I* am missing something, and the

answer is yes. I am missing your report. It was due on my desk this morning."

"It was?"

"Do you know how to operate a calendar, Deere? By the way, I've been ringing you all day. Haven't you had your phone on?"

"It kind of fell by the wayside."

"Wonderful. That's simply wonderful. All right, don't let me waste any more of your valuable time. I assume I *will* have your report in one form or another by the time you leave the office."

Gene mused. The fact of the matter was, his report was drafted and ready to zap through the office e-mail, as it had been for the past week. Some lingering uncertainty had kept his finger off the SEND button, though. The final section, Prioritized Recommendations, still seemed a bit undercooked. As he stood in Chas's office, his toes on the concrete floor less than a centimeter shy of the kilim rug, he got an inkling of what had been troubling him.

"Actually," he said to Chas, "I could give you the gist of it right now, if you like."

"Orally?" said Chas, in evident distaste.

"Straight from the horse's mouth."

Chas frowned. Then he opened his lone desk drawer and pulled out a small Sony DAT recorder. "Get Sefyn to transcribe this when you're done," he said, sliding the machine across the expanse of oiled walnut.

Gene picked up the recorder and examined it. It is strange and wonderful, he thought, what technology can do. The two security experts were staring up at him, looking impatient, as though he were a web site they were speed-surfing through.

"I've been thinking," said Gene, "about palm trees."

"Cool," said Expert #2.

Chas scarcely seemed to pay attention. Presumably he intended to let the transcript do the talking.

"There's this Indian guy I met," said Gene, "and he's got this little palm tree growing—it's a saw palmetto, *Rhapidophyllum hystrix,* which used to be widespread in the Southeast until developers took care of it. Only this particular tree is growing in Maine, not all that far away from here."

"Is your report," wondered Chas, courteously enough, "going to be all about this palm tree? Or can we expect you to move on eventually to the subject of replanting the North Woods?"

"I'm not sure there's any difference," said Gene. "See, my point is, I've been monitoring all these trial plots out here, and I've been doing extensive field surveys of patterns of tree growth and natural reforestation in the wild—but the whole time, I find that I've got this little palm tree stuck in my head. And finally it hits me what the palm tree is trying to tell me."

"You've shifted into the present tense," said Chas. "Would you like the grammar checker to straighten this out for you?"

Gene shrugged. He felt like a present-tense kind of guy. "It's a question," he said. "Here it is. If you can grow palm trees in a place like Applemont, Maine, then why grow nothing but a single variety of transgenic spruce? In other words, if local conditions are such that the forest is driven naturally toward complexity and diversification, then doesn't it seem misguided to override Nature and push the system back toward species reduction, and eventually monoculture? This is just a *question,* keep in mind. I'm not necessarily advocating a hands-off approach to the working forest. What I *am* saying is that one of the great lessons of science is that Nature does not operate in a casual or accidental fashion. Nature winnows and optimizes. So if Nature is casting a strong vote in favor of diversity and system complexity, then the only explanation is that millennia of evolution have demonstrated that this is the wisest long-range approach. And indeed, that seems to be borne out even in the limited field tests I've been running. In terms of simple productivity, for instance—which we can define in terms of vegetal tissue production per unit of area—the mixed-species plots have a clear edge over their single-species competitors. That's not even factoring in such things as heightened resiliency in the face of atypical meteorological events, fluctuations in the predation cycle, and so forth."

"I'm sorry, Deere," said Chas, "but you seem to be speaking in very broad philosophical terms here. Is there any way you can boil your thoughts down to a set of definite recommendations?"

Gene took a few steps across the concrete floor. He found himself in a corner of the office, from where the place looked large, impersonal, and barren. The two data guys had lost interest in all this plant talk and gone back to poking holes in the local-area network.

"Okay," he said, "here's a recommendation. Shit-can the X *dawkinsia* 4.3.2. At least go back to an earlier version. Without the suckering rhizomes, for example."

"No can do," said Chas. "I'm just telling you that parenthetically. You may, of course, make any recommendation you like. But I can tell you that the Company is not going to walk away from this significant investment, nor abandon this lucrative proprietary technology."

"Well, fine. But we're not really talking about technology, are we? We're talking about a living forest. At least, that's what *I'm* talking about. And my concern is that the X *dawkinsia* will be two undesirable things at once: it will be unnaturally formidable, and it will be unnaturally vulnerable."

"Say again?" said Chas—military radio talk, his Annapolis education cropping up.

"In the short term it will be too strong and aggressive a competitor, bringing about a serious reduction in the complexity of the forest. This will, as I'm arguing, be accompanied by a loss of overall productivity, at the very least. But in the long run you encounter a deeper problem, which is that a system dominated by any single variety will be insufficiently flexible and dynamic to respond to changes in the environment. One serious insect problem or climate flip-over, or one virus the plant has never seen, and there goes your crop."

"People have been predicting such a thing," Chas noted, "for 20 or 30 years now. Hasn't happened."

"Just wait," said Gene. "Nature is opportunistic. You dangle a monocrop out there long enough and some critter will figure out how to make a banquet out of it. You've got to keep in mind that X *dawkinsia* is something that we created in a laboratory. And of course, we did our usual fine job of anticipating the survival traits it will require. But our knowledge is necessarily limited. Even if we think of *everything*, we're only thinking of everything that exists *today*. Ten years from now, twenty years—not long at all, from the standpoint of a forest—this proprietary supertree of ours may be the Edsel of transgenic cultivars."

Chas leaned back in his chair and thumped his thumbs against each other. "This is the extent of your recommendation?" he said. "Scrap the 4.3.2?"

"No," said Gene.

But Chas evidently had done enough listening for one day. "Well, Deere, your wishes may have already been fulfilled. The lab techs have reported such a fall-off in heliotropic response and all the other parameters that I've ordered them yanked off life support."

"You're . . . killing them?"

"No. I'm having several thousand of them potted up. Some others—a quantity I have yet to determine—I'm sending out to the field-test grounds around Applemont. It's a big job, and I'm still weighing options. My inclination is to run tissue cultures off the individuals in your trial plots. To the best of my knowledge that's the only source of unaltered genetic material we've got left. *N'est-ce pas?*"

Gene was flummoxed. He couldn't believe Chas would have done any of this without consulting him. On the other hand, he hadn't exactly been readily at hand to consult.

"Now, Deere," said Chas, "for formality's sake, will you *please* go back to your office and sit down at your desk and not get up again until your report is finalized? Ask Sefyn to order a pizza if you become weak from hunger."

"Suppose I need to go to the bathroom?" said Gene, still irked at having been run around.

"Piss on one of the palm trees," Chas suggested.

ESSENCE OF ROCKNESS

On the *Linear Bee,* Ludi held a first reading of her latest script-in-progress. This time at least the sketchy, open-ended quality of the piece did not disturb her. Open-endedness had become the whole point of the performance. Her chief anxiety now was whether the audience would pick up the ball.

Pippa Rede and Eben Creek and Deep Herb showed up, but for most of the time all they wanted to talk about was Guillermo.

"He was *so cool* on the news," Pippa said. "You could tell it was him, even though they did that thing where they electronically scrambled his face up so the police couldn't use the tape as evidence."

Ludi had thought this was stupid. Making himself out to be some kind of hero of a nonexistent Underground.

"Yeah," said Herb. "His voice sounded like Dr. Spock."

"You mean Mr. Spock," said Eben. "From *Star Trek,* right?"

"Wow," said Herb. "Was he on there, too?"

"Could we do the business part first?" implored Ludi.

"I didn't get what he was saying, though," said Pippa, "about shifting the struggle from digital to analog."

Eben said, "I think he meant like, it's time to get past the concept stage and really take the struggle to the streets."

"What streets?" said Ludi—then she realized she was doing it, too.

"What's this about a Corporate Executive?" Pippa Moss wanted to know. "Hello? Anybody home?"

It took Ludi a second to get that they were back to talking

about her script. "A Corporate Executive," she repeated. "Right. That's a character. What about it?"

"Well, do we really want somebody like that in the play? I mean, won't he start ranting about how he deserves a bigger tax cut and people who don't like it can go live in New York?"

Ludi shrugged. "That's up to the character. I don't think we ought to leave anybody out. Anyway, aren't you stereotyping the guy? Maybe he's really okay and just happens to have a lot of money."

"Ha," said Eben.

"And what's this about a Rock?" said Deep Herb.

"Why? Do you think it's too . . . static?"

"No, man," said Herb. "I was just wondering, like how you would do the makeup and all."

"We're not going to use any makeup," Ludi explained, for the umpteenth time. "Just a sign that designates the character. And a mask, for anonymity. It's up to the person who plays the Rock to convey, you know—the essence of Rockness."

"Suppose he just sits there?" said Eben.

"Then he—or she—will contribute a solid Rocklike presence," Ludi said, feeling impatient, then feeling bad about her impatience. Maybe it *was* a boneheaded idea. But it was too late to back out now. Flyers were tacked up around town, and a p.s.a. was being read several times a day over WURS. Besides, the Midsummer Night performance was an annual event. It was like Easter mass for the rite-of-intensification set.

"Tell me this, then," said Eben. "What are we going to do if the thing gets out of control? I mean, suppose this Radical Faerie should get into it with the Evangelical Protestant. Or suppose the Chamber of Commerce Type should start screaming at the Welfare Witch. Suppose a big fight breaks out."

"That hasn't happened in real life," said Pippa, meekly. "At least, not around here. Why should it happen in a play?"

"Because it's dark," said Deep Herb. His voice struck Ludi as odd—as though for once he had a grip on what he was talking about. "And people are wearing masks, so they feel like they can do anything. Some of them have had a few drinks with dinner. And others are on vacation, so they're like, set free. Anyway it's Midsummer, when the wild spirits come out. That's why."

The Players exchanged glances. One at a time, they began to smile.

"We can hope, anyway," said Pippa.

"Yeah," said Eben. "Now that you put it that way. Maybe it *will* get out of control."

Ludi wondered what Gene would say. Something about order and chaos: new forms emerging from the Void. Things appearing that no one has ever seen before.

"It ought to be interesting," she said. She pronounced all four syllables distinctly.

MUTATIS

The song of a tree is not the tree. Still, a tree without a song is a pulp machine.

Out of deep and distant folds in the æther (the akasha, the whome), Beale's fellow dryads (sentient form-fields, matrices of organization) drifted (became explicate, emerged into the Manifest) toward the morphic space generated by the millions of genetically identical tissue-cultured specimens of the tree known as X *dawkinsia* 4.3.2.

From the dryads' standpoint (granting that they *had* a standpoint, despite being nonmaterial entities occupying a multidimensional phase-space), the 4.3.2 saplings appeared alien, unnatural, vaguely menacing, and tone-deaf. This is not anthropomorphizing. From a dryad's point of view, attributing consciousness to human beings is *deimorphizing*. Nonetheless it is evident from patient observation that human beings do behave in a purposive and loosely "organized" fashion—albeit not so organized or purposive as, say, a colony of termites. Let alone a healthy forest. So humans *can* be said to possess awareness of a certain, limited kind.

But these are philosophical problems. There were practical matters at hand. In any case, dryads prefer to do their thinking in the winter, when things are calm.

Hesitantly, the form-fields entered the morphic space of the young trees. It was (in human terms) like stepping into a cold and featureless room. There was the smell of recent construction about it. Proportions were bad. Lighting was inadequate. Who designed this thing—a chimpanzee with a draw program?

Well, still, it was a *place*. (A room. A tree.) It was better, arguably, than floating around in the Implicate with nothing to do. It presented a certain aesthetic challenge.

The dryads did what all sentient beings would do (and "thinking machines" would not) in such a situation. They relaxed. They began to make themselves at home. They set about decorating, renovating, sprucing the old spruce up. A displaced American chestnut dryad (one of many, many), homesick for great spreading branches, turned off a timing mechanism that would have caused its lower limbs to fall. An elm dryad redesigned its canopy to widen into the shape of a vase. A fringe tree dryad developed showy flowers. A swamp maple dryad decided to go deciduous. The yew dryad made no changes at all, only hunkered down sullenly—possibly out of spite.

Enterprising microbes opened a gene market. Insects swarmed in, eager to acquire some of the chemical resistance bred into the 4.3.2 tissues. Bacteria founded colonies, way stations, lonely outposts. Viruses shuttled back and forth, some leaving deposits, others making withdrawals. Fungi planted themselves like shrubbery around the trees' foundations. Some of the dryads welcomed the color and vivacity of the new arrivals; others tried to discourage them, making them biochemically unwelcome; a desperate few slaughtered them outright.

It was all business as usual in Nature, though not in a large-scale commercial greenhouse.

Last came the mites. They arrived first in small numbers: a cautious, exploratory delegation. Beale learned of their arrival through a pheromonic broadcast that flashed through the network of intertwined roots. He took it upon himself personally to see that the newcomers were properly welcomed. Mites are notoriously picky, overbred, refined and highly specialized creatures, and they are capable of doing as much harm as good, given sufficient provocation. Beale fussed over them, fed them, bedded them down. That was all you could do. After that, you could only sit back and hope.

Somewhere, Beale knew, the Bishop of Worms was keeping himself apprised of all this. His agents were everywhere—in every fleck of water, every dust mote, every subtle current of air—and already in countless ways He was making His presence known. Decay, tissue necrosis, root predation, insects devouring microbes, microbes devouring smaller microbes, fungal blight striking tender stems, plant-generated toxins poisoning symbiotes—the Worm never rested; always hungered; ate and ate but never became full.

Fuck him, Beale thought. Thinking this is what Tex might have said. Wondering if Tex would have been proud of him. Of how he and his fellow dryads had gotten themselves organized. Form a union, Tex had said. A political action committee.

Make your voices *heard*, man.

Beale laughed (insofar as sentient form-fields can be said to laugh). He raised his voice. He sang.

The other dryads joined in. They all sang together.

All the songs were different.

Many of them contained strands of melody that had never been heard before. They were new creations—undreamt, unpredicted, never sung until this instant.

The songs blended. They clashed. They rose and fell, harmonized, grated, crescendoed, faded, and began again, with variations. They went on and on.

It was a wondrous sound, but not yet a beautiful one. It was clamorous, noisy, chaotic. Many of the parts were splendid (and some were horrible), but they were not yet a whole. Many instruments, but no symphony.

Many trees. But not yet a forest.

PASSIO

From a Gulfstream II turbojet flying at 18,000 feet, approaching the Bangor International Airport—closer to his ancestral home in Scotland, he reflected, than to corporate headquarters in Houston—Burdock Herne enjoyed a sweeping view of some of the Gulf Atlantic real estate holdings in the Northeast. It was not a strategically vital sector in the overall scheme of Company operations. Gulf Atlantic had only recently arrived on scene here in any major way, having acquired some territory that had been harvested and turned over by a South African concern, then piecing together an assortment of third-party holdings. Graphically, when color-coded on a map, the territory resembled that new Xerox logo: a couple of big geometric patches plus a lot of smaller bits and dots. It was dwarfed by the core Gulf Atlantic operations in the Southeastern U.S., in the Tongass National Forest, and in Malaysia. Nonetheless, the Company considered this to be a region of nearly incalculable promise: an important working asset for the future.

Burdock Herne had personally invested an increasing amount of his attention up here, over the past several months. The more probable it looked that the global climate change scenario was, in fact, going to play out, the more confident he became in a certain personal vision that he called the Great Green North. As the value of the Southeastern Sector declined (perhaps precipi-

tously, over the next decade), so the value of these northern holdings, here and in Canada, proportionately increased. As yet,
however, Gulf Atlantic's competitors had failed to move decisively to solidify their positions, particularly in Maine, where the
regulatory climate was congenial. This opened a window of opportunity that Herne felt could not be—and had not been—left
unexploited. The Company was actively acquiring land from
Goddin northward, and plans were in the final stages to nail
down the productive viability of this land before any shifting of
the regulatory winds should occur. Not that any was anticipated;
but where politics came into play, you had to hedge your bets.

All this was, of course, closely held information, and much of
it was forbiddingly technical, even for Herne. He had put one of
his hardest-charging young field managers in charge of the operation up here, and he did not believe in Monday morning quarter-
backing. Hand the boy the ball and let him run with it.

The airplane banked. Sunlight flashed off ponds that looked
shallow and almost perfectly round, like holes on a green. The
surrounding forest spoiled the effect, though, because its texture
was bumpy and its summer coloration far from uniform. Where
timber production had come fully up to speed, the landscape had
the deep glaucous hue of Kentucky bluegrass. Where the forest
remained in a wild, uncultivated state, you had pale greens and
black-greens and yellow-greens and spots of purple and even
patches of washed-out magenta that must be fireweed, moving
in quickly to colonize a fresh cut or an opening left by a burn.
It boggled Herne's mind that such vast expanses of land should
be underutilized. On the other hand, it gave him a pleasant feeling
of standing on a frontier, looking out (so to speak) across broad
sweeps of prairie that had never known the plow. It buoyed him
up, thinking of new fields that remained to be conquered. The old
world was not yet done with its need for men like Burdock Herne.

"We're about 15 minutes out of Bangor, sir," the pilot called
back over the intercom. "Want me to place any calls for you?"

"No thank you," said Herne. "They know I'm coming."

He settled back into his seat as the plane eased down through
the thermal layers of air. Bit of an onshore breeze, this time of
year. Sun warming the land, heating the air up, lifting it, creating
a low-pressure region and hence an inflow off the ocean. Herne
enjoyed thinking about such things: big things, large-scale phe-
nomena, supra-human forces constantly at work. It gave him
comfort, somehow, to think of himself as only an agent, an opera-
tive—a point man, as he phrased it—carrying out his assigned

role in a greater drama: the drama of History, of the unfolding of Western Civilization, the grand movement of humankind toward its unforeseeable destiny.

Herne did not pretend to know any better than the next person how things were going to turn out. He was as troubled as anyone else by the trends of modern times. He was no shortsighted fool, eyes only on the next quarterly earnings report. At times his position seemed a lonely and even an anonymous one—keeping a steady hand on the tiller through the dark passage of a stormy night. At other times he felt exhilarated, lucky to have been born who he was, to be alive in this minute, doing the things he was so perfectly suited for.

Well, life was complicated. You couldn't reduce it to a simple formula. It was tempting to try; Herne had seen many of his peers give in to that, especially as they got along in years. You can reach a point where you know so much and you've seen so much that you start to mistake your store of information for wisdom. But information is not wisdom. Experience and knowledge are valuable things, but if that were all it took, then any 80-year-old could come creaking out of his golf cart and take a seat at Herne's desk and do a better job than Herne himself was doing. Respecting the wisdom of the elders is one thing. Recognizing the difference between what is wisdom and what is just accumulated belief—that's where the problem lies.

Herne felt his heart pound once, unusually hard: an interruption of its smoothly regulated rhythm. He felt a strange kind of pressure at his throat, as though something were wrong with the cabin air supply. He laid a finger on the intercom button but held off from pushing it. The change in pressure, he thought, was coming from somewhere else. It was coming from inside.

Hastily he reviewed his recent train of thoughts, looking for a thread of anxiety that might have crept in. He found none. Rumination, a general taking stock of things, that's all it had been. The sort of thinking you do while coming down in a plane from cruising altitude—those drawn-out moments before you stretch your legs and enter the terminal and click over into moving-and-shaking mode again.

What, then, could be the trouble?

Herne touched a hand lightly to his chest, just by the rib cage on the left-hand side. The heart was doing fine now. It was strong and well cared-for and it had many good years left. He touched his throat. His breathing had normalized. Whatever disturbance had passed through him had not left any physiological trace.

Suddenly he understood. For an instant, like an echo, he heard in his mind the word *wisdom*. That's the word that had triggered the strange episode. Wisdom, he thought. He placed a question mark at the end of it.

Wisdom?

No answer came.

Then it hit him with double force—triple, quadruple force—in his heart and the throat and now other places as well. The lungs. The stomach. The head. And the eyes, especially the eyes.

Burdock Herne, he told himself, *thou art a fool.*

He sat there clutching the armrests with both hands. His eyes were pressed firmly shut. He took breaths in and blew them out slowly, at a deliberate pace. He was not going mad. Not having an attack of any sort. He was not even losing self-control: not really.

A crackle of radio chatter came from the cockpit. He could not make out the words through the closed compartment door, but he could imagine them well enough. The practiced, almost unconscious repartee between pilot and tower. Between the firm, unmoving ground and the swirling, flighty, capricious airplane. *Cleared for landing,* he imagined the tower saying. That universal Chuck Yeager drawl. Y'all come on in, now. We'll see ya back earthside.

"It'll just be a couple more minutes, Mr. Herne," said the voice on the intercom.

But Herne did not hear that. He pressed his forehead to the double-paned polycarbonate window, wishing it were cooler than it was. His eyes fluttered without opening. "Thistle," he whispered, in a voice that did not seem to be his own.

"Thistle, where are you?" the voice cried.
"Why won't you come back
to your daddy?"

or
could it be real?

Can all of these things really be happening? Tex thought probably not. Probably this was some kind of post-life dementia. Probably this is what happens when your physical body is dead but your etheric or dark-matter body still hangs together in scraps and tatters, like Miss Haversham's wedding gown. Maybe this—what would you call it?—slow fade-out just goes on, gradually lessening in intensity, for however long it takes for the thing to come unraveled, or succumb to entropic rot, or get chewed apart by astral moths. Until in the end you're only a memory. A lingering echo in the life-field.

"Bear," said Molly. Kind of an edge to her voice.

Tex lay with his eyes closed. The clock radio was playing dead air. He could hear the hiss of white noise through tiny speakers, the slap of water against the hull, the splutter of a lone lobster boat.

"Bear." She shook him. "Wake up."

And for an instant

—everything inside him crackled with energy, like a circuit suddenly electrified

—he thought

It was all a dream!

"Wake up," Molly commanded.

"Raven," he croaked, eyes flashing open. "You won't believe—"

Beside them, between them—interpenetrating them, for the Goddess's sake—lay Gene and Ludi, slumbering peaceably, innocently, the timeless look of blissed-out lovers on their still faces, like masks.

"Won't believe what?" said Molly. She sat on the edge of the bed with one of Ludi's knees sticking into her hip. The ultramarine murmur of dawn gathered itself behind the curtains. The clock radio read

AM 4:32

Tex sighed. "Never mind."

"Come look, then," said Molly. "You've got to see this."

No more surprises, Tex thought. Not just yet. He pulled himself up and loped out to the aft deck, facing east, where daybreak might or might not have been under way, depending on how strict your standards were. As far as Tex was concerned, it was still the middle of the night.

"Look," said Molly.

Tex looked. He saw the ghost-white cylinders of petroleum tanks across Cold Bay. He saw the silhouetted hump of Cadillac Mountain waiting to receive the morning's first sunbeams. He saw Ursa Major. He saw the fragile crescent of a waning moon, like a thin piece of bone.

"Look at what?" he said sleepily.

"It hasn't happened *yet*." Molly stopped short of adding, *you silly old Bear.*

"That's good," said Tex. "I'd really hate to miss it."

He eased himself down into one of the deck chairs.

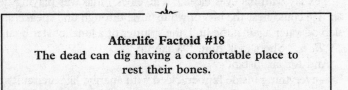

Afterlife Factoid #18
The dead can dig having a comfortable place to
rest their bones.

The blue glow brightened by some small measure. Was this a digital or an analog calculation? Are we talking quantized photons or continuous waves?

"Raven," he said, "if you don't mind my asking, what the hell are we looking for?"

She looked at him round-eyed, open-faced. Grandly she said: "Dawn. On Midsummer Day."

"Oh," he said. "That's cool. Why didn't you say so?"

He straightened in his deck chair. He declaimed:

"And the dawn comes down like bird poop
Out of seagulls on Cold Bay."

"That's beautiful, Bear," said Molly.

Then the dawn did come up. But first, something else happened.

GOD STUFF

"Where do you stand," asked Ludi, lifting the turquoise fetish of Bear, his back laden with a tiny medicine bundle, "on this god stuff?"

"What?" said Gene, who stood sleepily beside her, facing the altar in the pilot house. "Where do I stand on what?" He put a hand on her neck, moved it down softly to her shoulder. He kissed the skin there that still held the warm, breadlike smell of sleep.

The hiss of the clock radio had woken them up. Gene had turned the radio off, but Ludi got up anyway and wandered over to the altar, which seemed like the place to be on Midsummer Day. So Gene—like a sweet but pesky puppy dog—padded in after her.

He breathed deeply at her neck, as though trying to inhale her.

Ludi jostled him off. "*This* stuff," she said, waving her hand: the fetish, raven feathers, black and white candles, an arrangement of rocks. "Gods, goddesses, spirits. Higher powers. Whatever."

"Ah," said Gene. He blinked. He yawned.

Ludi poked him in the ribs.

"*Aagh,*" he gasped, faking great distress.

She laughed. "Maybe I do love you. It depends."

"Not on where I stand on feathers and incense, I hope." He scratched his chest, naked except for the skull pendant dangling from its neon green shoelace.

"Why do men do that?" Ludi asked him. "Scratch and stretch and yawn like that? Why not just open your eyes and be awake?"

Gene shrugged. He had never in his life felt so precariously happy. Not even as a 9-year-old kid when his secretly acquired model rocket had shot *straight* up in the air and then come *right* down through the canvas top of the neighbors' convertible.

"That's an interesting question," he said, after some swirly and chaotic early-morning-type thought.

"About why men scratch themselves?"

He shook his head. "The god thing," he said. "I suppose you expect me to take some hard rationalist line. And in a way that's how I feel. That what we believe ought to make sense. But I'm not sure. There's this almost religious belief among cognitive science types that the problem of consciousness—intelligence and self-awareness and all that—eventually will be explained as a function of information processing and feedback loops and things like that. In other words, consciousness isn't a mystical thing, it's just an emergent property in systems that reach a certain level of complexity. So I ask myself, Where do we find systems of great complexity? And the answer is, Everywhere. Throughout the Universe. In fact, the complex system par excellence is the biosphere of Earth. So I have to think—if it's true that someday you'll have a computer, or something like a computer, that will achieve genuine awareness—why can't *living* systems of sufficient complexity also achieve awareness? Why can't there be some form of emergent consciousness in the living Earth? Am I right? And if there *is* such a thing, it seems to me that we might as well refer to it as Gaia, the Earth Goddess. I mean, consciousness does imply personality, right? It's like the Anthropic Principle, only applied to godhood."

"Oh, yeah," said Ludi. "That really clarifies things for me."

"Oh, come on. It's not *that* technical. Why don't people *know* anything anymore? The Anthropic Principle is just a common-sense idea in physics. It says, One thing we know for sure about the Universe is that it *has* to be the sort of place where intelligent carbon-based life-forms will naturally tend to arise. We know this because *we* are an intelligent carbon-based life-form, and we are here thinking about the Universe. So you could say, as an earthly corollary, that one thing we know for sure about consciousness is that it must arise naturally in complex living systems. We know this because we are complex living systems, ourselves, and we are conscious. So this being the case, it makes no sense to assume that consciousness would arise *only* in a single type of organism. Nature does not restrict itself that way. Once a trait is evolved— say, vision—then it tends to pop up everywhere. It even makes no sense, probably, to assume that consciousness arises only at the organism level. As opposed to, say, the hive level, or the pod-of-dolphins level, or the ecosystem level. This is probably something we'll understand a lot better in 100 years."

"Except that we'll be dead."

"Maybe. Don't count on it." He wiggled his eyebrows, as though he were in on something.

"You," she told him, "are a very strange man." She picked up the Bear fetish and tickled its polished round belly. "Isn't he, little Bear?" she said. "Sweet old thing. Come here and let Ludi give you a kiss."

"Can we go back to bed now?" said Gene.

Ludi shook her head. "Don't you want to see the sun come up? Like, just as a matter of scientific curiosity?"

"There is very little that I can learn from watching the sun come up. I've already seen it very many times."

"But this is Midsummer Day."

Gene could think of nothing to say about that. Like much else about Ludi, it was not a well-posed problem. Maybe it wasn't a problem at all.

"Which way is east?" he said.

Her long finger stretched out at the end of her long slender arm. She was very beautiful. In physics and sometimes in biology, it is often said that things that are sufficiently beautiful must, at some level, be true. "Stick with me," Ludi told him. "Maybe you'll learn something."

UP LIKE THUNDER

Gulls swirled around the mast. Their predawn screeches—louder, it seemed, than at any other time of day—began low-pitched, then rose abruptly to become piercing and shrill. They sounded like synthesized effects. So much of the natural world you wouldn't believe if you saw it in a movie.

Tex was just dozing off when dawn surprised him. It would have surprised anyone. Strange colors moved in the atmosphere: wide gashes of orange and indigo, with a lavender aura fading to barely perceptible pink. As the sky brightened, the mountaintops seemed to grow darker, even impossibly to swell, as though pushed up by pressure building within the planet. That was how mountains formed, Tex believed. But these were old mountains, eroded and weary. The Earth slid further down its gravitational trench and the great glob of thermonuclear radiance all those millions of miles away—a safe distance, but just barely—could almost be seen along the fringe of the horizon. And that is when Dawn arrived.

Tex had never seen it this way, face-to-face. He supposed it must have slipped past him every day of his life; but you could not imagine that, really, when you looked at it.

It was gold. It was huge and terrifying and covered with glowing fibers of pure light, like luminous fur. It rose from its dark lair beyond the sea and it came forward violently, like a predator. Its eyes were starry infinitudes. Its mouth was the Void where things vanish and do not reappear. Its nostrils exhaled the first air of the new day.

Its paws touched first upon Cadillac Mountain, as Tex had known they would. Then it reached out and touched other peaks nearby, one by one, until the whole range above Mount Desert Island lay beneath its vast golden body. Briefly it rested a paw on Awonadjo Mountain, brushing the antenna of WURS; then with a single bound it leapt all the way across Cold Bay and landed on the aft deck of the *Linear Bee*.

Tex felt the luminous fur brushing against him and he thought, Even for an afterlife trip, this is getting a little weird.

"*Arth Vawr*," said Molly. "I'd like you to meet my husband Tex."

Then the *Dawn* was staring at Tex and no shit, burning right through him. Tex was afraid to look back. But how could you avoid a gaze like that? The eyes glowed at him from everywhere. The mouth yawned black above him. For a moment Tex thought he had been swallowed up. Then from deep inside that space an Awareness spoke to him.

YOU ARE THE ONE,

said *Arth Vawr,*

WHO IS CALLED BEAR.

It didn't sound like a question and Tex was inclined not to answer it. But one great foot with claws that could possibly have shredded a planet came down beside him and he said weakly:

"Yeah. I guess that's me."

Arth Vawr said:

> I HAVE ALSO BEEN CALLED BEAR. I HAVE BEEN VENERATED. I HAVE BEEN FORGOTTEN. I HAVE BEEN PAINTED ON CAVE WALLS AND BURIED AND BETRAYED AND REMEMBERED AND EXHUMED. I HAVE DIED. I HAVE SLEPT. I HAVE REAWAKENED. I HAVE BEEN PASSED FROM ONE PEOPLE TO ANOTHER, AND MY APPEARANCE HAS BEEN ALTERED MANY TIMES. DON'T BE CONCERNED IF YOU FEEL A LITTLE DISORIENTED. IT GOES WITH THE TERRITORY.

"Yeah, thanks," said Tex uncertainly.
Arth Vawr turned to Molly.

WAS IT YOU WHO SUMMONED ME?

he asked.
"I don't think so," she said. "Not lately, I mean."
Arth Vawr said:

THEN WHO?

And with proper dramatic flair, Ludi climbed out onto the flying bridge, just over Tex's head. She was wrapped in a Chief Joseph blanket. Gene emerged behind her, in paisley boxer shorts. The skull pendant seemed to glow like moonlight above his heart.

AH,

said *Arth Vawr*.

IT MUST BE THAT THE TIME HAS COME.

Tex and Molly looked at one another.
"The Time?" one of them said. Neither one was sure who.
Arth Vawr made a sound like a heavenly sigh.

MY DESTINY IS BOUNDED BY MY NATURE,

he said.

> UNLIKE YOURS. I SHALL CONTINUE TO DO WHAT I CAN
> ONLY DO—AND WHAT ONLY I CAN DO—FOR AS LONG AS I
> AM CALLED BACK HERE. WHEN I AM NO LONGER NEEDED,
> OR FORGOTTEN AT LAST, OR ALLOWED TO SINK INTO NON-
> EXISTENCE, THEN MY GREAT TASK MUST GO UNFULFILLED.
> BUT I AM HERE AGAIN, FOR AT LEAST THIS ONE MORE DAY.
> I MUST MOVE NOW.

With that He leapt from the houseboat onto the shore, where His light like melting gold seemed to smother the dead chicken plant. Then He was gone, pressing inland. He got along pretty quickly, for a deity of his age.

On the flying bridge, Ludi squeezed her arms tight, keeping warm in the cool ocean breeze. Gene stepped close and wrapped an arm around her. Light of incomparable purity washed over their two fresh faces, down their firm shoulders and their strong young arms.

"Isn't it incredible?" she said. "I really can't remember a more amazing sunrise."

They stared over the bay, past the mountains, into the blinding immanence of the newborn day.

"What do you think He meant?" Molly asked Tex—whispering, though Gene and Ludi could not have heard her.

Tex peered at the shoreline, where the ancient bear-god had merged, it seemed, with the sun-drenched Earth.

"Offhand," he told her, "I'd venture to say old *Arth Vawr* is fixing to kick ass and take names."

WILDLIFE SIGHTINGS

The light of dawn struck a sign declaring FREE TERRITORY deep in the unincorporated township of Applemont. Near the sign it fell upon Wild Jag Eckhart's dirty brown Suburban, where it annoyed the yearling wolf (whom Eckhart, as a private joke, had named Hoot) already in ill temper at having been locked in the rear compartment for the past hour. Eckhart had arisen in darkness and brewed a strong thermos jug of coffee and begun loading canisters with unusual care into the backseat. The coffee was for later, to help pass the hours until nightfall. The canisters were for later than that. The wolf was for company. Eckhart had decided he loved the animal. There is no knowing how the wolf felt about Eckhart in return. Thus far it had not taken any bites out of him, though the temptation must surely have arisen.

By the time the sun began to clear the hemlocks along the paved state highway, the Suburban was breezing past the Irving Mart outside the main entrance to the Goddin Base. Eckhart recognized a couple of the pickups parked outside, but decided not to stop and say hey. He turned onto a road that ran northward, along the chain-link and barbed-wire perimeter fence. His radio caused the dashboard to vibrate, pumping out the base line of some love song over 92 MOOSE.

DEATH & COMIX

On WURS, Indigo Jones began his show with a wrap-up of local news. He liked to get this out of the way early, so he could get down to raving about politics.

"It says here that down in Pickup City," he said—you could tell he was skimming—"the Ravens Motorcycle Club has announced the opening of a Retox Center. Apparently it's for folks trying to kick the 12-step habit. The Center will hold a two-day intensive workshop this weekend, and your admission fee of $89.50 covers both nutrients and inspirational videos, including Sam Peckinpah's *The Wild Bunch,* considered by many to be the greatest American film. Whatever happened to *Citizen Kane?* I guess the world marches on, folks. Participants are advised to bring their own sleeping bags. Here's a little thing by Ned Lagin called *Seastones,* and it says here this is the original February 1975 version. Enjoy."

Saintstephen Bax and Shadow Malqvist shook their heads at each other. They had possibly never been awake this early in their lives. And look what they had been missing. Thistle Herne, rising from her nest of magazines on the official Pod sofa, said:

"Who does that person's voice remind you of?"

"L. Ron Hubbard," said Saintstephen.

"The guy in Crash Test Dummies," said Shadow.

"Jimmy Carl Black," said Ari, a local elf. "The Indian of the group."

Saintstephen swung an arm around and pretended to cuff him. "What you been listening to, boy?" he said.

"You guys," said Thistle, shaking her head.

Over the radio, Gracie Slick and David Crosby seemed to be experiencing simultaneous personality crises.

"Crank that sucker *up,*" shouted Saintstephen. "I *love* it."

Shadow ignored him. He was poring over a defunct serial comic called *Anima.* "I can't believe it," he said. "They've got lütkvisk in here."

Across the big open room of the Pod Lodge, Guillermo Gobán sat alone and in silence before the computer workstation.

"What's going on here?" he said. "What're they doing?"

Shadow and Saintstephen glanced over, squinted at the huge Radius monitor, and went back to their previous amusements.

"Just poking around," said Shadow.

"They're a bunch of lightweights," said Saintstephen. "Looking for us, probably."

"Yeah," said Shadow. "But their LAN thinks we're just another node. So not to worry."

Guillermo looked worried anyway. Thistle offered him a can of Jolt and he shook his head. "Don't need it," he said.

He was dressed in olive coveralls. He looked like something between a guerrilla and a tree surgeon.

"Nervous?" asked Thistle, sympathetically.

He smiled at her. It was a handsome, winning smile, with just enough hint of soul-deep suffering to really reel them in. Thistle wasn't buying it.

"Don't blow our cover if you get caught," she said. "It'll piss off Syzygy."

"Yeah," said Ari.

Guillermo lowered his eyes, perhaps recalling those deer remains—bones and skin, tied with an apron string. He said:

"I'll take your secret to my grave."

The door opened and Gus the timber wolf trotted in, wagging his tail, and began hunting for stray Cheez-Its. He was followed by Jesse Openhood. Today Jesse's black hair had a hawk feather braided into it. He looked unusually sharp-eyed and present.

"Did you see?" he asked them—or perhaps only said rhetorically, to the Lodge at large. "One of the death traps has been broken."

"Cool," said Shadow.

"Which one?" said Ari.

"The east."

"What does that mean?" said Guillermo. His voice was measured, but spooked.

"It's means time's a-wasting," said Jesse. "Something out there's going to kick some ass today. Take some names."

Gus wrapped up a quick patrol of the room, disappointed. He had found only pretzels and the remains of a peanut butter sandwich.

"Come on, boy," Jesse told him. "Let's go down to the Long House and throw some beers in the cooler."

SOULS UP FOR GRABS

Sun bounced off the corrugated metal sides of the converted hangar at the Goddin Forest Research Station. Inside, Burdock Herne was presiding over a get-acquainted breakfast. The food was mediocre but abundant, served buffet-style in the vast cavern where once B-52's had parked. The guest list included not only Gulf Atlantic employees but also representatives of the local community, including

Donna di Fuora, Chair of the Dublin County Chamber of Commerce
Rev. Hobart Banebook, member of the local clergy
Samantha Sorensen, reporter for Channel 5 News

"You know, it's very important to us," Herne recited, "to be genuinely active and involved members of the community. We want to be good citizens. We want to be good *neighbors*."

"No complaints here," said di Fuora. "I think the initial concern some of the locals felt has dissipated, especially since your company underwrote the construction of a new high school gymnasium."

Herne slapped the table, palm down. It was a startling gesture to those seated within Richter-range, but not out of proportion with the man himself.

"That's *exactly* what I'm talking about," he declared. "That's what I mean by being a good neighbor. In addition to creating high-wage jobs, of course. A new gymnasium? *Excellent* work there, Sauvage."

Chas Sauvage sat two chairs down from Herne, pressed between the flesh of Banebook and the spinning tape recorder of that reporter. What was her name? All Chas could think of was Gidget. He turned and gave her a confident, clubby sort of wink. She looked back in surprise. Chas didn't care. He sensed a crisp wind blowing his way. He tacked smartly to return the C.E.O.'s smile.

"Thank you, sir," he said. "But you know, I have to thank Reverend Banebook here for making us aware of situations of that type. The Reverend—"

"Please," Banebook said, waving a fork laden with scrambled eggs, "everybody, call me Hoot."

"Hoot," said Herne, decisively.

"—has his *finger*," Chas continued, "very much on the local pulse. Ear to the ground. Very little escapes his notice."

Hoot nodded as he chewed; his fleshy cheeks pouched out squirrelishly.

"Well, then, Hoot," said Herne, "any concerns out there now you'd like to share with us?"

"Nothing that comes to mind," said Banebook. "Apart from the usual community issues."

A moment followed that was like a hollow container of possibilities, out of which might have tumbled anything, or nothing much. The Channel 5 reporter—whose name was *not* Gidget—gave destiny a nudge by repeating into her recorder:

"The usual community issues."

Then she pointed the recorder at Hoot, thereby coming between Chas Sauvage and a speared sausage.

Banebook gestured with dangerous expansiveness, given the

bulk of his upper body. "I'm talking about the battle for the minds and souls of our youth," he said. "For example, the popular notion of the forest as some kind of holy sanctuary."

"We at Gulf Atlantic," Burdock Herne declared, "are fully committed to the idea that the forests of this country are not just vital economic resources, they are part of the sacred patrimony we will hand down to our children and our grandchildren."

Herne smiled past Banebook to meet Chas's stern eye. Chas gave a very slight shake of the head.

Banebook said, "That's an interesting way of putting it." He selected his words with the care of a child prying the good bits out of a pizza. "And I suppose I would only differ with you when it comes to your use of the term *sacred*. I'm sure folks down in Texas are more levelheaded about things like this. But here in what remains, your fine efforts notwithstanding, a wild and unsettled part of the country, there is a certain body of opinion—especially among the young—that there is something sacrosanct, something shall we say *divine*, about these woods around here. To put it bluntly, you're up against a gang of tree-worshipers. You can't so much as crank up a chainsaw without some trust-fund hippie quoting Thoreau at you. I realize you're a businessman, Mr. Herne, and you have to answer to the concerns of all your customers. But I ask you: don't you find a certain ominous note—a certain moral danger—in dealing with modern-day practitioners of the oldest blasphemy in the world?"

Herne wore a look of unalloyed fascination. You might (with due caution) have used the term *rapture*. Never in his life, his expression seemed to say, had he heard words of such finely whetted reason as those uttered by the Reverend Banebook. Even Hoot himself appeared to find the C.E.O.'s attentiveness a trifle unnerving.

"I only bring this up," Hoot said, "because of the emphasis being given to so-called environmental issues in the media nowadays."

He paused; he waited. Still Herne did not react.

"It's the *kids* I'm worried about, Mr. Herne," Hoot went on. (Gidget's recording would reveal a faint but perceptible timbre of desperation in his voice.) "The rising generation. Souls up for grabs, is how I look at them. Are you a father yourself, Mr. Herne?"

All at once—jarring the gestalt of the breakfast table—Herne raised his hand to shoulder level. He held it there a moment, as though calling for quiet, for thunderous silence; then he eased it slowly back down. He placed the large palm flat, fingers splayed, on the table.

"I assure you, Hoot," he said, smiling with the attractive lethality of a laser beam, "that we will take these heathen eco-kooks and crush them into the very ground they worship until their shit comes oozing out of their eyeballs."

The hand on the table rotated clockwise and then counterclockwise, as though reducing something imaginary to the consistency of wood pulp soaking in a vat of sulfuric acid.

DAY CARE & OTHER ITEMS ON THE DOMESTIC AGENDA

Gene Deere excused himself early. He had to go home and feed his bear. He had taken to calling the bear Tex, despite his intention not to grow attached to it. When he arrived at his rented bungalow he found that Tex had knocked down the barrier at the foot of the steps and climbed to the master bedroom and defecated on a recent issue of *Nature*. Then he had gone to sleep on the unmade bed.

"I thought wild bears shat in the woods," said Gene—softly, so as not to wake Tex, who would become excited and possibly claw a hole through his chinos.

Tunes from Ludi's damned Music of Your Life station ran through his head. "Moon River." "Some Enchanted Evening." Music of *whose* life? he wondered.

His own, if something didn't change.

For an instant he had a hellish vision: himself spending the rest of his mortal existence listening to low-fidelity recordings over a crappy clock radio in somebody's walk-up apartment. Or worse: aboard a missing hippie's houseboat.

What a horrifying concept, thought Gene, shaking his head.

He was not aware that he was smiling.

COLLAPSE OF THE WAVE PACKET

The Witches of Pickup City processed into the magic circle behind Pippa Rede's Lighthouse through the opening in the east and turned clockwise, deosil, to close it behind them. While the circle was intact, no malign or unsympathetic spirits could gain entry. Invited guests only, please. After the women were in their places and the circle safely closed, Syzygy Prague, the high priestess, peered around at them—seven in all, quite good for short notice (it helped that so few local Witches held ordinary jobs)—and she said portentously:

"Today we will take extra precautions."

Her accent, usually dormant, returned strongly at certain times. Pippa wondered whether Syzygy turned it on and off deliberately, for theurgic effect. If so, it worked. She sounded exotic and somewhat dangerous. Witchy, in a word.

"This is a Time that is not time," she declared, "in a Place that is not a place. I stand at the threshold between this world and the Other, between the manifest and the possible."

She reached into a pocket of her deep violet sweatshirt (the day was too warm for cloaks) and drew out her athame, or ceremonial blade. Most Witches take pains to acquire an athame of just the right sort: proper wood for the handle, ritually cured steel, sigils of power on the haft. Syzygy used a plain kitchen knife. The other women imagined that this was the knife with which she had (famously) hacked the deer up. In their minds, this charged the athame with special and rather hideous energy. In actuality, the knife was a nicked-up old thing of no culinary value. Generally speaking with magic it is the mental component that is most crucial.

Syzygy moved slowly around the circle, stopping at each of the four quarters and tapping the soil three times with the blade. In the east she said: "I call upon you, Powers of Air, to witness this rite and to guard our company."

In the south she called upon the Powers of Fire; in the west and north, Water and Earth. Then, kneeling, she swept off her 99¢ cowboy bandana and laid it on the tree-stump altar. From a pocket of her jeans she produced a pair of votive candles, white and red—the Goddess and the God—which she placed on the altar cloth and lit with a blue-tip safety match scraped on a thumbnail. Through the flames she passed a sprig of dry catmint. The smoke smelled uncannily like sage, which did not grow so well this far north. At least three Witches made mental notes to remember this. So many books about magic seemed to be written with the climate of California in mind. Always the adaptable one, our Syzygy.

"I invoke *Gort*," the priestess declared, "spirit of Ivy, the tree of protection. I invoke the *Twrc* the boar, ruthless and red. I invoke *Geis,* the mute swan. I call upon you to join your power with ours, so that we may accomplish the working that lies ahead of us."

The women felt a tingling move among them. They shivered pleasurably.

Syzygy fished in another pocket and pulled out a medicine vial, the kind eardrops come in. She squirted this liberally about the altar, nearly extinguishing one of the candles.

"By this tincture of male fern, whose uncurled fronds we gathered today at Midsummer Dawn, I call upon *Flidais,* protectress of woodlands and wild things. I invite her to attend with us also, and help us in our task."

The women shared an inquisitive look. Syzygy was famous for issuing wake-up calls to obscure and long-slumbering deities. Sometimes she got an answer and sometimes she did not. Out on Route 1, an RV horn bleated. A chancy breeze swirled through the stand of rugosa roses that blocked the view of the I.G.A. parking lot. Their smell was heady.

Syzygy scratched in the ground with her athame. She inscribed a circular form, a spiral or labyrinth. Then she spat into the center of it.

"I call upon *Nantosuelta,*" she said loudly, "keeper of holy wells, attendant at troubled births, patron of the domestic arts, friend of bees and doves, cousin of the great dark goddess Morrigu, also known as Battle-Raven and as Morgan la Fay."

The women perked up at this. Something about the invocation seemed right to them. At least the résumé was impressive.

"*Nantosuelta,*" repeated Pippa.

The Witches murmured the name. Syzygy laid her athame on the altar. She ran a hand through her disorganized hair.

"All of you who have come to our circle," she said, "mortal and ever-living, visible and unseen: hear me. Today we reach a turning point in the wheel of the year. The energies of growth and fertility that were born at Beltane are today coming to full flower. In a few weeks the flower will bear fruit and we will celebrate Lugnassad, the beginning of the harvest. But today is the turning point. Today is the day of election. At Midsummer, the Earth moves from a time of opening to a time of enfoldment. We pass from the open petals of the flower, which welcome the sun and the pollinating bee, to the closed and secret world within the pistil, where the embryo of the seed is nurtured. Midsummer is the instant when the infinite possibilities of the past converge into the singular destiny of the future. The open bid becomes the sealed contract. The wave packet collapses to reveal the particle. Do you follow me?"

Yes & no. The Witches understood Midsummer in their hearts

and their bones and possibly in their wombs; not necessarily in their minds. Syzygy knew it as a song in her blood.

She said, "This is where we must put our energies, then. We will help Nature choose the best outcome. So that when the many grains of pollen race down the style to reach the innermost sanctum of the ovule, the best grain will win."

"That sounds pretty heterosexist," one of the Witches said.

Syzygy shrugged. "It's Nature's way. If we're going to have a future, somebody's got to get fucked."

The women, for the most part, enjoyed this sort of thing—the Earthy touch. They smiled and shook their heads. Syzygy, they thought. That Syzygy.

"Are we going to do scrying or something?" asked Pippa.

"Better than that," said Syzygy. "We're going to cast a spell."

So saying, she whipped her violet sweatshirt over her head and kicked out of her jeans. It was the Witches' custom to perform spell-workings naked, or (to use the ecclesiastically correct term) skyclad. Happily the women pulled their clothes off. Sunshine and a chancy breeze danced across their skin, made them feel deliciously free, stoked on power, at one with the ecstatic spirits.

Then they cast their spell. But we may know nothing about that, because spells are secret.

WORLD BEAT

Sefyn Hunter took the day off. He wanted to get a little drumming in. Anyway he had been working hard lately, picking up the slack for Gene Deere—whom, please don't take this wrong, he absolutely adored. But let's face it: Gene just wasn't cut out to be an organization man.

On a bluff overlooking the ocean, surrounded by boulders and naturalized heather and an occasional candelabra of woolly thistle, *Onopordum acanthum*—which would have been the first thing Sefyn planted in his own backyard garden, if he had one—he carefully folded his clothes and stacked them in a soft pile. He took a tube of woad blue cream makeup and smeared it over his cheeks, around his eyes, down his throat, around his nipples, and in a line bisecting his stomach, crossing the navel, and terminating in his pubic hair. Then he sat cross-legged and placed his double-doumbek between his knees. Lightly, tentatively, he tapped the acrylic skin. He listened to the wind that scoured the hillside, distant applause of the surf, occasional cries of gulls or squonks of ravens that circled in the sky before him, apparently for the fun of it.

After a few minutes he picked up the pulse of the day. It was strong but changeable, now moving slow deep in the Earth, now picking up speed and racing skyward. Sefyn followed it as best he could, bending low over his drums and then arching back, stretching his spine into an inverse comma. Staring in wonder at the glassy cerulean of the heavens. After a while he ceased to hear his drumming as a thing separate from the rest of the world. The air that entered his lungs took on a rich and nutritive quality. He felt he could live on it. Of course, in a sense he *was* living on it. Heedlessly, Sefyn laughed.

After an hour or so his arms lost all feeling and his back was sore and his stomach felt tight, his eyes dry, his mind empty. He saw nothing now and heard nothing outside the infinitely resonant life-sound of his drums, which seemed more intimately connected to the essence of Sefyn than his own heartbeat.

The sun reached its highest point in the sky. Sefyn's penis followed it, pointing upward, tilting slightly south. All his blood seemed to have gone there, because his head felt empty and for a moment or two he wondered if he actually had fainted— whether he was lying on the ground, and if so, whether he had fallen onto his drums. Then he understood that he hadn't fainted; he had had an orgasm. It had knocked him just about senseless, but even so, he remained upright. The drums were silent. All he was doing was sitting there. More or less in amazement.

Watching his millions of fallen sperm cells
swim down into the body
of the Earth.

or
maybe the world is not a stage

at all. Maybe the world is a totally real and very serious place, and all the people in it are exactly what they appear to be.

Maybe the Normal People (i.e., who think their jobs are important, get regular haircuts, mow their lawns) are the ones who have it right, who really understand the way the Universe is wired.

Maybe having a sense of humor is okay—at least in your own private time—but not strictly necessary for a good and valuable life. Maybe life, in the end, is no laughing matter. Maybe death is no laughing matter. Maybe God does not make jokes, does not laugh at *your* jokes, and is not amused by this sort of speculation.

Maybe the way teenagers feel is just a phase.

Maybe you have to give up your youthful illusions sooner or later.

Maybe the suburbs are really good, healthy environments.

Maybe young minds need to be shielded from dangerous ideas and pictures of naked people touching each other.

Maybe the thinning of the ozone layer is due to natural cyclic factors unrelated to the Gulf Atlantic quarterly earnings report.

Maybe rich people need a tax break so they can save and invest and create a climate of economic vitality which will benefit all Americans in the long run.

Maybe people like you should go live somewhere else.

Maybe humankind's destiny is in the stars. Or in digital circuits. Or pure thought. So the "natural" world is not that big a deal, in the long run.

TEX & MOLLY DELIBERATE UPON THESE AND OTHER ISSUES, FINALLY REACHING A VERDICT

Nah.

THE THING; THE PLAY

Ludi could hardly have been more nervous if she were trapped between a baby bear and its mommy.

She passed through the crowd of people who had gathered around the gazebo at the center of the Dublin green: one of those quaint New England photo ops that serve no known function in modern community life. In her arms she clutched a cardboard box scrounged from the back of the I.G.A. and filled with drama-related paraphernalia:

> Masks
> Silly hats
> ID tags to be hung around people's necks
> Sheets of paper summarizing the Start-up Conditions
> Index cards bearing the title and meme of each character
> Flyers
> Fireworks
> Noisemakers
> Child-safe plastic light sticks
> Noncompetitive judging cards
> Fabulous prizes! (remaindered copies of
> *I'm OK, You're DOA* by Franz Bibfeldt)

"Drama in a box," Gene had declared, surveying the contents happily.

But that had been this morning, before he drove off to attend something he called, in the bleakest tones, a power breakfast. Leaving Ludi alone today of all days. She had tried calling Eben, who was not home, and then Pippa, who was getting ready for a ritual. Finally she reached Deep Herb, hanging around Dan Dan's apartment upstairs from the Pizza Scene, having apparently forgotten to go home the previous night. Deep Herb agreed to come help her get set up on the green—which was no guarantee that he would materialize. Somewhat to her surprise, he not only showed up—3 reefers later, however—but also brought along Dan Dan, Sara Clump (who had splintered from Guil-

lermo's splinter group after a quarrel over ideology), and an off-
duty deputy sheriff whom they had found puzzling over the
bumper stickers on Sara's illegally parked car.

"I keep seeing this little rainbow decal everywhere," the deputy
had said. His name was Doug. "Does it mean anything? Or I
mean, is it just pretty or what?"

"Come with us," Deep Herb told the deputy. "You'll see."

And because of the way Deep Herb was—guileless, unthreaten-
ing—Deputy Doug consulted his watch and scratched his closely
cropped head and climbed into Deep Herb's backseat. They left
Sara's car where it was parked (illegally), figuring they now had
official Sheriff's Department sanction. By the time the four of
them finished the drive to Dublin, Dan Dan and the deputy had
discovered a mutual interest in tattoos, and Sara and the deputy
had discovered a mutual interest in Ludi. Nobody discovered any
mutual interest with Deep Herb, other than perhaps a shared
hope that his car not execute an auto-da-fé.

"What a perfect day!" Sara exclaimed, extracting herself from
the backseat.

Ludi handed her a stack of flyers. "Maybe you could start
passing these around," she said. "So people will know about the
performance."

"Maybe it should be a surprise," said Sara, who only wanted
to hang in the sunshine.

"It'll *be* a surprise," said Ludi. "Don't worry about that."

"Yeah," said Deep Herb, gravely. "Spontaneous, man."

Dan Dan took off his shirt. Ludi could not help admiring the
spiderweb that (in lieu of actual body hair) filled in the space
between his nipples. His stomach was as flat as a boy's. What is
the matter with me? she wondered.

Deputy Doug tried to engage her in conversation. She thought
there was something strangely mechanical about him. Cast him
against type, she decided.

"Here," she said, pulling a mask-and-meme set out of the grocery box. "You be the Lipstick Lesbian."

"Pardon me?" he said, courteously.

"Remember the rainbow sticker?" Sara Clump reminded him.
He nodded, still somewhat perplexed.

"You don't have to put the mask on yet," said Ludi. "Wait
till dark."

Dark would not come for another few hours. No one was sure
how many. Something about the way time moves at this time of
year—jaggedly, like a sailboat tacking into the wind—keeps you

in a state of chronic uncertainty as to such matters as duration, minutes elapsed, hours yet to go. It is as though you are traveling across some unvarying, though beautiful, landscape. There is no way to gauge your speed or the rate of your progress. Suddenly you have arrived someplace. How did it happen? Is this a good place to be? Could you have stayed in that other place, that unbroken journeying, forever? You aren't sure.

They handed out flyers, hung streamers from the gazebo, took breaks to stroll to the Real Food Co-op for raspberry-creme soda. Eben Creek arrived with Indigo's boom box. It was tuned to WURS, where Bad Cathy was playing a totally inappropriate Leonard Cohen set. "Jazz police are looking through my folder," sang the Buddhist in black. Ludi spun the dial. Soon they were swirling around to the theme from the Warner Brothers classic *Unchained*. Deep Herb and Dan Dan got more spaced. Ludi assigned a Fleet Bank loan officer the role of Gun-Toting Survivalist, and asked an elderly tourist from Delaware if he would like to be a Rock. He examined the meme card, which read:

Meme R
Dresses down-market; regards political change with equanimity.

The tourist agreed. Ludi suggested that he might want to sit in the middle of the green. "Where you'll be in everybody's way," she said. "That's what rocks do here in Maine."

The Rock seemed to grasp this readily. A natural, empathetic performer.

Things were falling into place. Anyway, that's what Ludi thought.

IN THE WINGS

Wild Jag Eckhart drove his Suburban slowly along the road just inside the perimeter fence of the Goddin Forest Research Station. He passed the trial plots containing X *dawkinsia*. He passed stands of mixed softwoods, spruce and pine and fir. He passed plots where spruce trees were planted on a low-density grid, interplanted with transgenic fiber-maximized *Cannabis sativa*. He came at last to the plots where hard- and softwoods grew together in considerable diversity, approximating conditions in the wild. One of these patches reminded Eckhart of the woods around the Sovereign Citizens'

Militia Training Camp and Nature Preserve (tax and land-use classification pending). He braked the Suburban. He decided that here was where the first canister ought to go.

Eckhart had been, regrettably, too young for Vietnam. By the time of the later, more limited overseas engagements he had lost interest in organized governmental forms of warfare. Too tame, he thought; like fighting in a ring with gloves on, surrounded by ropes, and watched over by a referee. Besides which the government was not to be trusted.

Nonetheless Eckhart retained certain military or paramilitary enthusiasms, most of them acquired from watching movies like *Platoon* and *Apocalypse Now*. One of his greatest fascinations was with napalm. He had read articles about napalm in *Soldier of Fortune* and had ordered a book from Paladin Press on how to make the stuff yourself, right in your own workshop or garage. It was pretty easy, though you had to understand that you were violating a Dow Chemical Corporation patent if you followed the standard recipe. Eckhart was basically a law-abiding man, when it came to laws he considered just. So he tinkered with the recipe, scorching a number of acres of marketable timber in the process, until he hit upon a formula he could live with. It was a little slower to ignite, but when you got it going it burned like a son of a bitch. He had happened to mention this personal interest of his to Chas Sauvage one day—it was funny how that man could get you talking, even though he seldom showed much interest in what you were actually talking about—and Sauvage had come up to him later, months later, and said, "Wild Jag, I think I've got an interesting application for that hobby of yours."

Now, Eckhart understood without having to be told that he was getting into kind of a tricky area here. Because on the one hand you could say that what he was about to do was all in the line of duty, following orders from the boss, et cetera. But on the other he knew something sneaky or shady was going on. You didn't have to be a gene-splicer to figure that out. Just the way Sauvage acted when you talked to him—slipperier than a snake in a bucket of snot—was enough to put you wise. Beyond that, there was the strange assignment itself.

"Take out," Sauvage had said, speaking slowly and clearly, as though explaining something to a child, "the mixed-growth plots. All the naturalistic or quasi-naturalistic areas. I want them taken out of the equation. Do you understand?"

Sure thing, boss. Eckhart found it entertaining when people

underestimated him. That put *you* in the position of knowing something *they* did not, which was always an advantage.

"Then you can go for the hemp stands, the SPF plots—whatever seems appropriate. I don't care so much about that. Only, it should not look specifically targeted, you understand? It should not look as though any particular area had been singled out. As though the station itself—the whole operation, the Company—were the target."

He had not asked Eckhart if he understood, after that. Presumably because Eckhart was not meant to understand. Whatever this was about, it was Chas Sauvage's little secret. Eckhart guessed that much, but little more. Though he could have made a few guesses, if the question had been put to him. Not that he expected it ever would be; especially now, when the blame would fall so clearly on that band of greenie hackers. But if the question *had* been put to him, hypothetically, he might have guessed that the whole thing had to do with this very quiet struggle that was being waged between Sauvage and his chief of research, Eugene Deere. Eckhart was not sure what the struggle was all about; and between the two of them, Deere and Sauvage, he could not have said whom he cared for less. Mostly they were both the kind of people he didn't waste time thinking about. But he suspected that Deere was turning out to be a little too touchy-feely for Sauvage's liking: too much in tune with the times, sympathetic to the demonstrators that showed up outside the front gate now and again. Too close to being a pointy-headed McNeil-Lehrer type of person. And somehow this had translated into a disagreement over the trial plots and what to make of them. Which in turn probably fed into the visit by the Mondo Jefe from Texas, and from there into God knew what little twists and turns in Chas Sauvage's personal career plan.

So much Eckhart knew or could have guessed. But it was not his job to know, nor to guess, nor even to wonder. It was his job, in essence, to light the match. (In this case, the match was actually a digital timer, set for a little past sunset.) And until then, it was his job to set out the canisters, drive a safe distance away, and hunker down in the Suburban. Then wait.

Eckhart was lugging the first canister into a patch of baby woodland when his eye fell on something lying at the base of the sign that said PLOT 28b. He bent to look at this and saw that it was a denim jacket. One of the lab techs', probably. As a matter of common decency, Eckhart would have picked the thing up, dropped it off later at the front office; but he realized that doing so would connect him to this place where the jacket had been lost. Not that it would matter, probably. But you never knew.

By now, damn it, his curiosity was stirred up. He lowered the canister of homemade napalm. The jacket was a nicely made thing—not a piece of working apparel but the sort of thing you'd order out of a catalog. In fact, it might belong to a woman.

Eckhart thought about this. About a woman's jacket being left out here in Trial Plot 28b. Somehow, the idea pleased him. He did not know what to make of it, but he liked the idea of a woman taking her jacket off in this almost-wild place, with nothing but the trees and the bugs and the breeze any the wiser. And because he liked it, and because it wouldn't matter one way or the other in a few hours, he slung the jacket over his arm. Then he picked up the canister and went back to work.

IMITATIO

 Pippa Rede wore a peculiar smile on her face.

"I just have a really major feeling," she said, "something *amazing* is going to happen tonight."

"If this show comes off," said Ludi, "it'll be amazing, for sure."

She glanced at the sky. The sun was low. People were milling around the green. At the entrance of Cold Bay, the red light of the sea buoy had come on, flashing the Morse code for Alpha:

■ ▬

Sort of a Yin thing; appropriate for the great briny Mother.

Pippa said, "Something *unusual* happened in our circle today."

Ludi kind of heard her and kind of did not. She was scrounging through the grocery box to see how many character masks remained to be handed out. Not too many. The time must be getting close.

"I can't really talk about it," said Pippa. "Because, you know— a secret ritual and all."

"Yeah," said Ludi. "That makes sense."

Nothing about Witches makes sense, of course. The terms are antithetical. If you want sense, talk to a liberal Episcopalian. Ludi wondered who had gotten the Aging Hippie assignments. Those seemed rather pivotal to her. And how about the Minimum Wage Gen-X Type?

"Have you ever heard of Nantosuelta?" said Pippa.

"Nope," said Ludi. "Should I?" She thought about those tragic Latina pop stars to whom now and then terrible things happened before Ludi ever got a handle on who they were, exactly.

"I really shouldn't be telling you this," said Pippa. "But you're cool, right? I mean, you're not like, Xian or anything, are you?"

"Like what?" said Ludi.

For the first time she looked at Pippa—really *looked* at her—and what she saw was a pleasantly flushed and bright-eyed woman who was beaming like maybe her Food Stamp entitlement had just been adjusted upward.

"Xian," said Pippa. "That means Christian. Like Xmas."

"Ha." Ludi smiled, and Pippa smiled back, and then the two friends hugged each other.

"Anyway," said Pippa, "there's this ancient raven goddess who's in charge of wells or something, and Syzygy invoked Her today at our Midsummer circle and guess what."

"Hey Ludi," someone called.

She turned to see Sefyn Hunter, the guy from Guillermo's men's group.

He said, "I hear you're giving out parts for a play."

"Not exactly a *play*," she said.

Sefyn looked puzzled and intrigued. Ludi rummaged in the box.

"Feel like being a Native American?" she asked.

"That's *exactly* what I'm in the mood for," he said.

She handed over his mask. "Do you have a watch?" she asked him.

"Yeah. At home."

Pippa was edging this way and that, trying to stay in Ludi's line of vision. It was kind of appealingly pathetic. Around the gazebo, people had already put their masks on, despite clear instructions to wait until dark. Ludi reflected that nobody reads instructions anymore. This was the era of point-and-shoot, point-and-click, point-and-blame.

My god, she thought—am I turning into a Young Fogy?

The green was getting crowded. Over Indigo's boom box, the Music of Your Life station was doing its regular evening "Stardust" feature, in which a different version of everybody's favorite pop standard was played every night. The theory was, apparently, that this could continue forever. So you'd just have to keep listening, even if this entailed unimaginable suffering in the form of commercials for the hearing-aid center by whom this popular feature was brought to you, nightly.

Nightly at what? Ludi tried to remember. Seven o'clock? Eight?

"It has something," Pippa whispered, as soon as Sefyn had wandered out of earshot, "to do with Tex and Molly. Which of them was called Raven?"

"Melo-*dee*," sang the boom box, "haunts my memory."

"Molly," said Ludi. "Why do you say *was?*"

Deep Herb, appearing from nowhere, said, "Can I be the token African-American?"

"Somebody's already taken that," Ludi told him. "Why don't you be the Corporate Executive?"

"Hey, look," said Herb, digging through the drama box. "A Vegetable!"

Innocent Pippa said, "Perfect."

BEDROOM SCENE

Gene Deere was awakened by his beeper. He opened his eyes on the unmade bed next to Tex the bear, who was just waking also. The two of them looked at each other. The beeper continued to beep. Gene smiled helplessly at the animal in his bed and the bear pounced on top of him and promptly clawed a hole through his chinos.

"Damn it," said Gene—not at the bear, nor even the beeper, but at himself for the way he felt: confused and headachy from having slept at the wrong time and awakened at dusk. He lurched upright and went over to the telephone, dragging the animal that had wrapped its paws around one leg. Step and drag, step and drag. Dance of Yu, he thought. Then he wondered what *that* meant. Something Ludi had mentioned?

"Deere," said the voice of the Antichrist over the handset. "What's become of you? I had to give the King a tour of your cloning lab all by myself."

"Sorry," Gene said untruthfully.

"Don't fret. You can make it up to me."

Chas sounded jolly. The day must be going well for him.

"The security types from Houston want you to go through your logs and pinpoint the time the irregularities occurred. S'pose you can take care of that tonight?"

"Tonight?"

"Is there a problem?"

Gene thought about Ludi's play. Presumably this would not constitute a problem in Chas's eyes. "Can I do it over the modem?" he asked.

"Negatory. The security guys are worried about the integrity of our data lines. Some network node they can't account for. Got to do this in situ, I'm afraid."

Chas did not sound afraid. Of *anything*. He sounded like a man who's got the world by the short hairs.

"So," said Gene, conversationally, "was the King pleased with your presentation?"

"Too early to tell. No indication to the contrary, however. He didn't seem concerned about the problem with the 4.3.2. As long as we've got enough tissue stock to repropagate. I showed him the damaged trees we've potted up and he mentioned maybe doing some kind of public relations thing."

"Great," said Gene, thinking this at least had nothing to do with Operations. "Then I guess I'll be there in a half hour or so."

"I won't," said Chas. "The King wants to do a little tour of Dublin, so I thought we'd drive down to the village green in a bit. Some kind of annual hoopla going on there tonight, I hear."

"So I hear."

"Toodles, amigo."

Gene looked at Tex. The bear was growing bigger. As well he should, having chewed on everything in the bungalow.

"Want to go for a ride?" Gene asked him. "Want to see where Daddy works?"

CREATURES OF DARKNESS

Guillermo stepped through the hole in the chain-link and entered enemy territory. His olive drab coveralls were all but invisible in the fading light. Besides the heavy-duty wire snippers which he now returned to his backpack, he carried a flashlight, a collapsible shovel, a plastic trash bag, a canteen of water and seaweed extract (to lessen the shock of root disturbance), a QuickTake point-and-shoot digital camera, and a small electronic device whose function he did not understand but which he was supposed to clip around an L.A.N. cable somewhere, assuming he could identify one.

His mission tonight:

1. To obtain evidence of corporate misdeeds, and

2. To lay the groundwork for the next phase of the campaign to save the Great North Woods.

What he wanted, above all, was to obtain an actual specimen of the gonzo killer hybrid spruce that Gulf Atlantic intended to *insert,* as the in-house jargon went, *by the earliest and most expeditious means,* in order that *the long-term position of Gulf Atlantic in the Great North Woods will have been definitively secured.* Guillermo still felt a shiver when the words of the stolen briefing document ran through his mind. But tonight the shiver included an element of excitement. Because tonight the North Woods were striking back.

Behind him, in the tall grass and black-eyed Susans and goldenrod, he heard a rustling. A faint sound, not much louder than the wind might have made. But it had not come from the wind; Guillermo's instincts told him that. (He *had* instincts for such things, no matter what Ludi thought.) He dropped to a crouch and moved quietly around a signpost, reasoning that the white-enameled placard that identified this patch of trees as "Plot 29d" would make him even more inconspicuous.

He rested on his haunches, waiting.

The sound behind him came again, at regular intervals. There could be no doubt now that he was listening to footsteps. They drew closer and closer, then seemed to hesitate, and stopped. Guillermo tried to silence his breathing. He was afraid even to open his eyes.

Very nearby—within kicking distance—a voice whispered:

"Hey, are you there?"

Not the sort of voice he expected: it sounded young—kidlike.

Then there was a new set of footsteps. These came from behind, among the trees. Guillermo turned, too late—someone's hands dropped over his eyes, and a weight fell onto his back, pushing him forward. His elbows broke his fall, scuffing on gravel.

With a burst of violent energy, Guillermo twisted in the grip of his assailant. He threw the person to the ground and fumbled in his pack for the high-intensity flashlight.

"Hey," the first voice said again, louder now. "What are you guys doing?"

Guillermo flicked the flashlight on. In the oval of bluish light, Ari Prague, dressed in his crazy-quilt hand-sewn clothes, lay blinking and shielding his eyes.

"Surprise," the boy said. He raised a dirty bare foot to fend the flashlight away.

"What the fuck," said Guillermo. He swung the beam around

and caught Thistle Herne just as she got a hand up to cover the lens.

"Would you *please* put that out?" she whispered forcefully. "What're you trying to do, get us caught?"

Baffled into obedience, Guillermo clicked off the light. "What are you kids doing here?" he demanded.

"Kids?" said Thistle, bristling. "Who are you—somebody's dad?"

"Sorry," said Guillermo. Wondering what he should have said.

"Anyway, Ari's an elf," Thistle reminded him.

"That's right," said Ari.

Guillermo sighed.

"We hid in the back of your car," Ari told him, proudly. "Underneath that old blanket."

"That blanket," said Guillermo, "was intended to conceal the evidence while I get away from here."

"That's cool," said Thistle. "We'll ride up front on the drive back."

Guillermo looked at them seriously. "Now listen. If you two are going to come along, then you've got to stick to the plan, okay? Keep close to me and don't make any ruckus. Thistle, you can help me figure out what an L.A.N. cable looks like. And, Ari, maybe you can hold the flashlight or something, while I'm bagging the plant."

"*Yeah,*" said Ari.

"Don't worry," said Thistle. "This isn't exactly like breaking into Fort Knox."

"I wouldn't take too much for granted," said Guillermo. "These big corporations have tighter security than the Feds, nowadays."

"Not Gulf Atlantic"—with a clear note of disdain in her voice. As though she really knew what she was talking about.

"No?" said Guillermo, trying to study her expression in the dark.

She only shrugged. "So why don't we get moving? I kind of wanted to catch the show in Dublin after this is done."

Guillermo shook his head. Youth, he thought. No sense of priorities.

MASQUE

Ludi was down to the last couple of characters. Which was good because it was definitely just about dark. There was a moon—2nd quarter, still waxing, moving up off Cold Bay and glowing the color of a night-light in a child's bedroom.

Rose Moon, Ludi thought.

Near the gazebo, a middle-aged man strolled dreamily over the green, hands in his pockets, looking at everything closely as though appraising it for resale value. The man was dressed in the kind of expensive but personality-deficient clothing that Ludi diagnosed as a symptom of aesthetic impairment. She thought, Now this is the kind of guy who, if you read him a beautiful poem, would listen carefully and then say: *Is that it?* Which is fine—it takes all kinds; there's no need for everyone in the world to recognize the beauty in things—except that these people then conclude that there is no such *thing* as beauty, or at least nothing important about it, and they try to take it away from everyone else. To stamp it out, or pave over it, or at the very least make damned good and sure their tax dollars aren't being spent to perpetuate it.

Or I don't know, thought Ludi. Maybe I just don't know the guy.

She approached him, carrying her box. The man didn't notice her until he was about to knock her over. He blinked and saw the box and drew back; like maybe she was a Hari Krishna or Scientologist or something.

"Would you like a part in our performance?" she asked him.

The man seemed puzzled for a moment and then he smiled. "Ah," he said grandly: "a thespian."

Ludi shook her head. "You're the thespian," she said. "I'm just the author."

This seemed to please him even more. "So very nice," he said, "to meet a young person nowadays who actually *writes*."

Ludi sized him up. His face possessed that refined, overelaborated ugliness that she associated with unusual breeds of dogs. "Let's see now," she said, shuffling through her masks. "You could be the Welfare Witch. No, I don't think so. How about a Gun-Toting Survivalist?"

The man frowned. Ludi guessed he preferred to let somebody else do the shooting for him.

"Well, there's not much left," she said. "How about Somebody's Dad?"

The man looked surprised. He stared into her eyes for a moment as though trying to remember if he'd ever met her before. Majorca? Last year, the end of the season? No?

"Take this," she told him. "Really. You'll do a great job, I can tell. You *look* like somebody's dad."

He took the mask. He glanced at the card, which read:

Meme SD
Just hanging on till he can get the kids through college.

He looked up at Ludi again. Something wistful in his expression now.

"Do I put this on?" he said.

"That's all there is to it." She smiled, to reassure him. "Then if you'll just glance over this sheet of paper here, it explains what the start-up conditions are. Then it's totally up to you."

The man glanced quickly through the instructional material, as though accustomed to processing information rapidly. "What's this here," he said, without glancing up, "about an Unforeseen Development?"

"I can't tell you *that*," Ludi said, "or it wouldn't be Unforeseen, would it?"

He smiled at her, patricianly. He slipped the mask over his face. He looked neither more nor less imposingly bland than before.

She patted his arm. "Look, I've got to take off now. We're about to get started. I hope."

"A pleasure meeting the author *herself*," said the man in the mask, as Ludi was walking away.

It always disturbed her to meet someone of this type and to discover that he might be all right; he might not be totally heartless. At least as long as he got his daily feeding of raw meat at the appointed time.

At the gazebo, two dozen people were hanging out with masks on. Some of them had taken it upon themselves to supplement the masks with odds and ends of costumes, props, set pieces. The Law Enforcement Officer, whose ponytail hung down to his colorfully stained painter's pants, carried a neon water pistol. The Ancient White Oak wore branches strapped to her head, like antlers. The TV News Reporter—who appeared to be a polite Canadian tourist—was videotaping everything in sight, and asking people to say things into his microphone. The Guy Slinging Pizza had slicked his hair back, trying to look Italian. Deputy Doug (the Lipstick Lesbian) had tramped himself up in thrift-store regalia, right down to the trailer-park-queen high heels. Ludi felt sort of touched, seeing everybody getting into it like this.

She climbed up on the deck of the gazebo, staring apprehensively over the crowd. It felt funny, looking at all these people and not being able to tell who was who, behind the masks; then realizing that they weren't the audience, they were the *actors*, and everything that happened next was going to be up to them; and then thinking that she herself was sort of invisible, now. Refined out of existence.

"Okay, everybody," she called out. "It's finally dark, I guess. Time to get the shoe on the road."

Molly's customary pun. How she wished Molly were here! If only just to beam out her earth-mama smile and tell Ludi to break a leg. When you heard that, you knew there was nothing to worry about. Even if you blew your part and everything went as bad as it could possibly go—which happened—there was *still* nothing to worry about.

But that was Molly. And this was Ludi's show. Or shoe.

She bit her lip. The noise on the green subsided, except for the boom box, which continued to play "That Old Black Magic"—the Louis Prima version, with its infectious, distracting rhythm. People looked at Ludi and back and forth at one another and up at Rose Moon, sailing over the water. The night was warm and the soft wind smelled of peonies, old-fashioned roses, evening primrose, night-blooming stock.

"First I want to thank so many of you for coming and for agreeing to take part in our performance. As you've read, I guess, by now, or maybe you haven't, we're calling this *A Midsummer Night's Surprise,* and that's because we really don't know, any of us, what's going to happen. None of us knew what roles anybody was going to play tonight, until we got here. And now, as we're starting things off, we only know what's going to happen up to the big Unforeseen Development. After that, it's in your hands. Or in your heads. Wherever you want it to be."

She paused. She looked out at the crowd, the Players, the creators of their own drama. What a cool idea, she suddenly thought. Everyone the master of her fate. The teller of her own story. Everyone *together* collaborators making up their shared future. And all of them (she realized, with a hollowed-out sensation) looking at Ludi for direction. To point the way into the unknown, into the darkness.

"Here's the deal, then," she said. "Could I ask the person playing the Amoral Trickster to come up here, please?"

From the shadows at the corner of the gazebo, a tall figure shuffled through the crowd. He or she, you couldn't tell which, was wearing gym pants and a nice Liberty Graphics T-shirt that said

THREE CORVIDS

and depicted highly realistic images of a crow, a raven, and a clough—members of the genus *Corvax,* among the most intelligent, widespread and adaptable birds in the world. The Trickster's mask was black, with a headpiece drawn back to cover the hair of the person wearing it. Ludi hadn't intended the mask to be *scary*—more like mysterious—but the way it looked in the darkness, perched on top of this particular, rather skeletal body, gave her a mild case of goose bumps. The Trickster edged forward slowly, as though allowing the eerie tension to build.

"In the *meantime*," said Ludi, temporizing, "maybe it would be good if you all sort of looked around at each other's ID tags, so you get a sense of who's who in the story. And maybe you can think about the way your character might relate to other people's. Okay? Then if there's some character you feel drawn to—or whatever—then when things get started you can seek that other person out. So. Are we ready now?"

The Trickster reached the edge of the platform. Ludi extended a hand and the person, he or she, grabbed it with thin fingers and came lunging upward, the T-shirt flapping loosely, almost like wings. Ludi stepped back, out the way. She was about to say something else—like, *Break a leg* (an exceedingly odd expression when you thought about it)—but before she could, the Trickster apparently decided to get things rolling without her. Which was cool, Ludi guessed.

The Trickster turned to the masked crowd and raised both arms in a dramatic fashion: slowly, starting at the sides and ending at a level with the black headpiece—something like a conductor standing before an orchestra, hamming it up a little so as to capture the attention of the audience.

Okay, thought Ludi, my attention's captured. What happens now?

What happened now was an Unforeseen Development. But not the one Ludi had planned.

PRESENT AT THE CREATION

Gene looked up from the computer at his desk. The office was still, and it was dark except for the glow of the screen and a single HID bulb that Sefyn had connected to a 24-hour timer and suspended over a cycad from Australia, a *Macrozamia,* which was just now in the act of producing its one new leaf per annum. How these things ever grew large enough to be munched on by dinosaurs was a mystery to Gene. Probably it had been a mystery to the dinosaurs too.

He looked up because he thought he heard a noise from somewhere inside the converted hangar. It wasn't the bear: Tex was tethered to the desk by a long dog leash. Gene listened for a few seconds, but the sound did not come again. So he went back to browsing through screen after screen full of colorful but boring graphical data. The software was not something he had needed to get familiar with before now—it was tech stuff, concerned with regulating the growth conditions inside the cloning lab—yet it seemed to him as he stared at it that the layout was oddly familiar. Running down one side was a text-box of parameters, CALCIUM ION CONCENTRATION and NUTRIENT INJECTION RATE and things like that. You clicked on any of the parameters to call up a graph tracking the history of that particular thing. You could combine the parameters to get an overview, and you could adjust the time-scale: 50 hours, 50 days, 50 weeks and so forth.

Suddenly he saw it. Or rather recognized it. The thing about this software that looked so familiar. He remembered—clearly now—where he had seen it before. He had supposed it was a simulation, an A–L thing. But no. It was the control software for his own damned lab.

The noise came again—somewhere down the corridor. It might be anything. It might be nothing.

But Gene felt agitated, trying to fit things together in his mind, and the excuse to get away from his desk was—as usual—more than welcome. So he stood up and walked through the jungly office. Then he halted again.

Voices were coming from just outside the door.

Gene wasn't afraid. It was hard to imagine what there could have been to be afraid of, in a place like this, even after hours and in the dark.

A voice—youngish, he thought—said, "Guys. Look at *this*."

"Quiet," hissed someone older. Then a third—female? and more heedless—said, "Yeah, so what? It's a bunch of plants, is all. What did you think they do here, build robots?"

"Would you *please* keep your voice down," the older voice said. "Sometimes these places are equipped with audio surveillance equipment."

"Are you *kidding?*" said the second voice—definitely female.

Yeah, thought Gene. Are you kidding?

"This place is bush league," the female said.

"You seem to know an awful lot about Gulf Atlantic."

They were all talking loudly, now.

"I don't know shit," the female said, "and I don't want to."

Gene felt ridiculous, cowering in his own office, eavesdropping on trespassers, two of whom sounded like children. He stepped

out from behind a giant potted sentry palm. Then footsteps
sounded at the doorway, and all at once the main overhead lights
flashed on.

"Wow," said the kid in the doorway. "This place is *awesome.*"

Then he saw Gene. He froze. A feral look came over his face—
like an animal you had surprised in the middle of a forest. And
so Gene found himself face-to-face with Ari the elf.

Into the room behind him stepped Thistle, the girl with long
pretty legs. Gene recognized her right away. She recognized him,
though it took a moment. Finally there was Guillermo. Ludi's old
boyfriend—or whatever he was—done up in full commando gear,
and hefting (rather ludicrously) a collapsible shovel.

"Gardening at night?" Gene asked him.

"Hey, look," said Ari. "It's a little *bear.*"

Gene was at the point of deciding that the whole thing was not
just amazing but also amusing; then everything changed. Again.

From somewhere outside came a deep, resonant noise like a
heavy object falling from a great height and striking the ground.
This was followed by a series of other, similar noises that grew
louder and louder, one by one. They seemed to grow closer as
well.

Gene and Guillermo and Thistle and Ari all looked at each
other. Tex strained at his leash and let out a long throaty cry of
distress. After the fifth or sixth detonation (which is what these
sounds had to be) Guillermo made eye contact with Gene and
raised his arms, inadvertently just missing Thistle's chin with his
shovel, and said:

"We've got nothing to do with that. Whatever it is. I swear it."

Gene didn't doubt this, but it seemed beside the point. He ran
out the door and down the hallway and into the cavernous body
of the hangar. From there, through the open bomber doors, you
could see it: a wall of fire stretching from horizon to horizon. Or
no: it was several distinct fires, the closest perhaps a few hundred
yards away. And rapidly spreading. The flames leapt with an
intensity that seemed artificial—like movie special effects—and
they burned a funny color: yellow tending toward peach-pink,
with bands of methane blue. It was really spectacular.

Gene felt so scared he was afraid he might lose control of
his bowels.

Guillermo caught up to him and the others stopped a little way
back. This far off, you could feel the intense radiant heat.

"I *swear*—" Guillermo began, but Gene held a hand up to
stop him.

"I know, I know."

The two of them stood together for a couple of moments, thinking hard.

Behind them, Thistle said, "What kind of hazardous stuff do you keep around here? Anything that could give off poisonous fumes?"

Gene groaned. He thought of his laboratory: mutagenic and cytophagic and otherwise unpleasant substances up the yin-yang. "A million things," he said. He wondered what fire would do to the nitrous compounds in the greenhouse. Barrels of herbicides. Tanks of JP-5 for the dusting planes. He shuddered.

"Ah, the wonders of modern forestry," said Guillermo.

"Wow," said Ari. "I've never seen anything *like* this."

"We better do something," said Gene.

They looked at him. For several seconds nobody asked, *But what?*

SMELLS LIKE VICTORY

Wild Jag Eckhart began to suspect that maybe he had accomplished a little bit more than he had actually set out to do by the time the third or fourth canister detonated and he realized that with the wind coming the way it was, and the flames as hot as they were, and the weather as dry as it had been—well, adding it all up, and seeing what he was now seeing, he couldn't really imagine there was going to be any way to stop this. He had seen fires before, big ones and small ones, and he figured that he had a pretty good idea of how they operated. This fire looked like one that would take the whole base out. Lock, stock, barrel and parking lot. That was just about the size of it.

Having gotten that figured out, Eckhart moved quickly to the next set of calculations. Which had to do with who was going to take the rap for this. As he saw it, the only thing connecting him to the fire would be Chas Sauvage. Even if the Suburban was found—or what would be left of the Suburban—it would be a simple matter to explain that he had just been doing his Chief of Security thing, what with all these threats from environmental terrorists and whatnot. Sauvage would surely back him up. If they hung, they were going to hang together, and Sauvage did not seem like the sort of fellow that would let a little conflagration sidetrack his promising career.

As far as Eckhart could figure, then, he was just about a lock to get away with it.

And that was as far as he really needed to think.

ON A HILL

From his vantage point on a bluff above Cold Bay, Jesse Openhood could see the flames spreading across the flat dark landscape where Goddin Air Force Base ought to be. And he could see the moon riding over the bay—Moose in Low Places Moon, his mother would have called it. And he could see streetlights spun through Dublin village, like the glowing filaments of a web. Somewhere in the center of that web lay a black patch that was the village green.

Jesse looked back and forth between these sights: the fire, the moon, the darkness at the center of the web. It seemed to him that they were all connected, one to the others. He felt that if he concentrated, he might make a guess as to what the connections might be. Of course, it was hard to concentrate under the circumstances. Midsummer Night was not a time to try any serious thinking. So Jesse reached into his cooler and he pulled out another Andrew's Dark Brown Ale. He was pretty sure that's what his old friend Tex would have advised.

"What do you think, Gus?" he asked.

The big timber wolf answered with a low, anxious, deep-in-the-throat noise—less a howl, Jesse thought, than a sort of incantation. Like he was calling for something, or for someone. Just sort of calling into the night.

UNDER A RAVEN SKY

There wasn't a whole lot of talking going on around the Dublin green, but Ludi was almost certain everybody was thinking the same thing.

Could this be the Unforeseen Development they were all waiting for?

She started to make an announcement—tell everybody that, no, this great orange glow in the western sky, somewhere beyond the edge of town, how far away was anybody's guess, was not part of the evening's drama. But something stopped her from doing this.

"It's out at Goddin," she heard somebody say. "It's got to be."

Why has it got to be? she wondered.

Then she thought:

Gene.

Of course, there was no reason to suppose that Gene might be anywhere near his office. Even assuming that Goddin was, in fact, where the strange orange light was coming from. But this did not stop a terrible cold feeling from entering her stomach—seeping in from below, coming through her bowels, but before that coming up out of the cold dark ground. That's how it felt. Suddenly the world was skewed or knocked sideways and nothing made sense to her. She could not remember what she was doing on the platform of the gazebo.

"What should we do?" someone asked.

Funny: she could distinguish certain voices from here and there, out of the general murmuring, the sense of shared confusion that was passing in waves through the crowd. It was as though now and then the broad waves would contract into a single, isolated unit, and this unit would utter a phrase like:

"—go out there."

Or:

"—called the Fire Department?"

Then from this new center the waves would propagate outward again. All the while the whole thing, the mass of people wearing masks and crowded together on the green, was gaining in energy, in momentum, in volatility.

A movement of shadow, black within blackness, caught her attention. She turned to see the Amoral Trickster, still anonymous within the black mask; and beyond the Trickster, Pippa Rede. Pippa was not wearing a mask, and her expression, watching the Trickster, was clearly frightened. In one hand she carried something that, when she raised it, Ludi recognized as a 3-tined garden fork, the kind you use to make little trenches for seedlings to go in.

Pippa raised the fork until its steel points were aimed straight at the Trickster. Was she crazy? Was all this Witchy stuff getting to her malleable little mind?

"Out of the way, Ludi," she said, with uncharacteristic firmness.

Ludi didn't think she *was* in the way. But she got out of it anyway. Pippa's pale face was alight with the glow of the distant blaze. It flashed orange and yellow and white. The flames seemed to come not from the horizon but from within, from Pippa's eyes.

No kidding, thought Ludi. There *is* some kind of weird light in those eyes.

In fact, as she watched, the light seemed to move outward, to spread over Pippa's face and down to her shoulders and out along her skinny arms. Finally it reached the garden fork.

"Take my car!" somebody yelled.

And somebody else, a kid in the Token African-American mask, said, "Fuck that, man. I've got an *Eldorado*. We can get six or seven in, easy. What say, bro?"

"Seven or eight." The larger kid next to him was playing Corporate Executive.

"Eight or nine."

"Let's take *everybody*."

The Trickster turned. For an instant—an effect of the weird lighting, perhaps—Ludi was sure the Trickster was turning toward her, away from Pippa. Then she saw that it was the opposite. The tall figure loomed over the poor little Witch, spreading those skeletal arms as though threatening to engulf her.

"*Be gone from here,*" said Pippa, more loudly than Ludi had ever heard her speak before. And when she gestured with her garden fork

snapping tongues of blue light
flicked out of the three tines
like the tongues of electric serpents
and the Amoral Trickster made a raspy, screeching noise
and raised its arms high, then higher, spreading the Liberty
Graphics T-shirt
like billowy wings
and *poof*—

(was nowhere to be seen)

—and Pippa lowered the garden fork.

She looked normal again. Receding; almost unnoticeable.

Ludi took a moment to consider whether any of this had actually happened. Yes—or no? Both? Neither? She felt imperatively a need to decide.

"Well," said Pippa, "*that* was different, huh?"

"Hey," said Deep Herb, stepping up onto the platform, "I was wondering if I could cop a ride with you guys."

"A ride?" said Ludi. Like, incredulous at this interruption.

"Where to?" said Pippa.

"Out to the *fire*. That's where everybody's going. Haven't you been paying attention?" He turned to Ludi. "I thought you were in *charge* here, man."

"I'm not a man," she reminded him.

"But, Herb," said Pippa, "didn't we come in your car?"

"We did?"

Sara Clump showed up, with Deputy Doug hanging close. Ludi was now sure she was going crazy: the two of them appeared to be holding hands.

"Let's get moving," said the deputy, sounding grave and official, though his tangerine lipstick, which had gotten smeared, sort of diminished his credibility.

Everybody made for Deep Herb's car. All around the green, other people were climbing into other vehicles. It was just too much.

"Stop!" cried Ludi.

They stopped. They looked around at her. Pippa, as usual, moved behind the others, as though seeking to disappear.

"Isn't anybody going to tell me what just *happened?* Pippa Rede, I'm talking to you."

Pippa slunk out far enough to submit to being spoken to.

"Well?" said Ludi.

"It's, um—" Pippa cleared her throat. "It's what I was trying to tell you."

"Tell who?" said Deep Herb.

"About our *circle* today," Pippa went on, a little louder.

"Shouldn't you say *tell whom?*" said Deputy Doug, blinking beneath a heavy load of purple eye shadow. "I took a course in report writing last year, is how I happen to know."

I can't believe it, thought Ludi. This guy actually fits right in.

"At our *circle* today," said Pippa—sounding pissed, now, that nobody was paying attention—"there was this sort of manifestation of a raven goddess, and one of the women got this sort of message."

"*What* sort of message?" said Ludi.

"I *told* you," said Pippa. "About Tex and Molly."

And Ludi thought:

Yes. Yes, of course. Tex and Molly. Somehow all of this *has* to be about Tex and Molly, doesn't it?

Because nothing else is
crazy enough to
explain it.

or
"we could read in bed for a while,"

suggested Molly. "What do you think?"

You could tell by looking at Tex that he didn't think one thing or another. It was Midsummer Night and they had nowhere to go and nothing to do and not even Gene and Ludi for strictly vicarious entertainment.

On WURS, Pippa Rede's little daughter Winterbelle and some of her friends from the Waldorf School were filling in for the regular deejay, who was at tonight's shebang in Dublin. The children were doing a theme show: all the records they could find in the station library that looked like they might sound neat. Molly did not have to try hard to imagine what the studio must look like.

"That was 'Ancient Voices of Children' by somebody called George Crumb," said Winterbelle, over much giggling in the background. "Pretty weird, huh? Now we're going to try something called, let's see, 'The Good Humor Man He Sees Everything Like This' by Love. And if my mom is out there listening, I want to say, Hey, Mom, have you seen my ballerina slippers? I can't find them in my backpack. Okay, here it goes."

"They sound so cute," said Molly.

"Mm," said Tex. He shifted on the couch, unable to find a comfortable position. It was like he was waiting for something, expecting somebody.

Molly tried to distract him. "You know, Ludi's developed a

pretty good touch with the plants. Look how happy the begonias are."

"The pinanga's lost a leaf," he said, without looking up.

"Oh, the pinanga," said Molly, gently scoffing. "Who'd want
to grow palm trees in a place like Maine?"

Tex tensed. As though he had taken offense; but no, it
wasn't that.

On cue (or a little bit late) came a

KNOCK AT THE DOOR

"Ha!" Tex fairly crowed. "I *knew* it! I knew we weren't going
to be able to have one evening alone in peace."

Yeah, thought Molly. Like he really wanted one.

Then she thought: Wait. *A knock at the door?*

To the best of her recollection, there had never *been* a knock
at their door. The people she and Tex knew were not the knocking type. They were either the coming-right-in type or the yelling-
loud-enough-to-shake-the-pier type.

Who could this possibly be?

Tex crossed the room with pretty impressive alacrity, for a
dead guy. He opened the hatch to the foredeck and strained his
eyes in the dark.

At first there appeared to be nobody there. Nothing but drifting
shadows. Then one of the shadows drifted right on into the cabin,
and Tex exclaimed:

"Yo, Beale! What's up, bro?"

The shadow swirled around a bit and slowly Molly's left eye
was able to make out the shape of a down-at-the-heels-looking
man—no particular height and no particular age, just an air of
one of those vague psychic ailments that seem to strike mostly
Europeans: ennui, angst, weltschmertz, malaise—that kind of
thing.

Beale turned a gray and featureless face toward Molly. "How
do you do," he said glumly.

"Tex has told me so much about you," she said, which came
out sounding dumb. Somebody, she reflected, ought to write a
book of etiquette for the afterlife. There were so many odd and
potentially awkward social situations in which you might find
yourself.

"Want to sit down?" Tex asked his dryad buddy. "Can I get
you something to soak your roots in?"

Beale made a windy moan. His shadowy body appeared to flap

in an impalpable breeze. "No time left," he said. "No time to drink. It's over."

"No West for the reary, huh?" said Tex. "As the wagon masters used to say."

"Bear," said Molly. "Please. I think your friend Beale is trying to tell you something."

"He is?" Tex looked the dryad in the eye, or the bole, or something. He said, "Yeah—I think you're right."

"Fire," said Beale. "Fire at the shelter. The big greenhouse. Killing the trees. Everything is finished."

Then he seemed to run out of energy, as though the exertion of delivering this final message had exhausted him.

"At the Goddin place?" said Tex. "There's a fire?"

Beale feebly nodded.

"Then we've got to do something," said Tex. "We've got to fight it, man! We've got to stop it!"

Beale shook his head. "Too late," he said. "Nothing to do. The wind—the little trees—something burning, like gasoline."

He began to dematerialize.

"No!" shouted Tex, as though trying to breathe some life back into him. "It's never too late. Look at me—I'm *dead*, man, and I'm not ready to call it quits. Come on, let's go—you show me where the fire is, and I'll see if there's something we can do about it."

Beale shook his head; then he collapsed. The folds of shadow fluttered downward, into Tex's arms. In the end Tex found himself holding a single brown and withered leaf. Clutching it, he looked helplessly at Molly.

"I've never seen him like this," he said.

She moved over to touch his arm. "Bear? What are you going to do?"

"What else?" he said. "This is a definite emergency. I've got to get high."

WOUNDED KING (2)

While Tex fussed with the Tupperware container and Shelagh-na-gig, Molly carried the brown leaf that (she hoped) still held the earthly aspect of Beale into the galley and laid it gently on the counter. Altar or no altar, the kitchen is generally the most magical place in your average house. Humming the first tune that sprang to mind (if you must know, it was "Here Comes the Sun King"), she set about doctoring the leaf with an assortment of remedies: a squirt of Tex's ginseng, some dribs of Tabasco, a sprinkle of cumin (to ward off flatulence) and a fingerful of good black potting soil from an angel-wing begonia. After a minute or two, the leaf began to green up a bit.

"He's coming around," she called to Tex, who coughed stentoriously in reply.

"Ohhhh," moaned Beale, which Molly thought was a good sign, considering he was still only a leaf.

"Don't be discouraged," she told him, soothingly. She stroked the veins on his underside, rubbing some life back into him. "Maybe there's something Tex can do."

"Ohhhhhhh," Beale moaned, more vigorously—as though the very notion of what Tex might do was getting his pressure up.

Well, good, thought Molly.

"Too late," Beale finally managed to say. "All lost now. Hopeless."

By this time he was resuming some of his former human-like shape, though he remained essentially leaflike. He looked like something from the shadowy recesses of a Gothic cathedral.

Molly felt the taste of salmon tickling her palate. The know-it-all feeling came over her.

"Maybe there's something you're not thinking of," she said.

Beale shook his head, or crown, or whatever. But he was looking at her in a funny way. Like, she had gotten his attention.

"Did you ever hear the story," said Molly—having no concept when she began this sentence of how she was going to end it— "the story about the Hidden Castle in the Wasteland?"

Beale looked at her as though she, not Tex, were completely stoned.

"No," he said after a long time. "I have never heard that one."

"Well, then," said Molly, hoping she sounded jovial and not smug. "You haven't thought of *everything* then, have you?"

"I never claimed to have thought of everything," said Beale. But he sounded unsure of himself.

"Once there was a mighty king," said Molly. "His name was Anfortas. He lived in a castle surrounded by green and fertile pastures. Well, one day Anfortas rode out upon his great steed, when out of a nearby forest came a knight wearing green armor and riding a wild black mare. This knight was the Guardian of the Forest, and his horse was a nature-goddess in disguise. But see, Anfortas did not realize that. He didn't want this dangerous-looking knight crashing around in his nice, orderly realm. So he lowered his lance and shouted a challenge, and then he charged. The green knight lowered *his* lance, and the two collided. *Wham.* The Guardian of the Forest was killed, but King Anfortas was wounded, with the head of the other knight's lance in his thigh.

"After the battle, the mare-goddess galloped sadly back to the forest, where she placed a curse on Anfortas and all his kingdom: his injury would never heal, and the crops in his fields would wither, and his land would become barren. Because, see, Anfortas had forgotten that the natural world was the source of his great wealth and splendor, and had struck down its champion. So the king limped home, and he found his castle turned into a desolate prison, surrounded by a wasteland."

Molly paused. Tex made his way into the galley, clutching the clay pipe. His eyes appeared to rotate in opposite directions.

"Woo," he said.

"King Wen?" asked Molly.

"Definitely."

"Wait," said Beale.

Molly turned. The dryad was looking more human now, just as Tex was becoming more vegetal. If this kept up, the two of them were destined to intersect somewhere in the middle, between kingdoms.

Beale said, "What does this story have to do with *us*?"

"If you would let me finish," said Molly—not unkindly—but Tex broke in:

"Is that Tabasco? I'm totally starving."

"You're dead," Molly reminded him. "Now at the same time," she went on, "in a land far away, there lived a young knight named Parzival. Despite what you hear in later Christianized accounts, Parzival was neither virginal nor especially pure. In fact, he was living with a woman he wasn't married to, and they had had a child together. Also there was trouble with the authorities back in Camelot, so Parzival roamed the distant reaches of the world with a price on his head. One day he came upon a man fishing on a lake, very richly dressed. He asked where he could find lodging, and the man gave him directions to a castle. But he warned Parzival that the castle was hard to find—you could ride straight through its grounds without seeing it.

"Which was a major clue, of course. Because that's how it is with entrances to the Otherworld.

"So Parzival set off, and lo and behold, he found his way to the castle. It was a god-awful mess—the fields were dead, the wells were poisoned, the trees bore no fruit, and everyone was depressed. And of course, the lord of the castle was King Anfortas himself.

"Now to Parzival, this was all very mysterious. He could see that the king was hurt, and the whole realm was afflicted. But Parzival was just an ordinary, natural sort of guy, accustomed to living by his instincts, following the promptings of his heart. When he looked around the castle, he saw that *these* people were very refined and sophisticated. So instead of asking questions, or offering to help, he kept his mouth politely shut and ate his dinner.

"This was a terrible mistake. In fact, it was the first time in his life that Parzival failed to act on his natural impulse, heedless of the consequence. He kept quiet because he felt out of his element. When all he had to do was ask a simple and obvious question—like, What's the matter? Are you hurt? Can I help? And this would have mended the broken link between Anfortas and the natural world: the world of spontaneity and feeling and growth, which Parzival represented. Instead, by entering into the narrowness of the other world, the world of intellect and refinement, Parzival missed his chance. He rode away from the castle not knowing how he had failed, and condemned never to find his way back again."

Molly smiled confidently, as though this ought to have cleared up *everything*. She was unruffled when Beale (after a lapse of time) spoke balefully:

"Is that all? What is the point of it?"

"Oh, come *on*," said Molly. "Surely that's obvious to a wise old spirit like *you*."

The dryad rustled and fidgeted.

"*I* know," said Tex. He looked excited, like a grade-schooler eager to be called on.

"You do?" said Molly and Beale together.

"It's simple. The story says, No matter how hard a problem looks—even if it looks impossible—you've already got the solution right in your hand. Or in your heart. You've just got to do like, what comes naturally."

Beale stared at him. Not for a very long time by dryad standards, but long enough.

"You are suggesting, then," said Beale, "that we are not behaving according to our true natures?"

"I don't think—" began Molly.

"I'm *suggesting*," Tex said, "that you're a bunch of pretty damn smart growth-fields. And it seems like there's something you guys could *do,* if you really wanted to. You could, you know—make something up. Something *new.* Isn't that what you're supposed to be good at?"

"But why?" Beale said wearily. "It is too late for that. All we could accomplish is staving off the inevitable."

"You don't *know* what's inevitable. Nobody does. Nature is inherently creative. You explained all this to me yourself."

"I did?" Beale shook his head. "We are boundlessly creative, it is true. But that creativity applies only to ourselves, to the forms we generate. We can do nothing to change *you.* And unless you are able to change yourselves, there is ultimately no hope."

"There's always hope," said Tex. "Anything can happen. Anybody can change."

And Beale, ever reluctant, and no more eager for action than an old oak ought to be, said:

"Prove it."

AS ABOVE

From the air, the areas covered by flame, contrasted with the surrounding lands that were smoky and dark, looked like computer-generated patterns illustrating some principle of chaos theory. A Mandelbrot apocalypse.

Back in the raven form to which he had grown well accustomed, with Beale's leaf clasped tightly in his beak, Tex began choking on noxious fumes even before the heat got to him. He spiraled lower, trying to orient himself in this hellish new landscape, where the old cardinal alignments—runways, hangars, perimeter fence—were completely irrelevant; the only geography that mattered now was the stark divide between darkness and light: that which was irrevocably being consumed by flame, and that which might still be saved.

He recognized, through a fog bank of smoke, the hangar that had been made into a greenhouse. As he came nearer he saw movement around it, just outside the giant bomber door. He swept beneath the suffocating clouds.

There was Gene Deere, running between rows of trees in gallon-size nursery pots—thousands of them, tossed by the hot wind, seeming to reach out their tiny limbs toward Tex, shrieking at him to save them.

"Are those your buds?" he asked Beale. "Those guys down there in the pots?"

The dryad rustled a dessicated *Yes*.

"Okay," said Tex. "It looks like somebody's trying to help them. Let's go down and see what we can do."

Beale said nothing and Tex banked gently for a second pass.

Gene was shouting to somebody, waving his arms. Tex tried to follow his gaze—raven eyes are not so great in the dark—and finally, just inside the hangar, he recognized the last person in the world he ever expected (or wanted) to find here.

"Guillermo!" he cawed.

The self-made jefe looked up, as though someone had spoken his name. Then he yelled to Gene Deere:

"I can't find the water valve!"

Gene yelled something back, but the wind carried it away. The *wind*: a mad rush of air sucked inward by the leaping, rolling, cancerously growing body of flame: the very howl of Death. And Tex figured that by this time he knew Death when he heard it.

Tex skimmed the rows of potted trees. He fancied that he could almost make out the faces—at least some distinctive attributes—of the dryads inside them.

"What's the *matter* with you guys?" he yelled as he coasted overhead. "Haven't you got any fight left in you? After all these thousands of years, you're going to let some little brushfire finish you off?"

The dryads did not answer, though he could have sworn he heard them conversing among themselves—a chorus of misery, hopelessless, desolation. Finally, just as Tex banked away, he thought he saw (or not saw: intuited) a nasty-minded yew dryad giving him the finger.

"Yeah, we'll see about that," he called down. "We'll see who fucks who around here."

Rising again, he flew straight into a cloud of smoke so thick and hot and heavy with poison that the issue was almost decided then and there.

Tex gagged. His wing-strokes became disorganized. He tumbled in the air.

"Hold on to your ass," he said to Beale. "We're going down."

He spread his wings into a parafoil. The ground came up fast, hard and black and dangerous, to receive him.

Broken leg or no broken leg—mythic prohibition or none—Tex was returning to Earth.

SO BELOW

The thing about Air Force bases is there is fire-fighting equipment everywhere. Miles and miles of hose, among other things.

The other thing about Air Force bases is that this equipment was designed to be operated by trained and coordinated teams of gung-ho young airmen. Not by a couple of guys who don't really care for one another. Plus a teenage girl. Plus a very young bear. Plus an elf.

But this was stopping nobody.

"I can't find the valve!" Guillermo shouted again from the door of the hangar.

"It's there someplace," Gene shouted back, but obviously Guillermo could not hear him. He ran down the rows of formerly identical X *dawkinsia* spruces (it was so strange: even tonight, by the raging fire, Gene could see inexplicable variations throughout the lot of them) to join Guillermo and Thistle and Ari just inside the greenhouse.

A fire hose fat as a mature boa constrictor lay flopped on the floor. Gene tried to trace this to its source, but his eye got lost in a system of pipes that crisscrossed the corrugated metal bulkhead. He saw no control mechanism, no shut-off valve.

"Fuck," he said.

Thistle smiled, as though it entertained her to hear grown-ups curse.

"Do you think," she said, "you might tap into the hydroponic tanks?"

Gene looked at her as though she were speaking in Martian.

"Sounds good to me," said Guillermo. "Come on, Deere. Let's give it a try."

"Yeah—okay, right." Gene felt confused. He wasn't sure who was in charge here.

"Try over there," suggested Thistle. She pointed up an aisle of soughing tanks. "You might find a water-duct that way."

"Hey, cool, look!" Ari yelled at them from somewhere in the darkness. "Check this out, guys. I've found *space suits*."

Guillermo went over with the flashlight. What Ari had found was a rack full of asbestos coveralls, complete with flameproof helmets, thick rectangular visors, and O.B.A.'s—oxygen breathing apparatuses, which could be successfully operated only by the kind of people to whom speaking in acronyms comes naturally. Gene and Guillermo were damned if they could get the hang of it.

"Let's just leave the helmets off," Guillermo said, "and take our chances."

Gene nodded.

Ari and Thistle, on the other hand, were having no trouble. They shouted back and forth at one another, their voices metallic, muffled by the helmets, incomprehensible. Ari tried to squeeze fireproof coveralls onto Tex. The bear wasn't digging it.

The two men looked each other over: bodies comically puffed out by the heavy suits. For an instant, the both of them began to smile, then they stifled the impulse. Instead, they gave one another a spontaneous high-5.

"Let's do it," said Guillermo.

"Right," said Gene. Thinking, Do what?

PLAYERS (2)

The town of Dublin never had much in the way of a Volunteer Fire Department. Why bother? Anything bigger than a burning outhouse was handled by the boys from the Air Force base. In the couple of years since the base had closed there had been some changes made, upgrades of equipment and so forth. But essentially if you lived in Dublin, you got used to the idea that

FIRE = TOTAL DESTRUCTION

Which did not make fires in Dublin any less common than elsewhere. It just instilled an attitude of Yankee stoicism.

The first vehicle on scene, then, was not a fire truck but a bargelike early-70's Eldorado, its convertible top down and its seats spilling over with people (mostly young, but also an elderly tourist from Delaware) wearing masks. An antique 8-track tape player blared Deep Purple, "Smoke on the Water." The Eldorado squealed through the main gate, from which security guards were notably absent, and onto an old runway leading out toward the fields that were now, it seemed, completely ablaze. There the driver, wearing a Token African-American mask, skidded to a rather exciting halt.

"*Killer* fire," he said.

His passengers climbed out. Now that they were here, what did they plan to do? Each of them wore a tag bearing the name of a fictional character—Rock, Aging Hippie (2), Corporate Executive, et cetera—and in their confusion they fell to scrutinizing one another's labels, as though some clue might be found there.

"Maybe we should resign ourselves to letting it burn," said a woman whose tag read Taoist Waiter.

"Cool," said the Aging Hippie.

"What a bunch of pantywaists," said the Corporate Executive. He shook a big ebony fist at the fire. "What'd we drive all the way out here for if we're not at least going to squirt some water around? Come on, let's think *teamwork*. Let's think *creative problem containment*."

"Cool," said the Aging Hippie.

The Token African-American switched his tape player off. "Are you brain-damaged?" he asked the Corporate Exec.

"Unquestionably," the Exec said.

The two of them bumped their foreheads together.

"Ah, so!" they said in unison.

Behind them, a second car screeched to a stop. This was a small, badly tuned Renault with a rusted-out undercarriage. Steam billowed from its hood. Out of its creaking doors a Vegetable and a Lipstick Lesbian emerged, followed by Ludi and Pippa, in mufti.

"All right, everybody," the Lesbian said, shaking his purse and attempting to exercise some authority. "The important thing here is not to—" He coughed as a false eyelash fell into his mouth.

"Can you believe this?" said Ludi. She meant the fire. It was absolutely the most horrendous thing she had ever seen. At the same time (she would never admit this) it was incredibly, somehow, *painterly*. Like a gigantic Turner, projected with high-intensity lasers onto a backdrop as wide as the sky. And it *changed*: rose in the air and fell; and its colors shifted across a spectrum that began at yellow and moved through orange and red into a plum or cerise, where it deepened to the heavy purple and near-black of smoke.

Then she remembered Gene. And whatever beauty there might be about this horrible thing went right up in flames with everything else.

"Where are you going?" Pippa yelled at her.

Ludi hadn't even known, until then, that she had started to run. She was sprinting toward the nearest building, which might or might not be the one where Gene's office was. Tonight everything looked different; everything was different; it was impossible to be sure. Of *anything*.

"I'll be back," she called to Pippa. Wondering if this was going to turn out to be true.

MOTIVATION

Burdock Herne was so shaken he had neglected to take off the mask and the name tag that identified him as Somebody's Dad. He leaned forward, gripping the dashboard of Chas Sauvage's Mercedes as it spun efficiently through the gate and into the parking lot. Five or six cars were there ahead of them, and still no Fire Department. The radiance of the flames was hot on his face, even filtered by the windshield's low-emissivity glass. Against the curtain of brightness he could make out two dozen small figures moving purposefully about, coming together and then breaking apart again, as though engaged in some form of collective activity whose nature he could not fathom.

"What are they doing out there, Sauvage?" he asked his field manager.

The young man at the wheel made a quiet grunt. "Getting themselves roasted, it looks like."

"For what?" said Herne. "I don't understand."

Sauvage turned to look at him, as though he didn't quite follow the line of questioning. "I suppose," he said, in a measured way, "they feel it's the thing they're supposed to do."

Herne stared out the windshield, hard. Then he unbuckled himself and climbed out of the car and looked around the former Air Force base. It was alien, unrecognizable. Terrifying. Herne could not remember clearly why his company had decided to move in here. Strategic considerations, he was sure. Long-range thinking. Planting the seeds of tomorrow. Was that a corporate slogan, or a proposal that had gotten knocked down, a dead possibility? Had it been his own idea, or somebody else's? Under the mask, he was perspiring heavily, and the sweat ran down into his eyes and into his mouth.

"Sauvage," he said, hoarsely.

"Yes, sir."

"Keep the car ready. Stay back. I'm going to tell those people out there to go home before somebody gets seriously hurt. Then I'm going inside the office there, see if anything can be saved. Do you have your phone with you?"

Sauvage nodded, patting a jacket pocket.

"Very well. If I need you, I'll give you a call. Meanwhile, you try to find out why there's been no response from the authorities. Are you with me?"

"All the way, sir," said Sauvage.

Herne halfway expected the young man to salute, and was disappointed when he did not. Instead Sauvage opened his glove box and pulled out a compact, metal-cased flashlight, which he offered to Herne.

"You'll need this, sir," he said.

"Very well," said Herne. "Carry on, then."

Chas Sauvage nodded, slipped the Mercedes in gear. And Burdock Herne turned to face the fire that besieged the northernmost fortress of his empire.

FRONT LINE

Gene Deere nearly fainted with relief when reinforcements arrived from the Dublin green. The first person to reach him was a tall black teenager wearing, for reasons he would never understand, a sign that said Corporate Executive. This person came up and stood beside Gene and wordlessly assessed the disaster.

They were standing in a field of closely mown grass, as far away from the hangar as Gene had been able to stretch the fire hose. The blasting of hot air past his ears was so loud and incessant that he felt numbed: boxed-in by a surfeit of sensation. Behind him, Guillermo and Thistle had been left to figure out how to activate a machine that produced, according to its brass faceplate, AFFF, aircraft fire-fighting foam. Ari was assigned to protect the bear at all costs. Gene had entrusted Guillermo with the keys to the Rover. Just in case.

"Could you give me a hand here?" Gene shouted to the kid. He had little notion of how well his voice could be heard. He struggled to manage the awkward bulk of the hose, now grown heavy and stiff with water. "We've finally got pressure up here, but every time I open the valve, the recoil just about knocks me down. I can't keep it pointed at the fire."

"Got you," said the kid, loudly. He stepped in behind Gene and took up most of the weight of the hose. He planted his feet widely and dropped into what seemed an immovable stance. "Try it now," he called.

With trepidation, Gene pulled back on the brass lever that opened the flow of water to the conical, wide-mouthed nozzle. There was no way to do this by halves; the pressure was such that as soon as the flow started, the water forced the valve wide open. Then, as a matter of pure Newtonian karma, the nozzle

bucked violently back, water spewed everywhere, and Gene struggled not to be thrown across the field.

This time, with the kid anchoring the hose behind him, he
managed to get a column of gushing water pointed more or less
in the direction of the nearest flames.

"Great," he yelled over his shoulder. "Now let's try raking it
back and forth."

Other people were showing up now. They kept their masks on,
presumably because this blocked some of the heat from scorching
their faces. Some of them tried to figure out how to be helpful
to Gene and the black kid; others just stood with the light of the
fire in their eyes, bedazzled and dumbstruck.

"Come *on,* everybody," shouted a guy in thrift-store drag.
"Let's try to keep ourselves in order here."

Concentration broken, Gene felt the hose getting away from
him.

"Damn," he muttered, slamming the valve shut. He leaned
back wearily against the kid behind him, who let out a breath for
the two of them.

"How long you been doing this?" the kid asked him.

"Not long," said Gene. "The fire's moving fast. I'm not sure
there's anything we can do. Did you happen to see a bear on
your way in?"

The kid looked at him gravely, as though wondering if the heat
was getting to him.

"No," he said. "Thought I might have seen a wolf, though."

Then the flames roared ahead, spreading from a nearby trial
plot to the field of grass, and Gene and the others were forced
into retreat.

"Listen," Gene said to the kid, while they were catching their
breath, "are you one of those guys in what was it called, the
Pod?"

The kid lifted the mask from his face. "Saintstephen Bax," he
said. "You're that biologist, right?"

Gene nodded. "Nice work on the software," he said. "You
really did something amazing to those trees. I'd love to hold this
fire off so I can get a closer look at them."

Saintstephen shrugged modestly. "Couldn't have done it without you."

"Okay," the Lipstick Lesbian shouted from behind the lines.
"Recess is over, gang. Let's get back to our hoses."

Gene sighed. Saintstephen slapped him on the back. Another
kid came up wearing a tag that read Token African-American.

"Where's the party?" he yelled, bouncing from one foot to the other.

"Right here, dude," Saintstephen said. "Take hold of this donkey dick and let our man have a little breather."

Gene handed the nozzle over to the newcomer, who said, "Hey, I remember you."

"He remembers you, too," said Saintstephen.

"Guess who I saw," said the new kid, "back at the hangar."

"Tyagi Nagasavi," guessed Saintstephen.

"Not even warm."

That was all Gene heard. The wind changed directions and the flames spread to the grass. Everybody began shouting at once and Gene had a sudden thought that if these people were here from the performance in Dublin, then Ludi might be here also. Which, if true, would be a serious error on her part. And he left the others standing and shouting and trying to get reorganized, while the phalanx of flame advanced relentlessly upon them, and ran back toward the big hangar that loomed before him through the smoke. He was not even sure if it was the same building he had come out of. He was hardly sure of anything.

One thing, maybe. And that's the one thing he was looking for.

PEP RALLY

Realistically, Tex knew, it did look hopeless. But he was not prepared, at this late stage of the game, to become a realist.

"Come on, dudes," he implored the rank-and-file dryads, each clinging to an imperiled sapling. "Let's get creative. Let's not just stand here and wait for this thing to destroy us."

Beale, sitting forlornly on his leaf, looked up at him. "But we're trees," he said. "Standing around is what we *do*."

"Yeah?" said Tex. "And where's it gotten you? Homeless, that's where."

The dryads stirred and rustled. Tex wished he could understand what the little bastards were saying. All he could make out was this kind of resigned, philosophical murmuration.

"If we *were* homeless," said Beale—maybe translating, maybe not—"we would surely be better off. But no: you found new homes for us, and *now* look. We're about to be immolated in them."

Tex had to admit, the guy had a point. He turned to pace up

the row of plants, but his compoundly fractured leg bent and twisted beneath him, and his entire being rattled with agony.

Beale watched him, showing remarkably little compassion.

In the background—somewhat dimmed-out and muted, from the vantage of this gathering of shades—people ran around and shot water from hoses and shouted instructions at one another. It was inspiring; but at the same time it was idiotic. Like watching a colony of insects busily and energetically shoring up their nest while the hungry insectivore implacably went about clawing it to pieces. You might admire the little bastards their courage and their perseverance, but still—they might as well save themselves the trouble. They were toast, one way or another.

Well, thought Tex, but does that make it all right to just sit around and do nothing? Are you really any smarter or cooler or highly evolved if you just sigh and give up?

"You guys disappoint me," he said, gritting his teeth against the pain in his leg.

He found that if he really tried hard enough, he could walk. It was a lurching, unbalanced, grossly inelegant kind of walk—one leg hopping forward, the other dragging behind—but the thing was, he could do it. And he thought that by doing it, maybe he could shame the dryads somewhat into thinking there might be something they could do, too. Something they didn't *want* to do, most likely, and something that might be awkward or uncomfortable for them—not to mention something nobody had actually thought of yet. But still. Something.

He took another step. He dragged his bad leg. "I have to tell you," he said, his voice becoming a growl, "that even though I like you guys, and I can understand what you're going through here, you totally and gravely disappoint me."

From somewhere in the back row, a yew dryad said, "Why don't you just get lost? You've caused us nothing but trouble. You and your whole species. From the very beginning. All those millions of years we had everything under control. No worries. A few bugs, the occasional leaf-muncher. Big deal. Then you guys. And bam. Slash and burn. The axe. The bulldozer. Ten thousand years, maybe less, and it's over. We're history. So okay. That's how you want it, that's how it is. You win. The world is yours. Use it in good health. In another hundred years—less, I bet—you'll be history yourselves. Not even history. Nobody'll want to remember you. Then we'll return, or somebody like us. We'll take everything back that you've stolen from us. We'll grow in your yards. We'll watch your buildings rot. We'll sink our roots in the rotting bodies of your children. It'll be sweet. Personally, I can't wait."

There was a brittle clicking of limbs in the torrid breeze. Tex felt waves of heat passing through him. He heard the shouts of the still-living humans. It was enough to tell him that the struggle was going badly.

"You have to understand," Beale told him, speaking kindly, wishing him no ill, "compared to us, you are very young. You are an infant. The human species itself is younger than many of these organizing fields here. You have to try to grasp that we see things in a different and much longer perspective. This or that calamity, however terrible it may appear to you, is just another of many difficult times that we have seen. Yes, I acknowledge that these are worse times than most. Many of us are going to be lost, perhaps forever. But Idho is correct—sooner or later, some kindred form to most of us will return. There will undoubtedly be many changes to adapt to—higher temperatures, more ultraviolet radiation, less rainfall, an absence of topsoil. But adapting is what we are made for. And after all, we are immortal. We pass from this plane and we return; our identities alter; we merge and dissociate; that is simply our nature. One way or another, we will be with the world as long as the world is alive."

He sighed. He gave Tex a sadly compassionate smile.

"The same cannot be said for you, I'm afraid. Nature may be forced to conclude that ceding dominance to an aggressive territorial primate was not the wisest course of action. I suspect things will be rather different the next time around."

Tex threw up his arms. He could not stand any more of this. There was just no arguing with these guys; he could see that now. It had been a mistake to try to sway them by reasoning. You couldn't give a pep talk to a bunch of candy-ass morphogenic fields who obviously were not psychically equipped to feel peppy. He stared at the thousands of dryads, and he felt them staring immaterially and unemotively back at him.

The way Tex saw it, there was only one hope.

He was going to have to bullshit them.

Fixing the yew dryad with one glaring, psychotically bright eye, he said in a wise-ass voice:

"Suppose I could do something to totally amaze you guys. Right here, right now. Totally knock your leaves off. Would you listen to me then?"

They looked at him as though he was speaking in Uranian.

"Amaze *us?*" said Beale said after a long time. As though such a thing was pretty much out of the question. (Sounding a little amazed already, though, at the very idea.)

"Big-time," affirmed Tex. "Just watch. I'll prove to you that we humans have a few tricks up our sleeves you haven't seen yet. Then it's your turn. You show *me* how great and powerful you are."

"Oh, sure," rasped the yew dryad, nastier than ever.

"Great," said Tex. "I'll take that as a Yes."

And while his dead-hippie brain churned at high rpm's, trying to think of like, *anything,* he asked himself fervently

Where's Molly

when you need her?

COFFEE BREAK

Gene Deere staggered, choking for air, through the darkened hangar. The power was dead and the hallways were filling with smoke. Gene reached his office and there, in the dark, stumbled into Sefyn Hunter, who was sitting on the floor surrounded by his cherished plants. His eyes were wet, either from smoke or from crying. He looked up at Gene, who could barely make out the tag that said Native American.

"It's all going to go, isn't it?" said Sefyn.

He sounded like a little boy.

"Everything," he went on. "We're going to lose it all."

"No," Gene said. He was not sure why, other than to give Sefyn some small momentary comfort. But no, it was more than that. He found that he really meant it, that he really believed, for reasons entirely obscure to him, that all was not lost. "Here, Sefyn, stand up. It might be safer if you get out of here. The fire's pretty close, the last I saw."

"What are *you* doing here, then?" Sefyn asked him. "I'd have thought this would be the *last* place you'd go."

Gene held out a hand and Sefyn took it; he allowed himself to be hauled up to his feet.

"Oh, damn," he said. "I just can't stand the thought of losing them."

He looked around helplessly at his plants, all the objects of his strange but undeniable passion. Gene, a professional plant man, could recognize but not quite understand the syndrome.

"Are you okay?" he asked Sefyn.

"Sure, boss," Sefyn said, lifting his shoulders a bit. "How about you?"

"I might be better in just a little while," said Gene, allowing himself some cautious optimism, though once again he could find no rational grounds for it.

They left the office together.

Out in the hallway, Gene heard someone calling his name.

"Ludi?" he yelled.

He heard a voice—it could have been hers, but there was a lot of acoustical confusion—and he thought it was coming from deeper in the hangar, away from the main entrance.

"Go on," he told Sefyn. "I've got to check on something."

He ran out into the empty cavern at the center of the building and paused in the nearly total blackness there.

"Gene?" the voice came again, more distinctly now. "Is that you?"

"Ludi!" he yelled.

He stepped forward, letting himself be guided by some faculty he could not recognize. Once or twice more he called Ludi's name, and she answered with his own. He thought they were getting closer together, but he could not tell for certain.

Then he bumped into something. It clattered away from him, and the sound it made—plus the throbbing in his upper thigh—told him that he had bumped into a metal chair. He had come, he realized, to the place where an impromptu buffet had been set up for the C.E.O.'s get-acquainted breakfast.

"Ludi," he called, "talk to me. I think I've got a fix on where we are."

"Over here," she said. Her voice sounded close by.

"Okay. Just hold still," he said, moving forward by feel and by memory. "I'm almost there."

"Check this out," said Ludi. They were close enough to be speaking in ordinary conversational voices. "It's something—hey, you know what, I think it's a coffee—oh darn."

Bang. Gene heard a large metal object strike the concrete floor, then roll a bit. After that, for a moment or two, he heard nothing. At last, Ludi made an unusual noise: surprise mixed with confusion, along with perhaps a dose of pain.

"Are you hurt?" he asked her.

"I can't decide," she said.

Her voice was practically underneath him. He bent down, felt the floor beneath his palms, and crawled forward gingerly until he touched her. Then his fingers clutched her clothing as though of their own accord, and he pulled himself to within centimeters of her face.

"Thank god you're okay," he said. He blinked, trying to make out her eyes in the darkness. "*Are* you okay?"

She sucked in her breath. "You know what I did?" she said. "I think I knocked over a big coffee urn."

"Yeah. That's right." Gene remembered it: a huge thing that hardly anybody had touched because the institutional coffee inside was so typically awful.

"Yeah. Well, so I knocked it over, and it fell on me. And I think it might have broken my leg."

"No," he said. He couldn't believe it. He ran his arm down her side, over her hip.

"Stop," she said. "I'm not kidding. I really think I broke my leg. Can you imagine? I mean, a *coffee* urn."

Gene let go of her and lay back, supporting himself on his elbows. He looked up at the invisible ceiling and he felt flooded with a dozen different emotions; a hundred. He opened his mouth to say something and he thought he heard himself laugh. Then he thought he might have heard himself cry. It was one or the other.

"Gene?" Ludi said, easing herself over to him. "Is something the matter?"

"I don't know," he said. "I mean yes. Your leg is broken."

"Yeah," she said. "Weird, huh?"

He hoped that weird was all it was. His hand found her head and gently stroked it. "I'll take care of you," he promised.

She kissed his fingers. "To tell you the truth," she said, "I was kind of counting on that."

LEAVING

Molly stood up, rocking easily with the sway of the *Linear Bee*. Tex was in trouble. She felt that. She *saw* that. She saw everything, by this time. Nothing escaped her.

Anyway, she was tired of sitting around. She felt cooped-up. She wanted to get out and *go* somewhere, *do* something, get herself involved. She had been out of the swing of things for too long. A member of the audience. When what she really wanted—what she had always wanted—was to be a player. Strutting and

fretting. Making a fool of herself, perhaps. But at least making a
show of it. Not sitting on the sofa and eating popcorn.

She walked into the galley and poured the contents of her
Moon mug into an angel-wing begonia. She placed the mug carefully in the sink.

In the pilot house, she ran her hands briefly over the collection
of stones, the framed pictures of fallen heroes, the cool brass of
the candlestick holder. She took the raven feathers and tucked
them securely into the braid in her long brown hair. Then she
picked up the tiny fetish of Bear, guardian of medicine, chief of
the spirits of Earth.

"*Arth Vawr*," she said. "I'm ready to go on."

And she took a deep breath.

And she closed her eyes.

And the Heavenly Bear came for her.

THE RAW & THE COOKED

When the Dublin Volunteer Fire Department arrived
(very late) on scene, the Chief could find no one to
give him directions. These people dashing about (a
lot of them—what was going on here?) seemed to know nothing
about the layout of the place. Many wore masks, as if they had
come from a costume party. Lacking other guidance, the Chief
decided to save what he could of the buildings, and let the fields
burn. If anybody had offered any better ideas, he would have
been glad to listen.

Chas Sauvage saw the red lights of the fire engines but decided
not to turn back. He was cruising in his Mercedes along the road
that ran just inside the perimeter fence. The fire had already
devastated the field he was driving past. Now it raged onward,
closer to the main installation. Chas could see nothing in that
direction but a humpbacked mountain of flame.

He wondered in passing about Gene Deere—whether he had
indeed come in to the office tonight, and if so whether he had
gotten out in time.

Well, that was not an immediate problem. Tomorrow he would
look into it, if there was anyplace left from which to look into
things. Tonight he had more urgent matters to attend to—first
among them, finding out from Jag Eckhart how this "controlled
burn" had gotten so quickly and dramatically out of control.

The Mercedes reached the area at the far northern end of the compound that had been, according to plan, Ground Zero of the operation. The plots of mixed hard- and softwoods—Gene Deere's little showpieces—were vaporized. Nothing remained but an even ground-coat of ash. There was not even enough wood left to smoulder. Despite what had evidently been a horrendous blaze, the dirty brown Suburban sat in plain view ahead of him, right at the fence line, exactly where Eckhart had said it would be. Chas braked the Mercedes to a halt a short distance away. The thought of the two cars parked in the same field of vision was mildly repugnant to him.

He got out and looked around and called Eckhart's name. There was no response. Or perhaps there was. Chas thought he might have heard some noise from the direction of Eckhart's battered vehicle. A muffled cry, perhaps. It occurred to him that Eckhart might have been injured somehow—badly burned, or overcome by smoke. He might have crawled back to his car and be lying there. Rapidly, in his mind, Chas explored the ramifying paths of evidence and culpability here: whether a surviving but injured Eckhart might somehow be the loose thread that caused a great many other threads to unravel. On the whole he thought not. At any rate he thought that whatever the situation might prove to be, it would be containable. In fact, he meant to take the first step toward containing it right now.

He reached the Suburban, walking very quietly, and peered within. It was empty. Then he saw something peculiar—a window of the rear compartment had been smashed, apparently from the inside. Chunks of glass lay scattered on the ground, catching a bit of the orange firelight and glowing dully, like imitation gems. Chas (who had no truck with imitations) kicked them out of his way.

He was about to go around to the driver's door, but the sound of the phone ringing in his jacket pocket made him start. He yanked it out, flipped open the plastic hatch that covered the mouthpiece.

"Sauvage?" said the voice of Burdock Herne. "Is that you?"

Chas Sauvage never replied. A large timber wolf leapt out of the shadows beneath the Suburban and caught him precisely by the throat, making a clean and quick kill of it.

"Sauvage?" Herne asked, more loudly. The noises coming from the other end of the phone puzzled him, but there was nothing he could identify. He would never in a million years have guessed that these were the sounds of his field manager's body being torn apart by an angry wolf.

WOUNDED KING (3)

 Burdock Herne laid down the telephone on Chas Sauvage's desk. The air inside the old hangar seemed to shudder, to resonate with the violence of the night. Herne played the flashlight over the shiny wood of the desk: a miniature landscape furnished with executive oddments in semicircular formation, waiting to be toyed with. From there the light-beam leapt like Tinkerbelle through empty space until it found a purchase on the wall, where it quivered. Herne found himself staring at something too large to fit all at once inside the tightly focused light-cone. He moved his wrist from side to side, mentally assembling the image like a jigsaw puzzle—the quality museum gift-shop kind: 4-color reproduction of an Old Master on heavy cardboard.

Suddenly, with a jolt, Herne realized that he was staring himself in the face. Staring, rather, into a likeness of his face, rendered in oil. The Official Portrait. Herne had seen it a thousand times before now, of course. Hell, he had *posed* for it. Yet tonight he scarcely recognized the thing. Scarcely recognized himself.

Those eyes: they glowed strangely, he thought. A little too much intensity there. The expression was wrong, too. That clench of the jaw; an affected raising of one brow. If you had to characterize this face, this expression, how would you do so? "Aggressive serenity," perhaps? "Kingly hubris"? "Conquistadorial bliss?"

Herne shook his head. He could not recall whether the portrait had even been his idea. It was something one *did*, was all he remembered. He turned the flashlight away; then on further thought switched it off. The darkness swarmed closely around him, and felt surprisingly comfortable. Creature of the night, he thought. Predator. Top of the food chain.

Nothing to be afraid of.

Gingerly, he felt his way around Sauvage's desk and moved out toward where he thought the door might be. *Following my instincts,* he told himself. Wondering actually if he still had any of them left.

Elsewhere in the cavelike depths of the hangar, a sound of metal striking metal clanged for an instant, echoed, and then died. There was no further sound that Herne could hear. Even the background noise seemed diminished, as though the struggle outdoors were being abandoned, or already was lost.

Bunk to that, he thought.

Can't give up without a fight. That's what I teach *my* kids, anyway.

Herne groped his way through the door and stood in the blackened hallway. He could sense the emptiness around him. He took a step—

but in that instant the emptiness moved from without to within—
bottomless

—and Herne felt as though he had stepped off the edge of a precipice. And the abyss into which he was falling was himself.

AS THE DAY DISSOLVES

From his vantage point high on the hill, Jesse could see the fires spreading, seemingly out of control, and for a time it seemed that the whole world was going to be consumed by them, that everything he could see would be relentlessly devoured by that strange growing and mutating mass of chaos. Still he felt reasonably certain that something would happen to prevent that. Some new thing would appear, a thing he could not have imagined, nor could anyone. And after a while—long or short, he didn't know—some Thing did.

Out of the darkness of the sky above Dublin Harbor, stars flashed coldly and variably, their rays oscillating as they raced toward the Earth, deflected by gravity and slightly refocused by the lens effect of the atmosphere. As Jesse watched, a group of these stars—seven of them, the cluster known as the Great Bear, Ursa Major—appeared to grow brighter and then to coalesce into a greater light: a newly formed heavenly object too warm and golden to be a star, or even many stars together. The light grew, and it moved closer. It assumed a form that was hard to recognize—too big to encompass with your mind, it might have been—but Jesse had the feeling it was something he had known, something he had seen or been told about.

This light-thing moved down and inward: out of the sky above the harbor, into the night-black landscape of Dublin, Maine. For an instant, it actually seemed to take notice of Jesse's presence. Two great eyes appeared to rest very briefly on him. He raised his arm to shield his face from their burning glow.

Beside him, Gus the timber wolf howled and pranced and leapt high in the air. It was like he was celebrating.

Then the light-thing moved on, and Jesse lowered his arm, and everything was the same again. The same in the sense that, for example, the world was still turning and would go on turning for a while. The sun would keep on coming up and the plants would continue to grow. In that way, the world was the same.

Otherwise, it was completely different.

And Jesse Openhood—let's be clear about this—was the very first person to notice the change. Jesse and his wolf. Though he reckoned that when he got back home, Syzygy would probably say she had known it was coming. And Ari would affect to have heard about it long before anyone. His raven Jack would have told him. Because they were all of them part of the world, and the world was like that.

KEEPER OF MEDICINE

Molly felt large.

Comically large. Cosmically large. She felt the whole world in her belly. She felt the stars in her eyes. She felt men and women scurrying around at her feet—or were they paws now? Men were on one side and women on the other. Don't ask Molly why.

Arth Vawr, she said. What do we do now?

But the Heavenly Bear said nothing. And Molly realized with some discomfort (and then elation) that *she* was the Bear now.

Far out, she thought. It's just like the bumper sticker. You know: THOU ART GODDESS. Temporarily, at least.

On a hillside below her, she noticed Jesse Openhood sitting with a bottle of Andrew's in his hand and Gus, the timber wolf, at his side. Molly winked at him. He raised his arm, possibly waving at her.

Enough socializing.

She turned to face the Goddin base, which was a mess. A typical male mess, if you don't mind her saying so. Lots of large-scale destruction. Teams, with leaders. Big fat hoses squirting fluids. Loud noise. Bad smells. What fun.

Molly sighed. It would serve them all right, in a way, if she did nothing. If she just let the fire burn and everything be lost. Maybe they'd learn something from their mistakes. But the problem was, as Molly knew, they *never* learn from their mistakes. Wars, car wrecks, drinking bouts, it makes no difference. They lie down and feel bad for a while, then they get up and do it all over again. And they leave the women to clean up after them.

Molly was tired of it, both as a woman and as a goddess (if

only a temporary one). But she couldn't think of anything else to do. It was infuriating, and it made no sense; but was it better to just give up? Let the world go all to hell?

There had to be a better way. Maybe in the next life, if there *was* a next life, she would think of one. In the meantime . . .

Molly sighed. The effect of this was a gust of wind out of the south, warm and moist. The flames moved over the fields, spreading to new territory. A fuel-storage building caught fire, to fairly spectacular effect.

Whoops, said Molly. *Sorry.*

She extended a paw and snuffed it out again. It was almost too easy.

Now, where in the world, she asked herself, *has Tex gotten off to?*

The question had barely formed in her mind when the answer (in the person of Tex himself) appeared beneath her. She saw him standing in the midst of a crowd of dryads, thousands of them—flapping his arms, beseeching them. They were for the most part ignoring him, sensibly enough. Still Tex threw himself about, limping badly, as though his injured leg was hurting again. The dryads continued to disregard him. The fires continued to burn. Tex kept railing, not ready even now to give it up.

Molly was touched.

She supposed she ought to help him.

She bent down, meaning to bestow upon him a blessing: the gift of strength and healing, straight from the Bear, divine Keeper of Medicine.

But as she drew near to Tex

Something

—a Power, nearly as great as herself—

rose to stand in her way, blocking her path. Molly saw dark wings unfolding before her, a Blackness deeper than night rising out of the flames. And a *Voice* said

NO. NOT TONIGHT.

DANCE OF YU

Is this a dream? wondered Burdock Herne.

Is it a drama?

Could it really, possibly, be happening?

Is there such a thing as a dream that is also a drama and yet remains part of actual time, of History—all at once?

Herne stood on a plain of tarmac where once giant bombers had rolled. B-52's: planes as old as Herne himself—scary and Strangelovian, carrying in their bellies the seeds of a new era that had never, mercifully, been brought to germination.

All around him he saw rows and rows of tiny plants. Saplings; evergreens. Spruces, he thought. Plastic tags that dangled from their . . . from their *necks,* Herne almost thought; but no, from their upper branches, of course . . . identified them as X 4.3.2. This meant something to Herne, but only distantly. The very fact of trees standing by their thousands in identical pots no longer conveyed much meaning for him. Trees were a commodity; they were the foundation of Herne's empire, the source of his power and wealth. Yet suddenly a Tree—the very idea of such a thing, a living entity rising between Earth and Sun—seemed an unfathomable mystery, something you could spend your whole life thinking about and still never feel that you had grasped.

Herne had a sense of standing at a meeting place, a point of friction or interpenetration between two different worlds. Between *this* world—the real one, the only one—and Someplace Else. Some place, or dimension, or order of being, that was opaque and vast and utterly unknown; like the Dark Matter thought by physicists to underlie the manifest universe, constituting upwards of 90% of all creation.

This was sheer delusion, of course. There was no other world, as Herne well knew. Dark Matter or no, *this* was the world where you sank or swam, won or lost, fished or cut bait.

And yet Something—some wholly different reality—seemed to press inward, from everywhere at once, within and without: testing all the weak spots in his weltanshauung, trying to break through. Herne attempted to push the feeling away. But the feeling pushed back. It was stronger than he was. Herne's shoulders sagged.

It would never in a million years—never in the entire remaining life of the universe—have occurred to Herne that what he felt were the eyes of ten thousand dryads, tree spirits, lying heavily upon him. He would never have accepted the notion (assuming it were presented to him for consideration) that the actions of his company might have caused widespread homelessness among discarnate spiritual entities. Herne considered himself a religious man, a Believer; but he was much too sensible to believe a thing like *that.*

Still, he sensed that he was not alone on this stretch of tarmac. Some Presence that had little to do with the dancers ranged against the fire (though nothing to do with the rows of trees standing cramped in their pots) seemed to him to be waiting or hovering nearby.

Herne looked around. Determined to make sense of things, if sense could still be made. Fully resolved to clear his head, make an accounting, chart a reasonable course.

The scene before him was pure Hieronymus Bosch, only freshly painted. The old Air Force base, recently calm and orderly, was transformed into a maelstrom of fire and destruction, as though at the whim of a particularly wrathful deity. The all-consuming blaze had no center, nor any limit that Herne could see. Turning this way and that, he stared into walls of incandescent horror that rose and fell and moved across the ground too fast to permit even rudimentary mapping. Herne found after several seconds that he was without any sense of direction. Even the most fundamental distinction—*up* versus *down*—had grown debatable. The tarmac seemed to lurch and yaw beneath his feet; and the markings painted there years ago, black and yellow lines and stripes and arrows, glared with terrible new portent, like the most hideous sigils of necromancy.

Herne turned and stumbled and (with difficulty) caught himself. All of his effort was required simply to remain on his feet. Sweat drenched his clothing; his heart strained against his rib cage, as though trying to wrench itself free.

There was nothing he could do. For once in his life, nothing. Only stand and stare for a few minutes longer, until the flames arrived. Then turn and flee like a hunted and helpless animal; like a deer on the run.

He had never imagined coming to a place like this.

Before him, as if they were demons spawned by his fevered consciousness, two dozen figures danced in the firelight. Herne perceived them first as silhouettes, black-on-orange. Then magically they took the form of ordinary men and women, though misshapen by waves of heat, and pale as spectres. Strangest of all, they wore *masks*, as though their dance were just one part of a larger, symbol-laden shadow-play. Madly they ran about— whether coming or going, guided by purpose or driven by panic, Herne could not tell—and their arms flew wildly, and their mouths opened wide, then shut. Some of them wrestled with long serpentine things that shuddered as though half-alive, and that threw out steamy jets like a dragon's hot sputum. Others carried tools that might have been weapons or tools or ritual objects, their intended function impossible to know. Others did nothing

at all—just stood possessed, like Herne, by the dread, or the riot-
ous fire-spirits, or the living *Darkness*.

There was about it all—dancers and set pieces and panoramic
backdrop—a striking, ceremonial quality. Not like an orderly kind
of ceremony (say, a funeral, or a mass). No: an ecstatic, frenzied,
moon- and fire-lit, Dionysian riot of murder and mutilation. A
ceremony saved from utter chaos only by the will of the shadowy
god whose favor the dancers sought.

The scene was irresistibly appalling. And for an indefinite time
Herne stood watching it, unable or unwilling to turn away.

Suddenly a great wave of orange light seemed to swell up out
of the roiling ocean of fire; and the wave broke over the tarmac,
and flecks of flame like sea-foam spewed over Herne and nearly
dragged him under.

He fell hard on the pavement. His hip crunched and he sucked
in a mouthful of burning air.

"My god," he croaked. To his amazement, and chagrin, the
words came out in a gasping sob.

The King was lying on the ground: helpless, crying.

A slap of footsteps came around him, hurrying by. Herne
strained to lift his head, to see who it was that was moving past;
he would have been little surprised had it proved to be a committee of goblins, wearing Brooks Brothers suits. What he saw instead did surprise him, and he lowered his eyes, wondering
whether in fact he had injured his head and was merely delirious,
or dying.

Overhead, a figure in a space suit (or something like it)
mooned above him. Flames reflected from the shiny helmet, the
smoky glass visor. The figure bent low.

Herne understood in that moment that he was insane. He realized at last that the strain of running a giant corporation, the
incessant meetings and phone calls, the disintegration of his family, years upon years spent mapping strategy, maneuvering in
secret, launching surprise attacks, fending off challenges from
without and from within—all these things, topped off most recently by his only daughter's declaring that she hated him and
disappearing from their home—had combined to upend his mental balance: to jar him utterly out of the rational world into a
completely different world in which he was not a powerful man,
a Chairman, a King. Here he was only a tired and sick and
possibly injured old man. Beset with demons. Suffering hallucina-
tions. Barely able to hold his head upright, much less stand and
walk.

The imaginary figure in the space suit lowered a large gloved hand toward him. From deep in the helmet, a metallic voice uttered words in no language Herne knew.

"What is it you want?" he asked it. "Let me alone here, won't you? I just need a moment to regain my bearings."

The figure spoke again, and the hand in its glove contracted until a single finger pointed toward Herne's chest. He deduced finally that the creature was asking him a question. He followed the finger down to the little placard (he had forgotten he was wearing it) that said

SOMEBODY'S DAD

—which, he gathered, was what the creature was asking him about.

"Yes," he said. "Yes, I am. I am Somebody's Dad."

The helmet of the space suit dipped and rose: a nod. The gloved hand reached out again.

Take it, the creature said; or at least Herne thought he heard. *Come on. Take it.*

Herne could see no reason not to obey. In this different world, where his own will was of no importance, obedience—even abject surrender—was probably the correct course to follow.

"All right," he said, willingly. He took the glove, clutched it firmly: surprised for an instant by how small and delicate-seeming was the hand inside. But what did he know?

The creature in the space suit tugged him upward. Herne allowed himself to be helped to his feet. To his surprise, he stood a head taller than the alien figure in front of him.

"Thank you," he said.

The creature nodded. Herne saw his own face, his staring eyes, in the glass of the visor. He recognized himself without difficulty: an ordinary face, an unexceptional man, his gaze full of emptiness and hunger. *That* is what I am, he thought. Not the pompous old fool in the Official Portrait.

Hey, the creature addressed him. (He could understand its speech more clearly now.) *What's the matter?*

The matter? thought Herne, wonderingly. He looked around at the field, the fire, the darkness. On all sides, amid shouts and hissing water and a roar of air being transmuted by combustion, the dance of death went on and on, fast approaching its climactic agony.

Herne said, "I don't . . . I—"

Are you hurt?—clearly sympathetic now. Perhaps not alien, after all. Reaching out a gloved hand; touching him. *Can I help?*

"You—" Herne felt his own words clotting in his throat. He felt some large new thing rising up in him. "Yes"—with surprise he heard his voice say—

"You can help."

QUESTS & QUESTIONS (2)

"*There,*" said Tex, pointing as though it were something he was proud of. "See that? What do you think?"

The dryads seemed to confer among themselves. They did so with no sense of urgency, as per custom.

This is *no time,* thought Tex, for a fucking Ent-moot.

"Think about what?" said Beale, glancing aside at his comrades. You could tell he was temporizing.

Before them, in the long aisle of potted spruces, the figure in the asbestos space suit held the hand of Burdock Herne and led him away. Down the rows of potted trees, toward the vast door of the greenhouse, they receded slowly, into the welcoming dark.

"Right there," said Tex, "you're looking at a little human miracle. You're looking at *proof* that people can change, if they take it into their heads to. Because see, you've got a screwed-up old guy there—a guy with, you know, something missing inside—who's being healed. The root of *heal,* you know, is the same as *whole.* So what you've got is a man who's been wandering in the Wasteland, who's out of touch with his own heart, but now he's being led back toward Whome."

"How do you *know* that?" said Beale. "How can you be sure what's going to happen? Nobody can foresee the future. Isn't that so?"

Tex leapt up into the air (as best he could) and landed on one foot, like a peg-legged pirate. He crowed:

"Aha! So you admit it, sucker. Now let's quit dicking around here and do what you promised."

Beale sighed. He seemed to debate the worth of arguing that, in fact, the dryads had promised nothing. The gleam in Tex's eye dissuaded him. Trees, as a class, have much strength but little willpower. When a strong wind blows, they bend before it.

"All right," said Beale. "We believe you. Humans can change. At least in theory. But what is it that you expect *us* to do?"

"Be creative," said Tex. "Surprise me."

"Surprise you." Beale shook his head. Then he closed his eyes.

His physical form faded: in a matter of seconds, it was gone. The other dryads vanished as well. There only remained Tex, and the fire, and the thousands of baby trees.

But in the next moment, from everywhere—the trees, the Earth, the heavens, the Otherworld, the Dark *Mater,* the Whome—

a golden *Presence* appeared or became or was seen to have been immanently close at hand all along.

The *Presence* might have had something of the likeness of a bear. A Great Bear whose teeth shone white and large as glaciers, whose ears jutted like mountaintops, whose glowing fur was all the waving grass of the plains, whose paws were archipelagos, whose eyes blazed like newborn suns. The *Presence* growled, and a rumble shuddered through the Earth like a grinding of tectonic strata.

Tex had to take a few steps back to grok all this. These steps moved him out to someplace in the vicinity of the Moon. The poor mortal humans closer at hand probably didn't have quite the same perspective. The Goddess only knows what *they* thought was happening.

Stately, the *Presence* turned itself about. Where its paws pressed on the Earth, the blaze was extinguished. Where its breath blew, new flames roared and entire buildings exploded.

Woo, thought Tex, appreciatively. This is one mean-ass teddy dude.

The *Presence* gave him a look: the sort of look that could shatter a polar ice cap.

WHAT MAKES YOU THINK I'M A *DUDE*?

the *Presence* demanded.

Uh-oh, thought Tex. That voice sounds strangely familiar.

"Sorry, ma'am," he said. "No offense, okay?"

HMMPH

grunted the *Presence.* It turned a shoulder to him. Which settled things, for Tex.

"Molly?" he said, incredulous. "Is that *you,* babe?"

The *Presence* had no time to answer.

Out of the night, a *Darkness* arose. At first it seemed immaterial, a mere shadow, some kind of visual illusion. But the shadow—whose degree of blackness was more profound than a mere paucity of light—acquired texture and depth; it rippled like heavy fabric; it drained light from the very air nearby; its surface radiated heat, while remaining as blank as the Void.

Then the *Darkness* took a Shape. And the Shape was that of a monstrous, evil-eyed *Raven*.

"Damn," said Tex. He recognized this one, too. It was getting to be a regular reunion around here; and not a happy one.

The *Raven* lifted its wings. It rose into the night sky, blocking out wide swaths of stars.

KEEP ON FLYING

the *Bear* advised it:

YOU'VE GOT NO BUSINESS HERE.

But the *Raven* said:

OH, YES. MUCH THE SAME BUSINESS AS YOU. I MADE A PACT WITH A MORTAL, AND I MEAN TO SEE IT TO AN END.

GET A LIFE

the *Bear* rumbled, its deep voice resonant with authority.

YOUR ROLE IS PLAYED OUT. YOU'VE MISSED YOUR EXIT. ANYWAY, I'M RUNNING THE SHOW NOW, AND I'M OLDER AND GREATER THAN YOU.

OLDER, PERHAPS,

the *Raven* conceded.

AND EVEN STRONGER. BUT I AM *MUCH* MORE CLEVER. CHECK THE RECORD. I WAS ODIN, RULER OF THE GODS. HAIDA THE TERRIBLE. BRAN, OF MANY BATTLES. RAVEN THE TRICKSTER.

A BUNCH OF UPSTARTS

sniffed the *Bear*.

I WAS A GODDESS BEFORE THERE WAS A LANGUAGE TO NAME ME. I BECAME ARTIO, AND THEN ARTEMIS, LONG BE-FORE ARTH VAWR—BUT EVEN *HE* IS OLDER AND WISER THAN YOUR DARK-EYED SCAMPS.

The *Raven* laughed: an awful sound, like bones being ground to powder.

NOT WISE ENOUGH. I WAS HIS UNDOING, AS MORRIGAN THE ENCHANTRESS.

I AM THE SEVEN BRIGHT STARS!

declared the *Bear,* rearing up to score the heavens with its claws.

BUT I,

said the *Raven,* smugly,

AM THE DARK FIRMAMENT THAT SWALLOWS THEM.

And with that, the winged *Darkness* launched itself high and higher, spreading its wings until all the sky and all the Earth grew black. Even Tex was quaking; while out of the fields far below he could hear people screaming in what must have been a final paroxysm of panic. He could see nothing at all, except for the folds of shadowy death that draped themselves over the head and eyes and massive haunches of the *Bear.*

And then . . .

(Tex chuckled: he had sensed there was going to be an *and then.*)

There was a

GIANT SLURPING SOUND

followed by a

HIDEOUS BELCH

and the *Raven* was no more.

Where It had filled the sky, there was now only emptiness. Or not just that; but a definitive embodiment of Nothing: vast and round and all-devouring—a veritable black hole among Nothings. Tex peered into it for a while, and as he watched, the black hole contracted. Finally, with a

WET SMACK

it slapped shut. And Tex realized that he had been staring, as it were, eyeball to molar with the Bishop of Worms.

But this (though it would have been enough) was not all.

Perched up high on the Bishop's slime-green, mucilaginous,

ever-spasming body—clutching some kind of tentacular cilium, like a hair growing out of a wart the size of a minivan—sat Beale the dryad. He gave Tex a weary, though not uncompanionable, wave.

Faintly he called out:

"Surprise."

DIGESTING

"Well," explained the dryad, "a deal is a deal, after all—even where humans are concerned. I merely *reminded* the Sublime Excrescence of his arrangement with you, and informed him of the raven-deity's interference. Naturally to a Primary Being like the Worm, a human god-form is not worth making a fuss over. Just a light snack, really."

Tex slapped Beale on the shoulder. He glanced about to make sure there was no further sign of the Bishop's presence. Or of his absence, or whatever he had. "Thank Goddess," he said, "the old bastard didn't gobble up Molly for dessert."

"Goddess had nothing to do with it," said the dryad.

And—*pffft!*—he vanished into the æther, whence he came.

Meanwhile, back at the former Goddin Air Force Base:

The *Great Bear* stood for a moment in the burning field. Then it lowered itself upon the ground—and the fires were gone.

The *Bear* breathed long, gently—and the air was free of smoke, clean and fresh and cool, with the newly made smell of young mountains.

Then the *Bear* nestled deeper, into the body of the Earth, rolling softly westward, where the sun had gone. And the fields were once again empty.

"Unbelievable," said Tex.

"No kidding," said Molly. She stood beside him, unobtrusively, just as though she had been hanging there all along.

"Hey, Raven," said Tex. He turned to kiss her on the forehead.

"Hey, Bear," she said, smiling peaceably.

"Well," he said, "I guess I've finally reached it."

"Reached what?" she asked him—suspicious, anticipating a punch line.

"The point where nothing can *possibly* surprise me anymore." He was quiet for a few moments, while they both digested this. "Do you think it represents some level of attainment? Like, have I *graduated* or something?"

"Transcended, maybe," Molly supposed. "I don't know. I'm hungry."

"That's impossible."

"Well . . . thirsty, then. Or maybe just tired."

"Maybe you're getting old."

Molly laughed. "I think it's a little late for that."

Tex kissed her again. This time like he meant it.

ASIDE TO YOUNG REDUCTIONISTS

Or I don't know. Maybe none of this really happened; maybe Tex and Molly tumbled down the Well and that was the end of it. Maybe all the rest was a series of coincidences, mass delusions, hoaxes, shaky conclusions founded upon inconclusive data. Maybe I'm just projecting something that I want to believe. There might have been a purely causal and reasonable explanation for everything. For example, it could have been caused by swamp gas.

The Universe itself, after all, still awaits a satisfactory accounting. The most logically compelling argument thus far advanced is that it was all a rather cosmically improbable statistical blurp.

TURNING MOMENTS INTO LINES

Tex stood up and his leg was better. Not *completely* better. It still hurt a bit, when he put his weight on it. But you wouldn't want to lose all your scars, would you? That would be like losing your stories. That would be worse than being dead. Which really, when you get right down to it, has its advantages, though these no doubt would be wasted on the young.

Out of hangars and parked automobiles and collapsed Quonset huts and other hidey-holes around the base, a crowd of Players began to emerge. They drifted by ones and twos and finally in a great clump out onto the scorched field where some of them thought they *might* have glimpsed Something, for just a moment, though then again probably they had not. They would have to think about this. Among the last to emerge was Gene Deere, who carried Ludi Skeistan in his arms like a beloved child. She did not look entirely happy. Though she did not look entirely unhappy, either.

"Is this as smoothly as you can walk?" she asked him.

"You gave *me* to understand," he said, breathing harder than seemed strictly necessary, "that you were not so heavy."

"You gave *me* to understand," she said, "that you weren't such a 90-pound weakling."

"I feel faint," he said, pretending to swoon and stagger. "I'm afraid I'm going to drop you."

"Great," she said. "Maybe Guillermo will pick me up."

Gene scowled. He scanned the tarmac quickly until he saw Guillermo in heavy schmooze mode with the Channel 5 reporter that reminded Gene pretty strongly of a character once played by Sally Field. But that hardly made her exceptional, because everywhere he looked he saw faces that seemed vaguely familiar— recognizable in the way you recognize a fragment of conversation, for instance, because once before, somewhere, you might have heard those very same words, maybe in some movie. He saw wild-looking teenagers and a pale, otherworldly-looking woman and a dark-skinned elfin boy. He saw a guy he had once bought a pizza from. He saw a deputy sheriff wearing a dress. He saw a waiter, a businesswoman, a man of the cloth. He saw somebody's dog. Or was it a dog? Could it actually have been a wolf? Could that have been blood, fresh blood, on its muzzle? Gene saw slackers and tourists and professionals and boat trash and he thought he saw Wild Jag Eckhart, who was making a weird sort of howling noise, as though he were trying to summon a lost pet.

Last to come out into the field was Burdock Herne, who was Gene's supreme high commander, the King of the Corp—assuming that, with the Goddin Forest Research Station now essentially destroyed, Gene still had a job. Herne was walking with, or being led by, a girl in a fireproof suit whom Gene gradually recognized as Thistle, the pretty teenager whom he had first seen swimming naked in a spring, like a creature out of a fairy tale. Her face was covered with soot but looked somehow even younger and prettier for that.

"What are you staring at?" said Ludi, in his arms.

"Nothing," he said quickly. "Are you still here?"

"Yes, I'm *still here.* But to tell you the truth, I'd just as soon be in Philadelphia."

Burdock Herne walked into the middle of the field, the middle of the crowd of dazed and tired and happy people. He held up his arms and he said:

"I want to thank you people. I want to thank all of you for coming here and working together to try to save my company's property. I want to thank you for letting me see that. And I want to thank you for being good neighbors. I only wish there was something, some way to even begin to repay you for all that you've done."

Thistle, his runaway daughter, said something to him that he didn't catch.

"Trees," she repeated. "Give them trees."

"Ah!" he cried. "Of course. Listen, everyone. I know this is a small gesture, but I hope you will all accept the gift of some of our little trees here. We have thousands—*thousands*—and since you've all been responsible for saving them from the terrible fire, why, it seems only fair—less than fair!—for you all to take them. Take them all! And plant them wherever you like. Give them new homes. That will be a start, at least, in expressing our thanks to you. Together we can start to repair all that's been damaged here. Here and elsewhere. We can make a new beginning."

And somewhere above, while music played softly out of a boom box in the dark,

Tex & Molly swirled lightly,
as though dancing
on a cloud.

or
maybe not "above"—

maybe "below" or "beside"—but at some remove in *some* dimension, at any rate, Tex and Molly looked on.

They were separated from the Players and the scorched-out field and Dublin Harbor and all the rest of it by a medium more viscous than Space. More cluttered than Time. Some translucent thickness of Akasha; of the Æther; of the Whome.

From this distance, they watched while the drama played itself out, the many threads and many stories and many lives moving further out in the night.

"Look at them," said Tex.

"Who?" said Molly, sounding dreamy. "Gene and Ludi?"

"No, the dryads. Don't they look happy? People are carrying them to their cars. Off to their new homes. Can you dig it? Look—that guy with the NRA cap must have a couple hundred in his pickup bed."

"That's nice," said Molly. She stretched and yawned. "Now listen, Bear—tell me honestly. What was your wish?"

"My what?"

"Your wish. That you made just before we fell in the Well."

He narrowed his eyes at her. "You tell first," he said.

"All right," said Molly. "I wished to be back on the houseboat, and to wake up nice and warm in my own bed."

Tex stared for a moment, cannily. "That's it? That's all of it?"

"What did you expect? You didn't exactly warn me it would be the last wish I'd ever make." She paused long enough for Tex to look sheepish. Then she poked his arm; only kidding, like. "Anyway, it came true, didn't it?"

Tex guessed it did.

"So what was yours?" said Molly. "Did yours come true, too?"

Tex shrugged. He thought so. Maybe. Probably. Glancing around the Air Force base, he said, "Where *are* Gene and Ludi, anyway?"

"You're changing the subject. Probably they're back at the houseboat by this time."

"*Our* houseboat? Why? What time is it?"

Molly gave him a worldly, or Otherworldly, lowering of the eyes. "Time for a final kiss, I'd imagine. And it's *their* houseboat, now."

"Why?" said Tex, imploringly.

"Bear. You're whimpering."

"I am not." But of course, he was. Adjusting his voice, he tried it again—this time managing a bit of a growl: *"I am not."*

"That's better." Molly stroked him. She pointed downward. "Look. There they are. What did I tell you?"

Implausibly, the *Linear Bee* lay directly below them. As Tex gazed in astonishment, he and Molly floated down to rest lightly upon the flying bridge.

Afterlife Factoid #19
Relax. Enjoy it. You're only as dead as you feel.

"I just thought we might pick up a couple of things," said Molly. She scooted below, disappearing through the hatch.

"A couple of *what* things?" Tex called after her. "For what? Are you planning a trip or something?"

By the time he caught up with her in the living quarters, Gene and Ludi appeared to be well past the Final Kiss stage. They were freshly damp from the shower and wrapped in bathrobes, which Tex supposed must be theirs, now, also. Gene paraded about, splashing champagne everywhere, while Ludi looked on placidly from the sofa. Her injured leg lay propped on a fat pillow, bracketed by ice packs.

"I guess it's not broken after all," she said, as though this were a cause of some regret.

"I knew you were faking," said Gene. He handed her a champagne flute—had Tex and Molly actually owned such things, or was this part of the new regime in the galley? Ludi accepted the glass with long, tapered fingers. Tex sighed.

"Here," called Molly, from the bedroom. "Grab this blanket, would you?"

The faded Chief Joseph came hurtling through the door. Tex, who was busy staring at Ludi's long pale legs, fumbled it.

"A blanket?" he said. "For what?"

"To stretch out on, of course." Molly emerged from the bedroom and made briskly for the galley. Discreetly, she avoided looking at the young couple now busily occupying most of the sofa. Tex was less concerned with discretion. Do what comes naturally, he thought.

Ludi said, "You know, Molly was always telling us, Break a leg. And it was like I really had gone and done it, you know? I kind of thought—"

"Mm," Gene said, or rather murmured, nuzzling up closer to Ludi, the lucky stiff. "Could we forget Tex and Molly, just for a little while?" Ludi spilled champagne on him. Deliberately, Tex believed. *That's my girl!* he thought.

Apropos of nothing, Ludi said, "What do you think's going to happen now?"

Gene glanced up in bemusement; and for a tiny instant, he and Tex *almost* caught one another's eyes. This seemed to puzzle Gene even more.

"What do you mean?" he said.

"I mean, to your job and all. The Goddin place, Gulf Atlantic. The whole operation." Ludi regarded him seriously, as though these questions were suddenly very important.

Gene pulled away, though only a little. He tried to think. "Well, I guess," he said, "things will take a while to settle down. The Big Boss wants to see me tomorrow, at his hotel. He said he wants to make some serious changes. Also something funny about Chas no longer being in the picture."

"Good," said Ludi. She snuggled into his chest, as though this information had put her back in the mood for romance.

Gene closed his eyes and held her tightly for a second or two, smiling at the wonder of it all. Then his eyes popped open again.

"Damn," he said. "I forgot to feed Tex."

"Can't he wait till morning?" said Ludi.

Gene labored to disentangle himself. "He's a growing animal. He's had a long day. It'll only take a minute. Just let me toss some food out on deck."

At this, Molly popped out of the galley, carrying snapshots and other mementos taken down from the refrigerator. She clucked her tongue. "I hope he can find something. The cupboard looks pretty bare."

"Hold on a minute," said Tex. "Are you saying there's a *bear* living on this houseboat?"

Molly stood close to him; she murmured, "There's *always* been a Bear living on this houseboat. Only now it's a real one."

Tex growled at her.

She pecked his cheek. "Glad you're feeling better. Well, I guess that's everything. Are you ready to go?"

Tex turned for a last glance at Ludi. He soaked up as much of it as he could. It would have to last a while, he guessed.

"Go where?" he said. But Molly had already started climbing up the ladder, and it is doubtful that Tex expected an answer, anyway.

FURTHER OUT IN TIME

On the flying bridge, they spread the blanket out. Molly smoothed down the edges and they sat close together. The old worn wool felt soft and familiar, awakening memories by the hundreds. Tex laid his head on Molly's shoulder. He breathed her familiar scent.

"I don't know, Raven," he said after some time. Minutes or hours might have passed. It didn't seem to matter. "It's weird— but I kind of feel like I've had enough of all that now."

"Of Gene and Ludi?" Molly asked.

"Kind of. But more like, of everything, really. All that stuff down there."

—And this time, he did mean *down there*. The blanket hovered at a great height above the harbor, floating in the night sky of Dublin, Maine. A warm breeze fluffed up around them. They drifted before it, moving southward.

Tex went on: "It's kind of like we've done what we set out to do. Or finished the stuff we left undone. We saved the forest. Or a little bit of it. Maybe. I hope. And we passed something on. Our houseboat, at least. But maybe something besides that. Something good."

Molly thought about this. She rubbed Tex's shoulder. Slowly, by degrees, she felt the wiry muscles unwind.

"So what about it, Bear?" she said. "What *was* your wish? Did it come true, or not?"

This time he smiled at her. "All right," he said. "I wished . . . to change the world."

Molly laughed out loud. She couldn't help herself.

"No, really," he said, sounding wounded.

"No, I believe you. Really. It's just—why did I even have to ask?"

"Yeah," said Tex. "And I guess it came true. At least a little bit. What do you think?"

Molly gave him a hug. She thought she still loved him, after all this time. They stayed that way, close together on the blanket, for a while, looking at things moving and changing and happening below. Down in the living world. Friends, dryads, kindred spirits, wild things—it seemed pretty complicated now. Hard to follow.

"I think you're right," said Molly, finally. "I think you did change the world. It's different now, that's for sure."

"But you know what?" said Tex. "Now it's like, we're not part of it anymore."

Molly nodded. "Not Players any longer."

"Right. It's like we're out in the audience just, you know— looking on."

"Or up in the rafters," Molly suggested. "Looking down."

"Or in the sky," said Tex. He looked up. "Hey, dig it. The *sky*."

Molly dug it. The heavens shone all around them, in every direction. In more directions than you could count. "Wow," she said.

They dug it together

"All the stars," whispered Tex.

"All the stories," said Molly.

She pressed against him, leaning back. He wrapped his arms around her.

The stars were *alive*, they realized. Teeming, seething with life. They jostled and spun and sang in their cosmic dance.

"Like that time in Arizona," said Tex. "Remember the sky then?"

"Jerome," said Molly. "We had just met. You had retired from being an acid-head."

"Oh, come on," Tex laughed. "You can never really *retire* from something like that."

Tex and Molly were young again: circa 1972. They were lying

out in the night air on a Chief Joseph blanket. Under the same stars, the same heaven. The blanket was rumpled, spread out on top of a hill. The ground underneath was soft with buffalo grass. They stared around them, then at one another, in amazement, in enchantment, in delight.

If you lie on your back and look deeply through the clear night sky, it's easy to imagine that you're falling into it—the whole spinning Universe is pulling you inward, while the heavens swirl around you. Even on a cold night, you can feel the warmth out there. Warmth and awareness and light.

Compassion.

Joy.

Life. Life without bounds. Without limit.

Tex could remember feeling, back then—the Then that had become, mysteriously, Now—that if he wanted to, he could just float up there among those stars. Just let go of the Earth and *float*, and keep floating. Floating forever, away and away. Only he had never wanted to, really. He had been afraid. And there had always been something to hold him down; some weight, some worldly attachment. Now, he was not so sure. He looked at Molly beside him.

She was looking back. The light of the stars shone in her eyes. The moon glimmered in her long brown hair.

"Raven," he said. As though he had never really seen her before. Never recognized or believed all that she was.

"Bear." She took his hand. Her touch was magical. The energy of the cosmos streamed through it. Tex felt himself growing lighter as it entered him: less substantial, as though his flesh were turning to spirit, to the purest star-stuff.

She said, "Let's keep going this time."

Tex took her hand and they left,

they went out there where they had been heading all along.

And Tex said, "What an
unbelievable
trip."